NEVER TOO CLOSE

She put her arms around his neck and held tight to keep from falling as his hands moved up and down her body with a light touch. He kissed her ear and then her cheek as she shook against him. "It's all right. Breathe, Maggie. This isn't going to hurt."

"I know. I'm just nervous. I've never . . ." she managed to say.

Sam's strong hands moved down past her waist and fanned out over her hips as his mouth opened against her throat. The warmth of his tongue circled her skin as his hands began to move up over her back, pressing her closer against him. He wasn't holding his feelings back and letting her remain safe from being involved. Tears trickled down her warm cheeks as she let herself drift with the moment and not worry about the pain that would surely come when she was alone again.

Melting against him, she breathed deep as he retraced his journey from her hip to the back of her hair. This time he pulled the tie holding her hair and dug his hands into her wavy curls. "God, I love the feel of you," he whispered as if to himself and not her. Gently he tugged a handful of her hair, pulling her head up. His warm breath brushed over her cheek a moment before his lips moved over hers. This time the kiss was light, teasing.

She cried out at the pure pleasure of it and heard him laugh softly against her cheek. Then he kissed her again and again, playing with her mouth but never kissing her deeply as he had before.

"I can't get eno st her throat as he tugge o he could taste the spot

Collections by Jodi Thomas, Linda Broday,
Phyliss Miranda, and DeWanna Pace

GIVE ME A TEXAN

GIVE ME A COWBOY

GIVE ME A TEXAS RANGER

GIVE ME A TEXAS OUTLAW

A TEXAS CHRISTMAS

BE MY TEXAS VALENTINE
(coming soon)

Published by Kensington Publishing Corporation

A Texas Christmas

JODI THOMAS
LINDA BRODAY
PHYLISS MIRANDA
DEWANNA PACE

ZEBRA BOOKS
KENSINGTON PUBLISHING CORP.
http://www.kensingtonbooks.com

ZEBRA BOOKS are published by

Kensington Publishing Corp.
119 West 40th Street
New York, NY 10018

All Kensington titles, imprints and distributed lines are available
at special quantity discounts for bulk purchases for sales promo-
tion, premiums, fund-raising, educational or institutional use.

Special book excerpts or customized printings can also be created to fit specific needs. For details, write or phone the office
of the Kensington Special Sales Manager: Attn. Special Sales
Department. Kensington Publishing Corp., 119 West 40th
Street, New York, NY 10018. Phone: 1-800-221-2647.

Zebra and the Z logo Reg. U.S. Pat. & TM Off.

ISBN-13: 978-1-4201-1966-4
ISBN-10: 1-4201-1966-4

First Printing: October 2011

10 9 8 7 6 5 4 3

Printed in the United States of America

Contents

ONE WISH: A CHRISTMAS STORY

JODI THOMAS

Chapter 1

December 1887
Kasota Springs, Texas

Sam Thompson stood in the blackened corner of the alley silently watching the mercantile across the street. Wind blew against his back as if trying to force him to move from the shadows. He needed to be heading home, but the woman inside the store kept him rooted in place.

She moved now and then past the windows, sometimes looking out as though hoping to see someone coming to shop. Her slender form drew him now just as her green eyes had the first day they met.

Sam shoved his hands farther into the pockets of his worn coat and prayed no one walked through her doors tonight. Margaret Allison had no idea of the danger she was in, and he had the feeling if he walked across the street to tell her, she wouldn't believe him.

He was a Thompson, and in this town that usually meant he was one step above the wolves who came down from the north on cold nights like this to hunt. Thompsons lived out along the southern breaks near the Palo Duro Canyon, not here in town among the civilized folks. Thompsons kept to themselves and minded their own business.

If Sam walked into the mercantile, Maggie Allison would be more likely to think he'd come to rob her than help her. He didn't much care about whether she lost money or not. Everyone knew that her parents always had money. After all, they sent her to a big school back East to grow up. They must have left it all to their only daughter. She could weather a robbery, but he didn't like to think about what the drunken gang of outlaws, now building courage by the mug, would do to her when they found her alone.

She had no one to protect her, but Sam was a man who didn't have the time to be her hero. If she'd just lock the door and go up to bed, he could get home before it started snowing.

He stomped his feet to keep them from freezing and tried to talk himself into leaving. Maggie Allison hadn't said more than a few words to him in twenty years. He didn't even think she remembered meeting him when they'd been six. It wasn't his job to worry about her. The town had a sheriff and plenty of upstanding men. She didn't need him.

So why didn't he get on home to his responsibilities and leave her to her fate?

The memory of Maggie in pigtails crossed his mind. Even at six she'd been prim and proper in her starched dresses covered with a white apron, her red hair always in place, her manners perfect, her green eyes wide open as if she was afraid she'd miss one moment of life if she wasn't alert. "I'll never tell you a lie, Sam Thompson," she'd said the day they'd met. "And I promise never to be mean to you, if you promise never to be mean to me."

He'd been six, but he swore she'd won his heart that first day of school.

When the teacher told her to sit next to him, she didn't

hesitate. However, she did spend the morning telling him he smelled bad and his fingernails were dirty and he needed new shoes and she didn't like the color orange.

Sam smiled remembering how she'd split her sandwich in half and shared with him that first day. Maggie Allison was different from anyone he'd ever met, and she fascinated him. She did everything right, learned everything first, said exactly what the teacher expected her to say. The only thing he had in common with the proper little red-haired girl was that no one liked her either. She didn't seem to mind. She read or stayed in with the teacher while other kids played, but Sam tried to join in and he'd been given more than one black eye to show for it.

It had taken him three years of walking four miles to school to figure out what his grandfather had told him all along: he didn't belong in town. Only, unlike his relatives, Sam had learned to read, and he'd impressed the teacher enough that she always packaged a few books for him and left them by the schoolhouse door. He'd walk to town on the first of every month and drop off the last books before he picked up the next set. Then, in the midnight hours, he'd sit by the fire and read. Over the years he sometimes thought of Maggie sitting beside him that first year encouraging him as she pointed out the words with her thin little finger.

In the shadow's cold, Sam saw her step near the window once more. Proper as ever, with her hair now pulled back in a knot behind her head. Her parents had sent her away to school after that first year. Folks said it was because she was too bright to stay here. Most said she'd probably never come back to a small town in the middle of nowhere, but she had. She came back to bury her parents last year, and to Sam's surprise, she took over the mercantile.

He studied her now, knowing he needed to go home, but

not being able to stomach the thought of her being hurt or
killed. The drunks he'd overheard talked of what they'd do to
her, how they'd make her scream even after they'd taken all
her valuables. They'd joked about how she was probably a
virgin, and virgins don't tell what happens, so they could
probably use her the next time they passed through town.

Sam forgot about the cold. He'd wait until she locked
the door.

Chapter 2

Margaret Allison paced the worn floors of her store. She'd told everyone she was staying open late every night this week before Christmas so folks could do any late shopping, but so far not one customer had come in.

She knew every respectable person in town was either at Wednesday-night prayer meeting or at one of the parties to celebrate Christmas. The Wilsons were having a huge dinner for fifty, the school was putting on the Christmas story tonight, and she'd heard even the saloon got in the mood and was running a special on beer. Everyone in town, even her two part-time helpers, had somewhere else to be tonight.

Everyone except her.

Sitting down behind the counter, she opened her journal. Over the years she'd kept several journals from time to time. Some about school, some about her thoughts, and one of poems she'd tried to write. But this one was different. This journal was just for wishes. It had pages of Christmas wishes; many she couldn't remember if she'd gotten or not. There were a few pages of shopping lists or packing lists when she'd gone away to school or traveled with her aunt. From the time she'd been thirteen, she'd kept a wish list on the back page of the requirements needed for the man she'd marry.

At first the list had been long and flowery, all about what he needed to look like and act like and have. Later the list became more practical. What profession he'd practice. How educated he'd be. How much money he'd make. What kind of house and hobbies he'd have.

Then a few years ago the list grew shorter and shorter until now she only had one thing on her list. One wish. She thought of making her one wish for a man to be *breathing,* but she couldn't be so pathetic. She knew she was twenty-six and one of those women who would remain forever unmarried, but something in her heart had to leave one requirement on her list. Any man she ever accepted would have to be *loving.*

One man who'd called on her because he was attracted to her money walked out saying simply that it wasn't worth it. He claimed she criticized everything about him from his dress to his breathing.

Maggie frowned, remembering. She'd thought the man simply overreacted. All she'd been trying to do was make him aware of his shortcomings. You'd think he'd want to know.

"If just one loving man could care about me for one day, I think I could survive on that little for the rest of my life," she said as she wrote *me* beside *loving* on her list.

She heard the door open and looked up as three rather shabbily dressed men entered. They spread out and began looking at the neat stacks of supplies and talking back and forth to one another about how late it was and how they were surprised to find the store still open. The heaviest of the three left mud on her clean floor with each step, while another lifted several garments and didn't bother to put them back like he found them. The third and youngest headed toward her with a long, lanky walk that reminded her of a rooster's strut. He stopped a few feet before he reached the counter she sat behind. He didn't look at her, didn't even seem to notice her. He lifted one of the cans of peaches stacked on the shelf. When he dropped it, his friends laughed.

She forced herself not to look to see if he dented it. Almost without care, he put it back on the shelf. The stranger turned her direction and glared at her with eyes dead of all expression.

Maggie looked away as she closed her journal and prepared to wait on her only customers of the night. His two friends were collecting a few things as they moved to join the rooster man. They laughed and talked with slurred speech, but the man before her seemed far more interested in watching her than in shopping.

She saw the door open slightly again and a tall man with a beard entered. She recognized him as a farmer who came in once a month, always near closing time. He usually seemed in a hurry, but tonight, he simply moved to the back and began looking at the tools.

She turned her attention to the three men who all seemed to be moving slowly toward her. She felt like a door was closing in front of her, shutting out the air in the room. They smelled of trail dust and sweat. One corner of the rooster man's lip went up as if he knew a secret he was about to share.

The heavy man set his things on the counter and leaned closer to look at her. "She's got nice hair, don't she, Boss."

"Yeah," the thin man answered as if she wasn't standing right there in front of them.

None appeared to notice the farmer near the back. The closest nodded his head toward her and said, "Evening, miss."

She could smell the liquor on his breath from three feet

away. The man reminded her of a snake about to strike. She straightened as she always did when nervous, as if the action would make her taller than everyone else.

"Is there something I can help you with?" she asked, doubting any of the three had a wife or sweetheart, but surely they had mothers, and it was Christmastime. "I could assist you in picking out a gift."

All three were now standing before her. One more step and they'd be within reach of her. Maggie had never been so glad to have the counter between her and customers.

"You might could help us." The stout one grinned. "We'd like you to empty that money box you keep beneath the counter and hand it over."

Maggie stared. "You're robbing me?"

The first man struck, covering her hand with his as he leaned close. He glared at her as he issued orders. "Lock the door, Barney, and blow out those lights in the front while the lady puts all her money in a bag, then we'll move to that office behind her where she probably keeps the real money." The dead-eyed man before her might be young, but he appeared to be the leader. His grip over her hand turned painful. "We're here to do a little business with you, lady, and we don't want no trouble."

Maggie fought down a scream as she nodded.

She watched as the shortest of the three rushed to the door. He pulled down the CLOSED sign as he locked up and began blowing out lights while he moved back toward her. She didn't dare look in the far corner to see if the farmer was still there. His only chance at staying alive might be to remain silent. These three might have been too drunk to notice him come in, but if they found him now, all they'd see was a witness.

The leader lifted his hand off hers and grabbed the front of her blouse. He jerked her hard toward him and whispered,

"We can do this easy, miss, or hard. It's up to you. All we want is your money."

The third man laughed. "And a little fun, remember, Adler. Don't forget that. You said we could all have a little fun. I say we gag her first. She looks like a screamer. I don't mind a screamer, but I don't want any company coming in on me while I'm having my turn with her."

The leader looked like a hungry coyote when he smiled at her. "You'll be quiet, won't you, miss. This ain't nothing personal, you understand. Louis ain't had a woman in a long time and I promised him."

She began to shake.

He let go of her blouse and spread the cotton out as if he were erasing his prints. "First business. Then, if you cooperate, I won't let the boys hurt you much."

Louis pulled his gun. "He's right. We get the money first."

The one named Barney made it back. All the lights in the store were out except for the small lamp just behind the counter. No one passing would be able to see her from the windows. Maggie felt trapped by the wall of robbers. All air had left her world.

She forced her mind to clear. She couldn't let fright cripple her. She stared at them and waited for a chance.

"Look at her, Boss." Barney smiled. "She ain't even going to scream. I heard she was a smart one. She knows it wouldn't do her no good." He leaned on the counter and bragged, "Boss told me I could slap you around if you start to put up a fight."

"We're wasting time. Get all the money in a bag and be quick about it." The boss seemed far more interested in the money.

Maggie nodded and reached her hand beneath the counter. Beside the money box was an old Walker Colt her father had carried years ago in the war. Just as she gripped the barrel, a long ax handle flew out of the shadows.

She watched as if everything were happening in one long, stretched-out second. The ax handle hit Barney hard in the back of the head, sending him halfway across the counter and tumbling like a rag doll.

Louis swung his gun around and fired blindly into the darkened store as another swing slapped against his jaw so hard she heard bone break. The one called Adler backed up, drawing his gun just as the farmer stepped from the shadows swinging.

Maggie lifted the Colt and fired toward Boss Adler more to save the farmer than trying to hurt the robber.

Two blasts rang as one. The farmer spun and tumbled as Boss ran for the door.

She rushed around the counter with the gun in her hand and fired again. Just as Boss barreled through the door, she heard him scream and grab his leg, then limp away.

Maggie dropped the gun and ran to the farmer. He'd risked his life to help her. If he'd just stayed in the darkness, he wouldn't have been hurt. Somehow this was all her fault.

It was too dark near the floor to see clearly. "Are you all right?" she yelled, brushing her hand over warm blood spilling across his shoulder. "I need to get you a doctor."

To her surprise, he sat up, pushing her hand away. "I'm fine," he said almost calmly. "And I'm not deaf, Maggie. Stop yelling at me."

She took a long breath. Before she could thank the farmer, the sheriff and several other men came running through the broken door. Sheriff Raines, his gun drawn, moved straight toward her as the others spread out, lighting lamps and looking around.

"Are you all right, Miss Allison?"

"Yes," she said. "This man stopped the others from robbing me."

The sheriff looked at the man next to her. "You sure he wasn't one of the robbers? He's a Thompson."

"I'm sure. Mr. Thompson saved my life, Sheriff. Those two," she pointed at Barney draped across her counter, still out cold, and Louis wailing as he held his bloody face, "were trying to not only take my money, but they were . . ." She couldn't say the words. She wouldn't.

Thompson filled in the blank. "They were planning to molest her and probably leave her dead. I heard them talking at the livery when I rode in to pick up one of my horses." He stood slowly but remained close to her. "The one called Boss mentioned to Louis that they didn't plan to leave a witness."

Maggie began to shake again and felt Thompson's arm go round her waist as if bracing her. He continued talking to the sheriff. "I saw the leader once a few years ago. He's Boss Adler, I think."

Sheriff Raines shook his head. "He's a bad one, but I've never been close enough to get a good look at him." Raising an eyebrow, he added, "Never known a Thompson to get involved with anything going on in town either. You folks don't seem to like kin, much less other people."

"Maybe we just like to be left alone." Sam was finished talking.

Louis stopped crying long enough to swear and say, "Boss'll kill every last one of you here. That's why he's never been caught. He don't leave no witnesses to testify against him."

Maggie didn't miss the way the sheriff and Thompson exchanged looks and, without another word, she knew she was in big trouble.

Chapter 3

Sam staggered a half step forward and was aware that suddenly Maggie was holding him up.

"Get him off his feet," Sheriff Raines ordered. "I'll go for the doctor."

Sam wanted to argue, but the room seemed to be moving. He felt like a leaf floating over turbulent water.

"Can you walk?" Maggie whispered from close by.

He nodded and let her help him up the stairs behind the counter. She felt good next to him, holding on to him, moving with him each step. He hadn't touched a woman in over two years, and the nearness of her shocked his system.

They stepped through a doorway into a small living quarters. As they moved to a table with only one chair, he tried to take in all that surrounded him. At first all he saw were colors. Reds and yellow and blues everywhere. Upholstered chairs and curtains and rugs. Shiny pots and glass ornaments, and flowers blooming indoors. This had to be Maggie's apartment, but he'd never have dreamed that she would live surrounded by color.

"If you'll tug off your coat and shirt, I'll see what I can do to clean up the wound before Doc Mitchell gets here." She turned around and began pouring water into a pan as if she expected him to follow orders.

"You don't—"

She cut in before he could finish. "Don't be a fool, Mr. Thompson. I've had training in nursing. I'm perfectly capable of cleaning the wound of the stranger who saved my life."

She tied an apron around her waist and began rummaging through a drawer.

"I'm not a stranger, Maggie," he said as he tugged off his coat. "We used to be friends. I'm . . ."

She looked up, her green eyes challenging. "You're Samuel Thompson. I remember you."

He smiled as he unbuttoned his shirt. "I'm glad."

She carried a bundle of cotton bandages toward the table. "You were the only one in the school here who was nice to me. I remember running home every day and crying. I'd tell my mother the only one who didn't yell at me was Samuel Thompson, and my mother would always say, 'That Samuel Thompson must be a saint.'"

He relaxed with a smile. "Funny, I remember you and those green eyes, but I'd forgotten Miss Rogers called me Samuel."

Maggie put her hand on his bare shoulder. "It's good to see you again, Samuel. I wish you'd told me who you were when you first came in."

He wished he had, also, but he wasn't sure how he would have reacted if he'd introduced himself and she'd said she didn't remember him. She'd meant so much to him growing up. Even though he rarely saw her after that year, she'd made him a better man. So many times when he'd almost given up on getting started and building a life, he'd thought of her and how she'd always pushed him to do his best.

Sitting very still, he watched her as she cleaned away the blood. "It's not bad. An entrance and an exit wound at your shoulder. Looks like it missed the bone, but it sure is bleeding. I'll try a cold compress." As she worked, she lectured him on how he shouldn't step into the middle of a robbery.

She was so close to him, he could feel her breath against his jaw and the slight hesitation of her touch as if she were afraid of hurting him. Taking a deep breath, he relaxed remembering the smell of her hair. Honeysuckle. Somehow he knew she'd still smell of honeysuckle.

"Can you clean it good and bandage it tight for me? I really need to be getting home. I've got a lot of work to do before this storm hits."

"Of course. Your wife is probably wondering about you." Her voice sounded more formal suddenly. "But I'd recommend you see—"

"My wife died two years ago in childbirth," he interrupted.

Green eyes filled with tears. "I'm sorry. Did the baby live?"

Sam watched her closely. "He only weighed a little over three pounds."

She shook her head. "I'm so sorry, Samuel." Her hand brushed his shoulder as she pressed against the wound to stop the bleeding.

They heard someone coming up the stairs and waited until the sheriff appeared, his hat in hand. He looked around and hesitated as if unsure if he should come inside.

"The doctor?" Maggie said without moving away from Sam.

Sheriff Raines seemed relieved to have something to say. "He ain't coming. I found him passed out at the Wilson party. Someone had propped him up in a chair, and I don't think anyone had noticed he was out cold."

"I don't need him," Sam snapped. "Maggie can bandage me up better than he could anyway."

Raines looked confused. "That right, Miss Allison?"

She smiled. "I'll do my best. Samuel and I have been

friends for years, Sheriff. I'd hate to lose him to poor skills. Though I'm no nurse, I have an ointment in my medical kit that will keep down the infection, and I do know how to dress a wound."

The sheriff looked confused. "You two are friends?"

Sam smiled at her as she worked. "We have been since the first grade."

"Well, good, 'cause my deputy says the two outlaws we got over in the jail are yelling about how Boss Adler will be back soon to kill both of you. I've been trying my best to think of somewhere Miss Allison could go to be safe, but I doubt anyone in town would want to risk their family to offer her a place. Now I know you two are friends, I think it might be a good idea if you took her home with you, Thompson. Nobody but your kin has ever been down in that part of the canyon, so she'd be safe there. If Boss does try to come after you and her, he'll never figure out which place is yours, and if he knocks on very many Thompson kin doors, they'll probably shoot him for being a bother."

"More than likely," Sam said as he agreed with the sheriff. "But I'm sure Maggie would be safer here." He couldn't shake the feeling that the sheriff wanted her gone more than he wanted her safe.

"No," she whispered. "I know of no one who'd risk his or her life to hide me, and I'd never ask you to."

When he turned to look at her, he knew she was telling the truth. In almost twenty years nothing had changed, he realized. Neither one of them had any friends in this place. He didn't want to take her home with him, but he couldn't leave her here.

She tied off the bandage as he looked at the sheriff. "If you'll stay here while she packs a few things, I'll go get my horses and take her with me, but you'll tell no one, not even the deputies, where she's gone."

Raines looked like he wasn't in favor of the idea he'd suggested, but he nodded as Sam pulled on his bloody shirt over the bandages. "No one would believe me anyway." The sheriff shrugged. "I've never known a Thompson to invite anyone down into that canyon."

Sam didn't argue. He just nodded once to Maggie and walked out.

Wrapped in his own thoughts, Sam walked back to where he'd tied his horses. He had little use for the sheriff. If it didn't happen in his town, he really wasn't interested. Three years ago when Otis Dolton, Sam's neighbor, beat his fifteen-year-old daughter half to death, the sheriff didn't bother to come out and talk to Otis.

The next time Danni Dolton was beaten, she made it as far as Sam's house, crying that if she'd gone toward town her father would just find her and beat her for running away. Sam took the kid in and cared for her. Danni was more girl than woman, afraid of the world. She'd been keeping house and cooking for her old man since her mother died. Even though Sam never hurt her, she was usually as far away as she could get from him in the house and she refused to go farther than the barn for fear her father would snatch her.

When her dad showed up to take her back, Sam stood between them while the old man yelled at her. Dolton swore he'd be back with the sheriff. Sam doubted that, but to make sure Danni never had to go back to hell, they went over to Tascosa and got married.

After that, she'd come by the fire at night and he'd read to her from one of his books. It didn't seem to matter what he read, she just liked listening. She never ate a meal with him or talked unless she had to. They'd been married about six months when she crawled in bed with him. She lay perfectly still without her nightgown on as if knowing what was to come. He rolled near her and asked her twice if she wanted this before he saw her nod in the shadows.

Without a word, he'd mated with her. After that, she'd come to him now and then. She never touched him. He never forced her or even touched her more than was necessary. He knew nothing of lovemaking, but he knew how to mate. When he finished, she'd move away and he'd feel so hollow inside he feared he might freeze to death.

After she died, he swore he'd never get involved with anyone again. Now he was taking the one woman he'd ever cared about home with him. If he hadn't stayed away from Danni when she was under his roof, how was he ever going to stay away from Maggie? Danni never even told him she liked him, much less loved him, and Maggie had just made it plain that he was probably the only friend she had.

He swore, suddenly realizing when Maggie got to his house she'd probably turn around and ride right back to town. What faced her at his place just might be more frightening than Boss Adler.

Chapter 4

Maggie moved through the small rooms of her apartment over the store. In the past hour she'd been frightened almost out of her mind. She'd shot a man and found a friend. She wasn't sure how much more excitement she could take, but now it seemed she was going home with a man so that an outlaw wouldn't kill her. Considering everything, packing seemed a simple thing to do, so she concentrated on that.

She'd need warm clothes. If he was a farmer, he might live in a shack where the wind circled through. She'd need sturdy shoes and warm socks. Maybe wool trousers would be more serviceable than a dress. With bag in hand she ran downstairs and pulled clothes from the shelves of her own store, something she rarely did.

By the time Samuel returned, she had two carpetbags full and was waiting by the back door. She'd also packed a tote sack of food. She didn't want to put Samuel out or shorten his winter food supply and, since she didn't know what he had, she didn't know what she needed, so she took one of everything. Sheriff Raines told her he'd send telegrams out tomorrow about Boss Adler, but he doubted with Christmas and the storm if anyone would have time to look at them for a week or so. With luck someone would spot Adler and hold him.

"A whole week," she whispered, almost afraid to be excited. She'd grown up traveling to school and on vacations with her aunt. Except for the summer, she'd spent all school holidays with teachers who'd offered her a place for a small fee. The past year she'd spent in Kasota Springs had been torture. Everyone welcomed her, but no one invited her anywhere. People her age were married with families of their own, and those older always seemed to have their settled groups. Maggie had no museums to wander through or libraries to spend her free afternoons in. No plays, no music, and most important, no one to talk to.

She'd grown from a bossy, know-it-all little girl to an opinionated, overeducated woman. It bothered her that she'd be spending another Christmas alone if it hadn't been for Boss Adler and the robbery. Maybe she should send the man a thank-you card once he was incarcerated. Even a drafty barn of a place sounded better than being all by herself.

"Oh, one more thing," she said as she passed the sheriff and ran back into the store. "Tell Samuel to wait for me."

She could hear the sheriff complaining that there couldn't possibly be anything else. He claimed to have seen wagon trains coming west with less baggage.

Maggie ignored him as she searched the counters. A watch—too much. A knife—too impersonal. Cuff links—too formal. A ring—too expensive. Then she saw it. A book. Not too personal, or formal, or expensive. She shoved it into a third carpetbag along with the cash box, her journal, and a shirt to replace his bloody one. As she passed the counter, she left a quick note to the woman who worked for her saying simply, "Take care of things for me until I return."

Sam and Raines were loading up her luggage when she

reached the porch. "Sheriff, will you have someone hammer a board over the broken door?"

"Sure," the sheriff answered as if bothered by the request.

"I'll ride the horse without the saddle," Sam said as he smiled at her, "but you'll have to carry most of the luggage tied behind you."

"I can't ride. I've only been on a horse one time in my life and I fell off then." Panic log-piled in her brain. "I don't know anything about how to handle a horse. Don't you have a buggy? I can handle a buggy with some skill."

The sheriff and Sam looked at her as if she wasn't speaking English. How could a woman in this part of the country not ride? It must seem as strange as saying she couldn't eat or breathe.

"You're joking." Sam raised an eyebrow. "Why would I own a buggy? I'm sorry, Maggie, but the only way down into the canyon is on horseback. You'll have to ride."

She shook her head and thought about informing him that many ladies in the cities didn't straddle a horse, but she didn't think now was the time to educate him since she seemed to be the one lacking in skill.

Raines stepped inside and grabbed a sawbuck from the store. He tossed the pack saddle over the extra horse. Without a word, the men moved all the luggage to the bareback horse. When the sheriff loaded the last bag, he turned and asked, "You sure that's all, miss?"

Before she could fire back an answer, Sam said simply, "Maggie, you take as much as you need to be comfortable. I don't want you feeling like you're doing without."

She almost kissed the man. If his cheek had been free of hair, she might have tried. She could never abide a man with hair on his face. It always seemed so backwoods somehow.

The sheriff helped her up into the saddle as if in a hurry to be rid of a problem. He didn't like trouble, and if Boss

Adler came back to kill her, there was bound to be trouble. He held the horse while Sam swung up behind her with one hand.

Sam reached around her for the reins. "I'll check in with you in about a week," he told Raines. "If you need us before then, leave a red bandanna on the north corner of Lamar's fence. I'll see it from the canyon."

"Don't suppose you want to tell me where you live?" the sheriff tried. "That canyon runs for a hundred miles."

"Not on your life. The only way I'll know Maggie is safe is if no one can find her." He looped the lead for the other horse around the saddle horn and urged his mount forward as his legs settled in behind her and he pulled her body back against his.

Maggie sat as still and straight as she could, but she was very much aware of the man behind her as they seemed to ride into complete blackness. In sudden panic, she glanced back at the fading lights of town.

"Don't worry, Maggie, I'll bring you back when this is all over." His words were low near her ear and she calmed.

She thought of saying she didn't want to go back. She'd rather face the night than have to be alone in a town full of people. This man she barely knew, this one friend, meant more to her than anyone. The town, even the store, meant little. If she could have sold it after her parents died, she'd be back teaching at the school she'd gone to for so many years.

"Thank you," she whispered, "for taking me in."

His arm closed gently around her waist. "Thank you for trusting me. There aren't many who would trust a Thompson."

"Why?"

"I don't really know. We keep to ourselves. Some of my relatives have been known to trade with outlaws and Apache from time to time, but I can't think of anyone I'm related to who has spent a night in jail. Rumor is we're a mixture of

Gypsy and Indian blood, but the truth is probably we're the stray dogs of civilization. Part everything but belonging to nothing." He thought about it for a moment and added, "Folks don't tend to trust people who aren't like them, and the Thompsons are just different."

She twisted until she could see the outline of his face. "You saved my life tonight, Samuel. As far as I'm concerned, that makes you a knight of the realm."

He smiled. "That would make you a lady fair."

She shook her head. "I'll settle for just being your friend."

"Fair enough," he said, "but it's been a long time since I've been around anyone who'll talk to me. I may not be good company."

In the darkness as he moved through trees and down into a valley, she decided now might be the time to talk about the rules. She had no idea what they were riding into, but if she was to act properly, she had to know what was expected of her. "Samuel, maybe we should talk about how it will be while I'm staying with you. We can set a few ground rules so I won't get in the way. First, I'd like you to know that I plan to help out and pay my way."

"I'll not take a dime of your money, Maggie, but I could use some help. With the storm coming in I'll have my hands full the next few days."

"Don't hesitate to ask if you think I can do anything to lighten your load." She almost giggled thinking of the excitement of doing new things. "I think there are those in town who think it would be most improper if we stay under the same roof without a proper chaperone."

"Are you worried about that?"

"Yes."

"Then rest easy. We won't be alone."

She took a deep breath and felt his arm tighten slightly as

if he feared she might fall off. "I'm not going to fall, Samuel. You don't have to hold me so tightly."

He laughed in her ear. "I kind of like holding you."

She patted his hand awkwardly. "I shouldn't be saying this, but I like having you close also. It's nice to have a friend."

"Same here," he answered.

"Then that can be our second rule, Samuel. We'll be respectful, but comfortable around one another." She didn't want him to step away from her when they reached his place. Once at a dance she'd attended while still in school, a boy had said he wouldn't touch her with a ten-foot pole. She hadn't known it then, but that seemed the standard for her life. People didn't come close.

Collecting her bravery, she added, "I think it would be fine if we touch now and then. Maybe even hug good night. I'm not from a family who ever touched, but I almost died tonight, and I think it might make me feel safer."

"You're such a gift." He laughed. "I think it would be real nice to have someone to hug good night, even if only for a week."

They were both silent as he crossed back and forth through a path she saw no markings for. It occurred to her if she had to leave alone, she might never find her way back to town. Slowly, she relaxed in his arms knowing he'd hold her safe even if she fell asleep. All her life she'd held herself in close check, but no longer. This was Samuel, the boy her mother had thought a saint, the man who'd risked his life for her.

A half hour later he helped her down. "We're home," he said.

He grabbed a few of her bags with one hand and walked ahead of her along a brick path to a door that looked like it had been built into a wall of stone. A few feet from the door he whispered, "There's something I haven't told you. It's too late to explain now, but promise me you won't say anything to anyone about what's in my house."

"All right," she whispered back frightened.

He laughed. "It's nothing terrible, but I won't promise he won't bite."

Without another word, he opened the door.

Chapter 5

Maggie stepped into a wide room with a polished brick floor and long beams running twenty feet above her. She'd expected a farmhouse with low ceilings and dirt floors. "How lovely," she whispered. A huge rock fireplace hugged one corner of the room, its chimney climbing a buckskin-colored wall made of stucco. There was a simple set of stairs running along the opposite wall leading to rooms above. Beneath the stairs was an arched doorway to what looked like a kitchen. Light from the fireplace danced around the room in welcome.

An old woman, round as a barrel, stepped to the doorway. Her face was scarred, the skin twisted like an ancient root across her throat. In her arms, she held a child dressed in a homespun tunic. "You said you'd be back in one hour," she said with a patchwork accent that seemed from no country but her own.

"I was delayed, Nina."

"I don't like walking back down the canyon after dark." The old woman glared at Maggie. "Next time do your business with your whore in town. Don't bring her here."

Maggie held her breath. No one had ever mistaken her for a soiled dove.

Samuel dropped her bags and took wide strides to the old woman. "That's enough, Nina."

Maggie wouldn't have been surprised if he'd slapped her. There was a wildness in the old woman's eyes as if she wanted to draw anger from all she met before she had time to see pity in their eyes. She glared at Maggie for a moment and then blinked a smile. "My mistake. If this one was a working girl, you couldn't afford her price."

Maggie didn't know whether to be insulted or flattered.

Sam lifted the child from the old woman's arm. His voice was calm, almost soothing. "You can go, Nina. We both know nothing will attack you on the way home. Even a coyote wouldn't eat your old flesh. But if you're so afraid, use the passage."

She snorted. "Did you bring my whiskey?"

"I did." He pulled the bottle from his pocket. "One pint for one hour. I'll bring an extra the next trip."

The old witch smiled a toothless grin. "Aren't you going to introduce me to your woman?"

"No," Sam snapped. "You didn't see her. Do you understand? No woman was here with me."

She shrugged. "Just like I don't see this baby or that blood all over your shirt. As long as you bring me my whiskey, I'll hold my tongue and not see a thing." She turned, pulling her shawl over her head, and walked to the back door. "There's stew on the stove and corn bread in the skillet. Nice to *not* meet you, miss."

Maggie watched her go. "Is that the woman they call the witch of Hideout Canyon?" Rumors had circulated about her for years. Maggie's mother used to whisper about her to some of the ladies who came in the store. People said the old witch could make potions and stop a woman from having a baby or keep a cheating husband from wandering. She used to be the only midwife who'd travel out to the ranches. Maggie's mother had been fascinated by legends and witches.

"That's her," Sam said, but his attention had turned to the child.

In her letters Maggie's mom wrote her about the witch. A dozen years ago a fire had run the canyon. Her place had burned to the ground, but the old woman walked out once the ground cooled, her little herd of goats around her. Some said no one could have survived the fire, but she came covered in ashes and moving slowly like black smoke on a still night. Others believed that the witch had already been scarred by a fire in childhood and this one hadn't touched her. Men even searched the canyon walls, but they found no cave wide enough to keep a woman and a dozen goats away from the fire.

After that the rumors grew. Some said any baby she delivered would be marked. People avoided her, and she took up the habit of yelling out at folks, calling them terrible names when she walked the roads. In an odd way Maggie felt lucky to have met her . . . pleased to know the legend was real.

Sam finally turned his attention back to her. "She's no witch, though I don't think all her mind remains." He held up the child in his arms. "This is my son, Webster. He's almost two and growing like a weed."

"I thought you said . . ." She couldn't bring herself to finish. The child obviously hadn't died.

"My wife died delivering him. I said he weighed three pounds. The midwife who pulled him out told me he was dead and even if we fought to make him take air, he wouldn't live more than a few days."

Maggie stared at this man she thought she was beginning to understand and realized she didn't know him at all. He didn't seem to notice that the child was tugging on his beard.

Sam grinned and continued talking, though his attention was now on the boy. "I couldn't do anything to help. The midwife just left him in the pan with the afterbirth while she tried to save my wife. When she ordered me out of the room, I took the pan. I thought he was dead and I ached to hear him cry out. I took him to the sink out by the barn and washed the blood off him, wanting to see my tiny son before I buried him. The cold water must have shocked his system. When he cried, I knew I had to help him fight for life. I picked him up and he grabbed my finger like he didn't plan to ever let go."

Maggie looked at the beautiful, healthy child leaning on Sam's unharmed shoulder. Sam's big hand patted him gently on the back as he walked slowly across the room.

He closed the door. "I'll put him to bed and get the rest of your things."

Maggie waited in the center of the big room as he walked up the stairs. She was almost afraid to touch anything. Not that there was much to touch. A high worktable with leather rigging stretched across it. A stool behind it. One rocker by the fire. One blue army-style blanket folded on the side of the wide hearth.

The room looked hollow.

She moved to the archway and peered into the kitchen. A stove, a sink, shelves set high on the wall with cans lined in order. Two hooks near the back door, one with chaps hanging from it and the other with a heavy, well-worn coat. A long table sat in the center of the room with two chairs. One had a pot turned over in the seat.

Again, Maggie had the feeling the room was hollow. Not lived in. Not a home. The house had enough to be serviceable, but not a home. There was no color, no keepsakes, nothing that told anything about the man and child who lived here, or the woman who'd once been the lady of the house. Maggie wondered if Sam's wife had put up curtains or covered the table with a cloth, then added flowers. Maybe he'd removed it all to push the sadness of her death aside, but that made no sense—he had the sandy-headed child, who must favor his mother, for the child had none of his father's dark hair or eyes.

"He's asleep." Sam startled her. "Nina always keeps him up talking to him, probably because no one else will listen to her. Luckily, Web doesn't understand a word."

"How did you keep him alive?" She saw this man before her in a totally different light.

"I took him to the canyon edge. Old Nina had built another dugout over the ruins of the one that had burned years ago. A few good rains brought back the grass, but the fired trees still stand like headstones around her place. I bought a goat from her and she said she'd keep the baby until I buried my wife. When I got back to the house, Danni's family had come and taken her body. They blamed me for her death, and her father, who'd beat her all her life, threatened to kill me if I caused any trouble over them taking her home. No one asked about the baby. The midwife had told them it was stillborn."

Maggie gulped down a sob.

Sam moved to the stove and shoved a log in. "I've never told anyone about the boy. My wife was fifteen when she crawled to my door and begged me to take her in. She'd been whipped until she couldn't walk for a month. I doctored her up, and when she did walk, she moved like a shadow about this place. I'd never seen anyone afraid of everything. If we hadn't married, her father would have taken her back home and continued abusing her until she died.

"If her father finds out the boy is here, he and his sons will come after Webster." Sam moved a pot to the stove, then turned to face her. "They'd have to kill me to take my son,

and I have no doubt they'd try. Old man Dolton placed no
value on girls, but he keeps his two boys close."

"Don't worry, Samuel, I'll keep your secret." She moved
toward him. "You could have told me earlier. I would have
helped. There must be things you need for a baby. I could
have helped you order them."

"I've made do. What I couldn't make, we did without, but
thanks for the offer."

She lifted her hands to his shoulders, carefully avoiding
the bandage as she hugged him.

For a moment he was stiff, cold, as if he didn't know what
to do, then he curled into her as if he'd been freezing for
years and she'd offered him the first warmth.

For a long while they just stood there, pressed together so
close she could feel his heart pounding against her. He'd
been standing so long against the world, she sensed he didn't
know how to let another person in.

Finally, he pulled away until she could look into his eyes.
"Do you think it would be all right if I kissed you, Maggie?"

She felt her cheeks redden. She nodded, not trusting
her voice.

He touched her lips lightly with his own, then straightened. "I've been wanting to do that for almost twenty years."

She laughed. "I wish you'd done it before you grew
that beard."

"I'll not do it again until the beard is gone."

"Fair enough."

Chapter 6

Sam had no idea what to do with Maggie. He'd only had one houseguest, and he'd ended up married to her. In the months Danni was with him she'd never said more than a few sentences to him. He didn't think he'd have that problem with Maggie.

He dipped her up a bowl of stew. When they sat down at the table he began eating in silence as always, but she cleared her throat.

He looked up at her. "Do you need something?"

She smiled. "Thank you for the meal."

He didn't think it was necessary, but he said, "You're welcome."

"You have a beautiful place here."

"Thank you." He stopped eating and waited for her to pick up her spoon.

"Did you build it yourself?"

"No." He thought maybe she was asking questions while she waited for her stew to cool, so he played along. "When I was twelve I went with my grandfather to take horses down to Fort Worth. He left me for over a year with a man who bred some of the finest horses I'd ever seen. That next summer when my grandfather came back to get me, the man paid me for the year's work in stock. They were the culls of his herd, but they were still the best horses I'd ever seen. I brought five mares and a stallion back with me."

"I'm surprised your parents let your grandfather take you away like that."

"My folks died before I had time to remember them, and Gran raised me like a free-range chicken. I remember once when I was five, I decided to stay out until he came looking for me. After two nights and nothing to eat but a few apples, I was so hungry I went home. I don't think he'd even noticed I'd been missing. Had the same feeling when I came back from Fort Worth.

"Gran took one look at the horses and told me I could have the canyon land he owned because it wasn't fit for farming. I was fifteen when I started this place. We built it together over three winters. I'd work for him all summer farming and raising grain, then he'd come over a few days a week all winter and tell me how to construct a house that would stand the winds. He thought I was crazy when I wanted to build the roof high and the doors wide. It took me all one winter to put the rock on the front, but it turned out like I hoped. From the road no one could make out my house from the wall of rock behind it. It's invisible, kind of like I was, growing up."

"I'll look forward to seeing it in the daylight." She finally lifted her spoon.

They were almost finished when he said, "I'll bunk in with Web. I do anyway when he's sick or wakes up in the night. You can have my room."

"I hate to put you out."

"No trouble," he lied. He loved his room, or rather the view of the canyon at dawn. Tomorrow she'd wake to that view, and the thought of it made him smile. Even though he'd been married, Danni had never slept in his bed. She'd come to him, then slip away as soon as he was finished. At first he thought she cared for him, but finally he'd decided she'd only wanted a child. As soon as she knew she was pregnant, she told him and never came to his bed again. He'd watched her growing and wanted to touch the place where his child grew, but she never came close.

Maggie stood and picked up his bowl. "You cooked. I'll do the dishes."

He watched her as she moved about his kitchen, washing up, then exploring. She was as different from Danni as night from day. He cared for Danni, protected her, tried to stay out of her way because he knew she couldn't stand to be too near, but Maggie was an equal—no, correction, she was so far his better he wasn't sure how to act. It never occurred to her that he might not want her to explore his world.

"You've a well-stocked kitchen, Samuel," she announced.

"I have a root cellar and a smokehouse out back." Sam felt a sense of pride. Before his grandfather died, he harped on the importance of being self-sufficient. By the time Sam was twenty he either grew all he needed or traded for it among his kin. Once his grandfather was gone, Sam worked from March to September on his ranch and the small plot of land that his grandfather called the farm. As his herd grew, so did barns and shelters in each pasture. From October through February he guarded his land and saw to his horses.

By the time his son was born, Sam was twenty-four and considered himself settled. He could afford to stay home more to take care of Webster for a few years and allow his herd to grow. It meant less farming and an occasional trip into town, but Sam thought the time with his son was well spent. Nina was the only person alive who knew of the baby. She came by to help out in the summer, trading watching the baby for stores of food. In the winter she traded her time for whiskey. She was dependable, but rarely said more than a few words to him.

Sam stood and faced Maggie. "I'll get my things out of my room and move your bags in."

She started to say something but stopped when he raised his hand. "It's decided."

And as simple as that, Maggie Allison moved in with Sam Thompson. He had a feeling if anyone in town knew it, they'd be the scandal of the year.

Chapter 7

Maggie woke at dawn. For a moment she couldn't remember where she was. Sun flooded a room bare of anything but a bed, a small trunk, and several hooks on the wall to serve as a wardrobe. The room was sterile, impersonal, cold; then she looked out at the sun rising over the canyon wall. The light turned the rocks into breathtaking colors. Rocks spread out in layers of earth colored like Spanish skirts dancing a thousand feet from sky to riverbed.

She crawled from the bed and wrapped a blanket around her shoulders. Maggie was drawn to the beauty of nature as she'd never been to any of the great paintings she'd seen in museums painted by masters.

When she turned, she saw Sam standing in the archway to her bedroom with his son on his arm.

"It's so beautiful," she whispered.

"That it is," he answered, but he was looking at her. "I love seeing your hair like that, so wild and grand. I remember when I was six I used to stare at it when I thought you weren't looking. I memorized that color. No other woman I've ever seen has that exact color."

She touched her hair. "I should have braided it last night, but I was too tired. I'm afraid it does tend to go wild."

"No. Don't tie it up today. Leave it down." He moved a few steps into the room. "Maggie, no one will see it but me, and I like seeing it down."

For the past year she'd felt so old. All she'd done was work and worry about what to do with her life. Most days she felt like she was trapped in a never-ending cycle of work. She worried when she couldn't sleep that she'd grow old without anything changing but the seasons. Like her parents, she'd fade year by year, until when she finally died, only a few would notice.

"I'll wear it down," she said. "But I'll tie it out of my face."

Reaching for her brush, she looked back at the archway and discovered he was gone. Quickly, she dropped the blanket and slipped into her robe. She was buttoning it when Webster toddled into the room carrying a long, thin strand of leather.

Maggie knelt down and accepted his gift. "Thank you," she said as the little boy smiled and ran back to his father.

Looking out the doorway, she saw Sam below, leaning over his workbench. Webster was bumping his way down the stairs on his bottom one step at a time.

"Sam, there are no doors."

He looked up. "I saw no use for them."

"But I need to change my clothes. Will you promise to stay down there?"

"I will."

She ran back to her bags and dressed as quickly as she could, then ran back to the landing. "Sam. There are no mirrors." He opened his mouth, but before he could form words, she shouted down, "I know, you have no use for them."

"Right." He grinned.

Maggie walked back into what was now her bedroom.

Her things were scattered across the floor. Evidently the man saw no use for chairs, tables, dressers, or wardrobes either.

Tying back her hair as best she could without a mirror, Maggie slipped into her boots and stormed down the stairs.

Sam didn't look up from his work, but Webster, who was sitting beneath the table playing with the scraps of leather, smiled at her. She noticed the legs of the table were connected by wide slats so that if Webster wanted out he would have to pass by his father's long legs. She also noticed that the hearth was built high so he couldn't have reached any fire within. Anywhere in this house would be safe for a toddler, except the stairs, and Sam had taught his son how to go down them.

"Does he go with you everywhere?"

"If I'm on my land he does." Sam watched her as if trying to guess what she was thinking. "It's cold and the snow is threatening, but if you like, you could walk with us through our morning chores before we fix breakfast."

"All right. Maybe I can even help."

"Maybe," he said as he lifted Webster up.

By the time she got back down with her coat and gloves, the two of them were dressed for the cold. Sam carried the little boy out and headed to the barn. Maggie hurried to keep up.

Once he'd closed them inside the barn, he sat Webster in a swing made from a high chair with the legs removed. While Sam worked, he'd pass by the chair and give it a shove. The boy would fly across the barn laughing as he swung out of any danger from the horses.

Maggie laughed. "You're a genius, Samuel." He didn't look her direction, but she had a feeling he was smiling.

While Sam milked the cow, Maggie tried to play with the little boy, but she'd been around so few children, she felt awkward.

"Can he talk?" she asked Sam as Web walked around her picking up straw.

"Sure. He talks all the time. I'm not sure what language it is, but he talks."

"Maybe he's just shy around strangers," she said as the boy handed her a handful of straw.

"Don't know if he's ever met one," Sam answered. "You're his first. He's probably trying to figure out what kind of animal you are. He knows most of the names."

She knelt to the boy's level. "Hello, Webster, I'm Maggie. Ma ... ma ... Maggie."

He didn't say a word.

"It's time to go back," Sam said as he walked toward them. "Web, take her hand and bring her to the house."

To Maggie's surprise, the boy reached for her hand and pulled her along behind his father. "He understood," she whispered.

"He understands more than he can say. He also knows he'd better stay up when I tell him to. I don't have time to go running around looking for him. If he's big enough to walk, he's big enough to keep up."

She smiled. Sam sounded so tough, but she noticed his steps were far slower now than they had been when he'd been carrying the boy.

She helped cook breakfast and Web sat on his father's knee while she removed the pot from the extra chair. They didn't talk much while they ate, but she caught Sam staring at her. Never one to ignore anything, Maggie commented, "You're making me nervous staring at me."

"I guess I'm not much more used to strangers than Web is. I mean you no disrespect."

"I know. Even though I see people all day long, I rarely spend more than a few minutes with them." She looked down at her empty plate. "It's so nice to sit down at a meal with someone."

He stood and sat Web near a stack of wooden boxes, then poured her another cup of coffee.

Maggie couldn't look up at him. She found herself fighting back tears. A lifetime of eating alone, of knowing it would never change, all bubbled up inside her. Even now, she hadn't been invited to stay; she'd been forced on him.

When she glanced up, she caught him rolling his shoulder as if in pain. "I forgot to check the wound."

"It's fine. Just aches a little."

"Let me check."

He shook his head. "I've got work to do. It'll keep until later. Don't worry about it."

She started to argue but guessed a stubborn streak ran deep in this man. She tried compromise. "When you get back we check the wound. Promise."

He gave in with a low voice. "Promise."

"It's almost like we're an old married couple," she whispered. "I've always wondered what it would be like eating all your meals across from someone day after day."

He shrugged. "Why don't we pretend to be just that for the week you're here? No one is around. No one will know. You'd still have your room at night, but during the day, we could take on the roles. You might decide the other side of the fence isn't so green."

She laughed. "You mean after pretending to be married to you for a week, I might remain an old maid all my life."

"Something like that."

Maggie had never heard something so outrageous in her life. People didn't go around pretending to be married. But if she never found someone, this might be her one chance to see what she was missing. Samuel didn't seem to talk to anyone. He wore his secrets close, so no one was likely to find out. When she went back to town, she'd simply say she'd been away. No one would pry. No one cared enough.

She leaned toward him as he drank the last of the coffee. "So what are the rules if we play this marrying game?"

He raised an eyebrow and she saw laughter in his dark eyes. He was liking the idea as much as she was. "From dawn to dusk you're my wife."

"Fair enough, but I'll not be bossed around."

"I already guessed that. We'll just do what we think we should, and if one of us has an idea what we think the other should do or say, we'll make a suggestion. Can you cook?"

"I love to cook. As of now, the kitchen is mine." She whirled around. "What's off-limits?"

He laughed. "Nothing. If you cook it, I'll eat it. With the storm coming in, you'll need to stay close to the house. Once I check the fences, I'll be working here or in the barn."

"What's off-limits between us?" She looked around.

"Nothing. For this week do whatever you want. Treat the place like your home and me like you would a husband. I'll take Web with me in the morning, but he likes to take a nap on that navy blanket in the other room after lunch. If you'll watch him then, I'll try to get everything ready for the storm while he's asleep."

"What do I do with him?"

"Talk to him. Hand him stuff to look at. He likes to stay close and think he's helping out." He studied her. "Are you sure you want to do this, Maggie? I'm not sure I'll make much of a pretend husband. Maybe you should back out."

She stood. "No. I want to do this."

He moved to the back door and began tying on his chaps. "Web. It's time to go to the outhouse."

The boy set his blocks down and hurried to his father. Sam pulled on his coat and folded the boy inside. "We'll be back in a few minutes."

With a gust of cold air, he was gone.

Maggie looked around as if making sure she was alone. Then she laughed. This was the wildest thing she'd ever done in her life. They were two grown-ups playing house.

She was still laughing when Sam stomped back in. Testing her limits, she said, "You're getting snow all over my floor."

He looked up as if about to challenge her bossy tone, then he grinned. "Sorry. It's really starting to come down."

He knelt and pulled a fur coat over Web. The sleeves hung long and the hood almost covered his face. "Tell your mom good-bye, son. We've got fences to ride before the snow gets any deeper."

Web didn't act like he understood, but Maggie fought back tears.

She knelt and kissed the boy's cheek. "Are you sure he's warm enough?"

Sam lifted a cradle board like she'd seen Apache women carry babies in. "He'll be warm in this, and I'll make sure the hood's low."

Sam strapped the boy in and lifted the pack to his back. Web laughed in excitement.

Maggie looked up at Sam. "I'll have lunch ready when you get back." She stood on her toes and kissed the one spot on his cheek not covered in hair.

A moment later he was gone, and for a while she wondered if she hadn't imagined the game they'd made up to play. It didn't seem possible that a grown man would suggest such a thing.

She walked through the house looking at everything. The only room she hadn't been in was Webster's room. It was small, but like everything else, organized. Books lined a shelf almost out of reach that circled the room. A hundred books, maybe more. Many of the classics and many she'd read in her childhood.

This room also had shelves built within the walls on either side of a crib. These shelves were filled with folded clothes and a few toys. A cot stretched in front of the crib, the blankets neatly folded at one end.

As she moved from room to room, one thought nagged at her mind. Nothing remained to show that a woman had ever lived here. If Sam didn't have Web to prove that he'd been married, she might have thought he was lying.

Chapter 8

Sam rode the fence lines of his property knowing that he'd lose horses in the canyon if one was down during this time. The walls of the Palo Duro Canyon protected his herd from the wind and from the worst of the weather. Years before, Quanah Parker and his tribe had wintered here. Some said Sam's people came during that time when the Indian Wars were going on, but Sam tended to think the legend was probably made up by his grandfather. Gran loved to tell stories about how his father once gave food to a starving Comanche band on the run and an hour later fed the troops from the fort chasing them.

Sam didn't know if there was any truth to it, but the Comanche never raided on Thompson land, and one of his ancestors did manage to get enough money to buy a long stretch along the canyon rim. He'd given it to his kids, who gave it to his kids until Sam's cousins owned most of the land down in the canyon below his property. They kept in contact, meeting in the fall and spring to trade. Sam laughed. Even those meetings were all business, not much hugging and helloing.

Sam often wished the relatives had bought the land all the

way to town. Then they wouldn't have the small farmers settling to the south of them. Men like Dolton and his like.

Web chattered behind him. He could say a few words like *bird* and *horse*, but most in between didn't make sense. Sometimes Sam felt like his heart hurt from loving the boy so much. "We'll be turning around soon, son."

Web made a laughing sound as they watched a deer bound out of the trees and run across the fresh snow.

Watching the deer's path, Sam spotted something in the snow.

Tracks.

One horse moving so slow no snow flew around the hoofprints. One rider crossing the edge of his land just beyond the fence line. In an hour the tracks would have been covered by the snow, but now they were clear.

Sam scanned the trees beyond his property. Someone could be watching him now. For two years he'd expected Danni's father to come back. He figured the man wouldn't face him straight on, but might take a shot at him from a distance. He'd have to be drunk and dumb enough to fire on Sam, and drunk men don't shoot straight. Sam had a feeling Otis Dolton knew if he missed, Sam would be coming for him.

So the men kept their distance and the strip of wooded land between their two ranches was never crossed. Until today.

Only, now, there was another threat. Boss Adler. He knew this valley. He'd stayed here with one of Sam's cousins before he was a wanted man. He'd even come to a cousin's fall meeting hoping to buy a horse.

Sam hadn't liked the look of the man so he didn't deal with him, but he'd recognized Adler once he stepped into the light of Maggie's store. Adler could pick him off from the tree line if he wanted to, but if he killed Sam out here in the open he wouldn't know where to look for Maggie. The shot would echo off the canyon walls, warning everyone to beware.

Sam kept his pace steady as he circled around, moving lower in the canyon. He wanted to make sure he wasn't followed. A half hour later, he passed Nina's dugout of a cabin and stopped in.

"Come to visit," she yelled, "or that woman run you off?"

Sam laughed. He'd decided a long time ago that if he had to depend on a crazy woman, he might as well join the insanity. "What makes you think she'd run me off?" He swung down from his horse and started toward her knowing she'd have coffee on a low boil at the back of her stove.

She giggled and followed him inside. "Oh, you're a looker, Sam, or you would be if you'd shave the terrible beard, but you Thompsons aren't friendly like normal folks. They say because of you and your kin there ain't no bears in these parts. They didn't want to put up with your un-friendly ways."

Sam pulled Web from his pack and let the boy walk around. Nina's three cats went on full alert as he headed toward them. "I came to make sure you have plenty of sup-plies. It looks like a bad storm coming in. If we get a few feet of snow, this little dugout will be buried."

"Afraid I'd come live with you if I ran out of supplies, and you'd have two women to put up with?"

"No. Just checking. I brought you a pound of coffee if you need it, but if you don't, I—"

"I could use it," she cut him off. "But don't think that takes the place of my whiskey."

"I didn't."

She handed him a cup of the dark brew as she asked, "You going to marry this one too?"

Sam didn't pretend not to know what she was talking

about. "Maybe I already have," he said, thinking about that morning and the pretend game they'd both decided to play.

Nina handed Web a ball of yarn to play with. "You were good to that other girl. I seen her now and then. She'd been hurt so bad I think she was more dead than alive, but this one ain't like that. She's full of spirit and heart."

Sam studied the old bag as he blew on his coffee. "Why do you say that?"

"She won't stay just because she ain't got nowhere else to go. She won't tiptoe around like a ghost. She'll want more. More than you know how to give, I'm guessing."

"You think so?" He knew the old woman was right about Maggie. Every part of him was aware she was in his house. She filled the place.

"This one you'll have to love to keep."

Sam decided to step back into reality. "She's only visiting."

Nina got busy playing with Web, and Sam thought about how much it hurt to say those last words. He didn't know Maggie anymore. Twenty years separated his memories from the woman now in his house, but he didn't want to think about her leaving. She was shy and bossy and hard to understand all rolled into one woman. When he hugged her she turned to stone, but when he let her go she didn't move away. She liked the idea of pretending to be married, but he had a feeling she didn't know any more about playing the role than he did.

He watched Nina show Web how to play with the cats instead of pulling their tails. The boy loved it when he dragged a string across the floor and one of the cats followed.

While they played, Sam pulled the coffee from the bottom of his pack. "I'll come by as soon as the snow clears."

"I know you'll come by when you can. You've been pestering me for years, and now you've bred I guess another generation will be pestering me for years to come. I just want you to know, I plan to live to be a hundred, so it might be a good idea if you produce a few more kids. Redheaded ones would be easy to spot."

Sam grinned. "She's only visiting." He swore he could read the old woman's thoughts in her eyes. "And I'm not taking her to my bed." In polite society he guessed what he'd just said would be scandalous, but the old woman just cackled.

Nina helped him load Web back into the pack, then she handed him a bundle of clean clothes for the boy. He thanked her even though he knew, like everything between them, it was just a trade.

He climbed on his horse, suddenly in a hurry to be home. The snow was falling hard now, and if he hadn't known the path to his place he would have never found it. Within minutes the snow would dust away his hoofprints. No one would be able to follow him through the rocks and trees. If someone was waiting for him to return to the pasture so they could follow him home, they'd be waiting a long time. For tonight and maybe tomorrow Sam knew they'd be safe.

Once he was home he took care of his horse and sat Web in his swing while he tried to shave in the icy water of the barn. He nicked himself a half dozen times, but finally stared at his face, reflected in water, for the first time in months. He couldn't remember the last time he'd looked at himself, but the man looking back seemed harder than he remembered. Maybe he was like Maggie, turning to stone as he aged.

Lifting Web, Sam asked, "How do I look?"

The baby patted his face, laughing.

"I know. You like the beard. I'll grow it back."

He cuddled Web close as he ran for the house. When he

barreled through the back door, the warmth washed over him like a welcoming wave.

"Don't forget to wipe your feet," Maggie called as if it were something she thought she should say. She was standing in front of the stove stirring a pot. A few strands of her dark red hair had broken free of the leather band.

Sam lowered Web and turned to pull off his coat and hat. When he turned back she knelt a few feet away, busily pulling the boy's coat off and paying little attention to her almost husband.

When she finally looked up he saw the surprise in her face. "You shaved."

He shrugged. "I did a lousy job."

She moved to him, touching his face almost as Web had. Without much thought, he pulled her into his arms, lifting her off the ground in a hug. "Oh, my," she said when he sat her back down.

"Did I hurt you?" he asked when she just stood still in front of him.

"No," she managed to say. "I'm just not used to being lifted off the ground."

"I thought that was what a pretend husband might do, but if you're not comfortable with it . . ."

"No. I didn't say that." She moved away. "Lunch is ready."

He grinned. She didn't mind him touching her, but she didn't know how to react. He could deal with that.

They ate the best soup he'd ever tasted. Once he stopped staring at her every move, he noticed a few changes in the kitchen. Things had been rearranged, some put on lower shelves so she could reach them, and a green and blue scarf was spread over the table. It was far too small to cover the length, but it looked good.

They ate in silence, both talking to the baby from time to time. As soon as he finished, Sam bundled Web up and took him to the outhouse. By the time they returned, she'd done the dishes.

Sam took the boy to the blue blanket resting on the hearth in the main room. They spread it out close to the warmth and Web curled around an old baby blanket. He was asleep within a few minutes to Sam's low voice telling him what a fine boy he was.

When Sam walked back to the kitchen, Maggie had the medical kit down and was prepared. He knew, much as he hated it, he'd have to let her change the bandage. She didn't seem to believe that wounds healed on their own.

"It's time."

He unbuttoned his heavy wool work shirt and pulled off his undershirt, which was stained with blood. She stared at him as if she'd never seen a man undressed from the waist up.

He'd never felt so naked in his life as he realized that she might not have ever seen so much of a male.

When she didn't move as he crossed the kitchen and sat down in the chair, he asked, "What's wrong?"

"Your chest is so hairy," she managed to say, as if she was looking at a freak show. "I didn't notice last night because of all the blood."

"I'm not shaving it." He smiled and she smiled back. "Still want to change the bandage?"

She went to work talking nonstop about the class she'd taken once in school. He had no idea why he needed to know all the details about a first aid class in some all-girls school, but he liked the sound of her voice. Finally, he decided she was nervous and somehow talking helped.

Blood had dried in spots, making the dressing hard to peel away, but he gave her credit for being gentle. Both holes had started scabbing over and he doubted there would be any more bleeding. He joked that he did more damage to himself shaving than the bullet did. She didn't laugh.

When she finished, he told her she'd done a fine job. She brushed her hand over the bandages, then looked away.

"Look at me, Maggie."

Slowly she met his gaze.

"Don't touch the bandage, touch me." Sam held his breath waiting. If he didn't tell her what he wanted, she might never figure it out.

She didn't look away as she raised her hand and brushed her fingers along the top of his shoulder to where the bandage ended and his throat began. She ran her fingers along his neck and he felt his muscles tightening to her touch.

With a sudden jerk, he circled his arm around her waist and pulled her down onto his lap. She was stiff, as if made of ice, but she didn't pull away. "What's wrong?" He thought of setting her back on her feet and pretending he'd never grabbed her.

"Nothing," she started, then gulped down a breath and said, "I don't like to be startled. If you plan to hug me or grab me, I would like to know in advance. I don't like surprises."

"Maggie, I don't want to talk you into anything, or bully you or force you. If you don't want this, we can go back to being little more than polite strangers. If you'd rather I didn't touch you, I give you my word I never will again." He figured he'd have to break both arms to keep that promise for a week, but he'd keep his word.

She stared at her hands and he felt like a fool for moving too fast. He should have been happy just to hug her good night or maybe hold her hand. He shouldn't have grabbed her in a bear hug or pulled her onto his lap. He'd been around people so little he didn't know how to act, and he'd never even tried to court.

Maybe the Thompsons hadn't run the bears off; maybe they'd married them all into the family. That would explain his hairy chest and his lack of manners.

He covered her hands with one of his. "I don't know how to do this. I never remember playing at anything as a child and I've never even thought about courting a woman. All I know is I want you near."

She looked up. "This near?"

He smiled. "This near is a start."

"All right, I'll stay this near while we talk."

He nodded, thinking he'd pretty much agree to anything if she'd stay right where she was.

She took a deep breath and started, "Tell me about your wife. Do you miss her dearly? Did you remove everything about her from the house to help with the pain of her loss? Did you love her deeply?"

Sam wished he could have made up something about a great love affair, but he'd lived an honest life and couldn't lie now. Even though he thought he might lose Maggie, he told her the truth. The whole truth about what Danni looked like when she arrived all bloody and broken. About how she never wanted him near even though with time he didn't think she was afraid of him. He told Maggie why he married her and how she never ate a meal with him or spoke to him unless he asked her a direct question. Sam even told her of Danni coming to his bed and how he understood she didn't want to be touched any more than necessary to breed.

"I'm not sure why, but she wanted a child and so did I. The mating never took more than a few minutes, and she was gone as soon as it was over. Maybe she wanted a child who'd love her."

"Did you love her?" Maggie rested her hand on his shoulder.

"No," he admitted. "I cared for her. I tried to be thoughtful and kind, but I never loved her. She was like a shadow moving in the house. She was broken inside and I didn't know how to help her. I don't think if we'd lived together a lifetime she'd ever have wanted me around. Not once did I touch her except to mate."

He sat in the kitchen a long time holding Maggie and remembering his wife for the first time in a long while. She'd come to him with nothing. He'd bought her a few dresses, but she only wore them when others wore out. He remembered coming back to the house after he'd dropped Web off at Nina's cabin. The midwife was loading up her things when he rode up. She told him his wife's family had come and taken the body and they'd sworn to kill him if he tried to follow.

Sam remembered walking back in the house thinking it didn't matter where she was now, no one could hurt her anymore. The bloody sheets were still on the bed, but nothing remained of her. It was almost as if they'd taken not only her few clothes, but also the footprints where she'd walked. It was as if she'd never been there.

He held Maggie a little tighter in his arms. He didn't want that happening when she left. He wanted to know she'd been there with him, if only for a few days. He wanted his house, his world, changed. Even if all he'd have left in a week were memories of Maggie, he wanted them.

"Maggie," he whispered as he brushed a strand of her hair away.

"Yes," she answered as if she too had been deep in thought.

"I don't want to startle you, but if you've no objection I thought I might try kissing you again." He didn't wait for her answer. Her slightly parted lips were all the invitation he needed.

He pressed his mouth over hers and felt her make a little sound against his lips. Moving his hand up her throat, he turned her head to just the right angle and tasted her lips. He felt her shudder like a frightened bird, but she didn't turn away from his kiss. When he heard her make a sound again, he slid his tongue between her open lips and tasted her.

Surprise rocked her body, but he held her to him and continued the kiss. Slowly, an inch at a time, she began to melt in his arms and the kiss turned to magic. He was learning. When he tried something new, a moment later she tried it also. He cradled her against him, hungry for more. She was hesitant, sometimes shy, but she didn't move away. She remained in his arms, letting him kiss her completely.

When he finally lifted his head and looked down at her, her cheeks were warmed with inner fire and her eyes sparkled like stars. He didn't try to stop her as she stood and turned away from him.

She walked to the window and stood, her hand spread flat against the cold glass.

He decided maybe she needed some time. "I have to go check the barn. I'll be back before Web wakes up."

Her nod was so slight he wasn't sure she'd heard him.

He grabbed his coat and walked out still pulling it on. In an hour he'd be back apologizing or kissing her again, but right now if he didn't put some distance between them, he'd be kissing her again.

Chapter 9

Maggie stood in the kitchen for a long while after Sam left. When she'd thought of playing like they were married she'd guessed there would be long talks over dinner and maybe enduring embraces good night. She'd never dreamed there would be kisses. Not just kisses, but one long kiss that shattered all she knew of kissing. One kiss that curled her toes and made her body feel like it was on fire.

Touching her lips, she could almost feel the way his mouth had covered hers. He'd held her close while she was falling as if to say he was there for her. This was nothing like what she thought the game would be between them . . . this was more. She'd wanted a tiny twinkling star moment to remember, and he'd offered her the universe.

The only remaining question seemed to be if she would be brave enough to accept his offer, and Maggie knew deep down in her soul that she'd never been brave.

Web was awake when Sam returned. He carried in wood and stoked the fire while she held the boy, then Sam sat him beneath his workbench as he started work. "I want to catch the last few hours of light," he said without looking at her.

Maggie felt in the way, so she went to the kitchen and decided to make bread. She had to do something besides stand around all day dreaming of one kiss. Sam would think she had only air for brains.

An hour later when she had the bread baking, she stood in the doorway and watched father and son. Both looked like they were doing the same thing, playing with leather straps, only Web's were just scraps and Sam's were blending into a harness.

She'd bought enough harnesses to know fine work. "Do you sell these?"

"A few, now and then. I take the train into Fort Worth every spring to sell horses. I've got a man near the livery who buys all these I have time to make."

"You wouldn't have to go all the way to Fort Worth. You could sell them in town." She bit her lip to keep from adding *in my store*. If he sold them to her, it would mean they would be talking on a regular basis even after this crisis was over. She could even imagine him coming in late with orders and her offering him supper before he had to head home.

He shattered her daydream by saying, "Don't want to sell them around here. I prefer to take them to people who don't know me."

She moved closer. "Afraid they might come looking for you when one of them breaks?"

"No. Afraid they might come looking for me to buy another one. I'd just as soon not have the grassland worn to my door."

"I understand. It's fine work, Sam."

"Not much else to do on a day like this. Snow's up to my knees. It'll be three feet deep by morning. Looks like we're going to have a white Christmas for sure."

Web caught her skirt and tugged as if wanting her to join him in his cage. Maggie laughed and held out her hands. "Come here, boy, and I'll let you taste the first slice of bread that's cooling." She glanced up at Sam, remembering the game they were playing, and added, "Come to your mama."

Webster came right to her and she laughed, thinking how good it felt to hold a child. A hundred times over this past year, she'd seen babies in the store and wanted to lift them up into her arms, but the few times she had she'd seen that sad look in the parent's eyes and known they were feeling sorry for her. To them she was always a woman without children, without a husband, without family.

Now, for a few days, she could hold Webster as if he were hers and no one would look at her with pity. Kissing his cheek, she took him into the kitchen and sat him at the table out of the reach of the warm bread and butter. He played with a spoon as she began slicing the bread.

Thirty minutes later Web was laughing as she tried to get butter out of his hair. She looked up and saw Sam in the doorway watching. "I had to come see what all the racket was about," he said.

"We're having a bread-and-butter tea." She giggled. "Without the tea."

Sam smiled at his son as he fought to keep Maggie from getting him clean.

"It's hopeless," she announced and brushed his hair in place before setting him down among his blocks. "He keeps using his two front teeth to scrape the butter off my bread."

Sam came near and knelt beside his son, handing him blocks one by one. His voice came easy to the boy, but when he looked up at her, the smile faded. "I saw tracks near my fence line this morning."

"Maybe someone is just passing," she said, trying to stay calm. Nothing had happened all day and she was starting to believe she was safe. The nightmare at her store seemed far removed from her.

He shook his head. "They headed out into nowhere. I've

never seen a rider travel that direction. Whoever it was had to be riding the fence hoping to spot my place."

She cut slice after slice of bread as if needing to keep her hands busy. "Who do you think it is?"

Sam shrugged. "Might be Boss Adler, but I doubt it. He doesn't know where you went, and even if he recognized me, he'd only know I lived in the canyon. I doubt any of my kin would tell him which place is mine even if he got close enough to their farms to ask."

"Or it might be Danni's father, Dolton." Maggie tried to think. "You said he hated you and blamed you for his daughter's death. Maybe he or one of his two sons decided to even the score."

"No. If he got drunk enough to do something about it, he'd just cut the fence and come after me. He knows where I am." Sam moved closer to her and helped himself to a slice of warm bread. "I heard his older boy, a horse of a man, got cut up pretty bad in a knife fight a few months back, and the younger one couldn't be more than sixteen." Sam thought, then added, "I doubt he's grown to his full meanness yet. One of my cousins told me the oldest boy is always getting in trouble for beating up the whores."

"Are you serious? If a man did that, wouldn't the law arrest him?"

Sam shrugged. "Probably not. I don't think Sheriff Raines worries about those kind of crimes."

"You are serious."

When he didn't deny it she wished she hadn't asked.

"Who else might be looking for you?" She didn't like the idea that there was a list of people coming carrying trouble with them. The man she was staying with didn't seem to have anyone except her on his friends list.

"The sheriff might be looking for us. He seemed awfully

interested in knowing where I lived. He asked me twice the other night."

Maggie shook her head. "Sheriff Raines is far more interested in retiring than anything else. Unless, of course, you committed a crime? He might hope to catch one more criminal before he hangs up his guns."

He raised one eyebrow. "I stole a kiss not too long ago. Does that count?"

Maggie fought down a giggle. She hadn't decided what to do about the last kiss, and the fire was back in his eyes. "It counts."

He smiled and leaned down beside Web as if letting her off the hook. "Your mama makes good bread, doesn't she?"

Web reached for his father's bread with sticky fingers and Sam laughed. "He's rarely had real bread. Corn bread now and then and sourdough biscuits sometimes, but never this. This," he lifted the piece he'd managed to hang on to, "is heaven and far beyond my skill."

"Didn't Danni make you bread?" Maggie wished she hadn't asked the minute the words were out of her mouth. She'd already asked enough questions about a woman two years dead.

"No," he said simply. "Her mother died when she was six. Her knowledge was limited in both cooking and sewing." As if he felt like he had to pay his wife a compliment, he added, "She could clean, though. For the time she lived here the place was always spotless."

"Maybe she was proud to be here," Maggie said.

"I never thought of it like that, but maybe."

As the light faded outside, Sam carefully drew the shutters before he lit the lamps. They ate an early supper talking of their lives, then played with Web on the blanket near the fire for a while before Sam reached for a book. "I usually read to Web before bedtime. I know he's too young to understand, but I'm hoping he hears the rhythm of the words. As soon as he's ready I'll teach him to read."

Maggie stretched her hand out. "I'll read tonight if you like."

Sam lifted Webster in his lap and began to rock as Maggie read. An hour later she looked up and found them both asleep. Smiling, she touched Sam's shoulder, loving that she felt so comfortable around him to do so.

He opened his eyes and looked at her as if he was trying to decide if she were real or only part of his dream.

"We should put him to bed," she whispered.

Sam lifted the boy to his shoulder and stood. Without a word, he carried his son to bed.

Maggie followed and watched for a moment in the doorway of the small second room before turning and moving down the hallway to what was now her room.

The moon was up and snow had stopped falling. The view from her window had changed completely since dawn. Yet another masterpiece spread out before her like a grand painting that covered the entire wall of a museum. This morning had been all fire and color. Tonight's world lay silent in blues and grays.

"I never light a lamp or candle in here. It would only take away from the beauty outside."

She smiled without turning around. She'd known he'd find her to say good night. What had started between them wasn't over, could never be over with one kiss.

But he didn't reach to touch her. He only walked past her to the window. She knew the memory of his tall dark outline against the moon's glow would hold to the corners of her mind until her last breath. He was a good man, she thought, more strong in mind and body than handsome. No matter how he dressed, no one would ever mistake him for a gentleman from the city, though, in his way, his ranch was very much a business and to her he seemed a very gentle man.

She liked the way he moved, always with purpose, never wasted energy, but best of all, she liked the way he was still, as if the world could circle around him.

Finally, he turned. "I need to tell you something, Maggie, I've never told anyone."

"All right." She hoped it wasn't some deep dark thing he'd done in the past that would stop her from liking him.

"There's a passage in the back of Webster's room behind one of the bookcases."

She breathed. Not much of a secret. She probably would have noticed it if she'd looked harder that morning when she'd walked through the baby's room.

"One of the reasons I built this house in this exact location was because there is a small entrance to a cave there. My grandfather hated two-story houses because he feared he'd be trapped by fire on the second floor. Like Nina, he lived through a terrible fire the year I was living in Fort Worth. That was one of the reasons it took him so long to come after me. He barely had enough supplies left to eat, much less feed me."

She smiled. "You found the way Old Nina saved her sheep and her life."

"I did, the summer I came back from working in Fort Worth. It became my quest for months."

She could almost see him as a boy climbing the cliffs and trails until he figured out the mystery, and then he hadn't told anyone, but used it to his advantage.

"I just wanted you to know about the passage, though it's probably filled with spiderwebs. If something happens and you're trapped upstairs, grab Web and go into the cave. Just feel your way along the narrow passage. You'll come out within sight of the old woman's house."

"I'm sure we won't have a fire the few days I'm here." Maggie understood why so many people feared fire. Even her parents checked and double-checked that all the lamps in the store were out before they climbed the stairs at night.

He grinned. "I don't know. I get warm just thinking about you."

She looked away, embarrassed by his directness and loving it at the same time. There was no need for them to follow proper rules. They were friends. They could be honest with one another, and she loved it.

"I don't want to startle you again, but I would like to say good night with a kiss. How about you come to me, Maggie?"

She took one step.

"Closer," he whispered.

She took one more step, feeling her own heart pound.

"Closer," he said again and raised his hand to take hers.

One step and she was so close she could feel the warmth of him.

Without holding anything but her hand, he leaned down and kissed her. A gentle kiss of promise. "Closer," he whispered against her ear as he tugged gently on her hand.

She leaned until her body touched his and she heard a low sigh of satisfaction against her ear.

"That's just about right." He moved his chin against her hair and lifted her hand to his shoulder. His fingers drifted along her arm and down the side of her body.

"I . . . I . . ." She tried to think of something to say.

"Don't talk. I just want to feel you near so I'll always remember what it was like." His hand moved to the small of her back and he tugged her until her body molded against his. "Relax. All I'm going to do is hold you for a while."

She put her arms around his neck and held tight to keep from falling as his hands moved up and down her body with a light touch. He kissed her ear and then her cheek as she shook against him. "It's all right. Breathe, Maggie. This isn't going to hurt."

"I know. I'm just nervous. I've never . . ." she managed to say.

"I know, me either. I wish I knew more about how a woman likes to be touched, but somehow I think we'll find our way."

He wasn't holding onto her; she could have stepped away. She'd spent her life stepping away from everyone. Her parents had started the pattern she'd followed all her life. Never get too close to anyone. Never care too much. Never feel too deeply. Her parents, even her teachers, must have thought they were saving her the pain of separating by never allowing her too close.

Sam's strong hands moved down past her waist and fanned out over her hips as his mouth opened against her throat. The warmth of his tongue circled her skin as his hands began to move up over her back, pressing her closer against him. He wasn't holding his feelings back and letting her remain safe from being involved. Tears trickled down her cheeks as she let herself drift with the moment and not worry about the pain that would surely come when she was alone again.

Melting against him, she breathed deep as he retraced his journey from her hip to the back of her hair. This time he pulled the tie holding her hair and dug his hands into her wavy curls. "God, I love the feel of you," he whispered as if to himself and not her. Gently he tugged a handful of her hair, pulling her head up. His warm breath brushed over her cheek a moment before his lips moved over hers. This time the kiss was light, teasing.

She cried out at the pure pleasure of it and heard him laugh softly against her cheek. Then he kissed her again and again, playing with her mouth but never kissing her deeply as he had before.

"I can't get enough of you," he whispered against her throat as he tugged a few buttons of her blouse free so he could taste a spot lower on her neck.

When he bit her lightly, she jerked away.

"Did I hurt you?"

"No," she managed to answer. "Do it again, please."

He laughed as he kissed her throat. "You'll never have to beg. I'm happy to do whatever pleases you."

Then he was kissing her again, and when his mouth journeyed down her throat she felt him loosen another button, pull the material back almost to her shoulder, and taste her once more. This time she made a little sound of pleasure and would have melted to the floor if he hadn't been holding her.

Finally, he raised his head and held her tightly against his chest. Both their breathing slowly returned to normal. His grip around her relaxed, but his hand still stroked her back. "You all right with this?" he whispered against her hair.

She wasn't sure what he meant. The kissing, the touching, the feel of his body pressed against hers. "No," she finally answered and felt him go very still. "I'd like to be kissed the way you kissed me in the kitchen at least once more."

She felt more than heard his laughter.

"You're a wonder, my Maggie." He moved to her mouth and granted her request.

"More," she whispered when he broke the kiss.

"You're a pretty demanding wife." His hand slid past her waist once more to rest on her hip. "I like the feel of you as well as the way you kiss me. I like the softness of your bottom beneath my hand. I like all of you."

She raised her head and waited to see what would happen next. His features were in the shadows, but she could feel the moonlight on her face, or maybe it was just the warmth of feeling desired for the first time in her life.

"Maggie," he said as he rubbed his cheek against hers. "I don't think I'll ever deny you anything in my power to give. If you want to be kissed all night long, I'll do my best."

With that, the conversation was over. He took her mouth with a hunger that surprised her. When she met his passion with her own, she felt him shake as if taken off balance for a moment.

For a while they kissed, sometimes deep, breathless kisses and sometimes light and playful. He couldn't seem to get enough of the feel of her hair in his hands, and she'd grown used to the rise and fall of his hard chest against her breasts.

She nestled beneath his arms. "Is this how it is between married couples?" she asked.

"Between some," he answered. "Very few, I think. Maggie, I kissed a few girls when I was more kid than man, but I've never touched or kissed anyone like I did you right now." He laughed against her hair. "If you had any sense, you'd slap me or have the sheriff toss me in jail."

"I wanted this. I wanted to feel." She drew in air and added, "I want more."

He was still for a while. "How much more?"

"Just a little more."

He lowered his mouth and she welcomed his gentle kiss as she raised her arms and moved her fingers into his midnight hair. One arm held her gently as she relaxed into the warmth spreading through her.

She was lost in the flood of feelings washing over her when he lifted her in his arms and carried her to the bed.

Without breaking the kiss, he lowered her on her back and rested his weight beside her.

"How about I just hold you all night?"

She made a sound but wasn't sure it made any sense. The feel of his long body running along her side warmed her completely.

"Go to sleep, Maggie," he whispered as he kissed her on the cheek.

She lay awake for a long while knowing he was doing the same. Finally, his breathing grew regular and slow. Rising, she spread a blanket over them both. When she lay back down beside him, he pulled her to him.

Late in the night, when she'd been half sleeping as she drifted between dreams and reality, she felt him move his hand over her body as if even in sleep, he needed to know she was there.

His hand stopped over her breast, cupping it.

She didn't move.

His fingers tightened slightly, then released her. In a sleepy voice he whispered against her hair. "I wish you were mine. All mine."

She tried to keep her breathing normal. She fell back asleep wondering if she'd really heard him say the words or if she'd simply dreamed it.

Chapter 10

Sam woke just before dawn. Maggie was curled beside him sound asleep. He smiled as he lifted her off his arm and tucked the blanket around her.

The air seemed bone cold, but any heat from the fire below had traveled up to keep the sleeping quarters above freezing. He checked on Webster curled in one corner of his crib. Sam knew if he was lucky, the boy might sleep another hour. By then he'd have the fires going and the first floor would be comfortable.

He'd just finished washing in the sink when he saw Maggie standing at the archway. Her hair was a mess and her clothes looked like she'd slept in them, which she had. She looked adorable. A few years ago he'd stopped dreaming, but if he still did, Maggie standing in his kitchen just as she was now would be his favorite dream.

"Morning," he said, watching her rub her eyes.

"Morning," she answered. "If you can wait a few minutes for breakfast, I'd like to clean up first."

"All right." He leaned against the counter and waited.

"Without you watching, if you don't mind."

"Oh, of course." He had no idea where he would go. Three feet of snow blocked both doors and if he went up-stairs he'd wake Web.

Finally, Sam decided to turn his rocking chair to the fire and pretend to be reading while she padded around.

First she tiptoed upstairs and brought down a load of her things, then he heard her pouring water in the tub.

Sam closed his eyes and swore. She was taking a bath in his kitchen only a few feet away and there wasn't even a door between them. Not that he really needed to look, he told himself. He'd imagine how she looked without clothes every time his hands had moved over her body last night. That might not be the same thing as looking, but it was probably as close as he would ever get.

He heard her splashing and decided she was torturing him. If she stayed the whole week he'd be building a door, not to offer her privacy, but to bolt him out.

She must have put on coffee because he could smell it. Maybe she wouldn't notice if he walked through the kitchen, got a cup, and poured himself coffee. He could even glance at her and apologize saying he'd forgotten she was bathing. That sounded like what married people might do.

Hell, he almost said aloud. She'd never believe him. Know-ing Maggie, the coffeepot would probably dent his skull on his way out. She wanted his kisses, she'd made that plain, but when he'd asked her if she wanted more she'd said *only a little,* as if she always rationed out pleasure. He could almost see her sitting in her tiny apartment above her store eating one biscuit from a decorative tin each night. Two or three would be too many. She could only have a little.

He leaned back in his chair and tried to think of anything else except Maggie nude in his kitchen.

"I'm finished." She startled him a few minutes later.

Sam opened his eyes. She was wearing some kind of fancy robe the color of a summer blue sky. It had tiny white pearl buttons running all the way down the front. He'd seen them in stores and guessed they cost more than a saddle. Her hair was tied up in a funny knot on top of her head.

"If you don't mind, I thought I'd dry my hair here by the fire."

"I don't mind."

She handed him a cup of coffee, then pulled a comb from her pocket and set to work on her hair.

"Mind if I watch?" he asked, knowing he'd fail miserably at pretending to read with her right in front of him.

He thought he saw her cheeks blush, but she shook her head slightly.

The house was silent except for the crackling of the fire. All the world outside his home could have vanished and Sam wouldn't have cared. He'd never thought watching a woman comb her hair would bring him such pleasure. The tangled mess slowly became silk.

"You look content," he said.

She smiled. "I am, but there is something I'd like to do."

"Me too," he answered, thinking his idea probably wasn't anywhere close to hers.

"I'd like to have a little Christmas here with you and Webster. I could make cookies and a fine dinner. Maybe we could have a small tree and decorate it with ribbons. It would be almost like a real Christmas."

"Sounds like a good idea. I'll shovel out enough to get to the barn. There are a few evergreens growing along the fence line of the corral."

She stood, her hair flowing round her like a beautiful cape. "It'll be great fun." She moved beside his chair. "You're the best almost husband in the world."

When she leaned to kiss him, he pulled her into his arms. After a light kiss, he whispered against her ear. "I don't want to startle you, Maggie, but I'd like to touch you if you have no objection."

She laughed. "You are touching me, Sam."

Moving his hand over the silk covering her breast, he whispered, "I'd like to touch you here."

She stilled for a moment.

He feared he'd stepped too far in this game they played. Touching a woman there seemed a very private place. The last thing he wanted to do was frighten her, but how could he explain that the closer they grew, the closer he wanted to be?

He bumped the back of his head against the rocker and swore. "Slap me if you want to, Maggie. I deserve it."

When she raised her hands to her throat, he knew he'd frightened her.

"Or maybe just shoot me. My brain hasn't worked right since I put my arm around you for the ride here." Even now he couldn't forget how his arm lightly brushed just under her breasts all the way home. He had a feeling he could pour hot lye-soapy water in one ear and let it drain out the other and it still wouldn't wash his mind clear of her.

An apology was on his lips when she began unbuttoning her robe. "We've only a short time before Webster wakes."

The robe opened an inch, then two as she moved down the buttons. When she'd opened almost to her waist, she leaned back against his arm and closed her eyes.

He couldn't move. He had trouble believing she was in his arms waiting for him to touch her where he was sure no other man ever had. He'd never touched a woman like this. He'd doctored Danni when she'd come to him that first night bleeding and cut, but there had been no enjoyment in it. To touch Maggie now for no other reason than to give and take pleasure seemed a luxury beyond any he'd known.

Leaning down, he touched his lips to hers, loving the way she smiled before opening her mouth slightly. He straightened and moved his hand down the opening of her robe. Her skin was softer than he'd expected. Slowly, he slipped his fingers over the rise of her breast as he watched her face.

When his hand covered one breast, she arched toward the warmth of it and made a little sound, but she didn't move away. She was so perfect, he thought. As he gripped her in his hand, he covered her mouth with his and kissed her deeply so the next sound she made was smothered. For a while he was lost in the need to hold her, touch her, taste her. She kissed him back, but she didn't move otherwise. Her hands remained tightly clasped at her waist.

He raised his head when he finally became aware of her stillness. "Are you all right?" he said, his fingers still caressing her.

"Yes," she answered, her words unsteady. "Is this thing done between husbands and wives?"

"I think so." He moved his hand away.

She straightened, sitting up in his lap. "Not in the mornings, I'd think. Otherwise no one would get to work on time."

He laughed. "So you liked it?"

She began buttoning her robe. "I did. Would you mind doing it again tonight, please?"

"I'd love to, Maggie, if it pleases you." He loved the honesty of this woman. Kissing her forehead, he added, "It pleased me greatly to touch you so. The softness of—"

"Samuel," she interrupted. "I don't think we should speak of such things."

He smiled. "As long as we do them, I think I can refrain from talking about it."

"Fair enough," she said.

When she slipped off his lap, he let his hand move down her back and pat her bottom. "Is it all right to say you're a beauty, my Maggie? A treasure to hold." He saw the blush rise in her cheeks.

"I'll go get dressed now. Promise you won't come up for five minutes."

He didn't trust himself to answer, but he did manage a nod. He was too busy wondering if she blushed all over.

When she came down a few minutes later she had on trousers tucked into boots and a man's wool shirt, but nothing about her reminded him of a male. She stood on the first step and raised her arms. "How do I look? I've never worn trousers, but they seemed appropriate for shoveling snow."

"It's still pretty cold out there. We may not get as much snow in the canyon as they do up top, but it is still just as cold."

"I was planning on my husband helping to warm me up when we're finished."

"I can do that, if it's what you want, but I'll respect my shy wife's request and not talk about the details." He thought it funny that she would do things she couldn't bring herself to talk about. Most men he knew talked about things they'd probably never do when it came to loving a woman.

She laughed as if she'd read his mind.

He walked to the bottom of the stairs, planning to pull her into his arms, but a pounding on the door stopped him.

No one had ever knocked on his front door. The few who visited him from time to time always came to the back. Sam reached for his rifle and motioned Maggie to go back upstairs. Whoever came knocking on a day like this had to want to see him badly.

He thought she might object to being ordered, but she ran up the stairs. With his hand on the lock, he glanced up to make sure she had vanished.

"Who is it?" he yelled through the solid wood.

"It's Sheriff Raines. I come out to tell you it's safe for Miss Allison to come on back to town."

Sam hesitated. He didn't want it to be over. For a few moments this morning he'd believed their game could almost be real.

Maggie appeared at the top of the stairs, Webster on her hip as if she'd been carrying the boy since he was born. "Really? We're no longer in danger?"

She looked so relieved Sam felt bad for wishing she'd stay here longer. He wanted a little more time, but she must be dying to get back to her world.

He threw the bolt, lowered his rifle, and opened the door. As the sheriff stomped in, Sam asked, "How'd you find me?"

"It wasn't hard," the man behind the sheriff answered as he leveled a Colt to Sam's chest, "but crossing a mile of snow wasn't easy."

Sam glared into the cold eyes of Boss Adler. He knew he'd never get his rifle up in time to fire before Adler killed him, but if he'd been alone, he might have tried. He was a dead man either way. All he could hope for was to buy enough time to let Maggie get away. Out of the corner of his vision he could see the empty balcony and guessed she'd slipped back before either of the men entering had a chance to see her.

Take the passage! he screamed inside. *Take the passage*.

The sheriff drew his attention. "Sorry about this, Sam, but Adler offered me enough money to retire in style. I don't have to kill anyone, all I have to do is look the other way."

Sam took a step backward. Icy wind blew into the house, but he couldn't feel it. There was no room in his mind for anything but fear for Maggie and his son. He had to give them time. Every second he could slow Adler down increased her chances. "How'd you find me?" he asked again.

Sheriff Raines laughed. "It took me a while to figure it out. Adler and his men were in town to case the bank. I didn't see any harm in helping them. After all, they wouldn't be robbing it until after I retired. But then it got messy when they decided to rob the mercantile. I planned to run in and fire a few shots while they rode away with the money, but you got in the way."

Sam saw the whole picture. "Then you decided to make sure we were hid away before you turned us over to Adler. That way there would be no killing of witnesses in town, right?"

"Something like that," the sheriff said. "Only you wouldn't tell me where you lived. I was about to lose a good deal of money before I remembered a few years back when you stole old man Dolton's daughter. I figured he knew where you lived and would be more than happy to tell me."

Sam took another step back, but Adler advanced like a cat playing with a mouse.

"So why weren't you here the first night?"

Raines frowned. "Strange, but it seems Dolton, much as he hated you, didn't seem willing to tell us. We had to wait around until his sons rode out. The big one headed into town to drink, and who knows where the kid went. We just waited until they were out of sight before we rode in to talk to Dolton. Adler had to carve on the old man several times before he started talking. He seemed more afraid of your kin than the knife. By the time he'd told us all we wanted to know, he'd bled out. I guess that makes his killing an accident. You can thank him and this storm that you lived one more day."

Sam looked at the man holding a Colt at his chest, but his words were for the sheriff. "Adler isn't going to let you go, Raines. You're as dead as I am."

The sheriff laughed. "You're wrong. Boss and I have

become friends. He needs me. I'm the one who will explain everything to the folks in town. Old man Dolton came over here, found Maggie Allison in your house, and killed her. You came home, found her body, and went over and killed Dolton at his place, after you tortured him, of course. The older son must have seen you and shot you, then I confronted him in town, and unfortunately, I'll have to shoot him before he tells us any more than what we can guess from the bodies."

The sheriff smiled. "I retire a hero. Adler goes about his business without a witness to testify against him. Since you and Miss Maggie are both alone without any family, there'll be no one to ask questions. By the time the snow melts no one will even care."

"Only one problem." Sam smiled. "Maggie isn't here."

Chapter 11

Maggie moved through the baby's room feeling panic dancing in her veins. For a moment she searched the walls looking for the door.

Nowhere.

She tried to think. Sam hadn't said a door. He'd called it a little passage, but she couldn't remember what else he'd said.

It wouldn't be in the floor or the ceiling. It had to be in the walls. She held a sleepy Webster close as she ran her free hand along the walls. When she reached the second built-in bookshelf, the frame gave slightly.

Maggie tugged and an opening appeared. She could hear Sam and the sheriff arguing downstairs. The moment she'd spotted Boss Adler coming through the door with his gun drawn, she knew they were in trouble. Her instinct was to run to Sam, but she knew he would want Web safe. That had to be her first priority.

Grabbing a blanket, she covered Web's head and moved into the dark passage. Once in, she tugged the bookshelf back into place. It crossed her thoughts that maybe she could hide there and wait until she knew it was safe, but if the baby made a sound, they'd be found. Her best plan of action was to be as far away as possible when someone opened the passage. If it was Sam, he'd come after them. He'd know where she was headed. If it was anyone else, her life would depend on finding somewhere safe to hide.

Maggie crossed her arms over Web and moved slowly along a tunnel that must have been an underground spring at one time. Water, a few inches deep, still trickled in the uneven grooves at her feet. She bumped along trying to protect the child and keep her balance as she moved down slippery rock.

Listening, she prayed she didn't hear a shot. The spiders and mud didn't matter. *Just don't let Sam die.* She knew Adler had come to kill them both. Maybe not being able to find her would buy Sam time.

She felt like she'd moved along the natural tunnel for half a mile before she saw light. Web hadn't made a sound until he saw the sun reflected off snow; then he began to cry.

Maggie's arms ached, but she held him close as she stepped from the blackness into the blinding light of snow. Wind whipped around her, turning the cold air to freezing. She couldn't see anything. She had no idea which way to go and she knew it wouldn't be wise to stay in the tunnel.

Sam had said something about being able to see the old woman's dugout from the cave entrance, but all she saw was snow.

Webster held to her tightly but she knew the blanket wouldn't keep him warm.

Panicking, she searched the horizon. All she could see was snow. Slowly she turned in a circle. Snow. A few rocks. The charred remains of what had once been trees.

Sam's description of Nina's place drifted across her panic. *Nothing left but burned tree trunks that stuck up like tombstones in her front yard.*

She stared at the dead trees and spotted a tiny curl of smoke from a cabin built half in the ground. The place was almost completely covered in snow. It looked to be only a hundred yards away, but the wind had whipped snow around, leaving drifts almost to her waist.

Step by step she moved toward the cabin. The snow fought her progress. Web wiggled, wanting down, but she couldn't risk it.

Finally, sweating and freezing at the same time, she made her way to the cabin door.

When Nina answered the knock, both Maggie and Webster were crying. Nina stepped outside and took the boy from Maggie.

For a moment, Maggie just stood still, trying to breathe as her muscles contracted in exhaustion.

"Come on, girl!" Nina yelled. "You made it this far. You can walk a few more steps."

Maggie forced one foot to move and then another. When she finally stepped inside, a blast of heat hit her as painfully as a hundred bee stings.

Nina dropped Web into her old chair and pulled the wet blanket away. The boy was sniffling from fright, but didn't look hurt. "Stay here and be still," Nina told him. "Maybe the cat will come sit on you if you do." She covered him with a quilt and shoved the chair closer to the fire.

Web stopped crying and watched the three cats.

Nina moved to Maggie. "You took good care of that boy, but you look terrible. Take off those wet boots and frozen trousers. I'll find you a blanket. We got to thaw you out a little at a time, so don't get any closer to the fire."

Nina helped her tug off her wet boots and trousers, then dropped a blanket over her head. "You got ice in your hair, girl. You came through that cave, didn't you?"

Maggie nodded.

"Then I'm guessing there's a world of trouble at Sam's place if you're here." The old woman stood and bolted the door before she sat an old gun on the kitchen table. "I can't do much about the trouble, but I can help you."

The clock on the old woman's mantel seemed to tick at half speed. Maggie finally sat by the fire, her hair drying wildly around her as she drank the strongest coffee she'd ever tasted. Nina fussed over the boy while she asked questions.

"They won't come here." The old woman was guessing the future. "Not that many folks know about my place. Not even Sam tries to stop by when it snows. The trail is too dangerous from above."

The day aged and Maggie thought she might go insane with worry over Sam. She guessed that if Adler didn't kill him outright, he'd start trying to beat her whereabouts out of Sam. She knew Sam would die before he said a word.

Nina circled past her and mumbled as if she'd read Maggie's thoughts, "He's alive, girl, don't you worry. I can feel things. I know."

"Would you tell me if you change your thinking?" Maggie didn't know whether to believe the old woman or not, but she had to ask.

"Of course I will. If Sam's dead, you'll have to start worrying about this baby. He'll be yours then."

"Mine?"

Nina barked a laugh. "He would have been anyway. That first time I saw you, you know what I saw in Sam's eyes?"

"What?"

"I saw longing. I saw need. The kind of need a man gets when he has to have a woman for a lifetime. I knew you were going to be his."

"But I'm not his."

Nina grinned. "Yeah, you are, girl, and if he dies today, you'll mourn him like a widow."

Maggie started to argue, but realized she couldn't. The old woman was right.

Chapter 12

Sam took the first few blows Adler gave him without even trying to duck. It wouldn't have mattered. The first time the Colt slammed against his head, the handle left a gash across his cheek and split his lip. The second time, he felt the blow at his hairline. Blood dripped in a steady stream over his left eye.

After that, Adler tied him to the worktable and took his anger out on Sam's body with the butt of his rifle. He kept yelling for Sam to tell him where Maggie was.

Sam never made a sound. The icy wind blew in the open door, numbing the pain.

Finally, the sheriff yelled and stopped the beating. He grabbed Sam by the hair and lifted his head off the table. "If you'll tell us where the woman is, I'll make him kill you and her quick."

Sam glared at the sheriff, thinking he was worse than the outlaw. Boss Adler was an animal, probably had been all his life. Rumor was he killed his mother when he was eleven and left his drunken father locked in the house to burn. But Raines had been a sheriff for several years, and before that he'd ridden with Colonel MacKenzie in the Red River Wars.

He must have been a good man once, but something inside him had twisted.

"How about I cut a few fingers off?" Adler suggested to the sheriff. "That sure got old Dolton talking."

"It wouldn't do any good. He'll never talk. Kill him and we'll go find the girl. She couldn't have gone far in this weather. I'll search the house, you take the barn. We'll find her."

Adler widened his stance and pulled his hunting knife. With both hands on the handle, he raised the knife above Sam's chest.

Sam closed his eyes and tried to picture Maggie holding his son. He wanted to walk into the hereafter with that one thought in his mind.

A blast of gunfire roared through the house like a freight train at full speed.

Sam jerked, thinking he was dead and the pain hadn't hit him.

Gunfire answered from somewhere close and another blast rattled the walls.

Then silence. Absolute silence. Sam wondered if this was what dying was like. Not painful or messy, just silent. His ears were ringing, but beyond that he heard nothing but his heart pounding.

He opened one eye. If his heart was making so much racket, he couldn't be dead.

Sam looked around the room and saw nothing. The sheriff and the outlaw seemed to have vanished. The door was still open, cold wind blowing in along with bright light.

Sam tugged at the ropes holding his hands and feet to the table.

"You still alive?" A voice came from nowhere.

Sam tried to see through the blood over his one eye that wasn't swollen, but he saw no one. "I'm alive. Untie me."

A shadow moved across the light at the door. The boy in the doorway couldn't be more than fifteen or sixteen. The buffalo gun he carried was bigger than him. Sam thought he looked like Dolton's youngest kid, but he couldn't be sure.

"I had to kill them," the boy said as he sat the rifle down and picked up Adler's knife from the floor. "You should have seen what they did to my pa."

"It's all right," Sam said in a low voice. "You did what you had to do."

As the kid cut the leather straps, Sam tried to sit up. As he did, he saw the bodies of both the sheriff and the outlaw. They'd been standing on either side of the table. The boy had shot them both in the head, and the buffalo gun hadn't left much of the skulls intact.

"You look terrible, Sam Thompson."

Sam would have smiled if he didn't hurt so badly. "You know me."

"Sure, my pa was always saying how he was going to ride over here and kill you one day. He hated you."

"You feel the same?" Sam coughed up blood.

The kid shook his head. "I used to come over here and visit my sister when you were out. She said you were good to her. She said she wanted to have your baby 'cause you were a good man, and that'd make the baby good."

Sam tried to breathe. He wished Danni had told him that once. Half the time he felt like she thought she was trapped in his house.

"What's your name?"

"Eben."

"Well, Eben, do you think you can get me to town? I've got an old sled that will hold us both." Sam could see the room darkening and knew he didn't have much time. "You'll have to get there fast. I think I'm bleeding inside."

"You're bleeding pretty good on the outside too, Sam."

The blackness claimed him before Sam could answer.

Chapter 13

Maggie waited at Nina's for two days without word from Sam. She was afraid to try to go back to the house even though the snow was melting. Sam could be dead and they could be waiting for her.

With each hour she felt safer knowing they hadn't found the passage. Nina's cabin was far enough down into the canyon that the sheriff wasn't likely to come down, and even if he did, Nina had a plan to meet him at the door.

The old woman kept telling her that Sam was still alive, but it made less and less sense. If he was alive, why hadn't he come after her? He could have walked the passage and been here even with the snow and mud.

On the third day, a tall man who had the same coloring as Sam knocked on Nina's door.

To Maggie's surprise the old woman opened the door and yelled, "What'd you want, Andrew? I don't have time to visit with no-good Thompsons passing by."

The tall man didn't seem to take offense. "I come by to see if you got the boy. We didn't find his body."

Maggie pushed past Nina. "What boy?"

The tall man was ten, maybe fifteen years older than Sam, but he had the same dark eyes. He removed his hat.

"Sam's boy. When I saw Sam's old sled headed into town I knew something was wrong. I know Sam don't want no one in his business, but all his kin know about the boy. I followed him to the doc's place in town. The Dolton kid was with him and he told me what happened. A man named Adler pretty near killed Sam, but the Dolton kid stopped it."

Maggie stood in the cold, trying to take in everything the stranger was saying. Sam was hurt, but he was alive.

"Well," Nina shouted. "What else, Andrew? I swear, getting anything out of you men is harder than milking a squash."

"I told the Dolton boy we'd bury his pa and whoever was in Sam's house. Less said about it the better." He stood swaying slightly like a tall pine, then he added, "It's the Thompson way, I guess."

Maggie couldn't believe what she was hearing. "We have to let the law handle this. Three men have been killed, and at least one of them tried to kill Sam."

Andrew looked at her like she wasn't too bright. "Town don't have any sheriff right now. The men who killed old man Dolton are both dead. There is no one to try and no one to tell."

"Where'd you bury the bodies?" Nina asked as if the matter of telling was settled.

"Over in the growth of trees between Dolton's land and Sam's. The ground was so frozen we couldn't dig deep, but we covered them good with rocks. By the time the oldest boy sobers up in a week or two, the brother will have thought of a good story. Their pa was fond of taking off for parts unknown. As far as Adler, I doubt anyone will look for him, and the folks in town will just think the sheriff started his retirement early."

"I want to go to Sam," Maggie asked. "Will you take me into town?"

"I'll take you home, but not to Sam. He wouldn't want people seeing you come to him. He knows there would be talk. If he makes it through this, he'll come to you. If he doesn't, he wouldn't want you to see him die."

Nina agreed. "No one needs to ever know you were here. That's how Sam would want it."

Maggie hadn't slept in two days. She was exhausted and frightened and worried. "What about Web?"

"I'll keep him here for a few days. You go rest. Sam will come to you as soon as he can."

Maggie could not bring herself to ask what would happen if Sam died. She couldn't think about it without falling completely apart. As if watching her own life happen mindlessly, she wrapped in a black shawl of Nina's and climbed up behind Andrew Thompson. He didn't say a word to her on the ride to town or when he helped her off the horse at her back door.

She climbed the stairs to her rooms and collapsed into bed. Sixteen hours later, she woke to the sun shining in. Like a wind-up toy, she moved about her rooms, taking a bath, dressing in the same dull clothes she always had dressed in, tying her hair back in a neat bun at the back of her neck.

Her time with Sam seemed more a dream than reality. The dullness covered her as she cleaned the glass from the store floor and decided to leave the storefront boarded up for a few days. The sheriff must have kept his word and told everyone she was visiting friends because no one came by to check on her and no one expected the store to reopen until the new year.

Every ounce of her body wanted to walk to the end of town and visit the doctor. If Sam was there, she told herself all she needed to do was see him and know he was alive. She didn't even need to talk to him. But deep down she knew she wouldn't be able to leave him if he was hurting or even dying, and she also knew he wouldn't want anyone to know.

Sam Thompson was a private man. Somehow if she told anyone her story of all that had happened since the robbery attempt, she'd be betraying him.

Three days passed, then four, then a week. Maggie no longer measured time. She'd set her logical mind in motion. She'd wait for Sam to come even if he only came to say good-bye. If he died, she'd somehow find Nina's cabin and take Webster. She'd sell the store and go back East where no one would know she wasn't the boy's natural mother. She'd live as a widow, for Nina was right—that was exactly how she would feel.

On the third day of January, Maggie reopened the store. Christmas and the storm were over, though snow remained packed on most of the roads. Every woman in town seemed to need to shop. A few asked about her broken door, but none asked about how her Christmas had been.

Midmorning Maggie was busy adding up purchases with both of her part-time employees restocking as fast as they could. Several women were shopping while an equal number just seemed to be visiting when suddenly a child's cry rattled the store.

Every mother reached for her children as a toddler shoved past ladies' skirts and ran toward Maggie.

She jumped from her stool and ran around the counter just in time to catch Webster.

"Ma Ma," he cried. "Ma Ma."

Maggie hugged him to her. "It's all right, Webster. I'm here." The sun had just come into her world.

The mercantile was silent as a tall man walked slowly toward her. His arm was in a sling and she noticed his hat hid a bandage, but no man in the world had ever looked better. Even with a thick start to a beard, she saw only perfection.

Maggie smiled at him and for a moment there was no one

else in the room. The hunger and love in his eyes told her all she needed to know.

Webster had stopped crying and was playing with the bun at the back of her neck. Though Sam only looked at her, Maggie became aware that everyone in the room was looking at him.

"Ladies," she said in a bold voice. "I don't believe you've met my husband."

Before anyone could think of a question, Sam circled her waist and pulled her around the counter to her small office.

He leaned over carefully as if he were still very sore and whispered in her ear. "You'll need your coat. I'm taking my wife home."

Maggie didn't hesitate; she turned to the coatrack and began pulling on her coat. The journal lay open on her desk to the page where she'd written *One wish—a loving man for one day.*

"One day's not enough. I'll take a lifetime."

"A lifetime of what?" Sam asked.

"Of loving you." She smiled at him. "And of doing all kinds of things we'll never speak of."

"I don't want to play a game, Maggie. If you come with me it's for real. Forever." He kissed her again with Webster wiggling between them. "And I'm not taking the time to shave before I kiss you again."

"I'd like to go home now. It's about time we had that Christmas we planned." For the first time in her life, she feared her heart might explode. "The girls can handle the store until I get back."

Sam took her hand and led her out the back door where an old sled waited. "On the snow, we can make it home in this, but as soon as I'm able, I plan to teach you to ride."

"How hurt are you?"

"Doc says I need several days of bed rest, so I thought I'd better come get my wife." He winked at her.

Maggie could hear all the ladies gossiping inside, but she no longer cared. After all, she was a Thompson now, and Thompsons keep to themselves.

NAUGHTY OR NICE

DEWANNA PACE

To Karen Kay Williams:
You are the epitome of what I think is best in a woman.
You're smart, you're loving,
and you don't take crap off anybody.

Love you, Sis.

Chapter 1

The Texas Panhandle
Wednesday, December 21, 1887

James Elliott III glanced up and squinted, finally noticing the angry grayish white clouds scowling on the northern horizon. Afternoon light had taken on an oddly brighter hue than what the morning offered, paling the prairie's beauty. Snow clouds.

Better watch out, he told himself as he rose from a bent-knee position where he'd been digging in the prairie, *or you'll wish you knew a little more about keeping warm in Texas and a little less about its so-called legends.*

If he'd been paying attention, the drop in soil temperature the past few hours should have warned him that some kind of storm was brewing. But he hadn't been. The excitement of knowing his search for the rosettes might finally be over had kept him absorbed and digging, ignoring caution.

This *was* the place he'd been seeking from one end of Texas to the other since spring. He knew it. Felt it to the marrow of his bones. Victory was so close he could almost imagine the tiny red bulbs that, come spring, might bloom into the mythical buffalo clover of Texas legend—pink bluebonnets.

All spring he'd found blue bluebonnets, even the somewhat rarer albino ones near the Alamo. A few of those had pink tips, but none were totally pink. A *curandera*, a half-Indian, half-Mexican medicine woman who had great knowledge of plants and herbs, had told him to seek the end of the buffalo trail and he would find what he sought, but to make sure it was what he truly wanted. He'd thought her mutterings odd at the time but found she had given sage advice. The last Indian uprisings had been quelled in the Texas Panhandle and the buffalo had met their end here on the Staked Plains of the Llano Estacado. Testing of the soil promised that this stretch of Texas might actually offer up the pink prize.

James dusted the dirt from his hands, then stretched his fingers and long, lanky legs to ward off the cold settling into them. He loved the feel of working with his hands and had elected not to wear gloves to work the soil. He'd wanted no hindrance to come between him and the first touch of his sought-after treasure.

Maybe finding your gloves and spectacles should be the first order of business, he told himself. James immediately patted the top of his head, remembering how many times he'd gone looking for his spectacles only to find them straddling the unmanageable dark tangle of curls he'd inherited from some family member he'd wished he'd known.

Not there.

He checked the lapel of his chambray shirt. No, he hadn't hooked one edge of the wire frames into the lapel where it gathered at the neck as he sometimes did. Where had he put them? *In the saddlebags with your gloves*, he remembered suddenly, not wanting to leave them somewhere out in the prairie in case he got distracted. Up close, he simply saw better without them and, since he'd planned to work in the soil all morning, logic had said it would be better to put them where he knew he could find them.

As he swung around, James's breath suddenly rushed from his lungs and lodged midway in his throat. Where in God's creation was his horse?

He'd left him hobbled near the cottonwood tree so the roan could forage some of the fresh mint growing near it, but there wasn't a tree in sight now. How far had he walked from his campsite that morning? The hours of the day ticked by in James's memory and he realized that in his growing sense of excitement, he'd covered more of the rolling prairie on foot than he meant to. *Absentminded, that's what you are*, he berated himself. *Mister I'll-Do-What-Nobody-Else-Can-Do. Now look at you. You've proven yourself nothing but a lost greenhorn.*

The reality of how deeply in danger he'd placed himself rooted James where he stood. He was out in the middle of nowhere. Wearing no coat. No gloves. All of those things and his spectacles were back at the tree with his horse. And . . . and it was a big *and* . . . he had no idea how far away he was from that tree or shelter.

A snowflake kissed the tip of his nose. Another cooled his cheek, dissolving as the heat of his hand brushed it away. Suddenly, a gust of wind swirled around him in a dervish of snowflakes, chilling him to the bone at the strangely beautiful sight of dancing white death.

"Better find the roan and save the beast from your stupidity," he warned, his words now rushing visibly from his mouth as frosty wisps of air, "so you can do the same for yourself."

Snow eddies rushed ahead of the whiskey wagon making its way down the rutted path that led from Old Mobeetie near the Oklahoma border toward the town of Kasota Springs. Already, snow piled in drifts against any barrier that opposed the growing force of the wind. Not that there were many in the long stretch of treeless prairie. The team of four oxen pulling the heavy load had slowed their steps considerably a couple of hours ago warning Anna Ross, their driver, that what she feared as possibility had become fact.

A blizzard had set in. The snow clouds from the north had rushed faster than she'd expected to belch white fury upon the Texas Panhandle. The poor ranchers had barely survived last winter's storms, the worst in Texas history. Now the fear of more to come sent a chill of foreboding through Anna, making her wish she could take her hands off the reins long enough to put another blanket over her lap and tug the yellow slicker she wore a little more securely up behind her neck.

Jack had refused to stay beneath the blanket she'd thrown around them, insisting to cast his one-eyed attention at the poor beasts making their way home in a lumbering race alongside them.

All morning she and her dog had watched cattle drifting down the two hundred miles of fence that the XIT ranch had built a year earlier to guide their stock home in case they wandered too far from food. For hours, the drift fence ran parallel to the wagon's path. If she hadn't already suspected the brewing storm would be a mighty one, the movement of the cattle trying to reach safety was evidence enough to warn of the approaching danger.

"We should've taken the train," she told the tiny golden-haired dog sitting next to her on the driver's seat, then called out encouragement to the oxen to keep pushing on. But if she had taken the train, she would have had to deal with all the fuss and bother with the people who were bringing in the new bell for the church steeple. And then there would be all those children on board headed for the orphanage. She just didn't have it in her to see those sad little faces. It was hard anytime to see such need, but at Christmas, it broke her heart.

No, taking the wagon to Mobeetie to fetch her saloon's supply of whiskey for the winter had been the right thing to do. She'd make it right. Come hell or a high-winded blizzard.

For friends, she had also picked up a list of merchandise meant to be used for the Christmas holiday. She couldn't let them down. Her friends in Kasota Springs weren't all that many, and disappointing them didn't set well with her. Anna flicked the reins and set her jaw to the task, giving the dog a quick wink. "Got to get these presents home, don't we, Jack? If Saint Nick can do it, so can we . . . huh, boy?"

Jack barked, making her laugh and easing some of the tension that gripped her. Jack might be all of five pounds, his head bigger than the rest of him, but he had the heart of a longhorn.

"You make one scrawny-looking reindeer, and I suppose with my red nose," she wiggled her nose trying to keep it from feeling so numb, "I could probably lead the team in the night sky. Do you think Santa would go for that, boy?"

Jack barked again, this time louder and with more intensity. Suddenly it became a continuous yapping that raised the hair on the back of his neck. He sprang to all four feet, then sailed off the wagon seat and into the air as if he were a bird taking flight.

"Jack, come back!" she yelled, jerking the team to a grounding halt. "You'll kill yourself out there!"

She could barely secure the reins and jump down herself before she lost sight of his tiny body bouncing through the drifts like some kind of crazed jackrabbit.

Anna thumbed up her slouch hat just enough to see better

where he was headed. A lone tree in the distance seemed to be her pet's intended destination. Of all times for him to need to relieve himself. Jack wouldn't hike his leg to mark his territory anywhere it was cold and didn't have plenty of bark. Leave it to him to find the only tree for a hundred miles.

She chased after him, fearing he would land in some high drift and be unable to bounce his way out. Thankfully, she'd worn a riding skirt for the return journey home, so her legs weren't as encumbered as they might have been. Still, they were getting colder by the minute as she trudged her way across the prairie after him. Good thing the dog had legs the size of buttonholes, or she'd never catch him. "Fool dog. When I get hold of you, I'm going to strap reins around you and make you lead the . . ."

The exaggerated threat died in her throat as she caught sight of the heap of snow where Jack had stopped, yards away from the tree, still yapping away. A horse lay on its side, its feet hobbled. Frosty air billowed from its nostrils with every breath. The snow around it was stained with blood. A whinny erupted from its throat and dark eyes stared at Anna as if asking for help.

"Be quiet, Jack. He's scared," she instructed, trying to take measure of the animal's injuries but, from this distance away, not finding any clue of why it was bleeding. A closer look would help if the horse would let her. "Move away, Jack. Let me see why he's down."

The tiny dog would not budge but quit yapping. Then Jack did something totally out of character. He stuck his nose in the snow and started digging. Jack hated cold. Sometimes shivered on even a warm day. Something under that drift of bloodstained snow near the horse had the dog's full attention.

All of a sudden the drift moved. Jack began to whine

and dig more. A man's bloody hand reached out, patted the dog, then fell back down and lay perfectly still.

Jack hiked his leg and peed on the man, marking his find.

"Oh my Lord." Anna bounced forward in the snow to reach the stranger's side and started brushing the snow away from him. How long had he been out here? How much blood had he lost? "Mister, can you hear me? Can you stand? How bad are you hurt?"

Her battery of questions was met with a groan and a shake of his head, but he managed to sit up just enough to brace his body with one palm. "My hand," he said in an accent that sounded from back East. "I cut my hand when I was trying to free the roan from the hobble." He shook his head, as if trying to gather his wits. "Don't know how much blood I lost. Must have gotten dizzy and lost consciousness."

He wasn't a line rider from the XIT, as she first suspected. The men who rode each twenty-five-mile stretch that made up the two-hundred-mile cattle fence would have greater skills than this man. They wouldn't have been so careless.

She took off the bandanna she wore around her neck and tied a makeshift tourniquet over the cut, stemming the flow. Anna reached out and raised the stranger's beardless chin, urging him to look up at her. Eyes the color of fine whiskey stared back at her, slightly glazed and surrounded by a forest of dark lashes. Though he was pale from being out in the elements too long with no coat and no gloves, his strong jaw and solid cheekbones carved his features handsomely. She had to force herself to look at his hand to keep from staring too intently at his face.

This was no time for the heat of attraction that instantly ignited in her bloodstream and raced to quell the chill bumps that had frosted her skin for hours now. The man was hurt.

She needed to get all of them to safety. "Can you walk by yourself?"

He nodded. "I think so. But first . . ." He motioned toward the horse. "Can you see if he can? I can't let him die out here. It would be my fault."

Anna moved to the roan and took a good look at the hobble. The beast had almost chewed it in half trying to finish the job the stranger had started with the knife. They must have been out here quite a while for the animal to have taken ground.

"Where's your knife?" she asked, looking around the snow but not finding it.

"It's got to be somewhere close by. I passed out almost immediately from the cut." He carefully brushed at the snow around him. "The sight of blood and I don't mix well."

That fact relieved Anna somewhat. Maybe he had merely been out for minutes. Maybe he was stronger than his pale face promised. Maybe he hadn't lost so much blood that she could still get him to safety in time. She couldn't be sure how tall he was until he stood, but she had to make sure he could stand on his own. Getting him, the horse, Jack, and herself back to the team was going to be hard enough without her having to carry him.

"If you don't mind getting my spectacles out of the saddlebags," the man requested, "I'll be more help trying to find the knife. Or maybe we can use one of the other tools in the bag."

Anna moved toward the saddlebags, whispering low words of reassurance to the roan that she didn't mean him any harm. "Better hope your luck is improving, mister. If they're not on this side of the bags, you can forget about those spectacles. They'll be crushed beneath all that weight. Why aren't you wearing them anyway?"

"I should have been but made an unfortunate choice.

Still . . . my luck's already improved. You came along. They'll be all right."

Anna searched through the bag and found an odd assortment of tools and, sure enough, the spectacles and some gloves. A long coat was rolled up behind the saddlebags. She grabbed it as well.

When she offered him the spectacles, he lifted his injured hand. "Would you mind putting them on me? I'm not sure I could do it at the moment and not get blood all over them. My hands are awfully cold."

She opened the wire frames and carefully slid them over his ears, intimately aware of how close their faces were now so she could make sure she didn't stick the frames inside his ear instead of over them. Their breaths mingled in a frosty dance and she had to gulp hers back when a glorious smile stretched across his lips. Yes, lips, jaw, cheeks, and pearly white teeth all added up to one fine-looking stranger.

"Thank you," those lips said, offering his gratitude.

"You're welcome," hers replied while Anna's mind tried to think of something to focus on other than the way his mouth moved. "How about the gloves? You want me to put at least one on you? I don't imagine you can fit one over that hand."

Whiskey-colored eyes darted to stare at the blood-soaked bandanna. All of a sudden the stranger's grin sank into a grim line.

"What's wrong?" she demanded, watching what little color he had drain from his face.

"Excuse me a moment, miss. I think I'm going to pass out again."

And he did.

Chapter 2

The amount of time and effort it had taken to get the horse on its feet, help the weakened man mount the roan, trudge their way back to the team, tie off the horse behind the wagon, and situate the stranger safely on the driver's seat so he wouldn't fall had almost proven Anna's undoing. She was so exhausted she could barely hold the reins.

But there was no time for exhaustion. The harder the team plowed through the snow, the more Anna realized that they could not possibly make it back to Kasota Springs in time. That meant they were going to have to take shelter somewhere before they found town. But where?

The tarpaulin that covered the whiskey cases and merchandise wouldn't be enough to provide any kind of relief from a blizzard. She couldn't use it for a makeshift tent. They'd freeze to death. She remembered one of her saloon patrons telling of a line rider caught out in last January's blizzard who had cut open the bowels of a beef and climbed inside the carcass to stay alive. She'd do that if she had to, but the prospect of taking an animal's life to save her own would be her last choice. There had to be another way.

It was difficult to tell just exactly where they were along

the road to Kasota unless she caught sight of something familiar in the distance. Piling drifts and blowing gusts made everything impossible to distinguish in the blinding fury of the storm. She'd thought she heard the train whistle once but couldn't have been sure it wasn't the wind misleading her. All Anna could do was keep the team moving as long as it would and pray it was headed the right way. Snow obliterated the rutted road in front of her, leaving nothing but a swirling white sheen.

The stranger shifted next to her, his head leaning against her shoulder as he slept. Only Jack's body shivering between them beneath the lap blanket they shared kept the man from any closer touch. At least she knew how tall he was now. He had to lean a considerable few inches to lie against her. At five feet, eight inches, she was taller than most women.

"I don't even know your name," she said, not realizing she spoke her thought aloud.

"James Elliott the Third. Yours?"

He was awake! She almost wished that if they were meant to meet their Maker today, he could have drifted off to gentle sleep and never known any more suffering than a cut hand. Her only consolation was that, at least now, they wouldn't die without knowing each other's names. "Anna Ross."

"Very glad to meet you, Miss Ross . . . or is it Mrs.?" His head lifted from her shoulder at the prospect. "I do apologize. I must have dozed."

"It's Miss, and you were exhausted," she reminded, taking no offense at his closeness. "I'm glad you could rest. You may need your strength."

"The storm's worsened."

"Quite a bit, but we seem to be staying ahead of it slightly. I'm hoping it veers off a little before we get where we're going. At least give us a little time to get inside somewhere."

She did her best to reassure him. "I've seen storms bull their way for hours then, all of a sudden, turn gentle as a lamb. Let's pray this particular temper tantrum is almost over."

His body shifted into a rigid alertness that hadn't been there moments before. "May I help with the reins?"

"Not with that hand you won't, but thank you for offering." She wished he could have. Her arms and shoulders were so tense from gripping the reins that she felt as if she'd tumbled down a cliff and somehow survived.

"Then what can I do? I must be of some help."

Anna nodded. "Keep watch for something, anything that might tell us where we are. With the snow so deep now, I'm not sure we're even on the road anymore."

"I'm new to the area," he informed her, "as you can probably tell. Any clues as to what I should be seeing?"

"A ranch house is what I'm hoping for. Maybe the train tracks that would at least tell me we're close to the road. I could follow those all the way into town." She didn't say they probably wouldn't make it that far in time. "Do you think you could turn around and open one of those crates?" She started to say *without hurting yourself again*, then thought better of it. No reason to die mean-mouthed.

He managed to accomplish the task.

"Now reach inside and get one of the bottles."

"Whiskey?" He shifted back around and held the bottle in his uninjured hand. "So that's the tinkling I heard in my sleep. Bottles clicking together."

His chuckle filled the space between them, delighting Anna. She liked the sound of it, deep-throated and unrestrained. His laughter was contagious, making her smile. "What's so funny?"

"I kept hearing the creaking of the reins and wagon tethers, combined with those tinkling bottles. I dreamed Santa was taking me for a ride on his sleigh."

The old German story of the toymaker Nicholas Klaus and his wife who had delivered toys to the children of their town sprang into Anna's mind. She started to laugh at the Third's joke . . . What was his name? She was so bad with names. Hell, she'd just call him Trey. But the reality of how that story had ended made her smile fade.

Klaus and his wife had died in a blizzard.

"Open that bottle and hold it up to my lips," she instructed him. "I need a drink and I don't want to let go of the reins."

He did as told and she took a long draw. The whiskey burned like liquid fire going down but, chilled as it was, the liquor warmed her to the frosty tip of her nose. "Now you take one. It'll help some with the cold."

He didn't bother to wipe the rim before he took a swig, and she wondered if he could taste anything about her. The thought of tasting *him* made Anna want him to hurry with the bottle so she could have another go at it. When his tongue flicked out to lick the drops that stained his lips, she almost let go of the reins and jerked the bottle from his hands.

"Easy, Miss Ross," he warned, holding the bottle to her lips again. "Slower is better, don't you think? We wouldn't want to put ourselves in any danger here."

Were they talking sips or something else? Whoo-howdy, but she was getting warmer by the minute. And the taste of him was definitely on the bottle. Pure scrumptiousness. Liquid lust. Man, muscles, and something else uniquely the Third that she decided she would check out a little deeper if they lived through the storm.

Anna girl, answer the man. "Frankly, slow never got me anywhere." She met his gaze directly. "In my experience, the faster done, the less it's gonna hurt."

Trey was gentleman enough to busy himself with another drink and not ask what she meant.

* * *

James was surprised to discover what fast friends he and Anna became. Perhaps it was merely the amount of whiskey the two of them had shared in the past few hours. Maybe it was the fact that they both thought they might be living their last moments on earth and didn't want to die with a stranger. She might not admit it, but he could see it in her face when she thought he wasn't watching. He could hear it in the way she kept trying to find humor in their situation and joked about it. He hoped their friendship was more than their circumstances and the fact that both of them were tipsy, but he would take whatever had spurred on their need to become more than strangers.

He never thought himself much of a talker but, apparently, Anna set him at ease like no other person in his life ever had. He always felt so on guard, so cautious of revealing anything about himself that might make him sound less than others. Mr. Must-Be-Perfect, he was, so he could prove his worth to those who had taken him in. So he could thank them for taking in the discarded.

That's why he had enjoyed himself here in Texas this past ten months. He was alone where no one knew him. Where he didn't have to live up to the expectations of being an Elliott. He could make a mistake and it didn't matter. He could discover his real self while he searched for the one thing that would, indeed, make him extraordinary among his adopted, well-accomplished family.

The pink bluebonnet. He had almost forgotten about his search. He'd been so intrigued with learning about Anna that he realized his search for the rosettes would now have to wait until the blizzard passed and possibly till spring.

Just how much of himself had he told her? He couldn't quite remember. Certainly not the fact that he'd been abandoned as a boy, or his need to prove himself to himself. The Elliotts loved him. He knew that in his heart. But he didn't know if he was worth that love. How could he? All he knew was that he had been a very lucky boy found on the streets and taken in by good-hearted people. What kind of man didn't know who he was? Have some sense of his own worth? He needed to prove himself worthy in some way and Anna, from what he could tell, was a woman of great confidence. She might laugh at his great secret. He had definitely not proven himself anything but a greenhorn to her.

She seemed to be an amazing woman. She made her own living and had the knack to easily draw someone into trusting her. Anna could drive a team and wasn't afraid to journey alone for her own supplies. She'd adeptly rescued him and his horse and maintained a calm certainty that they would survive their dour circumstances. James had always heard Texans had great bravado and tremendous strength of character, but he'd thought they were talking of their heroes. Now he could see that even their "ordinary" women were heroines in their own right.

His own great wish in life was to be extraordinary in some way. Maybe if they survived the storm, he would trust his secret with her. Maybe, if he knew her enough, she would help him discover how to become more than what he was. Maybe, he chuckled inwardly, he could become half the man she seemed to be. For now, he would settle for more simple conversation.

"You got awful quiet for a minute there, Trey." Anna broke into his thoughts. "You're not going to sleep again, are you? I need you to keep watching ahead."

"I'm awake. Just thinking." James studied the distance and decided he needed to wipe off his spectacles again. He took them off his face and rubbed the snow from the glass. "My spectacles keep frosting up."

"A lot of good they're doing you right now. We can barely see a few feet in front of us." She sighed. "I wish the wind would let up a little so we could see farther. You might as well take them off if they keep glazing over like that. You said you see better up close without them, right?"

He faced her and nodded. "Yes. Like just now I realize you have freckles on your nose and your eyes are sparkling blue."

"They always sparkle if I drink whiskey. Dead giveaway that I'm intoxicated." She batted her eyes playfully, deepening the twinkle in their depths. "Not that I drink all that often."

A muffled bark under the lap blanket made James laugh. "I think Jack just disputed your claim."

A tiny nose popped out from the cover, then the tiny brown body stretched itself awake. He hopped into Anna's lap and curled there, shivering.

"Can't keep a secret around Jack, can I, boy?" Anna nodded toward their laps. "Pull the blanket over him, will you? He thinks he's got to attach himself to me if he hasn't touched me in a few hours. I noticed he was snuggled up next to you for a while. You must be warm-natured."

"I usually don't sleep with any . . ." James pulled the blanket up to cover Jack. "I mean, I don't require as much clothing as most people. Well, I guess you would say I'm rather hot-blooded most of the time." James put back on his glasses and glanced away, finding no way to salvage his bad choice of words. "I don't think any of that came out as I had intended."

Anna laughed. "Maybe not, but it answered me rather well," she teased, trying to sound as formal as he meant to be. "You've got to get over that bashfulness around here, Third, or you'll become everyone's favorite stick to whittle."

It was then that he noticed it—her accent. Something not

quite as Texan as before. "Anna, are you from back East originally?"

Her spine straightened slightly. She shifted on the driver's seat and stared at the path ahead. "Isn't everybody?" she evaded.

"I hear New England in your voice sometimes. Muted by years in the South, but I'd bet you originally came from somewhere up north."

"If we're lucky enough to reach any place where there are people, Trey, you'll need to know something more about me."

She sounded hesitant, unlike the Anna Ross he had come to know in the past few hours. "I'm no one's judge. There's nothing about you that I find remotely problematic."

Despite her discomfort, she smiled. "Remind us to work on your speech in the next few miles. That kind of talk will get you plenty of fights in Texas." Then in a more serious tone, she added, "I was from back East once. Now I'm not. Some folks around here have forgotten that it's our days spent together here is all that matters. We can't change our pasts. It burns a few folks' tempers that I don't give a donkey's stubborn butt what they think of me one way or the other. But you may have to choose which side of the fence you want to stand on about me."

Anna stared at the road ahead. "I don't know you well enough yet to care which way you do, Third, but I thought I should be friend enough to tell you what you might be stepping into when you roll in on my wagon."

He didn't know whether to be upset that she didn't care about him yet or pleased that she cared enough to tell him the truth. She was honest to the bone, and he liked that best about her. Maybe she needed more time to get to know him. Maybe some of her might rub off on him. Maybe this delay in finding the rosettes could work to his benefit.

He was a man who made up his mind quickly because he knew by experience how fleeting happiness could be. Nothing ever lasted. Everything inside him said that Anna was meant to be part of his life. Whether as good friend or something more, he had no clue.

James stared at the snow coming down in all its wintry fury and decided he could either let it defeat him or use it to his advantage. This was Christmastime, and he believed in the magic of the season. As a boy he had weathered a worse storm than being out in a blizzard. He'd been alone, without anyone, and didn't know the first thing about changing himself to become more. Well, he'd wished for a family once and got one. He had soaked up every experience to make him a better son.

James now knew that there was something more he wanted as a man. He wanted to be with Anna this Christmas and any other that she cared to spend with him hereafter. Not just because she'd rescued him, but because he wanted to know who he could become with her. They just needed to find shelter.

Before he could tell her that it didn't matter what anyone else had to say about her, James saw something in the distance. Or at least he thought he saw something. Maybe it was just a product of the Christmas wish he'd just made. *Santa, were you listening?* "Anna, look to your left. About ten o'clock. Those bluish gray outlines. Are those buildings? That big one in the middle, apart from the others, looks like a house with lit windows. Candles, perhaps?"

Her head swung around to see where he pointed. She instantly reined the team to the left, exhaling a deep pent-up breath. "That could be the Henton place. It's got to be less than a mile, Trey. Think we can make it? Can't tell how far it is with the snow blowing so hard."

He leaned over and did something he would never have

done, not having known her less than a day. But he had offered up his wish to Santa. Now he had to help the magic take hold. He kissed her on the cheek. "A kiss for luck, Anna. I have complete faith you can do anything you set your mind to."

She did the last thing he expected her to. She let go of one of the reins, grabbed him around one shoulder, and kissed him right back.

Chapter 3

Anna deepened the kiss and all kinds of warmth blazed through her. Jack barked and tried to wiggle out from between where her and Trey's bodies nearly touched. *Down, boy*, she thought, but it was Trey who moved away.

"I didn't mean *you*." She tried to make light of his withdrawal, instantly cooled from the heat of his lips upon hers. "You didn't like the kiss?"

"I liked it too much, Anna," he admitted, taking the dog into his hands. "But we can't take our time with such things right now and, as I told you before, I prefer a little slower."

"A good boy, that's what you are, Third. And I, on the other hand, am not a woman to waste time."

"I think I should put away the whiskey bottle for a while, don't you?" He avoided her honesty and handed her back the reins. "Should I take the reins for a while?"

I wish you would, she thought, disappointed at his sound reasoning. *To see how well you handle things. The man was certainly right about one thing. The whiskey was definitely talking*. She hadn't felt this attracted to someone since . . . well . . . since never. What was it about this bespectacled, logical-minded, too-polite-for-his-own-good greenhorn that she found so darned appealing?

"Rest your hand." She continued to command the team. "I just want you to remember that I warned you, once we get to the Hentons' there will be plenty of people there to confirm it's not just the whiskey talking."

"How so?"

"Because it's Wednesday, isn't it?"

"I'd have to think about it with a clearer head. What does Wednesday have to do with anything?"

"It's the day of the Henton Christmas party. If their company couldn't get back to town before the storm set in and are stuck there, you'll be meeting a lot of people who might not be so eager to lend me shelter."

Trey's eyes examined her closely. "I haven't found you to be very troublesome."

"Well, that's worth something." She shrugged. "But I don't know all your deep secrets yet."

He studied her a moment as if trying to make sense of her words. "I suppose as a barkeeper people would naturally confide in you while they drink."

"Sometimes," she admitted, "but they won't be happy to take me in because I know *their* secrets." She flicked the reins to spur the oxen on. "It will be because they think they know mine."

Jack had the decency not to ask her what secret that might be. Instead, the man patted Jack and said, "Some secrets are what you do. Some you keep because you have no choice. And then there is the kind that needs to find the light of day so the darkness can finally go away."

Which was his? Anna wondered, surprised at the depth of yearning she could hear in his tone. He seemed such a simple man, but the more time they spent together, the more she realized she needed to take a closer look at him. Find out who he really was.

With each plod of the team's hooves through the snow, a

sense of dread gripped Anna in its icy clutches. The closer she got to the buildings, the more certain she was that they were heading into more trouble than the storm.

Jane Henton and her father would welcome her, no doubt. She and the schoolteacher at the orphanage were friends. But if others were still there from the party, she didn't know how her presence would be accepted in their midst. Everyone knew she had taken the wagon to Mobeetie so she would have an actual excuse not to attend the festivities. The invitation had been extended to everyone in town but a few. She hadn't cared that some of the men who had imbibed all month at her establishment thought she was one of the uninvited. They'd treaded carefully about discussing the party in front of her until she finally had enough of their whispering and flat-out told them she wouldn't be in town for it.

It was nobody's business that she had declined Jane's invitation.

She just didn't want the tension of her relationship with some of the townsfolk to taint Trey's welcome when they showed up. He didn't deserve that. It was bad enough that the fact he was a tenderfoot would reveal itself quickly. He didn't need to be a tenderfoot and in the company of a so-called soiled woman.

But she'd tried her best to warn him.

Maybe, just maybe, everyone had made it back to their own homes.

The team's lumbering gait took on more speed. "I think they've finally found a road again," Trey announced.

"They smell hay." Anna felt the animals' immense shoulders bending to their task, their hooves digging in deeper to hurry their gait. "I smell something wonderful cooking myself."

Smoke from the ranch house's high chimney drifted on the wind, revealing a glorious smell of chili spice and beef.

Jack sat up, his nose tilted to the wind as he sniffed. His little tummy grumbled loudly.

Trey patted him. "I agree wholeheartedly, boy. I could eat a cow, hooves and all, right now." As the team headed for the closest of the two buildings, he pointed to several carriages near the huge barn. "The animals that must have drawn the conveyances must be tucked away inside somewhere."

"Mr. Henton and some of his ranch hands would have made sure they were safe. He probably didn't have enough room to get all the buggies inside the barn, though. It looks like quite a few stayed."

The strands of a feisty foot-stomping song caught her attention, making Anna's jaw set. The party guests were obviously making the best of their circumstances and continuing on with their celebrations. The fiddle and banjo players weren't high on her list of admirers. And if that was who she thought was singing the tune, Anna knew this was going to be one miserably long visit.

"At least there should be enough people to help us get the oxen and your horse corralled," she told Trey, trying to find some benefit to such a crowd. "Think if I can get this to slow up just a little that you can hop down and ask some of the men for some help? I'm not sure the oxen will actually stop till they reach the corral."

Trey eyed the distance from the outbuildings to the house and the depth of snow that separated them. "It should be no problem. If I stumble, the snow will catch me."

He hadn't proven himself adept at much yet, but she had to trust that he could manage the task. "Take Jack with you. That way, they'll believe you're with me. Oh, and tie off a rope from the house to the barn if they've got one." She tried not to sound worried so he wouldn't be concerned about leaving her. "Just in case we can't see our way back to the house."

* * *

The party was full blown—merry, lively, and well attended. As James and Jack were invited in by a big-shouldered, gray-haired man standing at the door, a dozen people swirled around the dance floor that had been made from a rearranged great room. Cowhide furniture that could comfort large men had been moved to the far edges of the wall, some resting against the landing that formed the upper portion of the two-story house. Twin sweeping staircases allowed access to the landing, where several other people stopped their conversations and moved forward to look down at the visitor whose presence allowed in a rush of cold air.

"Welcome, stranger." The gray-haired man started to shake James's hand, then realized it was full of dog. "The name's Newpord Henton. It must be colder than Pike's Peak out there."

"It is indeed, sir." James smiled, trying to hide the chattering of his teeth.

As the door shut behind him, he noticed hat racks on one side of the parlor held every size bonnet and Boss of the Plains James had ever seen in one place. Stetsons, they called the wide-brimmed hats back East. Hats that instantly said a man hailed from the Lone Star State. Dressed in their prairie finest, the women looked like calico and paisley nymphs dancing in the arms of their beaus, all graceful and glowing from the abundance of male attention.

A long mahogany sideboy ran a good portion of the wall a few feet from the left stairway, filled with a punch bowl and glasses. On the opposing wall, a makeshift stage of sorts had been set up, allowing a reed-thin male fiddle player and plump female banjo picker to challenge each other with their instruments. Their feet were tapping as rapidly as their fingers moved. A woman who looked as if she were no more than four feet tall and had a mop of red curls that dangled every way but the right way on her head sang with such a booming voice, James thought it could have been a man's. Though she would never grace the cover of *Harper's Bazaar*, her voice could rival any of those he'd ever heard in New Orleans—raspy, full of sass and soul.

Jack didn't appreciate the sound as much as James did and commenced to howling a disapproving lament.

"I'd know that howl anywhere. I didn't see that one-eye till just now." Newpord Henton patted Jack's head and looked past James. "Is Miss Ross with you?"

James quickly explained the circumstances. A few of the women took steps backward or lifted their punch cups to their lips to hide their shared whispers.

His explanation was barely out of his mouth when their host called several names and men stopped what they were doing to follow his instructions. "Grab that length of rope from the mudroom, Luke, and anything else you find out there that looks long enough to tie us a guideline from here to the barn. Bo, tell Jane I need a heavy blanket. I'll bet Anna's freezing cold out there."

He started passing out hats. "A couple of you boys grab your coats and follow me. We've got a team to unhitch and we need to do it quick. I want us all to stay together and get back inside before anyone's lost out there. We all know what happened to the Murrays last winter."

The sudden quiet in the room spoke more clearly of whatever tragedy had befallen the Murrays than if someone had spoken it aloud. James would not have Anna experience anything remotely similar.

He held Jack out to one of the ladies standing nearby. "I'll go with them. Would you mind seeing that my little friend gets something to eat? He's really cold and hungry."

"You're hurt." The lady noticed James's hand as she took the dog.

"Get them both something to eat, Bess," Henton instructed, putting on his Stetson and coat.

James stepped closer to the door. "I'll help. Anna's—"

"You're my guest," their host countered, "and I insist. Ladies, make him feel at home. We'll be right back."

A beautiful blonde in a dress the color of mint moved through the crowd, holding a large blanket. "Here, Father. Do be careful."

"I will, darling. Now make Mr.—?"

"Elliott. James Elliott the Third." James half bowed and introduced himself.

His host stopped and stared at James, puzzlement creasing his brow. "From Boston?"

James nodded. "The accent is quite noticeable, I'm afraid."

"You don't look a bit like your father." Newpord moved past James, signaling the men forward who had gone to get the supplies. "But we can save that conversation until we have Miss Ross in out of the cold. Welcome to our home, Mr. Elliott."

The door flung open, the wind nearly snatching it from Newpord's hands as the men exited into the storm.

A hush fell over the remaining partygoers, a curiosity running the course of the room. James could feel it in each searching gaze, and he could sense that he was being measured in some way.

The blond, hazel-eyed beauty who had called their host Father linked one arm with James's elbow. "Don't mind us, Mr. Elliott. A stranger in these parts is always new fuel for conversation, and I'm sure some of us are wondering how you and Anna came to be traveling together. Did you meet in Mobeetie and hitch a ride? By the way, I'm Jane, one of her *friends*."

She made a great effort to stress the last word. James tried to remember everything Anna had told him earlier about the woman, but he was dreadfully tired, hungry, more than a little cold, and not at all up for any kind of interrogation no matter how innocent it might appear. Besides, he needed to determine how well Mr. Henton knew his father. That put a whole new manner in which he must conduct himself among the people of Kasota. He wouldn't want to embarrass the Second in any way.

And he didn't want anyone making Anna feel uneasy when she returned. It would be unkind and undeserving. She'd had a long afternoon and no telling how much longer trying to get the team to safety.

James wanted to set the record straight. In his book, Anna had been nothing but a heroine to him all day. If not for her, he and his horse would have probably met the fate he suspected of the poor Murray family. He quickly told the crowd how Anna had saved him.

"Oh, my goodness, Mr. Elliott. You must be starved," Jane insisted, parting a path to a room farther back into the house. "Won't you let me get you something to eat?"

The sight of all the plates of food on the heavy-laden kitchen table was enough to tempt anyone. The great room in the front of the house may have been decorated to please her father, but she was the master of this room. Everything matched. Everything had a particular place. She would make Sears, Roebuck proud with her ability to accessorize. Everything looked color-coordinated and meticulously arranged as if she were arranging them to paint them as art.

The pot of whatever spicy beef had drawn him and Anna into the ranch earlier bubbled at the giant hearth that held several small pots, as well. At least they wouldn't go hungry for a while. Still James didn't think he could eat a morsel until he knew Anna was safely inside. "I'll wait for Anna if you don't mind, but please feed Jack for me."

Jane let go of James's arm and took the one-eyed dog

from Bess, who followed close behind them, setting him down on the floor. Jack immediately ran over to the stack of logs meant to replenish the hearth and hiked his leg.

"No, boy," James admonished, but Jack continued to mark his territory. James offered Miss Henton a look of apology. "I'm sorry, miss. He's been cold for hours with nowhere to . . . well, I would be happy to remove the logs from the house, if you'll just show me your back door."

She laughed and bent down to scratch Jack's back. "The logs will burn that off just fine. We sometimes burn cow chips in here, if necessary. No need to concern yourself."

Jack growled as if he wasn't at all happy about the prospect.

"Here, boy, that ought to console you." Jane grabbed a tasty-looking rib from a platter of meat. "Go curl up somewhere and enjoy yourself."

The dog took the rib and trotted off to the braided rug that lay in front of the great hearth. He stretched his tiny body, shot James a sidelong glance, then gave all his attention to the bone.

"How about we see to your hand, then, if you won't eat?" Jane insisted, motioning James over to a basin used to wash dishes. "We can at least get it cleaned up and see how bad it is. You wash and I'll get my friend Marjorie to fetch some tincture of arnica and bandages from the medicine closet. Bess," she motioned to her guest, "go find Marjorie and tell her to meet me at the medicine cabinet."

The heat from the hearth was melting the chill from James's bones, and some of the tension of the day eased from his shoulders. At least taking care of his hand gave him time away from the crowd's curiosity. He untied the bandanna with a small amount of difficulty, since he had to do it one-handed, then set the bandanna to the side. He immediately looked the other direction, concentrating on the pitcher near the basin that offered water to pour over the wound. He did his best to pour and not look, but it stung like daggers jabbing into his hand. He gritted his teeth and bore through the pain. The injury wasn't anything he hadn't suffered before, because he was clumsy at times. Maybe Anna would help him with the stitching.

The thought of her touching him made James wish the men who were helping her would hurry up. The waiting was thrumming in his ears, making his head hurt. He didn't think it was the liquor wearing off, but it could have been. He hoped he didn't smell like the amount they had drunk. It was bad enough that Jack had urinated on him while he lay in the snow. He probably should have asked them to bring in a change of clothes from his saddlebags, but that had seemed a selfish request when all that mattered was that Anna got in safely. He should have gone out there to get her. A man worth his salt wouldn't have stayed inside while his woman was in danger. An extraordinary man would have.

His woman? When had he started thinking of Anna as his?

She's accustomed to those kind of men, he reminded himself. *Strong, confident, take charge and get things done kind of men. So be one yourself. Prove that you might not have been born a Texan but you are willing to learn to be one.*

Careful not to look at the cloth for fear of catching sight of blood, he washed out the bandanna and spread it over the mantel that rose above the cooking hearth. Once it was dry, it would add some warmth around Anna's neck.

James was drying his hand when Jane returned with tincture and bandages and a red-haired girl in tow. "I brought you a needle and a nurse to stitch you up in case you need it," she said. "Marj helps out at the orphanage with the kids. She knows how to make it hurt less."

"No thank you, both. I'll take care of that in a while. Could you do something else for me instead?"

It was then he noticed both had the same color eyes, and each set looked eager to help.

"Would you mind finding something warm for Anna to wear? I'm afraid she's cold to the bone, and her clothing is wet from all the snow."

"I love dress-up." Marjorie rocked back on the heel of her kid boots. "We could put her in something blue to match her eyes, and she'd look just lovely with her hair combed out of that braid she always wears. I never have been able to tell if it's curly or straight as a—"

"You know you like a good challenge of any kind," Jane teased. "Some of my mother's old trunks should have something her size." She blinked once, then twice, an edge of sadness taking away some of the sparkle that had been in the hazel depths only moments ago. "But I haven't been able to pick up the key to them since we lost her just last winter."

Marjorie patted Jane's shoulder. "Don't you worry, Janie. I'll do all the unlocking and moving stuff. You just do the choosing. You're the one with the eye for fashion. If it was me, I'd just pick something fun that would cause a stir!"

James nodded his appreciation. "Thank you for everything, ladies. For the bandages, the loan of the dress, but mostly for welcoming us in."

"It's no bother at all."

"Anna says you're a real friend to her, Jane."

"So is Marj."

"She's the real friend to a lot of us, and most of them don't even know it," Marjorie added. "And what's worse is, they don't want to know it."

"She won't let us tell them anything about her."

"What do you mean?" Marjorie insisted. "What has she told you that she hasn't told me?"

"That's not my secret to share." Jane frowned at her friend. "If she wants you to know, she'll tell you herself when she's ready."

"Why is she so disliked?" James tried to ease the tension that seemed to be growing between the pair.

"She told you that much?" Jane sounded surprised. "That must have been quite a journey you two had today. It took me two years to get her to open up to me."

"I noticed the look on some of the faces when I said that I rode in with Anna." James pilfered a cookie from the table and took a bite. A taste of cinnamony heaven slid down his throat. "I'm afraid I'm well aware when company is trying to be too polite. Yet the men didn't hesitate to go with your father to rescue her."

Hearing footsteps from beyond the kitchen door, Jane looked embarrassed. "I'm afraid we may be taking too long and everyone's getting curious about our delay. But to answer you before we go, I think the men were eager to help so they could have a moment alone with her away from the women." She continued in a conspiratorial whisper, "They're probably going to ask her not to reveal whatever they do in the Rusty Bucket—her saloon. They're most likely afraid she'll tell some of their Saturday-night secrets. But if they knew her at all, they'd know she wouldn't gossip about other people. Even though it seems some in this community are bent on spinning yarns about her."

"Besides, she barely remembers anyone's name half the time. She ends up calling us all whatever's on her mind at the moment."

James could relate. He had been Trey or the Third or just Third since he'd been with her. Not once had she said his real name. "Why do they feel the need to target her?"

"Partly because she's a woman of means and doesn't rely on anyone but herself to provide for her needs. Partly because she remains unmarried in a territory full of men who want to marry her." Jane's eyes shared a glance with Marjorie's that hinted she might be holding something back. "Mainly because someone heard a little of why she came to Kasota and couldn't wait to twist the tale so out of proportion that it couldn't be fixed unless Anna spoke up to unravel the mystery of it all. She's stubborn and acts like it doesn't matter what they say about her, but I think it hurts her very deeply."

"Do either of you know the truth?"

"No, not me." Marj waved her gloved palms as if warding off an advance. "If I know the truth about something, far be it from me not to tell it. Everybody in town would know it if I did. Not that I'm a gossiper or anything. I just don't like to lie."

"I don't need to know it." Jane's chin lifted defiantly. "I'm a schoolteacher, and I'm always handling arguments between children. And that's all this gossip about Anna or anyone else is, in my opinion. Adults acting like children being tattletales. What does it matter what she's done? I don't know any of us who are perfect, do you? The right or wrong of her past is her own business, not yours, mine, or anyone else's, Mr. Elliott."

"Call me . . . *Trey*. Anna does." Maybe Jane was right. Truth belonged to the person living it. It was Anna's to decide who to share it with and when to reveal it, if ever.

Maybe this was the real reason his and Anna's paths had crossed. Maybe she was meant to save him from the false life he led trying to become something perfect instead of finding happiness in what he was now. Maybe there was worth in discovering *Trey* Elliott, mistakes and all. "Everyone has secrets and reasons for them, ladies," he admitted.

"Maybe all we can do is hope they're like Christmas gifts—hidden for a while, then treasured when revealed."

"I know you're right, sir. And I also know that my guests better not push Anna too far," Jane forewarned, "or she'll show them just how truly naughty she can be."

Chapter 4

Anna waded through the river of white, the weight of the extra blanket that Newpord Henton had brought to warm her more cumbersome than helpful in her effort to reach the ranch house. The men had put her in front of them to edge her way up the guideline that now stretched from the barn to the main house. She felt like a grounded goose leading a formation of men behind her. Their thoughtfulness had been so she would find safety first, but it left her to battle the fierceness of the wind without any sort of human blockade to stave off some of its intensity. Occasionally the wind lifted the snow in whirling eddies, giving her moments of vision, but a white blast of hell wailed in madness through the unobstructed zone between the barn and the house, flinging swirls of driven snow and ice into her face and body.

Blasts of fury hit her from both sides, catching her off balance. She fell backward and the rope suddenly went slack. She instantly prayed she hadn't broken the whiskey bottles she had tied around her waist and legs.

"Did it break?"

They mean the rope, she told herself, *not the bottles*. She heard the sound of doom in the question asked from behind her, knowing if the rope had broken, she and all the men who followed might very well die out here just yards away from the house. The Murrays had met such a fate last winter. And they'd been feet away from safety. The blizzard had disoriented them, so bitter cold that it had frozen them until they were found a month later when the snows cleared.

She desperately inhaled, cold rushing through her nose and throat and stinging her with an iciness that hurt to the bone. Blistering wind sealed her eyelashes together with ice. Anna scrambled to her feet, clawing her way through the snow, grasping for the rope and praying that it still held.

Move. She willed herself into action. *You will not die. You will not let these men die. Rope or no rope.* "Hang on to my coat. Tell the next man to hang on to yours," she yelled. "The rope will hold or I will."

She couldn't tell if any bottle had broken. If it had, the liquor would have frozen the instant it soaked her clothing. If she was cut anywhere, she couldn't tell if it simply wasn't the icy wind making everything sting.

Suddenly the guideline pulled taut, jerking Anna forward and causing air to barrel from her lungs. She barely had time to suck in another breath before the rope moved forward on its own, inch by slow inch. They were being *pulled* toward the house!

"They're trying to pull us in!" she shouted back to the men. "They know we're in trouble."

Grunts of sheer effort echoed the men's approval behind her as they lent themselves to moving up the rope. Glove over glove passed along the guideline spurring their effort to reach their rescuers, forcing Anna to move faster than she thought possible.

Light beckoned from ahead. Shapes took human form in a doorway. Tears of gratitude moistened her eyes, making them burn worse from the bitter cold. Her teeth rattled like wagon wheels being driven over old bones. Every joint in her body felt as if it were being shaken loose, but by God's mercy they were going to make it in alive.

An avalanche of snow rushed over her head as the arms of the man standing in the doorway pulled her into his embrace.

"Anna, thank God, you're all right," the Third whispered as he gripped her tightly.

"Move," she whispered, wanting nothing more than to linger there and feel the sincerity of his welcome, but the others were not inside yet.

Trey immediately let go of her and helped with the next man and the next. When the last one found safety from the cold and the door shut behind them, a shout of victory echoed over the crowd.

Dusting the snow from his hat, Newpord Henton was the first to speak. "Whose idea was it to form a tug line at the door?"

Jane, who had been working behind Trey, pushed on Trey's back, making him move forward. "Mr. Elliott's, Father. He was worried it was taking too long and he meant to go out there himself. I suggested that he couldn't possibly grip the line with that hurt hand, but he insisted and flung open the door. It was just then that he saw the line go slack and managed to grab it anyway." She motioned toward his hand. "I think he's hurt himself all over again, tugging as hard as he did to get you all inside. We ladies tried to help all we could, but he took the brunt of the strain."

"Then I say we owe this young man a depth of gratitude and our lives." Newpord held his Stetson over his heart as if giving a solemn oath. "Ask anything of us and it's yours, Mr. Elliott."

Trey held out the edges of his coat. "If I could borrow some old clothes so these could dry, we can call it even."

"Help us get this rope off and I can do better than that,"

Anna said, holding up the end of the rope that still attached her to the others. "I brought some of your clothes out of your saddlebags."

All of a sudden a dozen hands mixed into the fray of un-knotting the guideline from around each of them. Several bottles slid down her legs and onto the floor before Anna could think to warn the helpers to be careful with her end. Luckily none of them shattered.

"Oops," she whispered, noticing several hems moving backward to step out of the way of the whiskey bottles. She picked them up and handed them to Newpord. "I thought I'd bring a party favor or two. It might help keep the old juices ginning if the firewood runs low."

"You bet it will, Miss Ross." Their host helped her gather the bottles, then set them on the sideboard near the punch.

Anna peeled off the layer of blanket and held out the fresh white shirt and black woolen trousers she had found rolled up in Trey's saddlebags. "Jane, could you show him some place to change?"

Jane grabbed both their hands and led them toward the staircase. "Father, if you'll show Mr. Elliott the study, he can change there. Marjorie and I will take Anna with us to my room." She faced the rest of her guests. "If you folks will excuse us a while, we'll be down as soon as possible, and, Luke," she nodded at one of the ranch hands who had helped with putting away the team, "you and the boys hang your coats up in the mudroom so they can dry faster. There are towels and some grooming things to freshen up with, if you like. I'm sure some of the ladies will have hot mugs of cider waiting for you when you're finished."

Anna allowed herself to be tugged up the stairs and into Jane's elaborate bedroom. The beauty of the room matched the loveliness of its owner. Trails of ivy interspersed with yellow daffodils swept upward to form a bright, cheery cloth that covered the walls. A four-poster bed, green and white cushioned settee, and chiffonier made of deep mahogany added a look of rich luxury. A low fire burned in the fire-place, making the room toasty and welcoming.

Anna sat on the bench at the foot of the bed, afraid she might stain anything else. Jane would never say anything about it, but Anna wanted to leave the room with as little mess as possible. "Whew, it's good to be inside." She finally breathed a sigh of relief.

"Tell us absolutely everything." Marjorie sat down beside her while Jane went to the chiffonier and pulled out a beau-tiful dress made of blue brocade trimmed in gold lace. "How did you meet him? How old is he?" the redhead asked. "Is he marri—?"

"Whoa, Marj." Anna laughed at her friend's curiosity. "I haven't even got one shoe off yet."

"Oh, sorry." The nurse bounced on the seat as if she had a burr in her bottom, tapping her foot while Anna took off both shoes.

"I can't wear that." Anna shook her head as Jane placed the blue dress on the bed beside her. "That was your mother's."

"Don't think for one minute she wouldn't have made you wear it herself if she were here. It's warm, it's pretty, and it matches your hair and eyes. Besides, my clothes are too small for you and you can't just sit here and let your clothes dry. I don't care how much you don't want to go back down there."

Anna knew to argue with her would do nothing but delay the inevitable. The teacher could be more stubborn than she at times. "Who all is downstairs?" Anna asked cautiously, needing to know from which direction she should expect all the impending daggers. "I thought I saw Cloris and Tinnie. And isn't that Izora Beavers I hear singing now?"

"You do," Marjorie confirmed. "And she's none too

pleased that you're here. That look she gave you when you came in could have melted the Rockies."

"Bless her front pew heart. She does hate my guts." Anna unrolled her wet stockings and sighed with relief as she peeled them off. "Ooh, that feels so much better."

"You should have never told her to quit sending her son in to your saloon." Marjorie reached out and tugged on Anna's braid. "You little sinful snot."

"The saloon is no place for a kid, I don't care how badly she says she needs his hard-drinking daddy. She just didn't like me telling her so. If she wants the man home in time for supper, let her come in after him herself."

"You're avoiding the real issue here. Izora's not going to change her opinion of you today, tomorrow, or any other time soon," she reminded. "Tell us about Mr. Elliott. How did you meet him?"

Needing the change from such a serious subject and knowing Marjorie wouldn't be satisfied until she knew as much of the details as Anna was willing to share, Anna laughed. "Actually, Jack peed on him."

"What?" teacher and nurse echoed in unison.

She told how she'd found Trey and most of what she'd learned about him. "Trey's definitely greener than newborn mesquite, but he seems to be a kind soul. We got along well coming here, but I warned him he might not discover me such a pleasant gal once he met some of the guests. Izora will see to it."

"If he's as kind as you say he is, he'll see right through Izora." Marjorie's forefinger wagged, punctuating each of her words.

"You didn't tell him *we* don't like you, did you?" Jane helped her strip from the riding skirt and shirtwaist that felt like it held ten extra pounds of ice.

"Not you, just most. And I didn't want there to be any

surprises if we happened to survive. Despite what some may think, I do care enough not to die with lies on my last breath."

"Why do you call him Trey?" Marjorie asked.

Anna giggled at her companion, who couldn't stay angry with anyone more than the amount of time it took to change her mind. "Well, I guess because he's the third mister whatever his name is. I don't know. You know me and how I am with names. What *is* his name?"

"James Elliott the Third."

Jane sounded duly impressed, and Anna was a little surprised at the instant temper that flared at the thought that her friend had wasted no time getting to make his acquaintance. Jane was considered one of the most eligible women in the territory, and she was extremely pretty.

He's not yours. Anna reminded herself that she'd barely known him a day. *He just rode in on your wagon. Calm your horses. She's got every right to know the man too.*

"Will you two please quit fussing over me so much." Anna moved away and faced the full-length oval mirror that showed off her pitiful-in-comparison-to-Jane's figure. Though both were blondes, Jane had a porcelain complexion and was slim and petite like the fashion of the day. Anna was pure Viking warrior woman, robust in breasts and hips, and her nose was sprinkled with freckles. The long braid that now rested over one shoulder hung to her waist. With a grumble, Anna flipped it behind her.

"Unbraid it," Jane insisted, holding the hem of her mother's dress up so Anna could put it over her shoulders. "Quit trying to look so much like a man. You'll be the prettiest girl at the party."

"I stopped being a girl a long time ago, Janie, and pretty is as pretty does. I didn't graduate from Miss Marabelle's Ladies' School of Charm and Social Graces, you know." She saw both friends frown and knew they were trying their best to make her feel welcome and help her to fit in, to make her feel more comfortable, if nothing less.

She allowed Jane to slip the dress over her head. "Okay, I'll be on my best behavior," she mumbled beneath the brocade as it settled onto her shoulders and beyond. When her head finally peeked out, she gave them both a stern look. "But the first time Izora opens up her big mouth about—"

"I'll stuff a cookie in it, I promise." Marjorie drew a cross over her ample bosom. "I'll keep a saucer right next to me at all times and she'll never know she's been plugged."

"You know, that just might work." Anna started fastening all the buttons and lace that adorned the gown. "And if it doesn't, I can always unleash Jack on her. He's not a bit bashful in how he feels about her singing and, despite that one eye, he has the deadliest aim in the territory."

James heard the laughter from somewhere nearby and recognized Anna's voice in the mix. Good, she must be feeling more composed now, more comfortable among her company. That would make the evening or however long they must stay at the Hentons' much easier.

The men who had brought her in seemed congenial enough, not at all guarded in her company. At least none who had returned from the barn had made any undue comments or shown any signs of snubbing her. Still, he decided to reserve his opinion of the men until after he had rejoined the party. Once he saw them interacting with Anna and the women, then he could determine more why she had cautioned him so emphatically about her position in the community.

Someone rapped on the door that separated the study from the other rooms along the second-story landing.

"May we come in? Are you finished dressing?"

Anna. The sound of her voice gave him a sense of not

being such an outsider. He was normally alone and not much in the company of others by choice. He loved people but cared too much whether or not they liked him. So he kept to himself, not wanting to deal with the rejection of someone not wanting his company. But with Anna he thought maybe it would hurt very deeply if she left him on his own to fend among the guests. She suddenly felt like a home he needed to rely on.

James brushed the wrinkles from his fresh white shirt and black trousers. Fortunately, she had wisely chosen to bring the warmer trousers rather than the denim, but the clothing was far less appropriate than what other party guests were wearing. He hoped he looked presentable enough not to embarrass her. "Just finished," he announced, putting on his spectacles. "You may come in."

"Don't you look like something the north wind blew in." Anna sashayed in with her friends in tow, her eyes twinkling from something she had probably been laughing at moments ago.

"Don't you look"—James's heart slowed to a single beat that caught and held as he took in the sight of her dressed in all her feminine regalia—"gorgeous."

"Breathe, Trey," Jane instructed from behind Anna. "You're turning blue."

"We came in to stitch you," Marjorie informed him, holding up a bandage and a needle, "which we've all decided is my job. Too bad you didn't come in unconscious or we would all have to arm wrestle to see which of us got to revive you."

"Marjorie!" Jane blushed.

"Well, we would and you know it." She laughed.

James exhaled his pent-up breath. "I hope this is suitable for your party, Miss Henton."

"You look fine, and nobody better tell you differently."

Anna reached for his hand. "Now let me see that cut. See, Marj, I told you he's got it bleeding again. I should have sent someone in to help him get dressed."

Bleeding again? Despite his reluctance to pull his hand from her gentle touch, James let it drop to his side. "There's no need for all this fuss and bother."

"I'll decide that." Anna motioned for Marjorie to come closer. "I'd say three good stitches will do it, but you see what you think."

James never had so much attention given to his hands before. All three women stood around him now, his palm resting in Anna's. He wished he hadn't spent the past few months digging in the prairie loam. His fingernails looked jagged and his hands scratched and rough from pulling away weeds and clumps of grass. They certainly didn't resemble a gentleman's hands. Did Anna think them too rough to the touch?

"We all agree on three." Marjorie tugged James away from Anna and led him to the desk that stood in front of a huge window along one wall of the study. "Kind of fitting, don't you think, since you're the Third. Just prop your hand on the corner here, and this will all be over in no time."

Pain pierced his palm and he glanced down at the needle Marjorie was using. A regrettable mistake. The needle blurred and all he could see was red, oozing blood. James's knees suddenly wobbled and he felt like a pine tree ready to topple. "I n-need a chair, please."

"It won't take that long," she insisted. "I'm really fast at this, and I'm just going to let this bleed out a lit—"

"Anna! Now!"

"Grab that chair, Jane, he's sinking fast," he heard Anna say from somewhere distantly above him. Suddenly, everything went black.

Seconds, or it could have been minutes, later his eyes

opened to see six eyes staring back at him. He started to sit up, but when he did the world whirled around him as if taking a spin around the dance floor. His eyes finally focused on Anna's. "Did I lose my wits about me again?"

"Again?" Two sets of hazel eyes turned to share a glance with Anna as the nurse and teacher voiced their curiosity.

"He sort of can't take the sight of blood," Anna explained. "He'll be fine in a moment now that we've got him stitched up and he can't see anything."

So he had been indisposed for several minutes. *Wonderful.* What a man they must think him. James forced himself to sit up in the chair and noticed his hand was well bandaged with no sign for further distress. He willed himself to stand without shaking. "I'm keeping you from your guests, ladies."

"They *are* probably wondering what's taking us so long," Marjorie agreed and packed up the medical supplies.

Anna linked her arm through his. "Let them wait a little longer. You girls go on down. I brought him and he's my responsibility. I'll see that he gets downstairs when he's ready."

Jane and Marjorie hurried away, leaving James and Anna finally alone again for the first time since their arrival.

"You don't have to go," Anna told him.

"And miss all the fun?" he teased, but he hoped Anna realized what he was really saying. He wouldn't leave her alone to face any guest who didn't show her proper propriety. "I say it's time I meet the good folk of Kasota Springs and see who I'll put on my naughty or nice list."

Anna laughed. "Better watch out, Third. You're beginning to sound a lot like someone I might grow fond of."

As she guided him out of the study and toward the stairwell, James noticed that she had deliberately linked her arm in such a way as to make it look as if she were leaning into him and not the other way around. She wanted him comfortable going down into strange company and didn't want him to feel as if he appeared weak in any manner. Being linked this way offered better balance if he happened to teeter going downstairs. Her thoughtfulness touched him, as had her remembering to bring his clothes inside. But would the others think her too close for propriety's sake? He didn't want to add to her discomfort with them. Yet when he tried to pull away, she wouldn't let him.

"Thank you, Anna, for the clothes and for not laughing at me just now about the fainting spell," he finally gave in, sensing she would not let him change positions, "or the earlier one. I'm not quite a Texan yet, I'm afraid, but I sure admire the kind of man who is."

"My pleasure, Third, and Texas doesn't make a man. You're ten gallons full of honor, and that's enough for any man to be."

Their eyes met and James felt as if some invisible thread had thrown a loop around his heart and tied the two of them together in some inexplicable way. No one had ever given him such a compliment. "I'm glad we met, Anna."

"Me too," she whispered, her smile warming him to the tip of his boots. But just as quickly as it was offered, the smile vanished. The crowd must have noticed their return and were moving forward to meet them at the bottom of the stairs. "But as I told you before, I'm usually not this pleasant. I must have finally gotten some Christmas spirit. Just don't expect it to last much longer."

Chapter 5

The roar of the fiddler's bow, the wail of a harmonica, and Izora Beavers's attempt to sing louder than the instruments made talking nearly impossible. As Anna paraded Trey around the room, everyone seemed intent upon stopping him every few steps and making his acquaintance. Anna could understand why. He had such a pleasant nature about him and handled himself well in conversation, despite how many times someone asked him, "Say, fella, would you say it in Texan?"

Though he never took offense, she sensed that he was trying very hard to fit in and not be so glaring a tenderfoot.

She encouraged him to move on quickly with each introduction, but Trey deliberately waited until the person he was meeting engaged her in the conversation too. The man was simply too polite, but she sort of liked the way he wanted to take care of her in that way. It endeared him to her and she felt herself growing more at ease with each person she talked to. He had a real knack for setting people at ease.

"Tell us more about your work here in the Panhandle," insisted Newpord Henton as he joined the latest group surrounding Anna and Trey. He offered them both a glass of punch. "What is a banker's son doing out on the plains digging in the dirt?"

Anna envisioned him behind a teller's cage dressed in a frock coat and tie. In fact, she could see him as a lot of things except a man who studied flowers for a living. What was he had said he was looking for? Bluebonnets? Hell, if he'd gone south, he would have found all the 'bonnets his eyes could see for miles. But he'd said something about a special one growing up here. One flower was the same as the next to her. And who could make a living off of studying flowers? Hadn't he said something about prize money from a foundation for research?

She tried to recall exactly what he'd said during their whiskey talk, but it was a haze at the moment. He'd droned on so much in some kind of scientific jargon only a professor could love, and she was no lover of science unless it was the mixing of whiskey. Whiskey gave her financial freedom. That was all the science she needed. So she'd more or less halfway listened to Trey's reason for being there. It was her great strength as a barkeep and her flaw as well. People shared their secrets with her and she only halfway listened, assuming they only needed an ear and not really an answer.

Now that she knew the Third a little better, she wished she'd paid more attention.

"You say you know my father." Trey accepted the punch and took a sip. "Ooh, goodness. What's in this?"

"A little Tennessee tail twister," Newpord laughed, "or rather some of Miss Ross's fine whiskey. It'll grow hair on your chest."

Anna sipped the punch. Sure enough, someone had seasoned the refreshment with a bottle or two of her liquor. "Well, I don't know about hair on our chests, but I don't think any of us will be getting cold any time soon." Her attention focused on their host. "How do you know his father?"

"I visited him a couple of times in Boston. He was interested in investing in some of the ranches around here, mine being one of them. Fine man, sweet-natured mother, and well-spoken older sister. All incredibly accomplished people in their own right. Wonderful bloodline."

"Yes, it is," Trey said and took another sip of punch, deliberately lingering at the rim of the cup.

It wasn't anything anyone else would have noticed, but when he turned slightly toward Anna as he did whenever he seemed uncomfortable, she knew talking about his family made him uneasy. Why, if they were so wonderful? Anna was a collector of secrets, and she knew when someone was holding one back. She would have to get to the bottom of this. See if she could help Trey find a way to deal with it. Even if all she did was listen when he was ready to talk about whatever he guarded so carefully.

"Come now, Mr. Elliott." A chubby redheaded woman wobbled up and the crowd immediately parted to give her access. "Do tell. We simply won't let you keep any secrets from us, will we, everyone? We want to know all about your family. We love to hear about things from"—she purposefully locked gazes with Anna—"back East. The news we get is usually so fretful."

All of a sudden Jack flew around the corner at a dead run, his teeth bared and his bark a howling yodel. He was like a bull at full charge. "Hold up, Jack." Anna tried to catch him but the little mutt was intent on reaching Izora's leg.

Marjorie and Jane moved in closer. Jane managed to grab Jack while Marjorie lifted a saucer and toyed with one of the cookies stacked on it.

"Keep that half-blind mongrel away from me." Izora glared at Jack as he continued to grumble at her. "He's already ruined my parasol. I'll never get the stain out. A party is no place for a dog."

"Where I go, Jack goes." Anna dared her to say something else. She was itching for a good coming-to-Jesus talk with Izora, no matter what season this was. Let the woman say anything else bad about her dog.

"You're the singer." Trey acknowledged the woman's unusual raspy, soulful voice.

"Izora Beavers," the redhead introduced herself, swinging her attention away from a confrontation with Anna. "Mrs. Izora Beavers."

Anna rolled her eyes before she could think fast enough to hide her disgust. As if Trey would be interested in anyone that wrapped up in her own self-importance. The man might wear spectacles but hc had enough eyesight to see a cocklebur in calico if it tumbled right past him.

"You must be exhausted from singing and need to rest your throat." Trey bowed slightly. "May I get you some punch, Mrs. Beavers?"

Nice way to tell her to shut up, Anna thought, proud of how easily he had handled the mean-mouthed harridan.

"No, thank you, Mr. Elliott, but that's very kind of you." Izora's double chins lifted as she stared down the length of her slightly pointed nose. "I hear you're from Boston. I think our Miss Ross and her little dog are originally from there too, aren't you, Anna?"

Anna glared at her foe. "I don't recall ever mentioning where we were from, Mrs. Beavers. I didn't know it was all that much of interest to folks around here since we all sort of made our way out west. Boston, New Orleans, the North Pole, what difference does it make? We're here now, and that's what matters."

"Well, I certainly wasn't implying anything." Izora's hand pressed against her ample bosom as if she were in distress.

"Care for a cookie?" Marjorie rushed one up to Izora's mouth and insisted that she take a bite. "There you go, Izora. Makes you want to stuff your face all night, doesn't it?"

Jane elbowed the nurse, jerking her slightly backward. "Marjie, get her some punch to go with that, won't you, dear."

"Anna was just saying that it's great that we all have a wonderful place like this to begin new lives and find whatever it is that will make us happy as people," Trey tried to ease the singer's animosity, "providing the storm abates."

"Is that one of those four-poster Eastern words?" a tall, thin man asked from nearby. "*Abates?*"

"It means providing the storm stops." Anna offered the explanation. "And I think it's just starting up, in my opinion." She shot Izora a warning glare. "Better button up your coats. It's going to get bitter cold before it ever warms up, you can bet on it. I just hope we all can find some way to keep triggers from being pulled so we don't have to ruin a good Christmas. Why don't we all have some of those cookies."

The music started up again and Trey took Anna's punch glass from her, asking Newpord if he would mind setting them down for him. "Anna promised me the next dance and I would very much like her to keep the promise."

He bowed to Anna. "Would you do me the honor?"

She'd made no such promise. Anna leaned in and whispered, "I'm not so good at it."

Before she could protest, he drew her into his embrace and waltzed her out into the swirling crowd. "It doesn't matter. Dancing is the one thing I do well."

They managed to make it several yards across the floor before he halted and asked, "What are you doing?"

"Counting. What does it look like?"

"The waltz is more of a slide this way up, down, then

slide that way, up, down. Yes, that's right. This way, up, down. Now that way, up, down. You're doing just . . . ouch!"

"Well, Jack got in the way." Anna noticed her pet dancing at their heels, trying to follow their steps. "He wants to dance with us."

Trey laughed. "I think he's got better rhythm than you do, my friend."

"Wait till he hears mariachi music. The dog can shake his hips better than any of us."

Anna concentrated on watching Trey's feet, but she kept getting distracted by the mass of heated faces, clinging arms, and twirling flounces whirling around her in a kaleidoscope of calico, lace, and paisley. Trey was good to his word. He could dance with the best of them, and it showed some interesting prospects about the man that made Anna want to find out for herself how else he moved well.

Be good, she reminded herself. *You'll send the man into a tizzy, if you act too bold.* It was just a shame that he was such a gentleman. She could think of a dozen better ways they could get to know each other during this storm than spending it dancing and talking with others. *Shameless, that's what you are, Anna Jolene Ross*, she silently reprimanded herself. *And you say people talk about you.*

She tried to talk and dance at the same time with Trey, but that didn't work. Too much sliding up and down while trying not to squish Jack's little body beneath her feet was becoming too much effort to think of as fun.

"Can we please stop for a minute?" she finally asked. "I'm afraid I'm going to take out his other eye."

"How did he lose the first one?" Trey escorted her to the edge of the crowd, Jack following closely behind. The dog kept looking one way, then the other, as if searching for Izora.

"By saving my life," Anna explained, picking up Jack and stroking his shoulders. Jack loved the way she stroked him from head to tail, warming his fur, so Anna made it a point to comfort him until he stopped shivering. "He took on a rattlesnake that almost bit me in the heel. I thought the poor thing was going to die, but after a few days he perked up and lived. Unfortunately, he lost an eye in the battle." She pressed Jack to her heart. "He may be little but he won't take guff off anybody."

"Sounds like his owner," Trey said softly.

No one had ever called her little. It seemed oddly endearing that Trey thought of her in that way. They were an odd threesome. A spectacled tenderfoot, a one-eyed ball of furry ferocity, and a freckled Viking. What kind of bloodline could that ever make?

A loud roar echoed up from the crowd as the fiddler announced a reel. "Grab your partners," he yelled and struck his bow to a lively tune.

Several men pulled out bandannas and wrapped them around their right arms.

"What are they doing?" Trey asked as the bandanna men lined up with male partners.

"They drew straws earlier to see who would be heifer and who would be bull. Short straws are heifers, or gals. Bulls, the men, get to lead. It happens at every gathering we have around here. Just not enough women to go around."

"Salute your partners!" the fiddler commanded.

Trey bowed as the others did, while Anna curtsied with Jack in her hands. She tried to keep up with others, backing away then moving forward only to lock the wrong arm with Trey. He spun her around the correct way, then gently pushed her toward her next partner. She looked back at Trey and realized that all pairs had exchanged partners.

"You haven't said anything to Izora about my account, have you, Anna?" Enoch Beavers held her at such a distance that they were barely touching. Though his head never turned, his eyes slanted to where Izora was dancing three couples away.

Anna would have put Jack down and let him go pee on Izora, but the woman might try to kick him and call it dancing. "No, Enoch, I haven't said a word, and I won't as long as you settle up soon after the new year. I want your children to have a good Christmas. Use your money for that."

His bulging cheeks blew out a great breath, fluttering his handlebar mustache. "You aren't at all what they say you are, you know."

Offering a smile that it took everything within her to give, she sweetly asked, "And who might *they* be?"

The command to change partners took his answer away with him, leaving her in the arms of yet another of the men who had not gone out to help her with the team.

"You're looking lovely tonight, Anna." Ward Crawford's hand settled a little too low on her hip.

The dandy thought himself quite the ladies' man, but she could barely tolerate serving him drinks at the saloon.

Jack growled.

"Good God, woman, do you have to take that one-eyed piss pot everywhere with you?"

Anna kicked Ward. "Oh, sorry. I'm not much of a dancer."

She allowed Ward to spin her once, just so that his hand would have to reach above her head instead of remaining at her hip. "And if you mean Jack, yes, he helps me *ward* off men with way*ward* hands. Now go away or I'll tell"—*What is his wife's name?* Anna hated being so bad with names— "where I found your hat last week."

Everyone knew Ward prided himself on buying big hats, had them made down in San Antonio at a special shop. One of a kind, they were. If one happened to wind up in a certain saloon girl's boudoir, then there would have to be plenty of explaining for the man who left it there. That was certainly something that man didn't want to have to tell his wife.

Not that Anna would ever hurt the wife in that manner. But the man better watch his mouth about Jack or else she might just alter her policy on not informing family members about her customers' Saturday-night shenanigans.

The floor quivered as those who did not dance clapped their hands and stamped their feet to the lively tune. Several exhausting partners and minutes later, Trey returned to Anna and the last round of the reel ended in thunderous applause.

"I think I'm ready for some more punch or maybe something to eat," Trey announced. "Will you excuse me while I sit out the next one?"

There was something strange in his tone, and his back was a little stiffer than it had been before. "Are you mad at me?" she asked, realizing that Jack was wiggling and wanted down. She let him go.

"Why should I be?" Trey moved away from the dance floor and headed for the kitchen.

He had no reason that she could think of, but he'd never felt so distant before. His words had never been so crisp and brief.

"I mean, if you prefer to dance with those other men rather than me, it's certainly your prerogative," he said over his shoulder.

"You're jealous," she announced, surprised by the fact. Deep within her two feelings flared—anger at his audacity and a certain pleasure in knowing that he cared. "I had nothing to do with who I danced with," she reminded him, following him. "The fiddler called the switch, so I switched. Believe me, some of them I wouldn't have ever danced with if it hadn't been for—" She stopped in her tracks, her fists knotting on her hips. He was being possessive, and no man possessed her. "Now, wait just a minute here. Why am I explaining this to you? You're the so-called expert dancer. You know how a reel goes."

"So-called?" Something etched in his face that she couldn't quite determine its source until he added, "I thought you said I danced quite well."

She'd hurt his feelings and she hadn't meant to, no matter how miffed at him she was at the moment. Anna noticed people staring at them now, listening. They would think she'd already attached herself to a stranger in a single day of knowing him. That was just great. They would leave this party with more fuel for the rumors that had been spread about her all over the territory.

Let them listen. It wasn't like arguing with him would make them dislike her any less. They would certainly take his side. He was company. She was old gossip. But she hadn't meant to make him feel less than he was. "You're a wonderful dancer. You just shouldn't have asked me to dance a reel if you didn't want me to be in other men's arms."

Trey stopped and faced her. "I didn't know how I was going to feel seeing you there. Now, will you stop staring a hole through me and show me where Miss Henton keeps her bowls for the chili? We'll talk about this later. *Alone.*"

"Fine. We definitely will." She'd never seen him mad, and he looked a whole lot more manly when he was angry. That appealed to her quite a lot. Maybe she needed to see what it would take to get him really steamed up.

Lord knew you didn't really know how much a man really cared for you until you had him riled at you. And there wasn't a man alive who had ever been brave enough to look her in the eye and tell her when she was going to do something.

Merry Christmas, Anna, she told herself. *Maybe you've finally got your wish. Someone brave enough to handle your secret. Someone man enough to handle you.*

Someone strong and true to spend your life with.

Chapter 6

James had no chance to talk to Anna alone as he hoped. Everyone had pitched in to help Jane and her father with seeing that all were fed. Some of the men had dared to open the mudroom door and scoop up buckets of the drift that had made opening the door nearly impossible. The snow was packed in so hard that the windows had frost on the inside of them and were bending inward. At least they'd managed to get enough snow to boil and let it cool into good drinking water.

Anna had insisted that she and the women use some of it to clean the dishes so that they would have enough to use for breakfast tomorrow. Most had lent a hand, but there were a stubborn few who didn't want to help because they didn't want to get their hands cold. Those guests were in the great room having a good time, from the sound of laughter and stamping of feet to the music.

James had been taught by his adoptive parents that if you ate at someone's house, you helped with the dishes. So he did what he could one-handed. He couldn't wash. He tried to dry, but it hurt to hold the dish with the injured hand while he dried with the other. So they allowed him to put away the dishes.

"You're a real help in the kitchen," Jane complimented

him, handing him another saucer to stack in the top of the cabinet.

"Being tall has its advantages," he said, taking the tiny china dish and putting it among the others.

"You wouldn't catch some of the men in here helping." Anna nodded toward the door that led out of the kitchen. "Unless it's proving who's strong enough to pry open a door. Women's work, they say. Not manly enough for them."

The moment the door had been opened and the buckets of snow scooped in, the other men had escaped to rooms deeper in the house. Only James and his host remained behind with the women. "If they're man enough to eat on it, they ought to be man enough to clean it," James informed, inspiring a feminine "amen" from the women that would have made any preacher proud.

"It's not that they wouldn't help, there's just so much room in here," Newpord defended his fellow men. "I chased most of them out. James here is new company, so I gave him his choice. Me? I like being crushed between a swarm of aprons and pretty gals. You don't get this old without getting this smart."

The women giggled and James eyed the man with fond respect. The widower must miss his wife deeply.

"Which brings me to the next thing we all need to do, not just us do-gooders," Newpord announced.

"What's that, Father? The gift giving?" Jane handed James another dish.

Gift giving? James didn't have anything he could give. Guess he'd have to sit out that part of the party. But what of Anna? She didn't have anything to offer either. Would she mind being left out?

"I was thinking maybe we better gather everyone and decide a few things before we continue with the party. There needs to be some organizing done, like where we will put everyone down for the night and how we're going to handle the outhouse needs, to state it bluntly. I don't think anyone could make it through those drifts to the shack, so we have to decide how we're going to handle the situation."

By the look of horrified feminine faces as they contemplated exactly what Newpord was implicating, James thought he might be of help with this particular problem. "Sir, I could offer a solution that might work."

Newpord held up a hand to stop him. "No, wait. Let's call a meeting in the parlor and we can all discuss it. It needs to be mutual agreement among us all. Looks like we're just about done here, so let's go call a council."

Everyone put down their dry towels and took off their aprons, following their host into the great room where the others were now visiting and talking, resting from their dancing and meal of chili-seasoned beans, beef, and corn muffins.

"Gather round, folks." Newpord's voice echoed over the room and up the stairs to those who rested on furniture there. "We're calling a powwow."

It took a couple of minutes for almost forty people to come together. Some were a little slower than others, having imbibed in the punch bowl a little too frequently. The women sat while the men stood behind them.

Newpord repeated what he'd said in the kitchen. "Now, I'd like to turn the floor over to our new friend, Mr. Elliott. Ah hell, let's call him James. If we're going to spend this much time with him, then he can allow us to call him James or Jim, can't he?"

A round of applause welcomed James into their fold. "Call me Trey." James glanced at Anna and was pleased when she smiled.

"Well, Trey, what did you have in mind instead of using the outhouse?" Newpord plunged ahead with their problem.

Embarrassed titters erupted in the room, then finally laughter, putting everybody a little more at ease about the subject.

"As some of you've learned, I'm a bit of a scientist. At least that's what I profess to be most of the time." Seeing a few nodding heads, he continued on, "As a scientist, I know that burning off waste seems to be the answer for our problem. I propose that we use the fire you've made in the mudroom chimney to burn off the excrement we gather in chamber pots, no matter what its . . . uh . . . *texture*. There are quite a few of us and so the amount may become substantial if the storm lasts."

"You mean gather our—?" Izora couldn't finish the words. "And burn it?"

"If we can't get doors open enough to toss it out, then it seems the logical solution to me. Even if we can get doors open, we should save that snow for use for drinking water and the like. We don't want anyone having to venture out too far into the snow and get lost." James searched their faces. "Of course, it won't be the most pleasant room to pay a visit, but it will do the job and not make any of us sick, should the storm linger longer than we hope. If anyone else knows a better way to accommodate this many people for that task, please speak up."

Anna raised her hand. "I vote we do as Trey says. It makes sense."

Other hands followed, and Newpord counted them. "Well, that's settled. That's most of us. Thank you, Trey. Now we need to decide where everyone's going to sleep. Do we take turns in shifts or try to bed everyone down at once?"

"I vote that we all sleep at once. We'll need to keep dancing when we're awake to keep warm." Izora looked at others for support. "It will be difficult to sleep with all that foot stomping."

They agreed to not take shifts.

"We have four bedrooms, the study, the upper landing, and the great room, the kitchen, and the mudroom," Jane's nose wrinkled as her mouth twisted disdainfully, "which now I'm sure we all agree we won't count. It will be hard enough trying to use the kitchen since it's next to the mudroom."

Everyone laughed.

"That makes seven rooms, if we use the kitchen," she continued. "There are thirty-eight of us here. That puts five or six of us in each room for the night."

No one disputed the teacher. After all, she'd taught the three Rs.

"We'll give you women the beds, so you'll have a place to stretch out," Newpord instructed. "We men will take the chairs, settees, and floors that have rugs on them near the chimneys. We don't want anyone catching cold on the floorboards. I'd prefer you figure out for yourselves who you want to share the room with, but if it seems to present a problem, we'll draw names."

Voices started exchanging their thoughts on the subject and choices were made. James could hear Izora's complaint that wives ought to get to stay with their husbands, but if she *had* to, she would share with other women. Finally, Izora insisted that Enoch sleep on the rug near whichever bed she was assigned, and Enoch nodded his agreement silently.

James moved over to Anna and leaned down to whisper in her ear. "Where are you sleeping?"

She looked up at him and one golden brow arched high over her left eye. "Why? Do you have something in mind?"

She was trying to flirt with him. She had been ever since he'd gotten mad at her earlier. All through the meal and dishwashing, she'd done nothing but find ways to accidentally brush her body against his, making him acutely aware of how well he liked the way she fit him.

Anna was playing with fire. He might be a tenderfoot in her territory and not any part Texan, but he was man enough to know when he wanted a woman. And he wanted her. He just didn't want her in the company of others. He would tell her just how much he liked the way she felt in his arms and brushing up against him, if they ever had a chance to be alone. Which didn't seem a likely possibility under these circumstances.

"I just wanted to know if you were going to have to spend it in Mrs. Beavers's room choice," he told her, realizing he hadn't answered her.

"Jane and Marjorie and I are taking Janie's room. We don't know yet who the other two will be." Her eyes twinkled like blue sapphires in the firelight. "Since there are more men than women, I don't know that it won't be a couple of men. On the floor, of course."

"Men, in your room?" James immediately excused himself and headed over to their host. "Mr. Henton, may I speak with you, sir?"

Newpord excused himself from the group surrounding him. "Yes, Trey?"

"I thought you and I should take the floor of your daughter's room for the night, if you have no objection." He realized how that had sounded when the gray-haired man's bushy eyebrows formed a V beneath his forehead. "I mean, sir. I assumed if unmarried men would be sharing some of the rooms with the women," he was stepping deeper into the quagmire of his words, "then you might want someone you trust to guard your daughter's room. Rather, I certainly would want to guard Miss Ross's."

The V eased up and a smile returned to Newpord's face as James continued, "And Anna just told me only she, your daughter, and Miss Schroeder are sharing your daughter's room at the moment. They need five people per room, is my understanding. We seemed the logical pair of men, due to the division requirement."

"Son, stop with all the twenty-dollar words." Newpord placed a hand on James's shoulder. "Just say you've got it bad for Anna and you don't want any other man in there."

James looked across the room at the saloonkeeper in all her sassy glory. "I'm afraid I do, sir. Does it show that much?"

The hand patted his shoulder. "It does to a man who felt the same way about his own woman once." The widower glanced Anna's way. "Sure. We'll claim that floor for us."

A sense of relief washed over James as that all-important matter was settled.

The hand left his shoulder as Newpord started chuckling.

"What's so humorous?" James hadn't seen anything that could have caused such a jolly reaction.

"I was just thinking that she must be at least part of what they claim of her."

James grew tired of all the innuendo and no one ever really saying what it was that Anna was guilty of. "What is that, Mr. Henton? No one seems willing to actually say it."

"She's supposed to be fast on her feet, son. She certainly roped you in. How long have you known her . . . less than twenty-four hours?"

"Fast on her feet?" James puzzled over the meaning. "What does that mean in Texas, exactly?" He knew what it meant up North.

Newpord hooked his thumbs in his belt and rocked back on his feet. "Well, that depends on who's telling you. Izora and some others think it means Anna's a soiled woman, a fast ruffle of petticoats. All because she came to town with money of her own and won't say where she got it. Jane and a group just like her think it means Anna's a woman who knows her own mind and means not to let anyone change it except herself. Me? This Texan thinks she's fast at finding the goodness of someone's heart. I'd say lucky is the man who wins her love."

James thought maybe she was all three of those definitions, the way she'd been acting toward him since the dance. Could he love a woman who might not be the perfect addition to take home to meet his family? After all, she'd warned him well enough how others thought of her.

How naughty had Anna been?

Chapter 7

The sound of a grandfather clock chiming from the study next door informed Anna that it was three in the morning. Jack stirred under the covers at her hip, shifting position so he could snuggle in closer. The house seemed quiet despite the numerous occupants, the silence broken occasionally by the howling wind that brushed branches against the windows to remind them that the blizzard raged on.

Jane rolled over in the bed beside Anna, throwing a hand over Anna's hip, accidentally touching Jack. The dog growled and let her know he didn't appreciate her disturbing his comfort. Marjorie followed suit, rolling closer to Jane and pushing Anna to the farthest edge of the bed that all three women shared. Jack went tumbling onto the floor, grumbling his discontent. He barked and ran over to the blanket huddled in front of the chimney on the rug, digging his nose into the folds of the blanket. When that didn't work, he started pawing the blanket to get the sleeper's attention.

Anna watched as Trey's hand reached out from beneath the blanket and pulled him in closer to snuggle. The Third's long, lanky body barely fit on the oval rug spread in front of the fireplace.

"Scoot over," whispered Anna, bumping her bottom up against Jane's belly, "You're hogging all the bed."

Jane giggled and flipped sideways. "Marjorie keeps calling me Bob, whoever that is, and hugging the breath out of me. He must be the knight in shining Stetson of her dreams."

"You bet he is." Marjorie yawned and rolled to her back, scooting over enough so Jane could do the same. "He'll show up someday on a white steed and ready for a redhead, you'll see. Got to have faith."

"You girls awake?" Newpord sat up from where he'd been lying on the bench at the foot of Jane's bed. He yawned and stretched. "I'm getting too old for this bunking somewhere other than my own bed. Hope the storm lets up tomorrow . . . I mean . . . today. It is today already, isn't it?"

"So the clock says." Trey added his complaint to the mix and sat up, throwing off the cover. "Although I've slept many a night out on the trail and this is a mighty comfortable rug, the fire's dying down and the floor's getting cold. I could use something warm to drink."

Jack blinked his one eye, his little head hanging like he could barely hold it up. He yawned so hard that his tongue rolled out almost the length of his body, then curled up like a pig's tail.

"Poor little guy. Won't anybody let you sleep?" Trey patted him and tried to wrap the blanket back around him, but Jack must have sensed everyone was getting up and refused to miss out on whatever they intended to do.

"Anybody else hungry but me?" Newpord stood and straightened the coat he had worn to bed to add more warmth for the night. Everyone had elected to wear their party clothes and coats to bed rather than make their hosts have to provide nightclothes for each. There simply hadn't been enough to go around, and the decision was made not to change out of their clothes so they wouldn't lose valuable body heat during the change. Izora had complained, of course, but after pleas from her husband not to make a scene, she finally agreed to follow majority rule.

Anna sat up and swung her feet around to touch the floor. The Third was right. The floor was cold, despite the low fire banked in Jane's room. Jane had offered an extra pair of stockings for Anna and Marjorie to put on before they'd gone to bed, but the chill seeped into both layers she wore. The upper floors always held heat better, so it must be freezing downstairs. The thought of going anywhere colder almost persuaded her to stay in bed.

"I say we all get up and sneak down to the kitchen, if we can," she suggested, "grab some hot cider and something to snack on, visit the mudroom, and hurry back. We can grab an extra log or two of the firewood, if there's any left."

"There should be plenty for tonight and part of tomorrow." Newpord tested the sturdiness of one of the chairs that provided a place to read in Jane's room. "After that, we might have to rely on burning off some of the furniture."

"Surely not, Father," Jane protested, pushing Marjorie to get out of bed so that she could too.

"Quit pushing," Marjorie protested. "I'm moving as fast as these cold bones can go. If my teeth don't quit chattering, I'm going to give Izora a run for her money in being the fastest talker in the territory. Perish the thought."

Jack started barking and everyone shushed him.

"No use destroying good furniture," Trey reassured Newpord. "We could always use the mudroom supply."

Everyone faced Trey at the ridiculous suggestion, but he sounded serious as a preacher passing the donation plate.

"That makes *scents*," Marjorie teased. "Get it?"

Jane shoved her friend again. "We got it."

"It would indeed be an option." James realized how utterly professorish he sounded and finally realized what Marjorie had said. "Oh, you were teasing me, weren't you, Miss

Schroeder? Though not a pleasant option, I admit, it would be one nonetheless and would save these lovely furnishings."

"Come with me, Mr. Fix-it. Let's go get a log. A wooden one." Anna offered him a hand up and laughed. "I'm already having a hard enough time trying to sleep without adding odor to it."

The sound of Jack's toenails clicking across the wooden floor said the dog intended to come too.

"Shh," Jane whispered, opening the door to her room. "If you make me laugh, I'll wake up everyone in the house. Now come on, everyone, let's form a tiptoe line."

Tiptoe they did indeed, like a fourteen-footed centipede weaving its way through a maze of male legs stretched one way or the other to find comfort and heat. Jack led the way, hurdling over blanketed bodies and not waiting to reach the mudroom before relieving himself of his own particular need.

"Stop it, Jack." Anna threatened to wring the dog's neck but he continued to mark his trail where he deemed suitable. "I'm going to owe you a house cleaning," she told Jane.

Snores echoed over the second landing, revealing that at least some of the guests had no trouble finding rest. The smell of body sweat from those who had danced and whiskey from others who had imbibed permeated the landing and great room. No, Anna decided, they definitely didn't need to add to the fragrance of too many people in one place. A log was needed and nothing else would be substituted. Jack, on the other hand, had his own plan in mind.

After a few minutes of trying not to swat the dog or wake anyone with their sidestepping, they managed to reach the kitchen and found it free of any sleepers. "I guess no one wanted to chance sleeping next to the mudroom, even though this is the toastiest room in the house." Newpord opened the door to the mudroom, and sure enough, it reeked of several visits. "You ladies want to go first?"

"I will, but I definitely won't be long," Jane said quickly and disappeared into the room, closing the door and its scent behind her as Jack slipped by to follow her in.

"I'll heat up some cider." Anna grabbed the blue speckled pot that Jane had earlier allotted for the cider and poured a jar of cider into it. Jane had insisted they leave the stove burning to help with the heat and in case anyone got up during the night wanting to warm up food. "Trey, will you grab five cups down for me and that tray there? Maybe take a few of those cookies and those cinnamon rolls."

Marjorie slapped at Trey's hand. "No, you don't. Leave the cookies for Izora. We wouldn't want her to run out before the storm ends, would we?"

Trey selected the cinnamon rolls instead. "She certainly is an intense woman. Why is she always so angry?"

"She's a bully. She's insecure about something as most bullies are, so she makes everyone think she's mean." Anna helped him settle the cups onto the platter, realizing he was having difficulty with his injured hand. "Is that hurting you?"

Trey shook his head. "Not really. It's just cold, I think."

"Here, let me finish that for you." Newpord started to take the platter from Anna, but she wouldn't let him. "Jane's finished, now it's your turn."

"Marjorie? You sure you don't need to?"

Marjorie shook her head. "I got a ten-gallon bladder. I think I'll wait till the sun's up and shining through the windows. I'd rather keep my drawers on for the moment. It's too cold to pull them down now."

"Marjie!" Jane's blush radiated through the firelight, making her look as if she could melt where she stood.

"Well, you know I speak bluntly. And that's the plain truth. Besides, we've been friends too long to worry about being polite."

"Then I'll be right back, ladies and gentleman, and we'll head back upstairs." Newpord disappeared into the mudroom with Jack following close on his heels.

"For that dog to be less than six pounds, four of it's got to be all pee." Anna sighed, knowing there wasn't a thing she could do about it except toss him outside, and that wasn't about to happen.

It didn't take Newpord and her pet long to return with their host carrying a log. "No need for distress, ladies. There's still more where this came from. I just had to find one Jack hadn't marked."

"Why don't you and the ladies head back upstairs. I'll wait for the cider to warm," Trey offered. "That way you can get that log burning and the warmth back into the room quicker."

"I'll stay with you, if you don't mind, Trey." Anna handed Marjorie the platter with cups. "He doesn't need to be trying to handle the hot pot with that hand."

All were in agreement and parted ways. Anna waved Trey into one of the kitchen chairs. "You might as well sit while we wait. It shouldn't take too long."

"Come here." Trey didn't sit. Instead his hand outstretched to her.

She searched his face and wondered if he could be as bold as she hoped he might be all evening. But that wasn't his way, or was it?

"We're finally alone," he reminded her.

"Almost," she whispered. "There's Jack."

"He won't mind this."

Maybe he was. She could hope. Anna accepted Trey's hand and walked up into his embrace. Leaning her head back, she shut her eyes, enjoying the timbre of his voice, the simplicity of his words and the promise they held.

She felt him tilt her chin back and brush a soft, slow,

sensuous kiss across her lips. Trey had been right. Slow was definitely better. This was far better than the hurried kiss on the wagon.

She opened her eyes and stared into his, searching for something she thought she might never see in those whiskey-colored depths—the sight of someone who would love her, no matter what anyone else thought of her.

Anna reached up and removed his spectacles, wanting nothing to keep her from reading the truth there, the hope and possibility of her future in this man's arms. She set them on the counter, then stood on her tiptoes and tangled her fingers in the back of his hair. She was mesmerized, wanting to look forever.

"Kiss me," he whispered, moving closer until her body touched his so intimately in every place that it ignited a fire within her stronger than any she'd ever known.

Trey didn't wait for her to answer his command. His lips pressed a lingering series of kisses against her lips, setting every nerve ablaze in her body as his tongue tangled tempestuously and oh-so-expertly with hers. The world spun out of control and she had to hold him tightly for fear that she might swoon, something she'd never done in her entire life.

"Trey," she whispered. "I didn't know it could feel like . . ."

"Say my name," he commanded. "I want you to know who you're kissing . . . who's kissing you."

Anna willed herself to remember. To make it important, because it was the most important thing she'd ever been asked to remember. From the first moment she'd met him, she'd known he would change her life. She'd felt it, an uncommon warmth that had blown in with the fiercest of winds. Every scene played out in her mind. Every word they'd shared, whiskey driven or sober. "It's James," she whispered. "James Elliott the Third."

He kissed her again so completely that Anna lost all sense

of anything but wanting to stay in his arms forever. *James*. The name branded itself into her heart. *James*. Her soul now knew its mate's name. *James*. The answer to all those wishes since leaving her home back East. Wishes from a heart that longed to be truly loved.

When he finally pulled away, he said, "I want you to remember that name, Anna. It's fine and good and the best that I can offer you. But I'm also Trey and the Third. I'm those things too. Absentminded, clumsy, ignorant of most of what you Texans count as common knowledge. Am I enough for you? Could you love a man like me?"

Could she love him? She already did. She loved all the things he was and what he tried so hard to be.

But could she let him love her? Not without him knowing the truth. The question she could not answer was if she was ready to tell him. To tell anyone, for that matter. She didn't know if she could. She'd kept the burden so long, it was hard to share it with anyone and trust that they might understand. It had been simply easier to keep the secret.

"I've been kissed before, James."

"I didn't expect anything less. You're a beautiful woman."

She stepped out of his embrace. "I've been more than kissed."

Hurt held him silent as he moved away from her and reclaimed his glasses. "So you've hinted many times." James's shoulders straightened, bringing him into his full height again. "Thank you for the kiss, Miss Ross. I'll remember it as one of the finest I've ever known."

"One of?" She nearly choked back the tears that welled from her heart and stuck in her throat. *It's not his fault,* she reminded herself. *He's only hurting you because you hurt him. Say something, fool.* But she couldn't saddle him to someone he might find shame in. "I see you're not a tenderfoot at everything."

He would hate her now. Leave her and always think of her as everything she'd told him she was. Worthy of gossip. Why did it matter now? She'd told herself she would never allow anyone to make her care what they thought of her. That way, it wouldn't hurt. That way, she could live with the choice she'd made long ago and never let anyone make her feel wrong about it. Now she had to hurt someone good because of it. Someone she knew she would love for the rest of her life.

"Shall we rejoin the others?" He reached for a pot holder to pick up the cider pot, but Anna wouldn't let him.

She grabbed another holder and took the pot before he could. "Let me. You'll burn yourself or hurt yourself again."

James tossed the pot holder he'd selected onto the table. "I'm afraid it's too late for that. I'm already burned."

Chapter 8

Thursday and Friday were a miserable attempt at keeping good humor among the crowd. Everyone did their utmost to be on their best behavior, but being cooped up with a few dozen people, some of whom they liked and some of whom they only socialized with on a limited basis, proved to wear thin on several of the guests' good manners.

The simple act of everyone getting meals, doing dishes that followed, taking a few moments of privacy to groom themselves in the bedrooms, and finding something to do to ward off the boredom of the storm became a massive effort for their hosts. Everyone tired of the dancing, the best of the foodstuffs were long gone, and now water gravy, biscuits, and coffee or cider were the only offerings. The storm hadn't let up so they hadn't dared attempt to reach the salt shack, where cured hams and beef hung in plenty.

James attempted to stir up what he thought was interesting conversation about the Panhandle and its plants and shrubs, but the men were more interested in discussions about how their cattle would fare during the storm. The women fretted over possibly having to miss the candlelight ceremony to celebrate their new church bell on Christmas

Eve, and the married women worried about their children
they had left with others while they were at the party.

No one would voice their real concern. What if this didn't
end soon enough to keep one or more of them from dying?
The past blizzards in this territory had claimed more than
their share of lives.

James had avoided Anna for days, his hurt over their kiss
so deep that he didn't know what to say to her. Last night had
been the worst, trying to sleep in her room without thinking
about her and what she'd said. Trying not to get up and demand that she tell him what she'd done that made her afraid
to trust him with her heart.

He'd caught her watching him as he'd talked to the various guests the past day and a half and wondered what she
must be thinking. He just couldn't bring himself to tell her
yet. He didn't know enough yet about what others knew of
her. Nothing he'd learned so far had seemed so terrible that
she had reason to try to scare him off. And that's what she'd
done after the kiss. Tried to frighten him away from loving
her. He had to find out the truth or his heart would forever
be broken. He had to fix this between them.

"Mr. Elliott, do you have a moment?" asked a woman he
remembered being introduced to as Cloris somebody. Crawford, he thought. Cloris Crawford, wife to Ward. "Certainly,
Mrs. Crawford. How can I help you?"

The woman led him to a group of women who were
having some sort of intense discussion in the great room.
"Ladies, Mr. Elliott's here." Cloris waved him to a chair near
one of the settees. "Will you join us, Mr. Elliott?"

Elliott bowed slightly, then took the offered seat, waiting
until Cloris was seated. "You all look deep in conversation."

Marjorie Schroeder spoke up first. "We were wondering
if you would like to conduct a game for us tonight. We need
a leader."

"What sort of game do you have in mind?" James thought

something to enliven the festivities might break some of the moods that were souring by the hour.

"A Christmas game. Not like the one we did last night where we chose a gift. That left you and Anna out. But we've thought of one that might sweeten our time together." Tears moistened Cloris's eyes as she said softly, "Some of us are having to remind ourselves that we came here to enjoy each other's company, and our group here thought if we called everyone together and asked each person to tell a story of how someone in the group had been kind to them, then that would remind us all of the Christmas spirit we should be sharing."

James felt deeply honored. "I'm sure Mr. Henton would be a fine leader of the storytelling. It's his home, after all."

Another lady spoke up. "We asked him, and he suggested that you should do the honors. That you are the newest member of our community and so would not have a story to tell about the rest of us. He wanted you to feel you were participating."

"Then what can I say but yes." James stood and thanked them. "Am I to spread the word and decide what time to start the storytelling?"

Marjorie shook her head. "We'll do it around dark, when we can light the candles and make it look more Christmasy. Let's meet upstairs in the study around six. It will be a tight fit, but it's warm there and the books and leather smell better than anywhere else in the house right now. We ladies will spread the word. You just decide how you're going to start the game."

"I have one request." James glanced at Anna where she stood talking to Jane across the room.

"Anything," Marjorie agreed.

"Make sure you bring Anna." James watched the saloon-keeper glance up and realized he was staring at her. She quickly avoided his gaze. "She hasn't participated in anything we'd done since Wednesday night. I don't want her going to Jane's room to spend the evening alone."

Something was definitely stirring among the guests. They'd all acted bored to death since early morning, the party mood long gone with the hours cooped up together. Marjorie and several of the women had been hatching something since noon and, knowing Marjorie, who couldn't stand to be bored, it would most likely be a game of some sort. She loved to keep things stirring.

Anna had watched James talk to various people the last day and a half and wondered what was so important that he'd made the rounds to everyone but Izora. She knew it was something more than just making acquaintances and being polite. He looked like a man on a mission. She only hoped she was not the purpose of that mission. The fact that he hadn't talked to Izora yet, however, hinted that the conversation did pertain to Anna in some way. Otherwise, why leave Izora out? He knew anything that woman told him about Anna would be negative.

Anna had done her best to stay away from him since the kiss. To stay away from everyone, for that matter. Even Jane and Marjorie, unless they specifically asked her to help them with a chore. Sharing Jane's room last night had been an act of silent compliance until she just couldn't take it anymore and got up and wandered the ranch house looking for a place of warmth that did not already hold a blanketed body for the night.

But the memory of his kiss had followed her wherever she went. His essence seemed to fill every corner of the Henton home because he'd made himself so much a part of everything that had gone on there since his arrival. He was a man of sweet goodness. A man who didn't know how not to be friendly. A man who had won her heart with his simple kindness and easy acceptance of who she was with him. That endeared James to her in a way no one in her life had ever done.

She stared out the window now and wiped away the frost that built there, peering into the distance and wishing away the storm, but all that happened was the cold at her fingertips and in her heart deepened. "I wish this storm would end," she whispered, knowing it was more than the one outside that she spoke of.

The storm of emotions that gripped her wouldn't ease its relentless pull on her heart nor her conscience that she'd treated him horribly and had been wrong in not trusting him to have faith in her.

"We'll ride it out," Jane assured her. "There's nothing too big for us to beat."

Marjorie joined Anna at the window and informed them of a gathering that would take place in the study tonight at six. Anna quickly shook her head. "I think I'll go to bed early, girls. I'm tired."

"You're not tired, and it's midafternoon." Jane refused to let Anna off so easily. "You're avoiding James. What happened the other night between you two in the kitchen? You were perfectly fine when we left you. Where's all that sass you usually have?"

"I don't know what you're talking about." Anna turned her back on her friends and moved away.

Marjorie reached out and stopped her. "We can ask him, Anna. He'll tell us the truth."

Anna stared into her friends' faces, knowing they spoke the truth. James wouldn't lie to them. He wasn't that kind of man. "Okay, I'll go to your storytelling tonight, but you'll wish I hadn't. And so will he. It's only going to hurt him more. You'll all see." She searched the room for sign of the one person who would put an end to all this guessing game that refused to end. To put an end to any chance of her and James getting past this chasm that separated them. "Has anyone seen Izora? We need to talk."

Chapter 9

The redhead sat across from Anna at Newpord's desk, looking like a queen holding court. Anna had asked their host if they could use his study before it was prepared for the evening festivities because it would offer privacy from the curiosity seekers. Most of the guests knew the animosity between Izora and Anna had festered for years, and most wondered when and if there would ever be a reckoning between the two women. Anna could just imagine the conversation going on outside of the room with everyone knowing she and Izora were alone together.

"I suppose you're wondering why I asked you in here." Anna met her foe's gaze and realized that Izora's double chins were slightly quivering. She was nervous!

"Whatever it is, let's be done with it, Miss Ross. I prefer better company, and thank you for not bringing your mutt."

Anna had to bite her tongue to keep from telling the woman what she could do with her better company, but she forced herself to remember she was doing this for James's sake. She would be arming the woman with all the power she needed to destroy her. "First of all, I want to know why you hate me so much," Anna began. "You've never really said it to my face."

Izora's curls bobbed as she tilted forward and splayed chubby hands on the desk. "I never said I hate you. I said I don't like what you are."

"What am I, then?" Anna's teeth gritted for a moment to bite back what she really wanted to say. Instead, she finally urged, "Tell me what you think I am."

"Must I say it?" Izora's eyes gleamed dark with criticism.

"I'd like to hear whatever it is you think I've done. I know what I've done, but it would be interesting to actually hear you say what you think that is. I've heard all manner of speculation from others."

"Very well, then, I won't mince any words." Izora leaned backward in the leather chair and triangled her fingers. "I think you are a woman who has used her wiles to convince a man to set her up in business. And you keep our husbands away from their homes with your whiskey, your employees, and your readiness to flirt with our men."

"Are you specifically talking about your husband, Enoch?"

"Don't you say his name like that."

"Like what?"

"All soft and fluttery."

"Good God, woman, I can't help the way I talk. If that were a sin, we'd all go to hell."

"Such brazen—"

"Tell the truth, Izora. You're mad because he wants to spend more time *away* from home than he does *at* home. The reason why is something you're afraid to ask yourself, so instead you take it out on me. Or anyone like me who's an unattached woman who spends her time around a lot of men. I'm not interested in your man, have never been interested in your man, and wouldn't put your children through the mess of wondering whose bed their father was sleeping in."

Izora gasped.

Anna leaned closer. "And while we're talking about that, you can just get over me telling you not to send your son into the saloon anymore. If you could see his face when he has to come take his daddy by the hand and lead him staggering out the door, well, you just shouldn't do that to the boy anymore."

"It's none of your business." Izora got enough gumption to look Anna in the eye.

"You're right, as long as your child stays out of my saloon. You'll make it mine if he comes back in."

"We've already been through this. Why did you call me in now to repeat it?"

Anna took in a deep breath, garnering her strength to do what she must. "Because I wanted you to know the truth finally. About me. About how much of what you know is fact and how much is what you've made up to spur others to believe you. Once I'm done telling you, you do with the information what you want."

Though Izora's eyes sparked with interest, her features became guarded. "Why are you telling me now? Why should I believe whatever you say?"

"Because I'm tired of bearing the burden of it alone. Of not caring what you or anyone else thinks of me. I'm tired of not feeling, Izora. Of being strong enough not to appear weak. If this gives you what you need to run me out of the territory, then so be it. If the people of Kasota want to judge me and deem me unfitting, then I'll go and leave you all to your precious perfections. I just refuse to hide anymore. It's made me lose something I couldn't afford to lose . . . someone who doesn't deserve to be hurt by my hard heart."

"Mr. Elliott?"

"Yes, if you must know."

"He's the only one it can be. You've known all the rest of us for years, and none of this has ever affected you."

"Oh really?" Anna wondered how ignorant the woman was of how the gossip she'd spread had affected her business and the way others viewed her. *But maybe that was my own fault*, Anna admitted. *I wouldn't let you know how much it bothered me, so it kept going on for years*. "I think you'd be surprised at how well you can set tongues to wagging."

"If you're going to insult me, I'm going to leave."

"Then you'll miss the part about me telling you that I did leave my home back East because I was caught sleeping with a man."

"I knew it!" Izora's eyes gleamed with triumph. "I knew from the first day I saw you." She leaned in over the desk, as if eager to hear more, the insult long forgotten. "Was he a married man?"

She *would* think the worst of her. Anna recalled Bartholomew's shame-filled face and whispered, "No, he was not married. He was a good friend, a young man who wanted to become a man of the cloth."

"A preacher!" Izora's hand splayed against her bosom. "You didn't seduce an innocent?"

"I slept with him," Anna admitted. "I had to."

"No woman has to seduce a man. It's her choice." Izora frowned, looking at Anna with even greater disdain.

"He had been raped . . . taken against his will . . . not by me," Anna said softly, not telling her the rest, for she had promised Bartholomew she would never tell anyone that particular horror. "I found him shortly after it happened and held him while he cried through the night. We fell asleep and were found in each other's arms the next morning. Of course there was lots of scandal and, everything considered, I decided to come west to start a new life."

"Then you didn't actually make love with him?"

"I said I slept with him."

"But you didn't say you shared your body with him."

"I loved him the way he needed it most that night. I held him." Anna waited for her to pass judgment on her. To criticize. To gloat.

"Did he give you the money for the saloon?" The redhead tried to hang on to the last shred of speculation.

"He didn't have a penny to his name. I'm from a wealthy family, and they were more than happy to give me my inheritance early if I would take my scandal and disappear. I'm sure you have your sources to check all I'm saying."

The burden of keeping the secret for years lifted from Anna's shoulders, making her suck in a deep, clean breath. "Now, Mrs. Beavers, you are armed with everything you ever wanted to know about me. I am a soiled woman, but then again I'm not. I won't deny a word of it, should you decide to use it to your advantage."

"I still don't like you," Izora's chins lifted, "and I don't appreciate you sharing this secret with me."

Of all the things Anna had expected Izora to say, that was the last of them. "Why?"

"Because if I tell it to anyone, then you'll look like some kind of saint and I a damn fool for gossiping about you. And I don't think I can stand the thought of becoming your friend."

"Then don't. We'll just stay enemies. It will keep things more interesting between us. I just wanted you to know the truth." A laugh bubbled up in Anna's throat and percolated there until it erupted into tears of laughter.

Izora, to Anna's great surprise, began laughing too.

Jane and Marjorie rushed into the room and stared at both of them as if they'd lost their minds.

Izora and Anna reached across the table, shook hands, and silently agreed that they would remain friendly enemies.

Chapter 10

"Tomorrow's Christmas Eve," James announced to all who gathered in the candlelit study, sitting with their legs crossed on the Aubusson rug that decorated the entire floor. "The ladies thought we should play a game that would help us recall the reason that you all came together for the party in the beginning. They want us to tell a story about someone here who has been kind to them."

Some of the men grumbled, but others encouraged them to participate and catch the spirit that they were trying to inspire.

Others came in late and took a seat. James waved them in. "There's room for all of us. Come on in." When everyone looked settled, he continued, "I was asked to lead the game because I am new to your community and several of you were afraid I wouldn't have anything to say. This was your way of allowing me to participate."

James searched through the crowd and was glad to see Anna sitting with Jane and Marjorie at the back of the group. The ladies had kept their word and managed to get Anna to join in. Jack was curled up on her lap, enjoying the strokes of her hand on his back. Lucky dog, James thought. He wished she would touch him so freely again, but he could only hope that what he was about to tell would help her change her mind about not getting close to him anymore.

"Well, I beg to differ. I can participate in another way," James said and stretched out his injured hand to encompass the crowd in his explanation. "I can tell the first story of how someone in this community has been kind to me in the past. My past with you is only three days old, but it's been a wonderful three days. Anna saved my life. Jane and her father took me into their home and gave me food, drink, and a warm rug to sleep on. Little Jack there marked me as his."

Everyone laughed when someone said, "Hasn't he done that to all of us and everything in this house?"

Jack barked and threatened to hike his leg. Anna soothed him. "It's okay, fella. They're just teasing."

"And the rest of you have been kind in ways you never knew you were being kind. Sharing your knowledge of Anna with me when I asked you about her." He faced Anna. "That's what I was doing, Anna, finding out everything I could about you so I could do the very thing you told me to do—decide for myself which side of the fence I stood on with you." James turned his attention back to the crowd. "Now let me tell you a story about myself. I faint at the sight of blood."

Some of the men guffawed.

"It's true," James admitted, "but Marjorie never laughed, even while she stitched me up while I was unconscious. I consider that terribly kind.

"Some of you have asked me to say it in Texan instead of whatever I was speaking in my own peculiar way. You didn't horsewhip me or throw me out into the snow. You just let me know you wanted to understand me better. I'd say that was an act of kindness. But most of all, every one of you showed me that I don't have to be perfect to be welcomed among you.

That whether I'm James Elliott the Third, or the Third," his eyes met Anna's gaze and held it, "or Trey, you've accepted me into your fold as all those things that I am."

Everyone clapped their hands.

Trey held up a palm to stop them. "It's yourselves you need to applaud. I learned something of the giving spirit from you. And isn't that what Christmas is all about? Not the physical presents we receive, but the gift of giving yourself to others however they need you. I needed to know I didn't have to be perfect to become your friend. You gave that to me, each of you in your own special way, and I thank you for it."

He got up and made his way to Anna. "May I sit by you?"

She looked up at him and patted the floor beside her, scooting over to give him room. He folded his long, lanky legs and took her hand in his, linking his fingers through hers.

Though his words were especially for Anna, he made sure everyone heard. "You see, Anna, I was lucky and was adopted by a very loving family one Christmas. They took me in and gave me everything a little discarded boy could ever want. But I thought I had to prove myself worthy of the magic that had happened to me. That I had to be as perfect as they seemed to be. They never once said anything to me about being more. I just didn't want them to ever regret taking on such an imperfect little boy. I wanted to be worth the love they extended to me. To reward them for their kindness to me."

Anna held his fingers up to her lips and kissed them, staining them with tears that trickled from her eyes. "You're perfect to me, James. I want nothing more, nothing less than who you are since I met you."

"And that's why I'm glad I came here. I was on a search for a myth—pure perfection. A pink bluebonnet. Well, I don't know if I'll ever find one, but the old *curandera* who told me that I would find what I was looking for up here in the place where the buffalo last roamed was right. You are my perfection, no matter what anyone says you've been before."

"Well, I can tell you what she's been." Izora Beavers stood up to her full four feet, eight inches in height.

It seemed as if everyone in the room except Anna sucked in their breath.

When Anna's hand squeezed his, James started to demand that Izora not utter another word.

"Let her speak, James." Anna watched the faces of the crowd and met Izora's gaze with her shoulders squared.

James thought her the bravest woman he'd ever met.

"She's been kind to me and my family," Izora began, surprisingly gentle in her speech. "My children would not be having Christmas if not for her. Enoch just told me." The woman started sobbing. "She delayed the payment we owed her so Enoch could buy toys and Christmas dinner."

Cloris Crawford stood. "And she donated money to the bazaar that's being held for the children of the orphanage."

"She paid for medical supplies that will be waiting for the new children coming in on the train," Marjorie Schroeder informed them.

"She's done a lot of things for the community the past few years that she never let anyone know about but me." Jane added her knowledge in the matter. "And she only told me so that I would make sure it got to the right sources. Funds coming from a teacher versus a saloonkeeper were more willingly accepted by some of you."

"I think some of us have been wrong about Anna." Izora's gaze swept over the crowd. "Myself included. I don't know about you, but I think we were all brought together by this storm on purpose, and I'm never going to forget what it's taught me."

"What's that, honey?" Enoch asked beside her.

"That I can be just as naughty as the next person if I don't know what the hell I'm talking about." She burst into tears and threw herself into his arms.

"What got into her?" Marjorie asked, looking stunned.

"I think some of that Christmas spirit you ladies wanted to stir up," James said, thinking that there was indeed a little magic going on in the house.

Izora's confession inspired others to speak up, and the guests began sharing their tales of kindnesses experienced among the Kasota community.

A sweetness of spirit settled over the crowd, a gentleness that they had lost trying to endure the storms both outside across the Panhandle and inside their own personal lives.

All of a sudden a loud rapping sounded from below. Jack began to bark and jumped up and ran for the study door.

"Someone's pounding on the door. We've got a visitor," Newpord shouted. "Let's get 'im inside."

A dozen feet jumped up and scurried out of the study and bounded down the huge staircase. The door that hadn't been opened in days now flung open wide to reveal a man dressed in a large white Stetson and yellow slicker. Standing behind him was a horse, frosted with a layer of snow.

"Evening, folks," the man said, "could I come in?"

"Look, everyone. It's stopped snowing!" Marjorie noticed and pointed behind the man.

"Come in, come in, stranger, and welcome," Newpord invited the man inside and helped him to take off his hat and coat. "Newpord Henton's the name and these are my guests. Make yourself acquainted."

"Bob's my name. Bob Schroeder," the man introduced himself.

Jane glanced at Marjorie. "Any relation?"

The nurse smiled and gave the man a good look from Stetson to boot. "No . . . not yet. That was a white horse you rode in on, wasn't it, Bob?"

"As a matter of fact it was, miss. I'd sure appreciate if you'd let me get him in out of the cold. He's brought me a long way to seek your help."

"What kind of help is that, Mr. Schroeder?" Jane asked.

"We need some men to help us clear the tracks. The train's stalled with lots of people aboard. We happened to see all the buggies and carriages near your barn and hoped that meant there were men available to help."

"You come in and have some coffee. We'll brush down your horse and give him some feed and saddle up some of our horses as well as hitch up a team of oxen. We'll be glad to help you and the crew, Mr. Schroeder."

"Here, let me take your hat, Bob," Marjorie offered. "Bob, that's a wonderful name. Is it short for Robert?"

James tugged on Anna's hand. "Will you come with me, Anna?"

"Wherever you want to go," she said. "To Kasota. To Boston. On your search for the pink bluebonnet."

"Right now, somewhere alone will do," he insisted. "I've got something I need to ask you, and I'm not sure when I'll get to once we go to help the people on the train."

James led her upstairs to Jane's room, pulling her into his arms once the door was closed. He kissed her with all the longing that he'd barely contained since Wednesday. His world was perfect now. He'd found where he truly belonged—where he was meant to be for the rest of his life—in Anna's arms.

Minutes later, they both came up for air, laughing from the sheer joy of knowing that each of them were loved and would never forget this particular Christmas that had brought them together.

Anna sat on the bed and pulled him down to sit beside her. "Ask me what you were going to ask me, Third."

James laughed. "What if someone comes in and sees us sitting here together? You'll start all kinds of rumors."

"Not if you ask me the right thing." She traced his lips with a slow fingertip. "And ask me fast, because as you know I'm not a patient woman."

James got down on one knee. "Anna Ross, will you become my bride and love me forever, come blizzard or shine? Love me for this Christmas and for every one from this day forward?"

"Uh-huh." She nodded and smiled. "But on one condition."

"What's that?"

"That if you feel yourself faint, make sure it's me reviving you and not Marjorie or Jane. I'm going to be a very jealous woman."

"I think you only have to worry about Jane now. Marjorie's got Bob."

Author's Note

The Lone Star flag was designed from the sight of albino bluebonnets in a field of blue ones.

The Texas state flower comes in a variety of colors—traditional blue with white tips, the pure albino bonnet, and even the pink-tipped ones that live along the walls of the Alamo. Legend says that the pink are the faded drops of blood that was spilled in that hallowed place when Texas won its freedom. So to find a full-colored pink one is a rare find indeed, and hints where a Texas hero now sleeps.

Yes, they really do exist.

THE CHRISTMAS BELL

LINDA BRODAY

Chapter 1

December 1887
Texas Panhandle

The morning was one of those where it paid to stay inside by the fire. Unless a man had cattle to feed and water.

Oh, the glorious life of a rancher.

Sloan Sullivan sighed, his breath creating vapor in the frigid air that stung when drawn into his lungs. His right leg had been injured when a horse fell on him several months ago and now protested the extreme temperature. He didn't have time to give it so much as a rub. He'd hurry and get the chores done so he could get off it and back to the cheery fire blazing in the old stone fireplace.

Shivering, he turned up the collar of his wool coat and pulled his hat down low, bracing himself against the biting wind that swirled around him like an insistent saloon girl wanting to dance. The heavy snowfall created a blanket of white in all directions and wiped away all traces of the footsteps he'd just made.

He'd seen storms like this on the Texas Panhandle, where no living thing survived long without refuge. But this particular storm was one of the fiercest he'd seen in years.

A faint black outline through the curtain of falling snow

caught his eye. He squinted. It looked to be the train, Engine 208 unless he missed his guess.

And it wasn't moving.

Furthermore, there was no smoke rising from the smokestack.

Fear tightened his chest. The Fort Worth and Denver City locomotive appeared stuck in the mountainous drifts that covered the tracks. The passengers would freeze when their supply of wood ran out . . . if it hadn't already. He had no way of knowing how long they'd been snowbound.

In the west pasture a good mile from the ranch house, Sloan limped to the rear of the sled he used to haul feed for the cattle during the winter months when snow and ice covered the ground. Grabbing the pitchfork, he made short work of forking the hay to the hungry, half-frozen cattle.

Throwing the implement into the back, he climbed up and prodded the horse into action. He had to hurry.

When he reached home, he drove the sled up to the kitchen door. Inside, he grabbed all the blankets and quilts he could find. Then he filled a wooden crate with food and supplies.

He loaded all of that into the sled and drove around to the woodpile. He filled the remainder of the space with enough kindling and logs to last for a few days. Covering everything with a length of canvas to keep it dry, he crawled into the seat and urged the horse toward the train.

It was slow going.

The animal floundered in the high drifts, doing his best to keep his footing.

The wind howled, pawing at the cracks of the passenger car like an icy snow monster bent on getting to them. Inside the Fort Worth and Denver City train, Tess Whitgrove shivered, chilled to the bone along with the other travelers who were trying to get home to Kasota Springs for Christmas.

Her desperate glance lit on the small black stove at the front end of the car. It had long grown cold. Each fall the engineer removed the first two rows of seats and added the stove to warm the travelers. Little good it did them without wood.

The blizzard had them in its grip and wasn't letting go. They'd been stuck since last night and were running out of patience, hope, and endurance.

And to make matters worse, the train engineer had put her in charge of the passengers while he, the conductor, and brakeman had worked tirelessly to try to free the locomotive. Unfortunately, their efforts had been for naught.

Tess had never asked for the responsibility of the passengers' welfare, and the heaviness weighed her down.

Despair filled her. Now, gazing desperately at the sea of white, she saw something move. She wiped a thick layer of frost from the train window and leaned closer to the icy glass.

All of a sudden a horse pulling a sled appeared in the breaks of the blowing snow. Whoever it was inched ever closer to the train.

Hallelujah! Their prayers had been answered.

Tucking a thin blanket, the only thing that had been available, more firmly around Ira Powell's feverish body, she turned to his wife, who hadn't left her husband's side. "Mrs. Powell, I have to find the engineer, but I'll be back soon."

"All right, dear. There isn't much else we can do anyway except pray." Weariness lined Omie Powell's sweet face.

Tess hurried to find Roe Rollins, the Fort Worth and Denver City Railroad engineer, to relay the good news that it seemed help had arrived.

She prayed the man coming was a doctor. Ira Powell wasn't going to last long without medical treatment. She couldn't be certain, but she feared he had black scarlet fever.

Lord knows, Tess had done all she could, and it was pitiful little.

If they could just get a fire lit in the stove at the front of the frigid passenger car, it would be an immense help. They'd exhausted their supply of wood over six long hours ago.

With thoughts rolling around inside her head like so many loose marbles, she found the train's engineer Roe Rollins doing his best to calm a prickly woman by the name of Mrs. Abner. She was traveling with four small children. The woman had certainly tried Tess's patience. From the exasperation written on Roe's face, it appeared he'd reached the end of his rope as well and was about to cut his red suspenders and go straight up.

"Now, Mrs. Abner, I don't care what kind of fit you pitch, you ain't getting off this train until I say." Rollins's words came through gritted teeth.

"You can't stop me, you old crow." The stout woman pushed back her black lace poke bonnet, which had slid over one eye. The hat had once been fashionable but now was a rather sad affair that had lost its ribbon.

Tess put her hand on the woman's arm and spoke gently. "Mrs. Abner, you wouldn't get more than a few feet before you'd freeze to death. You don't want that, do you? You're frightening your children."

Tess's glance swept to the frightened faces of the children, two boys and two girls, whose hats and heavy coats swallowed their thin faces. The youngest of the brood, a girl probably no more than two years old, coughed from deep inside her small chest. The sound worried Tess.

She gave them a bright smile and a wink, praying they wouldn't take ill.

Mrs. Abner stopped struggling with Rollins and drew up. "These children aren't mine. I'm taking them to the orphanage in Kasota Springs. But I'll allow you might have a point. I won't tolerate much more of this, though. I have connections, you know." The woman huffed, dropping into the seat. She gathered the children around her like a plump mother goose with her goslings.

Tess turned to Roe and spoke low. "There's someone coming. I saw a sled through the window."

"Won't be soon enough to suit me. I'll let him in."

"You may need my help." Tess followed close on the engineer's heels since the conductor and brakeman had braved the cold to get what supplies they could gather from the caboose.

Roe applied all his shoulder to the door, but it was frozen shut. Tess added her weight and pushed with all her might. At last the steel door broke loose.

And Tess's heart stopped.

The man on whom their survival depended was none other than rancher Sloan Sullivan. The blast of frigid air that entered with the man cavorted around her ankles and danced up her skirts. The weather reflected the icy scowl on Sullivan's face.

Why couldn't it have been someone else? Anyone else.

The measured assessment from the recluse's gunmetal gray eyes seemed to say he shared the sentiment.

The problem wasn't Sloan's looks. Her heart raced like a stampeding herd of buffalo each time she found herself in his vicinity. No, the point at issue was the way he went out of his way to avoid her. Several times he'd crossed the main street of Kasota Springs to avoid having to speak to her.

Tess knew the talk bandied back and forth about her. For one, that she was some kind of highbrow who thought her daddy's money could buy her whatever she set her heart on.

Particularly irksome was the spiteful gossip that her daddy hadn't been able to *buy* her a husband.

Even now, remembering the talk brought fresh pain.

As if a woman could shop for a husband the same way she bought a length of calico from the mercantile. Heaven forbid. She'd had her chances to wed and turned them all down. She'd wait for someone to come along who didn't have an eye on the size of her purse. And if such a man never crossed her path? She'd live out her days a spinster. She'd marry for love or not at all.

Sloan grabbed the handrail and pulled his tall form onto the train, ducking his head to get through the low entrance. He removed his battered felt hat and knocked the snow from the brim before settling it back on his dark head.

Tess steeled herself, certain he meant to ignore her.

After several long heartbeats, he reached up and touched his hat brim with two fingers. "Miss Whitgrove."

"Mr. Sullivan," she returned. "Welcome aboard."

The engineer pumped Sloan's hand. "Roe Rollins here. We're mighty glad to see help arrive. Yessiree."

"I brought a load of blankets, some food, and plenty of firewood for the stove. Thought you might use it. No telling how long you'll be snowbound. This weather is a wooly bear."

His deep baritone stirred the air and created a path of tingles up her spine. His ebony hair was so dark it had a blue cast to it, which only made his gray eyes more startling and clear. But it was the cleft in his chin and his full mouth that drew her attention. She'd lain awake many nights, fantasizing what it would be like to kiss him.

That was before he'd treated her like a case of poison ivy.

Now she barely gave him another thought. *Liar*, her conscience berated. She tamped it down and sneaked a look from the corner of her eye.

Rollins finally turned Sloan's hand loose. "I'll get some

men to help unload your sled. I'm sure you'd like to get back home while you still can."

Tess helplessly watched the old engineer disappear down the aisle. She didn't relish being alone with the antisocial rancher. Given his preference for doling out his words more frugally than a widow woman pinching pennies, she didn't know what exactly to say to him.

The silence grew uncomfortable. She finally managed to speak, the words coming no louder than a murmur. "Thank you for sharing what you have with us. We're badly in need."

He met her eyes briefly before he looked away. "I only did what any other man would do. I reckon this is one situation where a person's money is useless."

The words slapped her like a connecting open hand. A flush rose. "Have I done something to you, Mr. Sullivan?"

His frank gray stare swung to her. "No, ma'am. Things are the way they are, I suppose. Just remarking is all."

If only she could believe that. Unfortunately, he'd have a difficult time selling her that particular horse.

Although Tess didn't succeed in fully tamping down her anger, she managed to add a good helping of honey to her reply. "I assure you, Mr. Sullivan, that this silver spoon in my mouth doesn't interfere in the least with my ability to tell truth from untruth. You don't fool me. Just so you know."

Sloan was clearly ill at ease, shifting his weight from one foot to the other. Or maybe part of it was because his leg was hurting. She'd heard about his accident and had seen him limping when he made his monthly trip into town for supplies.

She was again searching for something to say when she noticed his attention drawn to Maryellen Langtry, who was heavy with child. With a struggle, the young woman pulled herself from her seat and lumbered toward the back. Probably going to visit the necessary again. Tess bit her bottom lip.

The woman would have to pass by Ira Powell, who lay on a bench seat near the back of the car. *Please, God, don't let the woman catch what Ira has.*

Rollins returned. He'd pressed into service Charles Flynn, who was traveling to Kasota Springs, and the conductor, who'd returned from the caboose in the nick of time.

Then the engineer, his helpers, and Sloan Sullivan turned up the collars of their coats, pulled on their gloves, and trudged into the howling wind and bitter cold. Tess shivered and pulled her coat tighter, thankful that the passengers would soon have a fire and food to put into their growling bellies.

Still reeling from her encounter with the aloof Mr. Sullivan, she switched her thoughts to another worry. The new bell that she'd gone all the way to Boston for might not make it to Kasota Springs in time for the Christmas service. Everyone would be heartbroken if it didn't arrive. And the way the weather was, it didn't appear they would break the train from the high drifts in time.

The likelihood of spending Christmas aboard the Fort Worth and Denver City train appeared pretty certain.

When she found a free moment, she'd go to the baggage car. The clothes, shoes, and toys she'd bought for the orphanage would help make Christmas bright for the children traveling with Mrs. Abner.

But first she needed to check on Ira Powell.

Omie Powell, his gray-haired wife, met her halfway down the aisle. "Come quickly. Ira's taken a turn for the worse."

Mr. Powell's breath was labored and shallow. He'd slipped into unconsciousness and burned with a high fever. Also, a strange sandpapery rash covered the right side of his neck. Tess's breath got caught on the sizable lump in her throat. All were signs of deadly scarlet fever that was sweeping the country.

A sudden gust of wind battered the side of the train, rocking it back and forth. Bone-chilling cold seeped into Tess. She didn't think she'd ever be warm again.

"It's bad, isn't it?" Omie clenched her hands together tightly until her blue veins stood out.

Tess was glad the woman had kept her voice low. The passengers didn't know the extent of the illness, and Tess wanted to keep it that way. If they got wind of what she suspected, there'd be overwhelming panic.

Mrs. Abner, who was always looking for something to raise a ruckus over, would seize the opportunity to lash out.

"Yes, Mrs. Powell, your husband's situation is very dire." She put her arm around the old woman's frail shoulders. "Just don't give up hope. As long as there's life, there's hope. You must be strong."

Omie straightened her five-foot frame. "I know what it is to wage a war with death. And often how futile it can be. I birthed six little ones and buried four of them before they were three years old." Tears filled the woman's brown eyes. The tragedy she'd suffered would've broken many a woman. "It's just that Ira is my life. I don't know how I'd make it without him."

Tess kissed the woman's wrinkled cheek. "Hopefully, you won't have to find out for a long while to come."

They needed a miracle—a Christmas miracle.

She laid a hand on Ira's chest, wishing she didn't feel so helpless.

A throat cleared behind her. She whirled and found herself face-to-face with the last person she wanted to see.

Sloan Sullivan thrust an armful of blankets at her. "Rollins said you needed these."

"Thank you." She wondered how long he'd been standing there as she accepted the load and promptly spread the blankets over Ira.

"What do you think he has?" Sullivan asked.

Tess pulled him out of earshot of the passengers. Her breath fogged in the air as she leaned close. "It looks to be scarlet fever, although I'm not certain. But for obvious reasons I don't want the rest of the passengers to overhear."

For once he'd appeared to put aside his ill feelings. "I agree. What can I do to help?"

"If you could get a fire going in the stove, we'd be in your debt. The children are freezing. I'm praying whatever Mr. Powell has won't spread."

"You were wise to keep him apart from the others as much as possible."

"I just followed my instincts, Sullivan, same as you would. It'll be a nightmare if this spreads to the others. It'll be especially bad if Maryellen Langtry, the woman who's in the family way, comes down with it."

His wintry gray eyes stared into hers before they flicked away. "I'd best get to that fire before I head back home."

"Sullivan?"

He'd shifted his weight and turned to go. He stopped. "Yes?"

"Maybe you'd better take a look out the window."

Sloan bent over to peer out. A low oath squeezed from between his full lips. "Reckon I'm not going anywhere in this whiteout."

Dismay settled like sour milk in Tess's stomach.

This was just dandy!

Chapter 2

Sloan jerked up straight. He was stuck on the train.

Fine rescuer he'd turned out to be.

Forced to share tight quarters with Tess Whitgrove, of all people. There'd be no way to avoid her.

A few seconds before, he'd been mulling over a plan to bundle Mr. Powell up good and haul him into Kasota Springs to the doctor. But it looked like Mother Nature had other ideas.

And he didn't dare set out for the ranch. He'd known of men who ventured out in a whiteout, lost their bearings, and ended up frozen stiff as a fireplace poker.

He gave Tess a wry grin. "Appears you won't get rid of me today."

"We have plenty of empty seats since most of the other passengers heard about the storm and got off in Farley Springs." Her pale amber eyes clouded and her mouth drew in a tight line.

It was evident to Sloan that she was none too pleased to be saddled with him. Well, he'd try not to add to her headaches. Staying entirely out of her way would be impossible, though, given the limited space.

Sloan shifted and rubbed his leg. "Guess I'd best unhitch

the horse from the sled and get him into the livestock car before he freezes to death."

"I'm sure the animal would appreciate that." Her silky golden hair that she'd tied back with a blue ribbon rippled down her back in curls as she turned to Mrs. Powell. "I can use your help seeing what kind of food Mr. Sullivan brought. Maybe we can find something for the children to nibble on."

"All right, dear," the older woman answered. "I need something to occupy myself with. Otherwise I'll just sit and fret over things that are beyond my control."

Sloan fidgeted. "Reckon I'd best see to my horse."

He watched Tess give her patient a lingering pat before herding Ira Powell's wife toward the supplies they'd unloaded in the front of the car. She seemed to care a lot about someone who was no kin. Could be an act for his benefit. Yet it appeared genuine enough. And there was Mrs. Abner and Mrs. Langtry, who could take on the chore of seeing what he'd brought and doling out some food, but they hadn't stepped up to offer. Maybe those rumors about Tess Whitgrove were unfounded.

If she were truly the selfish overindulged woman he'd heard she was, she'd sit on her hands and expect to be waited on like the Queen of Sheba.

Yes, he was beginning to have a new admiration for the lovely banker's daughter.

Prying his eyes off the gentle sway of her hips, he hurried to the woodstove that stood near the door of the passenger car. Someone had already piled a good stack of the wood he'd brought from the ranch beside it.

The train engineer knelt in front of the black iron stove and was busy laying a fire. The man looked up. "Go tend to your horse, Mr. Sullivan. I've got this."

"It's about time we got warm," huffed a stout woman who perched stiffly in a nearby seat. With all the children huddled around her, she looked like a stuffed Mother Goose. Only with her disapproving frown and sour disposition, she more resembled a nasty-tempered banty rooster.

"I'm doing the best I can, Mrs. Abner," Rollins answered.

Sloan shook his head at the irritating woman. Buttoning his coat and pulling on gloves, he limped out into the blizzard. He wasted no time in unhitching the horse and leading it into the livestock car out of the weather. Sloan even found some grain to feed the gelding. He checked on the other horse, a handsome dappled gray, and was satisfied it was in good shape. It must belong to the passenger Rollins had called Flynn in the shearling coat.

There was also a milk cow tied next to the horses. He saw that she had hay to eat. The milk would come in handy. He'd come back and milk her in a bit.

By the time Sloan made it back inside, a roaring fire greeted him. Glad to have gotten his horse out of the weather, he tugged off his gloves and backed up to the cast-iron stove to warm his bones.

His glance caught the children, who happily chewed on some of the jerky and hunks of cheese and bread he'd hauled from the ranch.

The woman who was clearly in the family way struggled from her seat and joined him. He caught the way the woman reached around to rub her back. As one who suffered his own pain, he knew her back was killing her.

And being a rancher and working with cows, he also knew her babe would arrive soon.

Heaven help them if they didn't get the train out of the drifts in time.

Sloan looked around. Not counting himself or the sick man in the back, there were three of the train crew and the land agent Flynn on board. That wasn't enough to dig out the huge locomotive even if Flynn hadn't appeared yet to be introduced to the business end of a shovel. No, Tess Whitgrove was more likely to ply her hand to the task than that fellow.

If the blizzard moved on out by tomorrow, he could bundle up Mr. Powell and this pregnant woman and take them to town.

That was a big if.

"Hello. I'm Maryellen Langtry." The woman offered a handshake. "We sure do appreciate you bringing supplies to us. Circumstances were getting pretty dire."

Sloan gave her hand a brief shake. "Out here we all help each other. It's the only way to survive."

"All the same, we're mighty grateful." The woman pulled out a handkerchief that she'd tucked into her sleeve at the wrist and wiped her nose. "I can't remember the last time I ate." All of a sudden she grabbed his arm and sagged against him.

He quickly helped her to the nearest seat. "Let me see if I can find you a drink of water, ma'am."

Problem was he didn't see any. His gaze swept the passenger car, landing on Tess, who was back with Powell. She met his glance and must've sensed trouble because the skirts of her gray wool traveling dress snapped around her feet as she hurried toward him.

"What's wrong, Sullivan?"

"It's Mrs. Langtry. She's feeling a mite faint. I think a drink of water would do her good."

"There's a bucket of melted snow and a cup next to the stove."

Tess's attention turned to Maryellen as Sloan went to fetch the water. "Maryellen, are you having pain?" she asked gently, laying her hand on the woman's brow, relieved to find Maryellen didn't have a fever.

"Only in my back. I just got a little dizzy." Maryellen flashed a wan smile and raised herself up straighter. "I'm feeling better already. Don't fret about me."

"Now, who else is going to worry if I don't?"

Maryellen's brow wrinkled. "Well, there's my husband Earl, who's the worrier in the family. I'm sure he's walking the floor, wondering where the train is. He must be beside himself."

There probably were a lot of anxious families, her own included. Her mother and father would be out looking for the train as soon as the weather permitted. Others in Kasota Springs would be out also. One thing about it, when the chips were down everyone banded together.

Then there was the mayor, who'd commissioned Boston Iron Works to design and pour the Christmas bell that now rested in a huge crate in the freight car. All the citizens of Kasota Springs had donated money to purchase it. Now it appeared the weather would prevent them from ringing the bell on Christmas Day. Once again, the day of the Lord's birth would be silent. And the newly erected bell tower would sit empty.

And Tess would have failed to show the townspeople once and for all she was something more than the pampered banker's daughter.

Failed.

She shriveled into a ball inside.

She'd been desperate to prove herself. That's why she'd volunteered to go after the bell and bring it home. She wanted to stop the jokes and gossip and innuendo.

"I wouldn't have been traveling in my advanced state except that my mother was very ill in Saints Roost," Maryellen said, tears filling her eyes. "I should've been home before this. And now . . ."

Tess patted Maryellen's hand. "We'll have you out of here and safely in your bed before you know it."

Sloan returned just then with a cup of water that he handed to Maryellen.

"Thank you, Mr. Sullivan." Maryellen took a deep drink.

All of a sudden a commotion at the rear of the train drew her attention. Tess's heart stopped and her breath got stuck in her chest. Mrs. Abner was leaning over Ira Powell.

The secret was a secret no longer.

"Get him off this train!" Mrs. Abner waved her hands, motioning toward the door. "He's going to kill us all. I won't have him exposing what he's got to me or my charges."

Omie Powell wrung her hands, tears filling her eyes.

"What's going on here?" asked Roe Rollins.

"I demand you put this man off this train at once."

This was exactly what Tess had feared. Anger rose. The old biddy wouldn't blink an eye at throwing Ira out into the snow.

"We'll do no such thing. That'd be a death sentence. Even if you don't mind that being on your conscience, Mrs. Abner, I'll not have it on mine." Rollins hooked his thumbs in his suspenders and squared his jaw.

Mrs. Abner sucked in air and glowered. "It's not like he's liable to live long nohow. If we don't protect ourselves, he's gonna pass what he's got on to me and the children."

Charles Flynn, the land agent on the way to Kasota Springs, stood and jerked his heavy shearling coat tighter around him. "Pass what on?"

"It's a deadly case of the fever, or I'll miss my guess," crowed Mrs. Abner.

"Now, Mrs. Abner, you're not a doctor. Goldarn it, you don't know what's making Mr. Powell sick. Go back to your seat and take care of those children and let us worry about this man." Again, Rollins did his best to keep the peace.

"I say we don't take any chances. I'm adding my vote to Mrs. Abner's here," said Charles Flynn.

Sloan held up his hands and raised his voice above the

racket. "Now, calm down, everyone. No need to get your tailfeathers in a wad."

Mrs. Abner pointed her finger at Sloan. "Don't you tell me to calm down. I have my rights, and I say we get rid of the problem before we all regret it."

Roe Rollins stood his ground. "Just wait a cotton-pickin' minute. He ain't going anywhere. This is my train, and I say who stays and who goes."

"You're being unreasonable, ma'am," growled Sloan.

"Mark my words. If this man gives us scarlet fever, your goose is gonna be the one in the grease. I have—"

"Connections," Rollins supplied for her. "Yes, I know. You've told me forty'leven times since you boarded."

Tess thought the situation had been defused and was breathing easier when Charles Flynn reached inside his coat and whipped out a pistol. She gasped in alarm and clutched Sloan's arm.

"This forty-five says you get that man off this train right now." Flynn's threat was as icy and hard as the frozen ground outside.

Glancing at Sloan, Tess saw a tic in the muscle of his jaw. Folks in town said he'd once been a lawman. They said he'd stood up to the Dooley Gang and single-handedly ended their reign of terror on the South Plains.

But he wasn't wearing a fire iron. How could he hope to handle Flynn?

Sloan took a step toward the land agent. "What are you going to do, shoot us all? Better use your head. Want to swing for murder?"

"I'm not going to sit here and catch scarlet fever, no matter what I have to do."

"And I'm not going to let you kill innocent people."

"How do you propose stopping me? I don't see a weapon on you. I don't see one on any of you."

"Just because you don't see one doesn't mean it's not there." Sloan's voice was deceptively soft. Tension gripped the passenger car, enveloping Tess. She wondered what Sloan meant. Did he have a hidden pistol?

Sloan took another step closer to Flynn, who was beginning to sweat, probably thinking his demand wasn't a good idea.

And rightly so, for Sloan didn't appear to be in the mood to back down.

When it seemed she could cut the air with a knife, someone pounded on the door of the passenger car. Tess almost jumped out of her skin.

But the distraction caused Flynn to lower his Colt. Sloan seized the opportunity. He lunged, tackling the land agent, bringing the man to the floor in the narrow aisle and grabbing the revolver. In the scuffle, the gun discharged, lodging in the back of a seat. The projectile barely missed the oldest orphan boy.

Again, someone pounded on the door.

Both the engineer and the conductor rushed to let the person in.

With jangled nerves and weak knees, Tess hurried to check on her patient. This promised to be a day that would burn in her memory.

Ira Powell's condition appeared unchanged. Dear precious Omie was caressing his hand.

"What was that noise?" Omie asked, her voice trembling.

Tess didn't know if the woman referred to the gunshot or the stranger intent on barging into their midst. "It was nothing to worry your head about. Just put all your thoughts on your husband getting well. Ira can feel your presence, you know. He'll draw on your strength."

"I don't feel very strong right now."

She put her arms around Omie and hugged her. "You're stronger than you think. Can I get you anything?"

"You don't have to wait on me hand and foot."

"I certainly don't mind. I don't want you getting sick too."

"I'm fine. Honestly. I'll just sit here and guard Ira. No telling what that spiteful Mrs. Abner will get in her head to do next."

Tess was grateful for a chance to see who'd been pounding on the door so insistently. Curiosity had gotten the best of her. Who was crazy enough to be out in the blizzard?

She passed Sloan, who was finishing tying up Flynn. She was grateful to the stranger who'd appeared on the train steps out of the blue. She shuddered to think what might've happened without the distraction. Without a doubt, Charles Flynn would've killed Sloan. And maybe anyone else who'd stood in his way.

As she neared the front of the car she could see Rollins and the conductor bending over a haggard-looking stranger lying on the floor. She could barely see the man's features for the shaggy red beard that covered most of his face. Ice and snow coated his beard and the buffalo robe he wore. From where she stood she could feel the numbing coldness radiating from his body.

Maryellen Langtry waddled forward as fast as she could in her condition, bringing a blanket. "We have to get him warmed up."

"C-coffee. I need some coffee if you can s-spare it." The stranger rose to a sitting position, his blue lips showing through his beard.

"Sorry, mister, we were just able to get a fire going in here. No way to cook except in the caboose."

"T-thought I was a g-goner out there," the man said through chattering teeth.

"You're all right now. What's your name?" asked Rollins.

"Does it matter?"

Chapter 3

Sloan froze. The hair on the back of his neck rose, compliments of old instincts from his days as a U.S. Marshal.

"Reckon a body's name, or the lack thereof, only matters to you and God," Rollins replied. "Regardless, you're welcome to what little we have."

Sloan didn't trust a man who refused to give his name. The stranger was either running from the law or gunning for someone. Both were reasons to be wary.

While he watched, the stranger tugged his hat lower on his forehead and drew the buffalo robe up around his ears.

Giving the rope that bound Flynn a tug to check the tightness, Sloan dropped into a nearby seat where he could listen.

"What are you doing out here in this weather, mister?" quizzed Rollins.

"Minding my own business." The man licked his cracked lips, staring at the floor. "Be nice if you could do the same."

Rollins spewed out a frustrated gust of air. "You're a disagreeable old cuss. Mind at least telling us where you're headed?"

The stranger's dark distrust was evident as he scanned the faces around him before he answered. "No place in particular, I reckon. I pretty much go where I want when I want.

Been doing that since I was out of knee britches. You folks are sure a nosy bunch. If the weather wasn't fit to freeze a man's innards solid, I'd mosey on."

And if Sloan wouldn't have to wrestle with his conscience, he'd boot Red Beard out the door and help him on his journey.

Though the man's shaking had slowed, he had to exert all his strength to get to his feet. He collapsed into the nearest seat, clutching the buffalo robe tightly around him.

The conductor watched Red Beard with narrowed eyes. "You got a horse outside that needs looking after, mister?"

Red Beard shook his head. "Broke his leg in a snowdrift a good ways back. Had to put him out of his misery."

So the stranger had a gun. Sloan took note of that tidbit and filed it away.

"Why is that man tied up?" Red Beard pointed to Flynn.

Rollins opened his mouth to reply when Mrs. Abner jumped in with both feet. "He was trying to save us from certain death, he was. We have a passenger sick with scarlet fever. Flynn and I were trying to put him off the train, which would've been the best for everyone."

"The fever, huh?" Red Beard's eyes widened a bit.

"Now, Mrs. Abner, we don't know that for sure. Ain't none of us here got doctor next to our name." Rollins clenched his hands, casting a look around, probably for something to hit that wouldn't land him in a heap of trouble. Sloan sympathized. He'd about had it himself with the old battle-ax and the close-mouthed stranger.

Tess looked up from where she stood with an arm around Maryellen Langtry. She met Sloan's gaze. He didn't know if the worry filling her pale amber eyes was the talk of scarlet fever or the fact that the stranger's sudden appearance would severely limit their food supply. He doubted what he'd brought would stretch far enough. The pinched faces of the children brought a lump to his throat. They slowly chewed the jerky. The poor things were starving.

Sloan made up his mind that he'd find some excuse to not be around when it came time to divvy up the food.

Tess stepped away from Maryellen and came toward him.

"May I have a word with you, Sullivan?" Her low drawl reminded him of a warm, sultry night under a full moon.

He nodded and rose, following her toward the rear of the train where Ira Powell lay still and pale.

When they were out of earshot of the others, she leaned close. "We need to move Mr. Powell to the caboose. He's not safe here. I don't trust Mrs. Abner, Flynn, or that stranger."

That made two of them.

He fought the headiness of the subtle scent of honeysuckle in her hair. "I agree. Besides, we really need to isolate Powell as much as possible. I'll clear it with Rollins."

"We couldn't move him before because we didn't have enough wood for both the stove here and the one in the caboose. Now we do." Tess's eyes glistened like stars.

"Rollins also mentioned that the stove serves as a cookstove for the train crew."

"Wonderful! We can make some coffee. I know that'd be welcome. And I can make some hot tea for Maryellen."

"I brought some things to make a stew if someone's willing to cook it." Sloan had the sudden urge to brush her cheek with a finger. But he resisted. He couldn't let her Southern charm weave past his defenses.

Her face lit up. "I'd love to make a pot of stew."

"There's a milk cow in the livestock car. I'll milk her. The children need nourishment."

Sloan gave thanks that he wouldn't have to carry Powell out into the blizzard. He was grateful for the way the cars were lined up. The baggage and livestock cars were immediately after the engine and coal car. Next came the passenger car, and the caboose lay beyond it. With doors opening at each end of the cars, a person could walk the entire length of the train without having to brave the weather except for brief moments on the metal platforms between.

Sloan shifted the weight off his sore leg. "I'll get a fire going in the caboose. Then I'll come back for Powell."

"After we get him moved, I've got to try to get his fever down."

"I'll help any way I can."

Tess chewed on her bottom lip as if undecided about what she was fixing to ask of him. "Would it be too much to ask if you could go to the baggage car and find my trunk? I have some clothing in there that I can tear up to make cloth for compresses. And I'll need more snow to melt."

Sloan nodded and turned to get some wood to make a fire in the caboose. When he headed down the aisle, Mrs. Abner was sitting next to Red Beard. The two of them had their heads together. Whatever they were talking about didn't bode well.

But at least Flynn was still tied up. Rollins was seeing to that, thank goodness.

The weight of Flynn's forty-five in Sloan's coat pocket felt reassuring in an odd way. He'd hung up his guns five years ago and swore he'd never touch another one. And he hadn't. Not since that horrible day in Panther Bluff, Texas.

A day that haunted his every waking minute and occupied his dreams at night.

He'd done the unthinkable.

And he could never undo those tragic events.

Hog-tying the painful memories, he dug a hole, pushed them in, and buried them. Rehashing things couldn't change the past.

Sloan turned to the business of loading his arms with firewood and made his way through the passenger car to the caboose. The cold potbellied stove was a welcome sight. Once he had a fire going, he got a pail, filled it with snow, and set it to melt inside the little train car.

Then he picked up the brakeman's lantern, touched a match to the wick, retraced his steps to the opposite end of the passenger car, and opened the door into the baggage car. He tried to ignore his throbbing leg. When they got Powell moved, he'd get off it, he promised himself.

Sloan would've had no trouble finding Tess's trunk even if it hadn't had her name etched in gold on top. It was handsome and made of the finest wood, by far the most well-constructed piece of baggage he'd ever seen.

He unlatched and lifted the lid, and promptly took a step back. Gossamer undergarments edged with rows of lace and ribbon lay neatly folded on top.

Sloan scratched his head.

He'd have to remove them to get to the clothing underneath. But what to lay them on to keep dirt and cobwebs off them?

Scanning the car, his gaze lit upon a length of canvas hanging from the wall. Carefully spreading it out on the floor, he lifted out a stack of unmentionables. It could've been an armful of dynamite with the slow painstaking movements. He'd about made it to the canvas when one lacy chemise on top slid off and landed in a heap on the floor.

Botheration!

Laying the fine clothing down, he looked at the offending piece, took off his hat, and scratched his head.

Well, pick it up, you fool.

But it might as well have been a coiled diamondback rattler.

He'd been more calm when he'd faced down the Dooley Gang. Then he'd only had to worry about flying bullets and getting filled with holes. This was a whole different matter.

Going through a woman's things was too personal.

Too . . . intimate.

Too . . . stressful.

Sloan wiped beads of sweat from his brow. He bent and picked the chemise up with a forefinger and thumb. Holding it up, light from the lantern shone through it. A vivid image of Tess wearing it crowded out everything else in his mind.

Heat rose and spread through his body in waves.

The garment was almost as sheer as a pane of glass. Every curve, every hill and valley would show through.

All that soft, supple skin.

He closed his eyes against the vision and forced air into his lungs before adding the undergarment to the pile he'd just removed. He'd just try to keep his eyes closed. But that wouldn't work either. He wouldn't be able to tell what he was picking up.

One of his problems was that these pieces of clothing didn't belong to just any woman. They belonged to Tess. Someone he'd entertained thoughts of more often than not, despite that her station in life was far above his. He'd never gotten up enough courage to say more than three words to her.

Before today she'd seemed aloof and unreachable.

And besides, all his mooning around would serve no purpose. From as far back as he could remember his mother had drilled one important rule into him. Stay within his class if he wanted to avoid a broken heart. Rich folks were too far above the Sullivans. His father had worked his fingers to the bone and ended up in a grave before he was forty. Tess was a banker's daughter, for Pete's sake. She had high expectations. She'd never settle for someone like him.

Especially after what had happened in Panther Bluff.

Taking a calming breath to stop his hand from trembling, he reached into the trunk. Whatever it was felt soft and warm and not sheer or delicate in the least. He looked and found himself holding a pair of ladies' flannel underdrawers.

He dropped them like a hot potato. Good Lord!

Why had he let her rope him into this?

But the soft flannel would make good compresses.

He picked the underdrawers back up and set them aside. Carefully transferring the lacy, ribbony stack of undergarments back into the trunk, he said a thankful prayer that the task was over.

Well, almost anyway. He closed the lid, picked up the pair of underdrawers, and scowled. He couldn't go wagging them into the passenger car footloose and fancy free.

He'd be a laughingstock.

Sloan rolled them up and stuck them inside his coat. That would do he guessed, although he felt a little funny having a pair of women's drawers nestling against his chest.

Tess breathed a sigh of relief at the sight of Sloan coming down the aisle. He'd been gone so long she started to worry.

She didn't know what it was about the man that she trusted, but she'd stake her life on him.

His quiet, calm manner was something to marvel. He hadn't even gotten in an uproar when Flynn had threatened to shoot them. But the closer he came to her now, the more she noticed his flushed face and reddened ears. Had something else happened? A quick glance found Flynn still bound. The stranger was still occupied with Mrs. Abner. And Maryellen Langtry appeared to be feeling fine, judging by the way she bustled around keeping the orphan children entertained.

"What's wrong, Sullivan?"

"If you need anything else from your trunk, you're going to have to somehow get it yourself."

"Then you didn't find anything from which to make compresses?"

"Oh, I got something all right." He glanced left and right before he reached into his coat and pulled out a piece of flannel rolled up tight and thrust it into her hands.

"This will do perfectly." Tess threw her arms around his neck. Realizing what she'd done and how it looked, she drew back. "I didn't mean to do that. I was just so grateful I got carried away."

"Let's get Powell moved." The huskiness of his voice vibrated along her nerve endings. "The sooner he's out of here, the better."

"Amen to that. If you'll carry him, I'll lead the way and open doors." She fastened her coat, knowing the stove wouldn't have had time to thaw the cold caboose.

Tess watched the great care with which Sloan tucked the blankets around Ira and lifted the old man into his arms. Her eyes stung with sudden tears. She wasn't in this fight alone. She didn't have to shoulder the full load. Whatever happened, she knew she could depend on this rancher.

She didn't know why he'd crossed the street in town to avoid talking to her, but they seemed to have moved past that.

Braving the icy blast that hit her when she opened the door, Tess held the door for Sloan. She carried the lantern, helping Omie navigate the narrow metal platform from one car to the next. Rollins dragged up the rear with the box of food.

Before long, they had Ira and Omie settled in the train brakeman's sanctuary. Tess borrowed Sloan's pocketknife to slit the flannel drawers he'd fetched from her trunk while he removed Ira's shirt and pants.

When she saw the extensive red rash covering her patient, she sucked in her breath. No one had to tell her Ira was in a bad way.

Sloan accepted his pocketknife back and closed the blade. "I'll get some coffee brewing while you and Mrs. Powell take care of things there. Then I'll carry it to the passengers. I know they'll feel almost human to get some hot coffee into them. And I want to keep an eye on that stranger."

Tess met his gray stare. "That's a wonderful idea all the way around. I'll wash my hands and get the stew cooking once I take care of Ira. Thank you for your help. I don't know what I'd have done if you hadn't been here."

He looked away and murmured, "Glad to do it."

A short while later Sloan turned to leave with the pot of coffee and an armful of cups. Tess caught his arm. "Will you please watch after Maryellen Langtry? I'm worried about her."

Sloan nodded and closed the door behind him. Tess keenly felt the emptiness in the small car. The tall man could certainly fill up a space with his large presence.

Chapter 4

Tess and Omie stopped long enough to get the stew cooking, then they resumed Ira's cold bath.

Tess dipped pieces of the soft flannel in the melted snow and applied them to Ira's fevered body. As the make-do compresses grew warm, Omie took them and handed Tess some cold ones. They had a good system going.

She just wished she could take the worry from Omie's gentle brown gaze.

But she couldn't. No one could.

When Tess's hands were frozen by the cold water, she dropped the flannel pieces in the bucket and rose from a chair she'd pulled over from the small eating table. Other than the table, there was a desk from which the conductor worked, keeping track of the tickets; the stove; and two small bunks.

Stretching, Tess moved to the wood-burning stove to thaw out.

Even though Omie's hands had to be as icy as hers, the old woman resumed where Tess left off. The woman wouldn't give up even though she had to be totally exhausted.

Standing by the fire, Tess watched the way Omie tenderly cared for her husband. The thing that struck her most was the deep love shining from Omie's eyes each time she looked at Ira. It was a beautiful thing to witness. Tess felt as though she was intruding on something rare and precious.

· She'd caught her mother and father stealing glances at each other in much the same way.

Tess wanted to find a love like that. She'd not settle for less. She'd rather go through life alone than to make do with second best.

While she was pondering the whys and wherefores of love and romance, the door opened and Sloan ducked his head as he walked through. He wore a look of puzzlement.

"Did that red-bearded stranger come in here?"

"No, we haven't seen him," Tess answered. "Why?"

"He's disappeared and I can't find him."

An uncomfortable stillness like the kind born from fear came over her. "I thought Rollins and the conductor were watching him."

"The oldest orphan boy's ball rolled under the stove and they were both trying to get it out. When they looked up, Red Beard had vanished."

"Do you think he left the train?"

Sloan wiped his eyes. "Frankly, I don't know what to think. Anything's possible I reckon."

"Have you checked the livestock car to see if your horse is still there?"

"Not yet. Thought I'd see if you ladies were all right first. Wish this door had a lock on it. If it did, I'd have you bolt it behind me."

Chills sashayed up Tess's spine. Sloan thought they were in danger. If the stranger came in here, Tess and Omie would be no match for him. She didn't relish being apart from the others but they'd had no choice. Mrs. Abner and Flynn were itching to put Ira off the train, and the devil take anyone who tried to stand in their way.

Tess balled her hand into a fist. She'd fight with the last breath she had to protect the kindly old gentleman. "If anyone comes in here with intentions of harming us, believe me, you'll know it. I can scream pretty loud."

He spared the barest flicker of a grin. "Just holler and I'll come running." Sloan stuck his hands in his pockets and shifted his weight. "Reckon I'll go check on my horse now."

"Sloan?"

"Yes?"

"Be careful. I don't trust that man."

His full mouth set in a grim line. "Makes two of us."

After he left, she looked for something to lodge in front of the door. But there wasn't a blasted thing that could keep a body out.

Sloan drew up the coat's high collar around his ears and stepped onto the metal platform between the caboose and passenger car. A wintry blast hit him. The wind hadn't died down one iota. The relentless gusts drove the heavy snow into drifts so high it reached up to the undercarriage of the train cars. He ducked through the door into the passenger car. Without pausing, he hurried down the aisle, opened the door, and proceeded across the metal platform on that end.

The dim interior of the livestock car made it difficult to see. Before his eyes could adjust, a fist swung, slamming into Sloan's jaw.

He'd found Red Beard.

Shaking his head to clear his vision, Sloan retaliated with a powerful jab to Red Beard's midsection. The force doubled the man over and left him gasping for air.

"Have you had enough or do I need to convince you a little harder?" Sloan asked.

Bent over like the man was, Sloan could barely make out

Red Beard's nod. "Enough," the man managed between grunts and groans.

Still Sloan needed some answers. "Why did you hit me?"

When the man seemed unwilling to reply, Sloan grabbed two handfuls of the buffalo robe and slung him against the inside wall of the boxcar. The force rattled the boards, shaking the car. The two horses skittered and raised a ruckus.

"Don't want any trouble. You startled me. I wasn't expecting anyone to come in here."

"I bet not." Sloan didn't try to hide his sarcasm. "I don't take kindly to a man trying to steal my horse, mister."

"Wasn't trying to steal no horse."

"Then you'd best get to explaining."

"I was just trying to see who they belonged to. All right?"

"What difference does it make who owns them? You don't have any right to be in this car."

"I'm looking for a man. Mrs. Abner told me you came from a nearby ranch bringing supplies, Sullivan."

Mrs. Abner was at it again. Sloan didn't know if she was deliberately trying to stir up more trouble or simply running her mouth in an attempt to look important. He'd wager she had a bone to pick with anyone who rubbed her the wrong way. She reminded him of a stout English bulldog with a short fuse.

"What of it?" He squinted at the stranger through narrowed eyes. "Do I know you, mister?"

"Far as I know we ain't ever met before."

"Who's this man you're looking for and what's your business with him?"

The stranger licked his lips. "Can't say."

"Can't or won't?"

"Some things a man oughta have a right to keep to hisself. I'm here because I promised my sister I'd come."

"Then you're meeting your sister?"

"Not exactly. Just taking care of something for her."

"What's your name and don't give me any backtalk."

The man's eyes darted around the car nervously. "I'd rather not say."

"I don't care what your druthers are." Sloan tightened his hand around Red Beard's throat. "Tell me and do it now."

"Deacon. Deacon Brown."

Sloan was surprised that it meant nothing to him. He would've wagered his ranch that he'd at least have heard the name. "You wanted by the law, Deacon? Is that the reason for stealing around and acting all secretlike?"

"I ain't broken any laws. If you don't mind, it feels like it's forty below out here. My toes are numb. Mind if we go back in by the fire?"

"You didn't seem to mind that before I appeared." With his free hand, Sloan felt inside the buffalo robe for a pistol. Finding one tucked in the waistband of Deacon's britches, Sloan put it in his coat pocket with Charles Flynn's.

"You ain't got no right to take that," Deacon protested.

"You'll get it back when you leave the train. Meantime, you don't have any need for it. Just think of it as protecting the passengers."

"I think we're done here, Sullivan. Let me go."

Reluctantly, Sloan released his hold on the man. "I catch you nosing around out here again I'll make you wish you'd never seen me or this train. Now git."

Deacon Brown gathered his buffalo robe close and left.

Though Sloan was by no means gratified by the turn of events, at least he'd gotten a few answers . . . if they were the truth. Time would tell on that. Sloan checked on the dappled gray and the gelding and calmed them down. Casting one last glance around the boxcar and finding nothing amiss, he followed Deacon Brown into the warmth of the passenger car.

He wondered what time of day it was, but he hadn't worn his pocket watch when he dressed that morning. And to judge by looking at the sky was impossible. Although the thick gray gloom made it seem near dusk, he had no idea if that was true.

Remembering his promise to milk the cow, he found a clean pail. Grabbing a lantern, he retraced his steps to the boxcar. It wasn't long before he returned with it brimming with milk.

"Thank you, mister," said the oldest orphan boy, smiling when Sloan handed him a cup of milk.

"You're very welcome, son."

His gaze was drawn toward the red caboose and Tess. He really should tell her he'd found the stranger. It was the right thing to do, he told himself.

No other reason. Definitely not.

But, as he limped in that direction, the door opened and Tess stepped into the car. She carried a steaming cup that bore the unmistakable aroma of hot tea.

"I was rummaging through the supplies and discovered a tin of tea. I know Maryellen can use some."

Sloan nodded. He knew how women prized their hot tea.

From the minute Tess had stepped from the caboose, the image of the very feminine, very revealing chemise he'd found in her trunk filled his head. No matter how hard he tried to get his mind on something else, he couldn't. It was hopeless. He wondered if she wore a similar undergarment now beneath her sedate gray wool traveling dress.

Heat rose and flooded his face.

Averting his eyes, he told her where he'd found the stranger.

"Deacon Brown, you say?" She wrinkled her forehead. Sloan nodded. "That's what he told me."

"I've never heard of him. Do you think he made the name up to cover for something he's done?" Her voice held a breathless quality and made him think of warm brandy and a flickering fire.

"I don't know what to believe. The man's sure acting suspicious. He had no reason to be messing with the horses. I intend to fill Rollins in on everything. Maybe between the train crew and me, we can keep him in our sights." He grabbed her arm to keep her from bumping into a row of empty seats. He could feel the jolt of electricity even through the layers of clothing. "How is Powell?"

Lamplight illuminated gold flecks in the pale amber of her eyes that reminded him of the color of whiskey. "His fever has come down some. Omie stayed with him while I got things ready in here for when it comes time to bring the stew over. And I wanted to check on Maryellen. I know she's all right or you'd have let me know, but I wanted to see for myself."

Lord knows they didn't need that baby to come now.

Sloan quickly scanned the length of the car, assessing things.

A sullen Charles Flynn was still tied up. Seated beside him, Rollins made sure the man stayed put.

Deacon Brown, if that's what his real name was, had taken a seat apart from the others. The man refused to meet Sloan's eyes. So be it. Nothing said the two had to be friends. In fact, it was more likely they never would be. Sloan raised a hand to his jaw and rubbed it. One thing about it, Deacon could pack a wallop.

Maryellen Langtry appeared in good spirits. Her thin face

lit up when Tess handed her the hot tea. You'd have thought Tess gave her a king's ransom in gold.

Mrs. Abner's head lolled back against the seat and her mouth gaped open. The woman was taking a snooze. Her charges played quietly across the aisle from her.

Seeing nothing amiss, Sloan caught Rollins's attention and motioned him toward the front. When the engineer joined him, Sloan relayed the scene in the livestock car with Deacon. "There's something not right about the man. Don't know what it is, or what he was doing with the horses, but we can't let him out of our sight."

"I've already thought about that. I spoke with my men and we're going to take turns keeping watch during the night."

"Good idea, Rollins."

"How's Mr. Powell?" Rollins asked.

"Tess . . . Miss Whitgrove said she managed to get the man's temperature down a bit."

"That's good. So far none of the others seem to have caught it. And Mrs. Abner has settled down, now that Powell is out of here. We might untie Flynn. What d'ya think?"

"Probably wouldn't hurt since I've got the only weapons on board. No, I can't see the harm, I don't suppose. But if he steps out of line again, I won't hesitate to truss him up like a Christmas turkey."

Rollins went to set Flynn free. Sloan's eyes wandered to Tess's trim figure, now that he could see it since she'd taken off her coat.

The woman would make some man a mighty fine wife. She had a way about her, and she certainly didn't shy away from work. She'd taken on the care of a seriously ill man without thought of catching what he had and cooked up a fine supper. The woman had shown an aptitude for whatever needed to be done.

Yep, she sure had a bunch of willowy curves.

Again the image of the thin lacy chemise passed in front of his eyes, and waves of heat rose.

He should go stick his head in a snowbank. Possibly that might cool him off.

He doubted it though.

Chapter 5

A few hours later in the train crew's quarters, Tess's gaze slammed into Sloan Sullivan's eyes and got tangled up in the fathomless gray depths. He looked at her in the oddest way, almost as though he'd never seen her before.

Then he smiled, actually and truly smiled, and her breath caught in her throat.

The slow, heart-stopping grin revealed rows of white teeth and crinkled the tiny lines at the corners of his eyes and around his mouth. The cleft in his chin deepened. All of that combined with the dark stubble on his square jaw set her pulse racing.

Sloan limped toward her, heavily favoring his good leg. "Here, let me help you."

She moved aside to give him room. Using some old rags for pot holders, he lifted the stew from the stove.

"I'll get the door for you," she said.

He carried the pot into the passenger car. The delicious aroma had everyone craning their necks. Tess followed behind with a box of tin plates, forks, and spoons that belonged to the train crew.

"It's about time you decided to feed us," Mrs. Abner complained, folding her ample arms across her chest. "These young'uns are a mite lean. Don't know what the world is coming to for a railroad to strand its passengers in the middle of nowhere and not give 'em nary a bite to eat."

Tess straightened her spine, trying her best to ignore the abhorrent woman. She clamped down on her tongue to keep back the words that ached to be said. Smiling brightly, she turned her attention to the orphans. "Soon as I get some ladled up, you'll be the first to eat."

The oldest boy swiped his sleeve across his nose. "Thank you, ma'am." He got his siblings in line, putting the youngest one first.

The boy's actions didn't escape her. She didn't know where they learned their manners, but someone had taught them well. The little dears made her heart melt. They'd borne the inconveniences of the blizzard with barely a peep. And when Mrs. Abner griped about the conditions, it appeared to embarrass them.

Sloan leaned close, his breath stirring the tendrils of hair at her ear. "Mrs. Abner could take a lesson from those children."

"My thoughts exactly." She took a tin plate from the box she'd brought from the caboose and ladled a helping of stew into it. Adding a spoon, she handed it to the first child. "Be careful now, sweetheart, it's a little hot."

Sloan helped the little girl to a seat, holding the plate while she climbed up. Then he placed a blanket on the child's lap to keep the warm plate from burning her and went back to help the next one. Tess's eyes watered at his gentle care of the youngsters. The rancher would make a wonderful father.

After he'd gotten each child situated with a plate of food in their lap, he turned to Tess. "I'll go sit with Powell while everyone eats. I'm sure Omie is starving. She needs to keep her strength up." A grin flickered for the briefest of seconds. "So do you, if you don't mind me saying."

Not trusting herself to do more than nod, Tess struggled with tears that hovered too close to the surface. The tall cattleman had a soft heart and knew exactly how to make each person feel special, their needs seen to.

Just then Mrs. Abner, who had sat like a swelled-up toad on a log while Tess and Sloan had seen to the children, got up and lumbered toward the pot of stew. Tess dragged her attention from Sloan's disappearing backside and hurriedly moved to man the pot. If she let Mrs. Abner ladle her own stew, she'd probably take every last bit that was left. Gritting her teeth, Tess was determined that would not happen.

Tess had everyone settled down eating when the door opened and Sloan helped Omie inside before he turned around and left again. The dear woman teetered a bit, unsteady on her feet. Tess hurried toward her and helped her down the narrow aisle.

She didn't know how they were going to get Omie to stay in the passenger car instead of going back to Ira's bedside. The woman positively had to get some rest.

Tess handed Omie a portion of the stew and took some herself. There was just enough left for Sloan in the bottom of the pot.

It was doubtful that everyone would get full, but they would all have some, and that was the important thing.

Maybe tomorrow the storm would move out and help would arrive.

And maybe they would get the Christmas bell to town in time.

When everyone had finished eating, she gathered up the dishes and silverware and put them back in the box. Tomorrow she and Omie would heat some snow on the stove and wash them, but not tonight.

It was pitch black outside. The passengers of the Fort Worth and Denver City Railroad were beginning to yawn. Maryellen Langtry busied herself making the children a bed. And when Tess glanced toward Omie, the old woman was sound asleep with her head resting against the back of the seat.

Seemed Tess's quandary was solved. She'd leave Omie asleep where she was. Sloan would keep her company in the caboose taking care of Ira. Or if he had other ideas, she'd stay by herself. She was a big girl.

Tess got one of the quilts Sloan had brought from his ranch and tucked it around Omie. Finding Roe Rollins, she asked him to keep an eye on things until morning. Then ladling up the last of the stew, she grabbed one of the lanterns and made her way to the caboose and Sloan Sullivan, or Sully, as she'd heard her father refer to the big rancher.

Sloan drew up his sprawling feet and rose when she opened the door. He cupped a steaming cup of coffee in his hands. His gray eyes swept the length of her. "I was about to come get you. Powell's fever appears to be back."

This was the first time she'd seen him without his hat. It lay on the floor beside the ladder-back chair. In the soft light from the lanterns his dark hair was the color of midnight.

"I brought you the last of the stew," she said, setting it on a small table opposite the bunks.

"There was enough to go around?"

To cover the embarrassment his sweeping perusal brought, she warmed her hands by the fire before she'd go to Ira. She'd hoped the desperately ill man had turned the corner.

"Yes. Everyone got a portion."

The howling wind pounded on the small windows of the caboose demanding entrance. The sound made her shiver. It was like an angry beast that wouldn't be denied. She leaned closer to the stove.

Sloan moved to the table with his coffee, brushing past her in the cramped space.

"Omie fell asleep after she ate, and I didn't have the heart to wake her. The poor woman is dead on her feet." She poured melted snow into a pan. "I asked Rollins to keep an eye on Flynn and Deacon in case you decide to stay here and help me. I hope that's all right since we didn't have a chance to discuss it beforehand."

Sloan nodded. "Rollins seems capable of handling the situation. I gave him Flynn's Colt just in case he needed it." He took a bite of the stew. "This is good."

"It's filling. I didn't have a lot to work with."

"You did better than all right." His smooth deep rumble brought warmth to her face.

The flutter of her pulse was like a million butterflies inside. Unsure how to reply, she moved to the chair at Ira's bedside. Applying wet compresses to her patient, Tess watched Sloan out of the corner of her eye. He was rubbing his leg. It must hurt something awful, but he'd never admit it to her. Guilt pricked her conscience. She'd kept him running from one end of the train to the other ever since he came aboard. It's no wonder it ached.

"Your leg . . . I heard you injured it."

The wry grin that flickered said he wished she hadn't noticed. "An accident several months ago, courtesy of a rattler and a spooked horse."

"I'm sorry I kept you running all day." Tess looked at the bunk bed above the one in which Ira lay. "I don't mean to tell you what to do, but why don't you lie down for a bit in this other bed?"

"I could ask the same of you. I'm betting you didn't get a wink of sleep last night. I did."

"We'll take turns. How about that? No use in us both wearing ourselves out." She wrung out a piece of flannel and placed it on Ira's feverish forehead. "Sloan, do you think the people in town might get to us tomorrow?"

"If this storm ends they'll sure try."

And if it kept right on snowing? Her stomach twisted in a knot. They could run out of food. And wood for the fire. They could all wind up freezing to death while they waited for help. She tried to put her worries out of her mind.

"Sullivan, why did you stop being a U.S. Marshal?"

"I'd rather not talk about it."

Tess had heard rumors floating around town about a shooting of some kind, but she'd never gotten the details. Didn't appear she would tonight either.

"Fair enough. Then tell me this. What do you do to celebrate Christmas?" She was suddenly curious to find out more about the reclusive cowboy. "Do you have family?"

"No, there's no one. Christmas is just another day on the calendar to me. Nothing special."

How sad to not have anyone to share the holidays with. It would be so lonely. She didn't know what she'd do if she didn't have the hustle and bustle that arrived with each Christmas.

"What do you and your family do?" Sloan's deep baritone seemed to stir the very air.

"With my grandparents and older brothers and sisters close by, we have quite a rambunctious time of it." She closed her eyes, her words growing soft as she remembered. "My parents and I rise early, and by the time we get dressed people have started arriving. The kitchen becomes quite lively. Everyone pitches in with breakfast. After we eat, we move to the parlor where the Christmas tree stands. With much laughter and teasing banter we exchange gifts. After that we head to church."

Her eyes misted with tears. She blinked them away. She'd not break down in front of Sloan Sullivan. She swallowed hard. "This will be the first Christmas I won't be there with them."

"Don't be too hasty in counting yourself out. Lots can happen in two days."

"I can't believe day after tomorrow is Christmas Eve. I thought . . ." Her voice trailed off. The lump in her throat made it difficult to go on.

"You thought you'd be back by then." Sloan gulped the last of the coffee and set down the cup. "If you don't mind me asking, why are you on the train?"

"The Christmas bell. It was my responsibility to go to Boston for it and bring it home." Again, tears stung her eyes.

"I can't imagine whose idea that was."

Tess bristled. "It was my idea. I volunteered for the job. I wanted to prove once and for all that I'm not the pampered banker's daughter. I wanted to lay all that petty talk to rest. Small chance of that happening." She wearily wiped her eyes.

"As I said, lots can happen in two days. Look at the bright side." A lazy grin played on his lips.

"Which is?"

"You're warm and dry and have food in your belly. My daddy always said things are not so bad that they can't be worse." He moved to the stove and put some water on to boil. "As for me, I'm spending the night in the company of a most fetching woman. Nothing can be better than that."

The unexpected compliment made her heart leap. She had a feeling he never said anything he didn't mean. Could she take that to indicate she was growing on him? That would be a miracle.

"That's awfully sweet of you to say, Sullivan." She dipped another rag in the cold water and wrung it out. "Mind if I ask you a question?"

"Shoot."

"Why did you treat me like I had the plague, crossing the street to avoid having to speak to me?"

"It wasn't anything personal against you. Passing the time of day with a beautiful woman . . . well, let's just say it's easier and safer to limit my conversational abilities to a herd of bawling cows. For me, it was best to avoid conversation altogether than having to rack my brain for something to say to the banker's daughter. We're not exactly in the same social circle."

"Of all the lamebrained excuses! Here you let me think you abhorred the very sight of me. Unbelievable."

Sloan shrugged. "Seems pretty silly, I guess. But there's also another reason. You remind me of someone that I'd do anything to forget."

Like a sharp stick, jealousy jabbed at Tess. An old girlfriend? She didn't like to think of another woman wrapped in his arms. Not that she had any claim on the cattleman or anything.

"Let's start over. I'd like to be friends." Well, more than friends, but if not that, anything would do. Tess rose and offered Sloan her hand. "To friends."

"Friends." His big hand closed around hers. "My Lord, woman, your fingers are like a chunk of ice."

Sloan pulled her to the warmth of the stove.

"I'm fine," she protested. "I don't have time to think about myself."

He still held her hand. "If you won't, I will."

Tess felt so small standing next to him. She tilted her head to look up at him. She drowned in his gaze. She sucked in a quick gasp of air as his head lowered toward her.

Sloan Sullivan was going to kiss her. Her pulse raced.

He released her hand and tenderly ran the pad of his thumb across her bottom lip. Cupping her jaw, he drew her against the length of him. She fit easily into his embrace, her palm resting lightly on the hard plane of his chest.

His warm breath teased, cajoling her.

Then silky little nibbles at her mouth prepared her for the fiery, passionate kiss that knocked her world off-kilter.

A slow sizzle tingled along her nerve endings, vibrating under her skin. This was what she'd waited her entire life for.

Tess sighed deeply, enjoying the gamut of emotions his kiss unleashed.

Chapter 6

"I'm sorry. I shouldn't have done that." Sloan dropped his hands to his sides, trying to remember all the reasons why he couldn't possibly entertain thoughts of letting Tess get close to him. "You have a way of tempting a man."

"Rule number one," his mother had preached with her dying breath. "Stay away from Jezebels and strumpets. And give a wide berth to women of privilege. Ain't nothing good can come of falling in love with someone outside your class. We're poor people and we don't know the ways of people with money. Remember where you came from and you won't get your heart broke."

Kissing Tess had sure felt good though. Her lips had been soft and pliable, her hair strands of spun gold.

The problem was those damn silky undergarments in her trunk. Every time he closed his eyes, that's all he saw. And he couldn't look at Tess without wondering what she wore beneath her dress.

Tess quickly turned away. "There's nothing to apologize for, Sullivan. Good heavens. We're not children."

Sloan ran his fingers through his hair. "I reckon you've been kissed more times than you can remember."

She spun around with fire in her eyes. "What's that

supposed to mean? Do you think I'm a loose woman? Do you think I run around tackling men on the street and kissing the daylights out of them?"

Oh Lord, how to get out of this mess. The little train car had grown extremely warm. Sloan tugged at the neck of his shirt, trying to loosen it. "Absolutely not. It's just that you're a very beautiful woman. You must have your fill of suitors. I didn't mean to suggest anything. . . . Let's just forget this whole conversation."

But he didn't want to forget the heady kiss that curled his toes. He knew it'd fill his dreams for days and weeks to come.

"Fine." Tess plopped down in the chair beside Ira.

"Fine." He turned, threw open the door to the metal landing between the caboose and passenger car, and stomped out into the cold. Without his hat or his coat. She had made him forget all about the frigid temperature.

Now he was stuck. He couldn't very well go back inside. Neither could he go into the passenger car and wake those sleeping travelers. And he couldn't stay outside for long, although he welcomed the coolness at the moment.

A moment or two later, the caboose door opened and his heavy coat lined with sheep's wool came flying out. He caught it before it could land in the snowdrift that stood as high as the platform he was on. Sloan took that to mean he'd just been evicted.

Tess Whitgrove made him madder than a castrated bull at finding out with one cut of the knife he was now a steer. The high-spirited filly could be so pigheaded. He grinned.

And so desirable.

And kissable.

Sloan groaned in frustration.

While he pondered his predicament, the door to the passenger car eased slowly open so as not to make noise. The mysterious stranger, Deacon Brown, stepped out onto the landing. The surly man was so engrossed in making sure the door didn't make a sound that he hadn't noticed Sloan. Deacon jolted in surprise when his gaze swung around and slammed into Sloan's.

Sloan straightened away from the handrail where he'd propped himself. "Mind explaining yourself, Mr. Brown? What are you doing out here?"

"I was just . . . I was . . . I couldn't sleep, so I came out to smoke."

"Likely story. Why is it that you're always sneaking around this train?"

Deacon's eyes hardened into bits of black flint as he fished cigarette makings from his pocket. The red-bearded man made a big show of measuring tobacco onto a thin paper. He rolled the paper around the crushed leaves and licked the edge before twisting the ends and sticking it in his mouth. He reached inside his buffalo robe for a match. The odor of sulfur crossed the space between them when he struck it on the railing.

Cupping his hands around the flame to protect it from the brutal wind, Deacon touched the match to the rolled cigarette before he spoke. "You don't like me very much, do you, Sullivan?"

Sloan snorted and slipped his arms into his coat. "And you figured that out all by yourself? I have nothing against an honest man. It's sneaks and liars I have a problem with. I've met your kind before."

Deacon shrugged. "Reckon you can believe what you want. It's a free country."

Sloan's eyes narrowed. "That it is."

He didn't buy the man's story any more than he could dig out the train from its snowy bonds by himself. Deacon was a man with secrets and would rather lie than tell the truth.

Sloan's initial instincts about him hadn't changed. In fact, they'd grown stronger with each passing moment.

Deacon inhaled, then blew out smoke that got swallowed up in the night. "How's the sick passenger?"

"Is that why you're out here? To check on Powell?"

"I told you, I came out here to smoke."

"So you said. And you're trying mighty hard to convince me that's your reason. You're a day late and a dollar short for that."

Silence reigned until Deacon finished his smoke. When the man turned to go back inside, Sloan followed on his heels, dusting the snow off his coat as he entered.

There'd be no sleeping for Sloan. He meant to keep the red-bearded stranger in his crosshairs. Sloan took a seat at the rear of the car and got comfortable. With the stove at the front of the long row of seats, it was a little nippy where he was, so he left his coat on.

Deacon dropped into a seat a few rows up. The conductor had stretched out on a bench seat and was snoring. Rollins was fast asleep, his head lolled back against the velvet cushion of his chair. No wonder Deacon had been able to slip past the two men.

In fact, there was no one awake except him and Deacon.

Sloan's thoughts turned to the irritating, exciting woman he'd just left.

Lord give him strength to keep from strangling her!

After all, it was Christmas, he reminded himself, a season of glad tidings, peace on earth, and goodwill to men.

But he wasn't feeling that charitable at the moment.

Bright and early the next morning Sloan felt eyes watching him. His glance swept the rows of seats but he didn't see anything amiss. All of a sudden he caught a furtive movement in the seat in front of him. Then four sets of eyes popped up over the back of the seat.

"Hi, mister," the children chimed in unison.

"Hey there. Did you sleep okay?" Sloan gently touched the back of the little girl's hand. She giggled.

All four nodded.

"Milk," said the small two-year-old.

"Oh, you want me to milk the cow. I see." Sloan stretched and yawned. "I'll have to get busy doing that. Are you hungry?"

"Uh-huh." The second oldest boy was quick to answer.

"We'll have to see what we can do about that." Sloan ruffled the top of the towheaded boy's hair.

The door to the passenger car opened then. Tess entered carrying a steaming pot. Sloan jumped to his feet to take the heavy pan from her. Their hands touched in the process of transferring it and Sloan felt a jolt run up his arm.

"I found some oatmeal and added some dried apples to it." She met his gaze unflinching. "I think it'll be quite filling."

Sloan opened his mouth to apologize for last night, but the maddening woman swung away from him before he could get a single word out. He ground his teeth.

"Hello, children. How are you this fine day?"

"We're good, Miss Whitgrove," said the oldest boy. "Mr. Sullivan's going to milk the cow so we can have some milk."

"That's excellent. That'll fill those empty bellies. I hope you like oatmeal and apples."

"We do."

"Okay, we'll have everything ready before you can shake a stick twice." Tess winked at them and returned to the caboose for the pot of coffee and the tin plates and silverware she'd washed up early that morning.

Omie Powell entered as she was gathering everything up. "How's my Ira?"

"He had a passable night. I managed to get his fever lowered and he took some sips of water. I'm going to thin the oatmeal down until it's soupy and see if we can get some of that into him. I think if we can get him to eat he'll do better."

"You shouldn't have left me asleep last night. I intended to help you with him." Omie smoothed back a worrisome strand of white hair that had escaped from her bun.

Tess kissed the woman on the cheek. "You were exhausted. I didn't have the heart to wake you. I did just fine by myself."

Fine if you didn't count the kicks she'd given herself over the turn of events last evening. Not for the kiss though. That had definitely set her head awhirl and her pulse racing.

What she regretted with all her heart was the words she'd had with Sloan afterward. And every bit of it was her fault. If she hadn't gotten her nose out of joint so easily, the cattleman would've spent the night with her in the caboose.

Not that anything would've happened.

But having him near, listening to his soft breaths would've been glorious. The thought of such intimacy should've scandalized her, but it didn't. She was getting quite long in the tooth at twenty-two and would soon be considered an old maid if she wasn't already. She longed for a husband and children of her own before that day came.

Suitors had come calling over the years, but Tess always had the feeling they were more enamored with her money than with her. It was different with Sloan. He saw her money as a stumbling block rather than an asset. She got the feeling he'd be more interested in her if she'd been a penniless pauper.

Omie leaned to touch her lips to Ira's. "Good morning, you old fool. I'd sure like it if you'd wake up and chat a spell.

I've missed our talks. Tomorrow's Christmas Eve, and here you are sleeping the day away."

Tess watched the tender way in which Omie caressed her husband's face. Tears filled her eyes. Omie and Ira were so much in love. It wasn't fair, what was happening to them.

With her vision blurred, Tess gathered up the coffee and the eating utensils and left the caboose. Taking it slow to keep from slipping on the ice that coated the platforms separating the two cars, she glanced at the overcast sky. White flakes were still coming down, but not as hard as the previous day. At least the wind had let up, even though everything was buried under a mountain of snow.

Rollins had estimated that they were probably ten miles outside of Kasota Springs. Perhaps folks from town would be able to get to them by tomorrow. She said another prayer that Doc Mitchell would be with the rescuers.

A short while later, everyone gathered around in the warm passenger car and shared oatmeal, milk, and coffee. It was just a simple meal but one that everyone seemed to appreciate, even the waspish Mrs. Abner.

Tess happened to glance up and fell headlong into Sloan's brooding gray stare. She quickly found something to ask the oldest orphan girl. When she next looked up, he was involved in a conversation with Roe Rollins.

She rose to gather up the dishes and silverware, enlisting the help of two of the children. They seemed delighted to be of assistance, probably glad to have something to do for a few minutes. She thanked her little helpers. But when she turned to head to the caboose, Sloan blocked her path. Without saying a word, he took the box of dirty dishes from her.

"You're avoiding me." he stated softly.

"I don't know what you want me to say." Tess pulled her coat closed as they stepped onto the platform.

"Just listening to me would be a start. I want to apologize. I made you angry and for the life of me, I can't figure out how. I never said or meant to imply that you're a loose woman."

Tess sighed. "It wasn't your fault, it's mine. I've been so accustomed to defending my every move that I reacted before I thought. I regret that such a pleasant evening ended on a sour note."

"Then you don't mind if I kiss you again?" His deep, smooth rumble caused her breath to catch.

"I would be most happy to have you kiss me." Breathless, she tilted her face.

"Pretend that a big clump of mistletoe is hanging over your head," Sloan whispered close, fluttering the wisps of hair at her ear. He nuzzled the curve of her neck before capturing her mouth.

Had the searing kiss landed on the platform instead of her lips, it would've melted the ice.

Chapter 7

Hours had passed and yet Tess couldn't keep the silly grin off her face as she went the length of the train to the baggage car. She'd determined to take some time that morning to get the little orphans some toys from the boxes of things she'd bought for the orphanage.

They were wonderful children and needed something to play with since it appeared they'd celebrate Christmas right where they were.

Inside the baggage car, she lit a lantern and opened a nearby box. She set aside a pretty doll with a porcelain face for the oldest girl and a soft rag doll with yarn hair for the baby. The dolls weren't awfully fancy but they'd give the girls hours of enjoyment.

For the boys she selected spinning tops and carved wooden horses. She added new scarves and gloves for all four to replace their threadbare ones.

Gathering up the loot, she placed it in a burlap sack. Then she extinguished the lantern and headed for the warmth of the passenger car. And Sloan Sullivan's company.

Her stomach fluttered at the thought.

* * *

Sloan admired the gentle sway of Tess's hips beneath the soft gray dress as she came down the aisle. She held something behind her back and acted mysterious.

Taking the seat beside him, she leaned close to whisper. "Will you do me a favor?"

"Name it."

"I want you to play Santa," she said, thrusting a burlap sack into his hands. "They're for the children."

"Why don't you hand them out?"

"I'd prefer they don't know who they came from. Go out like you're going to get coffee from the caboose. When you come in with the toys, pretend you found them in a snowdrift outside."

He didn't know why the secrecy. Couldn't she just give them the toys without making a big fuss over them? Those kids were smart. Surely they wouldn't buy a flimsy story like that. Would they? But then it'd been quite a few years since he was a child.

"Go on now. I'll wait here." She shooed him with her hands.

Her amber gaze followed him to the door. Her bright smile lit up everything that was dead inside him. If she asked him to walk on water, that's what he'd do, or die trying.

Sloan stood for a minute outside on the landing. Then he stomped his feet and made all kinds of racket coming back through the door.

"Ho, ho, ho! Look what I found."

The children, who'd been sitting quietly on the floor in front of the black railroad stove, jumped to their feet and ran to meet him. Their enthusiasm did his heart good to see. They'd been extraordinarily subdued and quiet. Being stuck on the train had been no fun for the little tykes.

"What's in there, Mr. Sullivan?" asked the oldest boy.

"Well, I don't rightly know. Let's take a look." He opened the sack and peered inside. "I can't believe this!"

"What, Mr. Sullivan?" They danced around him.

He pulled out the soft rag doll first and handed it to the youngest of the bunch, the two-year-old.

Her eyes lit up as she clasped it tightly. "Baby."

The doll with the porcelain head, hands, and feet came out next. He extended it to the oldest girl, who looked to be around five or six years old.

"Oh boy!" The girl held it, seeming in awe of the pretty doll. "It's beautiful."

The oldest boy looked worried. "Is there anything for boys in there, Mr. Sullivan?" he asked quietly as if he didn't dare hope.

"You mean like this?" Sloan hauled out a shiny red top and one of the wooden horses.

Excitement glittered in the boy's eyes, replacing the resigned look. He immediately plopped down on the floor to play with them.

Not wasting a second, Sloan handed a black top to the boy's little brother, followed by another carved wooden horse.

"Look what we got." The youngster waved the toys in the air.

Emptying the burlap sack, Sloan passed out a soft wool scarf and knitted gloves to each child. He never thought the gifts would make such a difference. Looking at the children, he suddenly remembered one long-ago Christmas when he was about six years old. His father had given him a small bag of marbles. It must've taken all year for his pa to save up enough to buy them. It was the only thing that he'd ever gotten as a boy that hadn't been handmade. His eyes misted and a lump filled his throat as he remembered what that little bag of marbles had meant to him.

His father had died two Christmases later.

How had he forgotten that?

Sloan's gaze found happiness shining in Tess's amber eyes. "Thank you," he mouthed over the children's heads.

It wouldn't have been possible if not for Tess's generous heart. Beautiful, sensitive Tess. It'd taken getting snowbound on the train with her to see how wrong he and the rest of Kasota Springs had been about the banker's daughter. She was quite something.

He didn't want to care about her, didn't want to see that she was no different from the next person.

But he did, and that would most likely be his downfall.

Had she always been this giving and no one had ever seen because she'd hidden it?

That didn't make any sense, though. She didn't have to go all the way to Boston for the bell in order to change people's opinion of her. She just had to be herself.

Tess rose and headed toward the caboose, probably to check on her patient, if he could hazard a guess. Sloan intercepted her before she reached the door.

He put a hand on her shoulder. "You're an amazing woman, Tess Whitgrove. What you did put joy on four little faces."

"I'm glad I could do it. Sometimes having money does have its benefits."

Sloan winced at her words. "That it does."

But it was more than having money. The way she'd taken on Ira Powell's care. The concern for Maryellen Langtry. And the way she'd shouldered getting tasty food into the travelers' stomachs. Not to mention going all the way to Boston for the Christmas bell. Those were the marks of a woman with a big heart.

He'd longed for a woman like Tess. Sometimes the loneliness pressed against him so hard it strangled the breath right out of him. He thought he'd accepted his lot, but when

Tess looked at him with her heart in her eyes and a soft smile on her rosy lips, he was far from satisfied.

"I'm sorry for the way I acted before. And the misunderstanding last night." He wanted to kiss her in the worst way. But with such limited space a moment of privacy was hard to come by.

"It's in the past. Let's let it stay there." She took the empty burlap bag from him. "I have to check on Ira first, but I'll make a pot of coffee. I have a feeling you can use some."

"I'm a rancher. I can always use coffee." But that wasn't all he could use. He'd be happy to demonstrate at the next opportunity. Until then, he might as well sit down and curb his impatience.

He took a seat and watched Rollins, the conductor, and the brakeman. They'd dug out a deck of cards from somewhere and had a lively game going.

Maryellen Langtry was playing with the children, and Mrs. Abner was asleep.

Charles Flynn and Deacon Brown had their heads together. Seeing that made his hackles rise. He'd give anything to know what they were talking about. While he watched, Deacon rose and ambled a short distance away and sat down. Sloan's eyes narrowed.

What were the two up to?

He was contemplating confronting the man when the oldest orphan girl started down the aisle with her arm tightly around her pretty doll. Sloan wondered if she was coming to talk to him.

But she wasn't. The girl stopped directly beside a glaring Deacon Brown and climbed into the seat beside the man.

"What'cha doing, mister?" she asked.

Sloan held his breath for a long second. He'd gladly throw the man into the snow if he as much as looked at the girl the wrong way. If Deacon knew what was best for him, he'd show the little girl some manners.

And if he made the girl cry . . . Sloan would wallop him within an inch of his life.

"I'm just sitting here wondering when this snow is gonna quit," Deacon finally answered. Sloan let the air out from his lungs. Looked like Deacon might be in the mood to pretend to be nice.

"Why are you so sad?"

"Just missing my family, I reckon."

"I'm real sad too."

"Why's that?"

"My mama and daddy died. They're in heaven. We don't have no one to take care of us."

Deacon put his hand on the girl's shoulder. "I'm sorry."

The girl squirmed around until she was almost sitting in Deacon's lap. "Do you have a little girl like me?"

"As a matter of fact, I guess you could say I do. I'm raising my sister's three young'uns, a girl and two boys."

There was another mention of that mysterious sister. Deacon's statement that he'd come to take care of some business for his sister came back. So the woman had three children. Why on earth was Deacon raising them, Sloan wondered.

Why wasn't the sister raising her own kids?

And why would Deacon leave the children right here at Christmas to traipse across the country in a blizzard?

"My name's Martha. What's your name?"

"You can call me Deacon."

Martha got on her knees and patted Deacon's red beard. The girl wasn't afraid of the man in the least. "Mr. Deacon, do you wanna play dolls?"

Again Sloan tensed. Deacon better give the right answer or he'd need God and all his angels to help him.

"I'd be right honored, Miss Martha."

Sloan couldn't hide the grin. He'd have to see this burly man playing dolls.

Martha's blue eyes twinkled. "I'll be the mama and you'll be the daddy and this is our baby."

Sloan settled back in his chair and watched Deacon play dolls with a lonely little girl. Her brothers were involved with spinning their tops, and the baby was too young to be an interesting playmate. Martha just wanted some attention. And she'd singled out the most unlikely man.

Tess returned as promised with a fresh pot of coffee for those who wanted it and a nice cup of hot tea for Maryellen, who seemed extremely grateful for the kindness. Sloan straightened his leg to get the kinks out and got painfully to his feet to help her with the welcome refreshments.

As he poured himself a cup of coffee he noticed the wrinkles on Tess's brow. "What's worrying you? Is it Powell?"

She captured her bottom lip between her teeth before she answered. "No, he's holding his own. I'm probably fretting for nothing, but I've caught Maryellen wincing and rubbing her stomach. I'm afraid it's her time."

"Have you asked her about it?"

"She assures me she's fine."

"Then I guess she should know, Miss Worrywart." He longed to smooth her brow and draw her into his arms, even if for a few minutes. But he couldn't.

"To be on the safe side, I think we should have a plan. Where are we going to put her, for one thing? We can't have her near Ira for fear of catching what he has."

"We'll have to make a place in here for her. Maybe we can rig some blankets around a section so she'll have some privacy at least. I'm sure we can make do with something. I'll pick Rollins's brain. He might think of something."

"I feel better now that we've talked about it." She glanced

around the car, her gaze landing on Deacon and little Martha. Tess cocked a questioning brow at Sloan.

After Sloan filled her in on the doll playing, she clasped her hand over her mouth to stifle the laughter. Her pale amber eyes glittered like precious stones. He was glad to have eased her worry for even a little while.

"Have you looked out lately?" she asked.

"Yes. The snow has almost stopped."

"When do you think the townsfolk can get to us?"

"The snow is really deep. A horse will have trouble pulling a sled through the high drifts." He ran a hand over his tired eyes, wishing he could soften the blow. "It'll take a miracle to get to us before Christmas Day."

"That's about what I figured." Her calm acceptance surprised him. But then the woman was full of surprises. She gave him a weary smile. "I've got to go check on a pot of potato soup I have cooking and relieve Omie for a spell. The woman has been at Ira's bedside nonstop since she woke."

"I don't think any of us are getting much sleep. I hope you at least managed to catch a few winks last night."

"Some. I dozed between taking care of Ira. I'm fine."

"I have a feeling you'd say that even if it weren't so."

"We do what we must. Our days are as long as they need to be. Do me a favor and keep an eye on Maryellen." Tess turned and strolled for the connecting door.

Sloan watched her go. He'd break his neck doing whatever she asked of him.

If only he could forget his promise to his mother.

He was seeing that having money didn't play a part in making a person who she really was deep inside. Tess had shown her big heart in so many ways since he'd boarded the train.

Still, there were huge differences between them that he couldn't overlook. He couldn't see her being content living in his small ranch house that always needed repairs. She deserved fine things. Things Sloan would never be able to give her.

And he couldn't see himself living in a mansion like the banker's and being comfortable.

He was kidding himself to entertain the notion for more than half a second.

All this thinking was premature though. For God's sake, he'd only kissed the woman twice. But he'd raised her dander umpteen times over the last two days. Was that a sign she was warming to him?

Sloan would give anything if he could share the tragic events that had led to him walking away from his U.S. Marshal job. But if she knew, she'd want nothing else to do with him.

A deep sigh filled the air. As he lifted his coffee cup to his mouth to finish it off, his gaze landed on Maryellen Langtry. Her eyes were large in her pale face and she had a death grip on the arm of her seat.

Chapter 8

They were just finishing the evening meal, such as it was, when Maryellen clutched her swollen stomach and moaned. Tess quickly put down her plate and sprinted for the woman. She was the first one to reach Maryellen.

Fear crowded her throat and threatened to choke her.

How were they going to save the woman and her infant? Tess had never been present during a birthing, not even her sister's. She wished she'd paid more attention to her mother's wisdom about the subject.

Sloan, evidently seeing the commotion, set his plate aside and came toward them as fast as his limp could carry him. Tess's gaze sought his. There was calm strength about the rancher. Probably of all the people on the train, Sloan would best know what to do, him being a cattleman and all. He must've helped some of his mama cows birth their calves when they couldn't do it alone.

That in itself didn't make him an expert on human births, but he was all they had.

"Let's get you lying down and as comfortable as we can make you," Tess said low.

"I'm scared." Maryellen gripped Tess's arm.

"I know. But we're right here, and we're not going to let

anything happen to you . . . or the baby." Tess prayed she didn't live to regret that vow.

"I was supposed to be back home in Kasota Springs before this happened. With Doc Mitchell close by."

"None of us expected to be snowbound, that's for sure. But we are and we have to make the best of it. You'll do fine. Let me and Sloan do the worrying. All right? You just concentrate on that precious little baby who's wanting to be born."

Maryellen nodded her head.

"What's going on here?" Mrs. Abner demanded around a mouth full of food.

"Mrs. Langtry is feeling a mite poorly," Sloan answered in a firm but polite tone. "She's just going to lie down for a spell. Nothing to cause concern."

"I knew Ira Powell would give us the fever!" Mrs. Abner drew her collar snugly around her throat.

Tess watched Sloan's gray eyes darken with fury. A good measure of steel in his voice spoke of his impatience with the prickly woman. "She's having a baby, for your information. Last I heard that's not contagious."

"Hmph!" Mrs. Abner got in the last word.

When Maryellen stood, her waters broke, spilling around her feet. She gave a frightened whimper.

"It's all right. Don't worry about that," Sloan gently reassured the woman. "It's perfectly natural."

Tess prayed he knew what he was talking about. He seemed confident enough though.

Sloan put his arm around her as a brace and helped her toward one of the bench seats at the rear. Tess quickly grabbed the quilt that Maryellen had been using to keep warm and hurried after the two. Thoughts of the panicky variety were running willy-nilly in her head like a flock of lost sheep.

She was trying to recall what she'd heard the first steps should be.

Boil water came to mind. Someone had told her that was the first thing to do, although she wasn't sure why. Maybe Sloan knew.

With tender care, Sloan eased the woman onto the bench seat.

Tess sat down next to their patient. "We need to get you out of those wet clothes. Do you have a nightgown in your bag, Maryellen?"

"Yes. My carpetbag is somewhere in the baggage car."

"I'll bring it to you," Sloan quickly volunteered. "That way you can get out what you want."

"We'll need to gather up some things and have them ready." Tess's mind whirled. "A soft blanket for the baby. Something to make diapers out of."

A voice behind interrupted her train of thought. "What can I do to help, Miss Whitgrove?" Roe Rollins was rocking back and forth on his toes, his thumbs anchored in his red suspenders. The man was clearly nervous. That made two of them.

"Maryellen needs some privacy. How about if you rig up something around this area to keep her from prying eyes?"

Seeming grateful to have something to do, the engineer surveyed the area. "Me and my crew should have something arranged in no time."

"After that, would you mind sitting with Mr. Powell so Omie can take a breather? The dear woman must be exhausted."

Tess meant to ask Omie what she knew of childbirth. Surely the sweet woman could give them some advice. Yes, Omie would know what to do. A measure of calm swept over her.

"Don't you worry, we'll handle things as best we can in the caboose. It's stopped snowing, so with any luck help could arrive tomorrow." The man turned and made his way up the aisle where the conductor and brakeman were.

Tess squeezed Maryellen's hands. "Did you hear that? Rollins thinks help could come tomorrow. I'm sure the rescuers will bring a doctor with them."

The woman's smile wobbled and her eyes filled with tears. "That's good news."

"Can I get you anything?"

Maryellen shook her head. Then a pain gripped her and she stiffened in alarm.

"Please try to relax," Tess coaxed. "Fighting the pain will make it worse."

While she wasn't sure that was right, it sounded logical.

Rollins and his men returned just then with an armful of blankets and a length of heavy cord. Within a short time they had the area closed off as a separate little room. Maryellen would be more at ease without the other passengers looking on, watching her every move.

The engineer, conductor, and brakeman left and a throat cleared outside the curtain. Tess recognized Sloan's deep rumble and swept the blanket aside.

The rancher held out a carpetbag. "I had a devil of a time finding this, but I think this is Mrs. Langtry's."

Maryellen gave it a brief glance. "Yes, that's it."

"Thank you, Mr. Sullivan." Tess took it from him.

"I'll leave you to your privacy. Holler if you need anything else."

Sloan disappeared and Tess got Maryellen into some dry clothes and made her comfortable.

Omie stuck her head into the enclosure. "I hear the little mama is ready to have that wee one."

Tess quickly turned to Maryellen. "I'm going to be right outside the curtain for a minute. I won't be long. Try to get some rest between the pains."

Wasting no time, Tess joined Omie and got right to the point. "I know nothing about birthing a babe. Tell me what I need to do, things to look for and that sort of thing."

"Honey, it's been many moons since I had my young'uns. Let me see." Omie pursed her thin lips. "Kinda keep track of the pains. The closer together they are, the quicker the baby will be here. You'll know when the time is here. You'll do fine, dear." Omie patted her hand.

"I hope so. I'm really nervous."

"Just try to keep Maryellen calm. That's the main thing. Panic makes a body tense up, and that won't be good for the babe."

Tess knew the kindly woman spoke the truth. A case of nerves wasn't good for anyone whether they were in the family way or not. "How's Ira? Any change?"

"He's resting better. And he opened his eyes for a short while. I got some more water and a few spoonfuls of the thin oatmeal down him."

"That's wonderful news." Tess hugged Omie. "I'm sorry I left his care totally up to you. I'm sure you're exhausted. Why don't you get some rest and let Rollins sit with him a bit?"

"I do appreciate everyone's kindness." Tears swam in Omie's eyes and her lip quivered. "Now, get back to Maryellen."

Before Tess returned to her patient, her gaze swept the dimly lit passenger car. The lanterns had been extinguished except for one or two that were turned low.

Her heart melted when she found Sloan. The littlest orphan girl, the baby of the bunch, was curled in his lap, one small hand clutching the rag doll and the other lying against his broad chest. Both man and child were fast asleep. For a second it was hard to breathe past the lump in her throat.

Sloan Sullivan had wiggled his way into her heart.

And what would happen once they were rescued? Would he revert back to his old ways of crossing the street to avoid her?

She stood with her hand on the curtain. Getting snowbound on the train with him had changed her life. And she didn't want to lose the bond they'd forged. In fact, she'd fight to keep it. No one quite made her feel like a woman like this long, lean Texas cattleman.

Maryellen's low moan interrupted her thoughts. She ducked into the curtained area and returned to her patient.

The long night dragged slowly. Maryellen's pains were very erratic. At times they were at regular intervals and other times they were further apart. Tess wished she knew what that signified, if anything.

Toward morning footsteps paused outside the curtain and Sloan peeked inside. Tess rose and joined him where they could talk without disturbing Maryellen.

"How is she doing?" His hair looked like he'd run his fingers through it a jillion times. And the dark stubble on his square jaw lent a dangerous attraction. It had almost covered the cleft in his strong chin.

Flutters in her stomach made her weak. Tess had trouble remembering his question. "I'm sorry, my mind was elsewhere. What did you ask?"

"Mrs. Langtry. How is she?"

"She's sleeping right now. The poor thing is exhausted. Birthing babies is hard work."

"Did you get some sleep yourself?"

"A little."

His hand rose as though he was going to caress her cheek. Evidently, he changed his mind, letting his hand fall to his side. Then she saw movement from the corner of her eye and knew someone was awake. It was the conductor. The man had gotten up to stir the fire. It touched her deeply that Sloan wanted to protect her reputation.

"You'll probably sleep a month of Sundays when you get back home and into your bed." A wry smile flitted, crinkling the corners of Sloan's gray eyes.

"Speaking of that . . . do you have any idea when that will be?"

"It's anyone's guess. We'll know more when daylight comes." He shoved his fingers through his hair. "By the way, it's Christmas Eve."

"It is, isn't it? Have too many things on my mind."

"Understandable. You've certainly had your hands full."

"I saw the little toddler fast asleep in your arms last night. She looked so peaceful and innocent."

"Yeah, the little darlin' tugs at my heartstrings. Probably missing her pa. I make a poor substitute I'm afraid."

Tess begged to differ. Sloan Sullivan seemed a natural.

The man in question laid a hand lightly on her arm. "Isn't this birthing business taking too long?"

"No. I've heard tales of labor sometimes lasting two or three days, especially for a first-time pregnancy. It just takes a while."

"On the ranch when a mama cow is having a difficult time, I tie a rope on the calf's leg and pull it out."

"My word, Sloan! Maryellen isn't having a calf. There's a big difference between a cow and a woman." She could just picture them tying a rope onto the baby and wrenching it free. "Besides, most babies come out headfirst. You'd hang the poor little thing."

"Just trying to help." Twinkles dancing in his eyes told her she'd been had.

"Another thing . . . my friends call me Sully. I'd like for you to do the same, Tess."

Tess's heart lurched, both at his familiar use of her name and the fact he evidently considered her a friend.

Her voice was breathless when she replied. "Are we friends, Mr. Sullivan?"

"Sully. And yes, I'd surely like to be friends. Unless you have an objection?"

"None at all . . . Sully."

He brushed back a strand of hair by her ear that had pulled free of the ribbon tying it back. The intimate touch released a swarm of tingles scurrying the length of her body. Though she'd been this near to other men, suitors who sought her favors, she'd never been lured by a single breath ruffling the tendrils at her temple or a hand carefully relishing the texture of her hair.

Not until now.

She'd stand neck-deep in an icy snowbank just to have Sully's hand tenderly caressing her.

Chapter 9

Sloan took a step back from Tess when the conductor ambled toward them, although it took all his effort to break the magnetism of her curvaceous body. Tess Whitgrove had put some kind of hold on him. Strange how he didn't feel a whole man unless he was near her.

And the reason why puzzled him. Before he'd come on the train he'd been unable to even speak to her. It had taken a blizzard to open his eyes. And his heart.

Truth of the matter, the pretty banker's daughter had a way of making him take stock of life and love. He didn't know if what he felt was love, but he wanted to be near her, wanted to do what he could to help her. And yes, he wanted to hold her in his arms and kiss her until neither had breath left. His mother's dire warning still sounded in his head, but it grew fainter by the hour.

Just before the conductor reached them, Tess disappeared behind the curtained-off section. He felt the loss acutely.

"Morning, Mr. Sullivan." The conductor gave him a cheery smile. "Couldn't sleep?"

"Too many things on my mind I reckon," Sloan answered. He tried to be civil but it was hard to keep the annoyance from his tone. It rankled that the man had interrupted the precious little private time with Tess. "What's your excuse?"

"I'm an early riser. Never catch more than five hours of shut-eye a night. Drives my wife plumb batty." The conductor's brown mustache wiggled when he talked. The man smoothed some of the wrinkles from his dark blue jacket. "I'm gonna make a pot of coffee. Want some?"

"It'd sure fit the bill." Sloan glanced around the train car. He found Mrs. Powell right away. The old woman's head was slumped onto her chest. That meant Rollins must be sitting with Ira. He'd not have wanted to disturb the sweet little woman if she'd been the one with her sick husband.

He followed the conductor toward the caboose, grateful to have something to do. All this sitting around was getting on his nerves, although his gimpy leg appreciated the rest he'd given it. He'd filled in the lulls between helping Tess by worrying about his cattle. He dreaded taking a tally of the dead cows after this storm was over and he could finally check on them. He just prayed the losses wouldn't completely do him in. The ranch had been barely surviving as it was. His deep sigh filled the air. Nothing he could do about anything now.

Pulling the door shut to the caboose, he decided when daylight came he'd take Tess's place on the cooking line. He could make the oatmeal. The children would be hungry when they woke up.

Rollins stood when they entered. From the haggard look on his face it didn't appear the engineer had gotten much sleep.

"How's Mr. Powell?" Sloan asked.

"About the same, I reckon. Sometimes the fellow's eyelids flutter and it seems like he's trying to wake up. But he just keeps sleeping."

"Maybe that's a good sign." Sloan hoped so anyway. Losing the man would take a terrible toll on Tess. She seemed to have a personal stake in the man's recovery. Sloan took a seat at the small table and watched the conductor put the coffee on.

Along about midmorning he was back in the passenger car helping entertain the children and diverting their attention from the increasing cries coming from behind the curtained area when a god-awful banging commenced on the outside metal door.

Hope leaped into his chest that the townsfolk had managed to get to them. He handed the youngest girl her rag doll and got to his feet.

He wasn't quick enough. Deacon Brown and Charles Flynn beat him to the door. They opened it to find a half-frozen stranger.

Sloan looked beyond the man for signs of others. But he was all alone except for a pitiful-looking mule out in the snow.

The stranger stared from one face to the next. "Saw the train stuck here and thought you might let me come in and warm up a spell."

"You're welcome to join us," Sloan said, closing the door against the bitter cold. "What are you doing out in this norther?"

The man's shaggy eyebrows were coated with ice. He made a beeline toward the stove, tugging off his gloves as he went. "Me an' old Jughead out there are what you might call roamers. We don't light in one place long. We just go wherever the wind blows us."

Seemed to be the norm these days. The stalled train was busier than a brothel in a cow town. First Deacon Brown and now this man. However, this stranger lacked Deacon's surly attitude.

Sloan poured him a cup of coffee from the pot that sat on top of the stove. "I'm Sloan Sullivan."

"Pleased to meet you, Sullivan. Big Jim Crockett."

Deacon and the rest introduced themselves in turn. Just then Maryellen let out a screeching wail behind the curtain. Jim Crockett jerked, sloshing his coffee onto his hand.

"Forgive the noise. We have a female passenger in the throes of childbirth," Sloan explained.

"No better time to welcome a new life into the world than Christmas Eve." Big Jim took a big swig of coffee.

"We've been expecting folks from Kasota Springs to come to our rescue since the snow stopped. In fact, when you hammered on the door I thought it might be them."

"Hate to break it to you folks, but they ain't gonna git to you today. Ain't never seen such huge snowdrifts in all my born days. Jughead floundered in some and like to not've gotten out. That snow is up to my waist in spots."

"Which direction did you come?" Sloan prayed the man hadn't come from Kasota Springs.

"I came from the northwest. The whole Panhandle is buried under a mountain of snow, mister. I'm about to freeze up here. Me and ol' Jughead are heading south where it's warmer. I'd like to find me a nice patch of sunshine." Big Jim chuckled. "Got a feelin' Jughead wouldn't mind that a bit either."

The last vestige of hope died that things weren't as bad as they appeared. Sloan would keep Big Jim's news to himself. The passengers needed to have faith that somehow, someway, the people in Kasota Springs would form a rescue party.

"When did you eat last, Big Jim?" Sloan asked.

The barrel-chested man rubbed his bristly graying whiskers. "I rightly recall it was yesterday sometime."

"You wait here and rest up. I'll be right back with some food."

Big Jim glanced around the car. "Are you right sure you can spare the vittles? No telling how long you'll be stuck."

"We're happy to share what we have. Isn't that what the

Good Book teaches us?" Sloan didn't give the man time to either agree or disagree. He limped down the aisle toward the caboose.

When he got even with the partitioned area, Maryellen let out a painful wail. He paused and stuck his head in. Tess looked up. "How are things going with the little mama?"

The black shadows under Tess's luminous amber eyes made him wince. Her face was haggard and she looked dead on her feet. "I don't know," she whispered, tears swimming in her eyes. "I wish I knew what I was doing. I don't know if this is normal or not."

Sloan stepped inside the cubicle and took her in his arms. He didn't say a word, just held her close and smoothed her hair, sucking in the faint fragrance of honeysuckle.

After some long moments he spoke. "I have to get some food from the caboose but I'll be right back. I'll sit with Mrs. Langtry for a while. I'm going to see to it that you get some rest."

She opened her mouth as though to argue, but Sloan would have none of that. "It's not open for discussion."

"You're awful bossy, Sully Sullivan." Her slight smile wobbled.

"These passengers have taken advantage of your generous nature and I'll have no more of it. It's time you got some rest or I'll know the reason why."

Sloan hated leaving her but he knew the faster he got Big Jim taken care of, the sooner Tess could rest.

A short time later, Sloan was back to sit with Maryellen. He'd fed Big Jim and seen the man on his way.

When Sloan had tried to get the man to stay the night, Big Jim had balked. "I was in a Yankee prison during the war. Ever since then I can't abide being indoors. I get the phobia. The walls start to close in, smotherin' and chokin' me."

And so Big Jim Crockett gathered up his mule and left.

Sloan gently pushed Tess toward an empty bench seat across the aisle and coaxed her into lying down. She'd no sooner curled up than her eyes had drifted shut. Sloan took her place by Maryellen's side. He wiped sweat from the woman's forehead and took her hand in his, rubbing the back of it lightly.

"Mr. Sullivan, it hurts so bad."

"I'm sorry, ma'am. Wish I could help you. But maybe it would make things easier if you keep your thoughts on that sweet little babe who's struggling to be born. I'll bet he's real anxious to see his mama. Think of the joy of holding him in your arms."

"I'll try."

"That's all I can ask. Just try to block out the pain."

An hour ticked by with Maryellen's pains coming one right after another. Laying a hand on her swollen stomach, he determined the babe was on the verge of entering the world.

While he contemplated the enormity of the situation, the curtain moved and Deacon Brown stepped around it.

"You'd better have a good reason for being back here, Deacon."

The man raised both hands as though to ward Sloan off. "We haven't seen eye to eye since I boarded the train, but just listen to what I have to say."

"Tell me why I should hear you out."

"On account of I'm a doctor."

Sloan snorted. "Yeah, and I'm President Grover Cleveland."

Deacon met his piercing gaze. "I don't blame you for doubting. I know I don't look much like a doctor, but it's the truth."

"And you didn't speak up before now because why? You knew we needed a doctor in the worst way."

"I swore I'd never practice medicine again after I made a grievous mistake that killed a patient." The red-bearded man wearily rubbed his eyes. "I never intended to come forward, but I can't sit by and keep listening to this woman who's in such obvious pain when there may be something I can do about it."

A scream erupted from Maryellen's throat. "Please help me. Please someone just help me."

Sloan knew they were wasting precious time. He motioned Deacon to the woman's side. "If you harm her you'll answer to me."

Tess leaped from the bench seat where she'd been sleeping as Sloan left the cubicle. "I heard Maryellen . . ." she began.

"Sorry she woke you." He wanted to pull her into his arms and bury his face in her hair. But there were too many eyes on them. Instead he took her hand. "You weren't asleep long enough."

"Why aren't you in there with her?"

"Because the doctor has taken over." He quickly told her about Deacon and his claim to be a doctor. "I don't know whether to trust him or not, but it seems we have little choice. Maryellen needs more skilled hands than ours."

Frankly, Sloan was relieved that they'd been replaced. Cows he knew about. Pregnant female passengers were another matter altogether.

"Well, I'm going to be with Maryellen or I'll know the reason why. She needs a woman by her side." And with that Tess tightened her jaw and pushed aside the blanket.

She was just in time to hear Deacon Brown say, "Mrs. Langtry, will you let me raise your nightgown and assess the situation?"

Maryellen gripped Tess's hand and nodded.

A second later, Deacon smiled. "I can see the babe's head. You're almost there. When the next pain comes, I want you to push as hard as you can."

"You hear that, Maryellen?" Tess's tremulous smile came as tears of relief filled her eyes.

With the next hard tightening of her body, Maryellen gritted her teeth and gave a mighty push. Deacon rose, cradling the newborn in his arms.

"You have a son, Mrs. Langtry." He laid the baby boy on Maryellen's stomach and cut the cord with his knife.

There was dead silence. No baby's lusty cry. No sounds from either inside or outside the curtained section. It seemed the world had gone quiet and deathly still.

Chapter 10

Maryellen lay spent, barely conscious. Tess wasn't even sure the woman had heard Deacon Brown. The new mother was exhausted and drenched with sweat despite the mounds and mounds of snow beyond the train windows.

Had Maryellen gone through such an ordeal only to have the fruits of her labor yanked from her arms?

Tess tried to swallow but found it impossible. The baby boy had turned blue. "Deacon, why isn't he crying?"

"Mucus. I've got to get the mucus out of his throat." He held the infant by the feet and dangled him.

Still no cry.

Suddenly the curtain parted and Sloan ordered, "Let me have him. I may be able to save him."

Deacon didn't argue, just passed the babe to Sloan.

Sloan gathered the tiny babe in his arms and pressed his mouth to the infant's. He blew gently several times. Tess held her breath, praying that God would have mercy.

And then there was a feeble cry.

And another.

Each one grew louder and lustier than the last.

Tess smiled through her tears as cheers of joy rose from the passenger car. Sloan handed her the small bundle and she wrapped the tiny infant in a knitted shawl that she'd dug out of Maryellen's carpetbag.

Her gaze met Sloan's. "How did you know what to do?"

"When calves aren't breathing after I pull them, I've been known to blow into their mouths. It usually does the trick. I figured the best way to get them breathing was to share some of my air. I figured if it worked for calves, it would work for infants."

"Thank God it did." She proudly carried the babe into the midst of the passengers to show him off. Everyone crowded around.

The oldest orphan girl, Martha, reverently touched the newborn's cheek. "It's baby Jesus."

A lump formed in Tess's throat and she blinked hard.

The littlest girl shyly kissed the top of the small head. And the two boys, one on each side, gently lifted each of the babe's hands, smiling when his fingers closed around theirs.

Mrs. Abner loudly harrumphed and held something toward Tess. "I bought these for my sister who's expecting a babe next month. I think you can use them."

Tess accepted a tiny soft gown and a baby blanket made from lamb's wool. "Thank you, Mrs. Abner. I'm sure this little tyke will appreciate your generosity."

From the corner of her eye she saw Rollins the engineer gather all the men together. He murmured something and Sloan and the others got their heavy coats, gloves, and hats on. One by one they exited the passenger car, venturing out into the white landscape. Tess watched them curiously, then rose and took the babe to his mother.

"My baby boy," Maryellen cried weakly.

Tess placed the infant in her arms and couldn't stop tears from welling. She was filled with the wonder and glory of it all. Happiness swept over her that she was a part of it.

She left Maryellen with her newborn son and made her

way to the caboose. It had been quite a while since she checked on Ira Powell.

Omie's bright smile greeted her. "I heard the news about Maryellen. I'm so happy mother and babe are both all right."

"Indeed, it's a miracle. I was very worried there for a while." Tess put an arm around the old woman's shoulders. "How are you doing? You look worn to a frazzle."

"I'm a little worse for wear but not complaining. Ira seems to be sleeping peacefully now."

"Hallelujah! That's wonderful news. I'm just sorry I threw his care onto you and Rollins. I had no choice though."

"Don't give it another thought, my dear. Everything worked out the way it was supposed to."

Tess got a large pan and went out to fill it with snow. She came back in and put it on the stove to heat. "I've got to get Maryellen and the babe cleaned up. Then I'll be able to focus on getting something cooking for supper."

"You just take care of Maryellen and the little one. I'll handle the meal," Omie said.

A little over an hour later Tess had washed Maryellen and her infant and had gotten a cup of hot tea into her. Tess was pleased at the color that had returned to the young mother's cheeks.

She was sitting with the children, relaxing a bit when she happened to glance out the window. She couldn't believe her eyes.

The rescuers had come!

Anxious to tell the others, she rose and made the announcement. Raucous cheers went up.

A short while later, the group of men that probably numbered twenty or more tromped in from outside, bringing lots of cold air with them. Tess's gaze locked with Sloan's. He had a wide smile on his full lips and a twinkle in his eye.

While the rest of the men hovered around the fire, he

made a beeline for Tess and took the seat beside her. "Good news. With a little luck we'll have you, your patients, and your Christmas bell to Kasota Springs in a couple of hours."

"I can't believe it."

"We went out to survey everything and discovered that once we shoveled the huge drifts from in front of the cowcatcher, the train should have no problem making it on down the track." He grasped her hand and raised the back of it to his lips. "But there's more. We're closer to town than anyone thought. Seems Rollins missed a mile marker because of the blowing snow. He thought we were ten miles out when in fact, we're only about five. We found a mile marker buried in a drift."

"This is indeed a season for miracles." Tess's heart swelled to near bursting. "If we can get the bell unloaded once we get there, we'll be able to ring it tomorrow."

"Not only on this Christmas Day but for years to come. And all because of you."

But now that she had the means within sight for the acceptance she'd sought, it had lost importance. They had survived unbelievable conditions. No one had died. And they'd welcomed a precious new life into the world. All that was far more important than whether narrow-minded people respected her.

Sloan threaded his fingers through hers and leaned his head against the back of the seat. A need for this tall rancher swept through Tess. She didn't know what she'd do if things went back the way they were a few days ago.

Her bottom lip trembled. "Sully, what's going to happen to us?"

"I wanted to talk to you about that." His shoulder rubbed hers in a companionable way. "How would you feel if I come courting?"

Ribbons of joy wound around her heart. "I'd like that."

"Would your father approve?"

That part didn't much matter. She'd fight with everything she had to hang on to what she'd found with Sully Sullivan. But the simple truth was that her father would welcome him with open arms. Benjamin Whitgrove didn't judge and didn't base a man's worth on the size of his bank account.

Her smile stretched wide. "My father will be overjoyed that there's hope for his spinster daughter yet."

"We still have lots of things to work out and some difficult decisions to make. But I'm willing to give it a try if you are, my dear Miss Whitgrove."

She watched Rollins leave the passenger car to go start the process of firing up the engine. Her heart was singing as she stood. "I think this calls for Christmas carols. How about it, everyone?"

"Yes!" three of the four orphans hollered.

And so she began with "O Little Town of Bethlehem."

At exactly 3:52 P.M., Engine Number 208 of the Fort Worth and Denver City Railroad chugged into the Texas Panhandle town of Kasota Springs. Christmas carols were still echoing up and down the train tracks, filling the air with glad tidings.

A group of townsfolk, led by the beautiful rancher, Tempest LeDoux, greeted the weary travelers. The train had barely stopped before she barged up the steps, firing orders right and left like a Gatling gun that had run amuck.

Sloan, who had left his sled behind and ridden the train into town, assisted Mrs. Abner and the little orphans off first. He was in the process of helping Tess get Maryellen Langtry and her new son bundled up when Tempest grabbed the reins right out of his hands.

"Maryellen, can't believe you decided to have this baby without us." Tempest tenderly cradled the small son.

"Mrs. LeDoux." Sloan addressed her that way because he could never keep count of which husband she was on at the moment. The last he knew was number five. "We appreciate your help, we truly do, but let us get our bearings first. We've had a rough few days."

Tempest grinned and drawled in that sultry Southern voice of hers, "I declare, Sully, I believe that's the most I've ever heard you say in one sitting."

And she went right on barking directions as if she'd never heard a word he'd said.

Sloan knew when he was whipped and quickly got out of her way. But then Maryellen Langtry's husband, Earl, almost plowed him down in his excitement to get to his wife and son.

Feeling as though he stood smack in the middle of a hurricane, he finally reached the door and assisted Tess to the platform where half the town milled about.

Farther down at the caboose, a bevy of men were carefully unloading Ira Powell, who was bundled from head to toe. Omie Powell trailed behind them. They were marching to Doc Mitchell's office like a group of soldiers, having to lift their feet high to clear the huge drifts.

Watching Tempest LeDoux's small army with amusement, Sloan put his arm around Tess to protect her from the onslaught.

Suddenly Tess broke free and flew into her parents' arms for a joyous reunion.

Acute loneliness swept over him. He had no one to welcome him. No one, possibly with the exception of Tess, who cared that he'd not frozen to death in the blizzard that was one for the record books.

He turned away, unable to bear the pain. Shoving his

hands into his coat pockets, he encountered the firearms he'd confiscated.

Finding Charles Flynn in the livestock car unloading his dappled gray, Sloan held out the man's pistol. "Hope there's no hard feelings."

Flynn took the pistol. "Guess I lost my head for a while. You see, I lost my wife to scarlet fever."

"You have my condolences."

Grateful that things had worked out, Sloan gathered his horse and led the gelding toward the livery for the night. Tess broke away from the homecoming with Mr. and Mrs. Whitgrove and fell into step with him.

"Randall Humphrey isn't at the livery." Tess pointed toward the freight and baggage car where the blacksmith/livery owner and a group of men were unloading the Christmas bell.

Sloan draped an arm casually around her shoulders, enjoying the sound of snow crunching under their feet. "You got it here in time. You have every right to be satisfied."

"For a fact I am. Sully, where . . . ?"

Deacon Brown suddenly appeared, interrupting Tess in midsentence. "Sullivan, can I have a word with you? I got something that needs saying."

"What's that, Deacon?"

"I'm sure you're wondering how I came to wander upon the train." Deacon squinted up at Sloan. "Well, I'll tell you. I was headed to your ranch to kill you."

Tess gasped in alarm and gripped Sloan's arm.

"What did I do to you that you wanted to take my life?" Sloan asked quietly.

"Not to me. My sister. Carrie Huxley ring a bell?"

Mention of the name knocked the breath from Sloan. An overwhelming stillness seeped into every crack and crevice of his soul. He knew what it must feel like to die. The quiet, the feeling of life leaving his body, and the empty void that was left.

Unable to look at Tess, unable to bear the questions he knew were in her eyes, he answered, "I remember her."

He'd not been able to forget the depth of Carrie's sorrow when he'd shot and killed her husband. Lord knows he'd tried. Some things stayed with a man and became a part of his fabric whether he wanted them to or not. It didn't matter that the shooting was a terrible tragic accident. The truth remained; the man had died by Sloan's hand.

The north wind ruffled Deacon's red beard. "My sister hanged herself two weeks ago. She couldn't live another day without her husband."

Shock rippled through Sloan. He momentarily closed his eyes to block out the rush of pain. "I'm truly sorry. If I could go back and undo the events of that day, I would in a heartbeat."

"You're not the man I thought you'd be. I thought I could hate you. I thought it would be easy to pull the trigger and end your life."

"What stopped you?"

"It was several things. The way you cared for the people on the train. The sweetness of that little orphan girl Martha who took a liking to me. The birth of Mrs. Langtry's babe. The beautiful Christmas carols that I'd not heard in a very long while." Deacon Brown drew his buffalo robe together. "I'll leave you and Miss Whitgrove now. Merry Christmas."

"Wait." Sloan reached out to stop him. "You didn't have to tell me your reason for being here. Why did you?"

"Felt I owed it to you."

"I appreciate that you did." He took Deacon's pistol from his pocket. "I need to return this. And do you mind if I ask you a few more questions?"

"Guess I rightly owe you that, Sullivan."

"What were you doing in the livestock car when I found you there?"

"Looking for an extra gun that Flynn said he had in his saddlebags. He was going to help me kill you."

"And the night I encountered you on the landing between the passenger car and caboose?"

"I wanted to get a look at Mr. Powell. Wondered if he really did have scarlet fever. Thought I might could help."

"I wish you'd have told us sooner that you were a doctor," Tess admonished.

"Well, I hadn't practiced in a while. Wasn't sure if I still had the skill I once had. I'd lost faith in my abilities and swore I'd never treat another patient."

Tess smiled. "I'm glad you were there, Dr. Brown. We had so many miracles over the last four days."

"Indeed we did, ma'am."

"Doctor, won't you join us for a candlelight service in a few hours?" Tess invited.

The red-bearded doctor thanked her, then turned and trudged toward the hotel.

Tess tilted her head to look up at Sloan. "Before Deacon interrupted us, I was about to ask what your plans are."

"I don't have any other than getting some shut-eye, probably in the loft of the livery if Humphrey doesn't mind."

"My mother and father want you to come home with us and accompany us to church tomorrow. They'd like to get to know you better. Especially since I told them you were going to court their spinster daughter."

Sloan squinted into the bright afternoon sun that glinted off the snow. "Before you decide about that, I need to tell you the full story of what happened in Panther Bluff. You may boot me out the door and out of your life."

He really wouldn't blame her.

"Not a chance, Sully."

After a relaxing bath and a huge meal of cured ham, sweet potatoes, and string beans, Sloan accompanied Tess and her family to the candlelight service held at the little white church.

Sloan gazed in wonder at the rows of packed pews. Seemed everyone had reason to give thanks. They'd all made it through the storm and they were grateful.

He cast a sidelong glance at Tess, who wore a resplendent green dress trimmed with red ribbon that reminded him of mistletoe. How would she react to what he needed to tell her? He tried to steel himself for her cold disdain that would rip his heart to shreds. But he had no choice. He'd not start off with secrets between them. She had a right to know what kind of man he was.

All too soon, they were back at the spacious Whitgrove house. Sloan and Tess took advantage of her father's invitation to use his study in which to talk. Tess took a seat on a leather settee while Sloan stood and paced . . . and worried.

"Carrie Huxley was the wife of my deputy, and they lived in Panther Bluff with their two children. You remind me so much of her, another reason I always avoided contact with you. Seeing you was simply too painful. Carrie was a pretty little thing with another babe on the way." He took a deep breath. "I stole all their hopes and dreams when I shot and killed her husband and my friend."

Tess was silent, absorbing everything. Quite possibly she was pondering how to tell him she didn't want him in her life. Sloan wished he was a better man, wished he was worthy of her faith and trust, and wished he had more to offer her.

After a moment or two she spoke, "I'm sure you didn't mean to. It was an accident and nothing else."

"Be that as it may, a man died for no reason by my hand. Deputy Huxley and I were in a shootout with a vicious outlaw gang. Huxley did the unthinkable. He stepped into my line of fire, trying to get into a better position. In one terrifying, senseless moment Carrie went from a happily married wife to a grieving widow with two young children and another on the way. She was Deacon's sister."

Sloan stopped pacing to stand gazing out the window into the blackness beyond. He couldn't bear to look at Tess and see loathing in her face. "That's when I walked away from my job and hung up my Colt."

"And you came here and took up ranching."

"I figured I couldn't hurt anybody else if I kept to myself and worked from daylight to dark." He struggled to get the next words through the tight opening in his throat. "I'll understand if you don't want me to court you."

Tess's heart ached for this proud, gentle man. With tears in her eyes, she rose and went to him. "Don't you dare think I'll let you go that easily."

He drew her into his embrace and buried his face in her hair. She breathed the honest scent that was Sully Sullivan.

"You've been my salvation." His hoarse whisper nearly undid her.

She had much to learn about this tall, lean rancher. The depth of love she had for him shook her. She'd never cared this much for anyone before. It was a total all-consuming love, the kind that would endure trials and triumphs.

Sloan put a finger under her chin and gently raised her face. "I'm not worthy of those tears, my darling Tess."

"I beg to differ. It's because you are worthy that I'm all choked up. I wouldn't waste tears on just anyone." A smile curved her lips as she smoothed back a single lock of hair that had fallen onto his forehead.

His head lowered and she rose on tiptoes to meet him.

His hand stole around her waist and tugged her closer.

His heart poured into the heated caresses along the column of her neck and jawline.

Tess shivered with longing as a deeper need for him tightened in her belly.

He finally pressed his lips to hers. The kiss was like a brand, erasing all logical thought from her head. She was his now. How could she ever have thought him cold and uncaring?

Then all of a sudden he raised his head. "Listen."

Melodious chimes filled the air as the clock in the study struck midnight.

"The Christmas bell!" Such a sense of love and well-being filled Tess's chest. She'd never known a more beautiful moment. Years from now she'd look back and remember the joy and complete awe of the night.

"It's Christmas Day." Sloan Sully Sullivan's low rumble stirred the tendrils of hair at her ear. "Merry Christmas, Tess."

Epilogue

On March 25, 1888, Tess Whitgrove and Sloan Sullivan wed. Family and friends, well-wishers and the curious packed the church in Kasota Springs. And Tempest LeDoux ramrodded the whole affair since she had such extensive experience in nuptial proceedings.

Following the ceremony, Sloan carried his bride across the threshold of his newly remodeled ranch house, which he finally considered halfway appropriate for his beloved Tess.

Shortly after their marriage, the Sullivans adopted the four orphan children who had stolen their hearts.

Each year they celebrated their love and the special joy of Christmas by remembering the blizzard of 1887 and being snowbound on Number 208 of the Fort Worth and Denver City train.

Dr. Deacon Brown came to visit often, bringing his sister's three children whose care he had taken over.

And on February 14, 1889, Mr. and Mrs. Sullivan welcomed the first of their five children.

AWAY IN THE MANGER

PHYLISS MIRANDA

To my precious grandchildren:
Emma Danielle, Alexander Patton, Emily Shay,
Abigail Miranda, McKenna Kathleen,
Christian Tyler, Parker Reagan, and
Addison Claire, who is my real-life Addie Claire.

You guys are my inspiration, and I love you.

Granny

Chapter 1

December 1887
Texas Panhandle

All Randall Humphrey wanted for Christmas was to be left alone and to celebrate in the only way he knew how—in solitude. He wasn't sure who thought up all the newfandangled Christmas festivities in Kasota Springs, Texas, but for him it only served as a reminder of the worst day of his life.

Rand cut into his rare steak just like he'd been doing every Thursday since he arrived in town, accompanied by his make-no-bones-about-it mother, floundering father, and his rebel half brother, a little over two years ago. The cook knew exactly how the blacksmith liked his beef. Just kick it in the butt and pass the dern thing over the fire without touching a skillet.

Rand would really appreciate his quiet dinner more if he wasn't so distracted by the townfolks who were fluttering around like a hive of bees, with Edwinna Dewey serving as the queen bee. Taking another bite, Rand figured if he could concentrate on his chewin' and less on the yammerin' around him, he might be able to drown out the incessant chatter of the town's number one gossipmonger.

His intentions to enjoy a quiet supper at the Springs Hotel, then stop by Slats and Fats Saloon for a cool beer before going back to the blacksmith shop was losing ground pretty damn fast. Right now, the possibilities were about as good as a tumbleweed would have of staying grounded on a windy day.

"Mr. Humphrey." Edwinna Dewey's trill voice penetrated Rand's thoughts. "Mr. Humphrey, you do remember that my niece and the children are due in from Carroll Creek tomorrow, don't you?"

"Yes, ma'am." He wiped his mouth on his napkin and laid it back in his lap. The thought of putting the woman six feet under if she asked him that question again briefly crossed his mind. Over the last two days, if she'd asked it once, she'd asked at least fifty more times.

"I just want to make sure that you have fresh horses for her and if there's any repair work that is needed on her carriage, you have a rental for her." She wiggled a bit, making him think maybe her high-pitched voice was the result of her corset being tightened a little bit too snug.

"Yes, ma'am." He knew exactly what her next question would be and fought off reciting it before she could.

"You haven't forgotten I've already paid you, have you?" Before he could answer, she continued, "I'll have one of my hands come to drive them to my place."

"No, ma'am, I haven't forgotten," he answered, after allowing her enough time to ramble on, if she wanted.

Sure enough, for the umpteenth time, she said, "Now, don't you forget, Mr. Humphrey."

"I won't. I'll get them on the road as quickly as possible."

"And you'll take care of their horses?"

"Yes, ma'am." He took a sip of coffee.

"I'm not sure if it was a good idea to send your brother to bring them here," she fretted.

"That was your decision, ma'am." He refrained from saying that he wouldn't have hired his good-for-nothing *half* brother, James Crockett, to fetch a lame mule. Of course, she hadn't asked his advice either.

"You know, Mr. Humphrey, you are so much like your father, except he was much more pleasant to be around. He kept his hair cut and shaved every day." A quirky smile came to her lips. "He was always smiling and smelled of bay rum and . . ."

And rye whiskey.

And you remind me of one of the many women he drank spirits with!

And . . . He clinched his jaw to keep from speaking the words, then he shot her a look that she could interpret any way she desired.

The ol' biddie sashayed back to her table, as though she was the only one in the room.

Three ladies sat cattycorner from him and were engrossed in conversation about the weather, amongst other things. They reminded him of a field of wildflowers on the last day of autumn, all decked out in patterned dresses in varying hues of dark, dull, and boring. Even their surnames reflected such: Mrs. Blackwell, Mrs. Brown, and Mrs. Redmond.

Mrs. Redmond was the loudest. "I'm so worried that the Whitgrove girl won't make it back from Boston with the bell in time for Christmas services." She buttered a piece of bread as she talked. "It'll just ruin the holidays, particularly after all the work we've done to raise the money for the bell. The train that she's due back on should be here at noon tomorrow or the next day. I hope Mr. Humphrey hasn't forgotten that he promised to install the bell."

Rand glanced up at the mention of his name and found all three women staring in his direction. Did every woman in town think he couldn't remember not to squat with his spurs on?

The woman answering reminded Rand of a black widow. "That is, if the snow doesn't hit. I've been around these parts for years, and I'm concerned that we're fixin' to get another snow and it's just now Christmas week," said Mrs. Blackwell.

Mrs. Brown nodded in agreement and chomped off a huge hunk of biscuit. Between bites she said, "It'll be one for the record books. I just pray we can have our Christmas Eve services before the snow hits." She stuffed another piece of bread in her mouth. "If it does, we'll be snowed in for days, and there'll be no Christmas with or without our new bell."

Rand didn't doubt the woman's words for a second; and a silent prayer for no snow touched his lips.

The cancellation of the Christmas festivities wouldn't be any skin off his nose, but he knew it'd be disheartening to the citizens of Kasota Springs. He didn't much want to admit it, but in his own way and for his own reasons, he might be disappointed just a smidgen, too; although he'd never let anyone know. After all, he had a reputation to uphold.

There had been little for Rand to be happy about for a while now. But his work with Tess Whitgrove, who had taken on the responsibilities of ramrodding the whole new Christmas bell shebang, had satisfied something in him. He'd reluctantly agreed to help her committee, making sure that the frame of the tower was adequately built and that the yoke was strong enough to handle the weight of the bell. Thankful for his experience building bridges before he came to Kasota Springs, the third-generation blacksmith didn't take long to be talked into installing the bell when it arrived. This was his one and only charitable event of the year. Deep inside he had to admit that nobody—absolutely nobody— would ever know he sorta enjoyed being asked to help.

His gut got a little tight at his own thoughts as he confessed to himself that he had an ulterior motive to agree to help. Thoughts of the toll of church bells resurrected fond childhood memories when his whole family attended Christmas Eve candlelight services.

The sounding of bells was about the only thing in life that could bring a smile to Randall's face. He hadn't found a reason to smile, really smile, for three years.

Rand could do without the rest of the festivities. His heart was still hurting, and it seemed nobody around noticed. Over the last few years, it'd become easier to stay out of the limelight because he felt less exposed.

Rand topped off his supper with a cup of coffee, which he hurriedly drank. Knowing he'd spent more time eating than he should have, he paid his bill and headed for the door. Since all three of the wildflowers were staring, he tipped his hat at them as he passed.

Outside the hotel's dining room, he had to wind his big frame through the crowd of people who had filled the front lobby with all of the hullabaloo taking place they called a bazaar—whatever in the hell that meant.

Tables were in every crook and cranny of the room, each covered with knitted thingamajigs, frilly doodads of all sorts, jars of jelly, and candies. He recognized some lace doilies and a quilt, only because his ma had made similar ones. But most of the items, he didn't know what they were even used for. One thing for sure, he wouldn't have any of them in his house if his life depended on it.

If the number of townfolks milling around like cattle awaiting a thunderstorm was an indicator, the event must be a success. That was good because the children's home needed all the money they could raise. He'd overheard the wildflower ladies talking about how the little cottage was busting at the seams with four orphans on the train with the new bell, and they could sure use every penny collected.

On second thought, a piece of Aunt Dixie's divinity sounded good. She wasn't his aunt, but surely was an aunt to someone. He hadn't had any candy since his mama died, so that'd be his one and only holiday treat. After all, Christmas Day was just another day in his life.

He left a silver dollar on the table, stuck the candy in his pocket, and walked off leaving Emma Mitchell's gasps hanging in the air. That was his one and only charitable donation for the year.

Pulling his Stetson low over his eyes, Randall sauntered toward the livery stable, avoiding the town square where a festive Christmas tree of no more than six or seven feet stood. Rows of strung berries, gingerbread men, and popcorn circled its scrawny girth, probably much to the pleasure of any rodents in the area. Light snow swathed its branches.

Even with his heavy sheepskin coat on, the wind whipped across Rand's face and chilled him to the core. The snow that had begun with light flakes now earnestly peppered the ground and everything in between. He could barely make out the corrals by the railhead off to the north.

Ever since Kasota Springs was established, they'd held dances, horse races, and box suppers twice a year—on the Fourth of July and Christmas, but unlike Independence Day, this year's holiday event depended on the weather. He just wished someone would realize that the weather wasn't likely to be fittin' for the holiday activities and call the whole thing off.

As soon as the bell arrived, Rand planned to finish the installation by Christmas Eve so he could spend the rest of the holiday alone wrapped in his own little world of solitude.

He had one stop to make before he got to his shop, but he had to hurry. His helper, Timmy, needed to get home to his sick mother. He was just a lad, but he could do the work of a grown man, mucking the stalls and feeding the animals.

Reaching the church, Rand continued up the hill to the

cemetery where he sought out the marker for his mother. Kneeling, he pulled a couple of weeds that struggled against the wind.

"Mama, I sure could use some advice." He brushed away the snow from the stone. "I think I'm gettin' about as grouchy as Pa was. Everyone says I'm just like him, except I don't smile as much. Sometimes I wonder if they even remember why I didn't have anything to smile about.

"You know, Miz Dewey challenged me on my attitude." He smiled inwardly. "If you'd been there, you would have set her straight, wouldn't you?"

Somewhere deep inside, Rand always thought he had every right to be as grumpy as he wanted to be. Although he'd just had his thirty-fifth birthday, he couldn't help himself if he had an attitude of an old man. How dare the loud-mouthed, frumpy Miz Dewey question his outlook on life. It was his and he had the right to do with it what he might. After all, he'd never had an easy life, and never had a home for any length of time until he got to Kasota Springs, a short two and a half years ago.

"You know, Mama, I vaguely remember Pa and Grandfather working until way after dark up in New York when they were building the Erie Canal. I can't believe they talked me into joining them on the Waco bridge job. I didn't think I had what it took, but they never lost faith in me . . . neither did you." He brushed snow off his full beard. "One of the happiest days of his life was when it was finished and we could move lock, stock, and barrel out of Waco, so we could all heal. I remember you telling me that we'd always live in Texas, but as far away from Waco as possible. Never thought the Texas Panhandle would be where we'd put down stakes."

What Rand had never told her, although he figured she knew, was exactly how much he really resented the Waco suspension bridge, because it had taken the soul from his father after his leg was mangled in a freak accident. That's when the drinking, gambling, and taking up with loose women began. His father had slid down a slippery slope, far away from his family. As much as Rand knew he needed to forgive his father, he hadn't been able to do so. To forgive was to forget, and he couldn't forget . . . not yet.

Rand had been away from the livery too long already, since he'd left earlier in the day to pick up extra supplies, just in case the winter snows showed up with vengeance in mind.

After hurrying back to the livery, he shucked his wet coat and Stetson and hung them on a nail inside the door. He stood by the raised brick hearth where a soft-coal fire fought for life and warmed his hands, as well as his backside. Melted snow dripped from the tips of his mustache down onto his beard.

"Mr. Humphrey." Timmy's voice broke with huskiness somewhere between grass and hay. "I've done all the chores. Horses are fed and I've checked and the carriage reserved for Ms. Dewey is dry, if she needs it. But Jughead won't come in."

"That old mule is a cantankerous ol' rascal, but as faithful a friend as any man could ever want." Rand wiped away the moisture from his beard with his handkerchief. "I want you to get yourself home and don't want to see you again until the day after Christmas unless I come for you. You hear?"

"Yes sir, I hear you. And I'll bring your milk later."

"Bring extra in case the storm gets us, if you've got it."

The lad nodded. "Guess Miss Margaret over at the mercantile got sick, 'cause there ain't nobody around today."

"Heard that." Rand pulled out a brand-spankin'-new double eagle from his pocket and tossed it to the lad. "Buy yourself something you've been wanting when they open. Maybe those boots you've been lookin' at."

Timmy grabbed his coat and pocketed the coin. "Thanks,

Mr. Humphrey, but I gotta pass on the boots. It's Christmas and I might've never been able to get Mama a present without you being so kindhearted." He neared the door and suddenly turned back to Rand. Lowering his eyes, his voice broke, as he said, "I'm not sure she'll make it to see another Christmas."

Rand took a deep breath and shielded himself from caring. "Timmy, thank your mama for the chicken and dumplin's she sent over and . . ." He took a second breath. "And Merry Christmas."

"Merry Christmas to you too, Mr. Humphrey, and don't forget Jughead." The lad shot out the door like Rand had kicked him out by the toe of his boots.

Now that Rand had all of the seasonal pleasantries out of the way, he could focus on his own priorities. After he got caught up on making a few household items that he'd promised to have ready for customers after the holiday, he figured on spending the rest of the holiday just the way he wanted it.

Alone with nothing but his animals and his memories.

His plan was simple. Work during the day with nobody to bother him. Take care of the horses. Eat what he wanted when he wanted and spend the evenings sitting by the fire, smoking his pipe and reading in the big room adjacent to the blacksmith's shop.

Tonight would be the start of the smoking and the reading. But first, he had to find his ol' tattered copy of Dickens's *A Tale of Two Cities*, and he was pretty sure it was still hidden away in his mother's Saratoga trunk upstairs. He had a hankering to see what kind of vengeance the remorseless Madame Defarge had been heaping on folks, but hadn't had time to find the book.

It took only a minute or two to locate the trunk and lift the lid, releasing the smell of stale air and cedar. The book lay beneath a quilt that had been pieced and stitching started but never got finished.

Over the last year, more than once the thought had occurred to him that he should donate the coverlet to the church's women's quilting group or whatever they called themselves, but he just couldn't bring himself to do it. For some reason, he couldn't stand the thought of someone else touching the piece of work.

At his age, he had little doubt that there'd never be a woman under his roof that he'd trust enough to finish it, so the quilt would stay buried in the trunk . . . like many of his memories.

Returning downstairs, he added logs to the fire before he settled in for the night in his comfortable chair near the hearth. He filled his favorite briar pipe and tamped the tobacco down. Taking a deep whiff, he enjoyed the pleasant, almost sweet scent. There was nothing better in life than good tobacco instead of the kind that smelled and tasted like yucca blended with cow chips and buffalo bones.

Even with a roaring fire, a chill hovered overhead. The temperature had noticeably dropped since he returned from supper, a sure sign that the winds had shifted to the north and would bring horrendous snows unless it skirted around Kasota Springs.

Heavy banging assaulted the door to the blacksmith's shop.

Rushing to get it opened as quick as possible, Randall came face-to-face with Edwinna Dewey, who stood outside with a fairly heavy layer of snow clinging to her hat and across the shoulders of her black coat. She seemed extraordinarily excited, more than usual, if that were possible. Her headpiece sat precariously on top of her head and her eyes bugged out with animation.

Over her shoulder he could make out people scurrying around like fire ants on a mission. A terrible commotion was going on, but the heavy snow kept him from seeing exactly what was taking place.

"Come quickly, Mr. Humphrey, we need your help." Edwinna steadied her hat with her gloved hands and rushed off, leaving Rand standing in the doorway wondering if this was her way of setting a trap for him, making certain that he couldn't enjoy a peaceful holiday alone.

On the other hand, what could have happened that would require the attention of the town's blacksmith?

Chapter 2

Rand threw on his coat and hat, not bothering with gloves, and hightailed it after Edwinna Dewey. The wind caused her umbrella to bobble along, proving little protection against the falling snow.

Across from the square, a crowd gathered near Dr. Mitchell's office. Most, including the wildflower ladies, stood on the sidewalk, craning their necks to see into the office.

As they neared, thanks to his height, Rand could easily see that the room was filled to the brim with townfolks. He recognized many of the faces from the holiday bazaar at the Springs Hotel, so evidently something had happened involving that event.

Edwinna elbowed and fussed her way through the crowd.

Rand was far enough behind that he couldn't hear her words clearly, but he was pretty sure many of them might not be suitable for ladies' ears.

"I've got him right here." Edwinna waved her parasol in Rand's face, as though she'd just caught Old St. Nick up to mischief. "He can tell you that his brother—"

"Half brother," Rand interjected.

"Half brother . . . was nowhere around, because he's driving my niece and the twins here from Carroll Creek." Again, her umbrella darted dangerously near his face. "Tell them, Mr. Humphrey. Tell them that my niece had nothing to do with stealing the money from the bazaar."

"Nobody has accused anybody of anything," warned Doc Mitchell.

Rand wasn't sure exactly what had happened, but apparently money for the children's home had been stolen. With the impetuous woman's open parasol flying from one shoulder to the other like a weapon, he was just about ready to confess to stealing the money himself, in order to save his eyesight. One wrong move and she'd blind him for sure.

"Miz Dewey, I have no idea where your niece and her family are, and *you* told *me* that *you* hired my half brother"— Rand held his tongue and didn't add *a no-good scoundrel of a man*. Rand continued—"to drive them here, but I can assure you I've seen none of them."

"That can't be true," said Emma.

Dr. Mitchell attempted to hold down his wife, and patient, who kept trying to stand. "Now, Emma, stay calm. Gettin' upset isn't good for your blood pressure." He tugged at her arm. "I'm sure Mr. Humphrey would know if a young woman and two children had arrived at his livery."

"Well, I'm not so sure," Emma shot back. "A man assaulted me in the alley and absconded with the bazaar money. He was tall and came up from behind me. I know it was Jim Crockett. I just know it."

"Now, Emma. It could have been someone else. Did you see his face?" Doc Mitchell asked. "You know Boss Adler and some of his gang was hangin' around the mercantile last night. Nothing good ever comes out of them when they come to town. Could it be them?"

"No! The man came up behind me," she huffed. "But I know who it was. He smelled like tobacco and bay rum, and was tall, just like . . ."

Someone in the crowd yelled, "Sheriff Raines has two of 'um in the hoosegow, and he went after Boss Adler. They were so liquored up he could hardly stand the smell of 'um."

Another male voice said, "All Raines is interested in is retiring, not capturing outlaws. Of course, except for some of the locals like the Thompson clan."

Emma Mitchell reared up and muttered, "If he doesn't get himself killed first . . ." A concerto of voices rippled through the crowd, drowning out her words, but Rand eventually heard her wail, "With all the money gone, there will be no Christmas for the children at the orphanage."

"Darlin', settle down." Doc Mitchell placed his arm around his wife's shoulder. "We'll have Christmas for the young'uns one way or another."

Emma Mitchell settled her head on her husband's shoulder and accepted his handkerchief, dabbing at her tears. "And it's snowing."

Edwinna Dewey said to no particular person, "I knew I shouldn't have hired a Humphrey." She whirled in Rand's direction. "I just know your brother—uh, half brother—let something happen to them and they're in a cold snowy pasture." She pulled her own hanky from her handbag and wiped away a tear then blew her nose, not so ladylike. "I know they're freezing and hungry, and . . ." She jerked up her opened umbrella and wheeled it in Rand's face. "And you're going to go find them."

"If I thought they were in danger, I'd be the first to be out there lookin' for them, but Miz Dewey—"

The sound of horse hooves pounding the hard clay street beneath the snow cut off Rand's words.

Tall and distinguished, the testy foreman of the Jacks Bluff Ranch, Teg Tegeler, dismounted. Without any pleasantries except for a tip of his hat to the ladies, he said, "Came to give y'all fair warning there's a storm a brewin'. And it ain't nothin' to snub your nose at either. Some of our hands jest got back from movin' cattle more south to try to avoid the worst of the storm, so wanted to warn you all."

Mrs. Redmond piped up and asked, "Do you think the train with the new bell on it will make it in before the worst of it hits?"

"I reckon not, ma'am. Guessin' from the way the railroad tracks cross over near the Sullivan Ranch, I suspect the train and the storm are on a collision course." He secured his big dun stud to the hitching post. "Best thing you all can do now is plan to hunker down for a spell. If you don't have extra supplies, better get 'um now, 'cause I think this might be the big one."

Tegeler excused himself, pulled the brim of his hat low over his eyes, and headed in the direction of Slats and Fats Saloon, most likely to get himself some warm liquid reinforcement before he took care of whatever business brought him to town so late in the day. And Rand was bettin' that the crusty cowboy's beeswax might well be Bonnie Lynn, the saucy redhead maid over at the Springs Hotel.

Suddenly, the loss of the money for the orphanage was overshadowed by the prediction of a winter storm; except, of course, to Mrs. Mitchell, who complained to her husband that she might have to take to her bed until Christmas Eve to get over her feeling poorly.

Edwinna Dewey got drawn into a conversation with the wildflower women.

With all the commotion, and a little luck, Rand could escape and get back to his warm chair, light his pipe, and begin to find out what Madame Defarge was up to before the coals in the hearth died out.

If he were playing poker he would have drawn the worst hand in the deck, because out of the corner of his eye he saw Edwinna Dewey hoofin' it his way. Even through the veil of light snow, he saw by the look on her face that she was about to have a conniption fit, and he had a notion he was fixin' to be the recipient of her poor humor.

"Oh, Mr. Humphrey." Her shrill voice caught on the wind and chased him down. "Oh, Mr. Humphrey, I'm not finished talking to you."

But I am with you! Rand rubbed away light snow on his mustache with the back of his very cold hand.

"You've got to go find my niece—" Edwinna demanded.

Although Rand's patience was a bit frayed, he tried to think how he'd feel if he were in her shoes. The thought made him shudder. There were a lot of places he'd like to be, but in her shoes wasn't one of them. "I can assure you, ma'am, Jim Crockett would have never left Carroll Creek if he suspected in the least there was bad weather. He'd never put the welfare of a woman, especially with children, in jeopardy."

"If you ask me, he's nothing but a scallywag."

"And I didn't ask you, ma'am." His blood boiled. After all, only kin was allowed to call out another family member—whether the accusations were true or not.

As though she hadn't heard him, she continued on her rant. "But you'll promise that you'll carry my niece and the twins to me the moment they arrive in town?"

"Yes ma'am, I promise." And he was being absolutely honest in making the promise, because if Miz Dewey's niece was anything like her aunt, he didn't want to spend a second more than was necessary with the woman. A cold chill ran down his spine.

The woman could be even worse!

Chapter 3

Fluffy snow churned from the heavens and blew against anything in its way, creating snowdrifts along the road leading into Kasota Springs.

In the distance, Sarah Callahan saw the soft flickering of lamplight from the window of the blacksmith shop.

Tucking three-year-old Damon to her side, she took a deep breath, then pulled Addie Claire closer, attempting to shield the twins from the snow freezing on their coats and hats.

"We're nearly there. You're safe," she reassured the children as they hurried through the ankle-deep snow toward the light.

She banged heavily on the door until a big, burly man opened it, allowing the heat from the forge to whisk out the door as though it were chasing away the snowflakes.

Aunt Edwinna had described the blacksmith as an old codger, as friendly as a coyote on a moonless night, but a man who was honest. At the moment, Sarah agreed with the old codger description, but her aunt had failed to say that he also looked like a big brown grizzly bear forced out of hibernation early.

"Mr. Humphrey?" As she spoke, opaque vapors swirled

from her breath. Instinctively, she gathered the little tykes closer, but she wasn't sure if it was to protect them from the howling wind or the giant of a man standing in the threshold.

"Yes, and you are?" he asked with an edge in his voice, leaving little doubt he wasn't all that keen on receiving visitors so late in the evening.

"Sarah Callahan." A gust of wind assaulted her, and the twins grabbed tightly to her legs, unsteadying her even more.

The man grabbed her by the arm and almost pulled her and the children clinging to her coattail inside. "Miz Dewey's niece?"

She nodded. "And this is Damon and Addie Claire." Sarah gently pulled back their hats so he could see their faces.

He tentatively smiled at the children before returning to the grumpy expression that she suspected life had etched on his face.

"I apologize, ma'am, for draggin' you in here like that, but I thought you were fixin' to land up in a snowbank."

The newfound warmth in his voice was in contradiction with his appearance. He offered his hand, and she accepted his welcome. Even through her gloves, she could feel the roughness in his grip, yet it gave her a sense of protection.

But it was his eyes that took her breath away. Deep, dark chocolate, and intense like he could see all the way to her soul.

She had to force herself away from her thoughts. "Pleased to meet you, Mr. Humphrey, and I apologize for coming unannounced."

"We can chat later. You all need to get out of the weather." He helped her remove her coat and hung it by the door. "Get those wet clothes off the children. Just drop them by the door, it won't hurt anything. There's a fire in the great room on the other side of the shop. I'll go find some blankets." He looked her straight in the eye and said in a commanding voice, "And get their wet socks off, too."

He lumbered away, leaving her to do as he'd instructed.

The scent of fire and smoke hung heavy in the air, and a layer of soot settled over every inch of the blacksmith's shop.

Depositing the soaking wet items by the door, she hurried the twins in the direction he had gone. To her surprise the living area was rather large, warm and inviting. Except for the size and sharing the building, it was in total contrast with the blacksmith's shop.

"I'm sorry these are so rough, but they are the first I found." Mr. Humphrey handed her three blankets and some socks. "I think gettin' you all warmed up right now is more important."

Sarah wrapped the freezing children in the heavy covering and huddled with them in front of the fire on a small rug, which she suspected he had hurriedly thrown on the floor.

"Mr. Humphrey—"

"Rand." His deep baritone voice was edged with years of control. "Short for Randall."

"And I'm Sarah." She stood. Tilting back her head, she boldly met his gaze. "Short for . . . uh, well, Sarah."

They exchanged cordial smiles.

"How about something to drink? Milk for them and some . . ." His voice trailed off, as though he wasn't sure what to offer her, but to her surprise, he continued, "Hot tea? If there's still some left in the canister."

"That would be lovely. May I help you, Mr. Hump . . . Rand?"

Before he could respond, little Addie Claire looked up. "May I have warm milkth, please, Mr. Humprand?"

Sarah took in a sharp breath, shocked that the little girl

had mispronounced his name so horribly. She softly corrected, "Mr. Humphrey."

"That's what I meant, Mummy." Addie Claire lay back down and curled up facing the fire. "Thank you, Mr. Grumpy."

Sarah looked up at Rand Humphrey expecting frustration to be etched on the big man's face, but to her surprise a tiny smile hugged the corner of his mouth, softening his features. "She has problems sometimes pronouncing some of her sounds," Sarah offered.

"And I have a problem being a tad grumpy and probably scary to a little girl." With a glimmer in his eye he added, "Even to big ones."

"You don't scare me, Mr. Humphrey." Sarah squatted down and put the oversized wool socks on each of the children, wishing inwardly she was as confident as she prayed her voice portrayed.

"Warm milk for the little ones and hot tea for the lady, comin' right up," Rand said before exiting the great room, undoubtedly headed for the kitchen. Over his shoulder he continued, "Then I must go find your aunt and let her know you all have arrived safely."

Sarah's heart sank, along with her spirits.

From the moment she saw the first snowflake, somewhere down deep inside she had found herself thinking that the snow surely had been a gift from the heavens and maybe, just maybe, she and the children would get snowed in at a warm, cheerful place—anywhere except at Aunt Edwinna's ranch.

Guilt overcame her for thinking such thoughts. The only reason Sarah had agreed to come to Kasota Springs for the holiday was because of the picture her aunt had painted of what a grand time the children would have going to all of the Christmas festivities—watching the horse races, the boxed supper—and she had even tempted Sarah by volunteering to look after the twins while she went to the holiday dance.

Aunt Edwinna had described a number of available men, the foreman of the Jacks Bluff Ranch, another rancher named Sullivan, and had warned her about two families to steer clear of, one named Thompson and the other Dolton. And she'd specifically cautioned her about the blacksmith, Randall Humphrey, leaving the impression that, although single, he was much too cranky for any woman to want to consort with.

Sarah reminded herself that she was in Kasota Springs for the holidays, not to consort with a man, whether he was cantankerous or not.

But now, with a blizzard dancing on a razor's edge, if Rand located Aunt Edwinna, Sarah and the twins would be stuck out on the ranch with the overbearing and oh-so-nosy sister of her mother.

Thoughts of getting snowbound with the big, testy blacksmith were more appealing than being stranded with her spinster aunt. Sarah hated to pray for more snow, but found herself closing her eyes and doing just that.

The oddest feeling washed over Sarah. Why did she feel so comfortable in her surroundings and not in the least threatened by a man she'd only met minutes before? A man who had a reputation for being as cantankerous as a lead steer on a trail drive?

By the time she had pulled on a pair of warm, woolen socks, the feeling in her toes had returned. She checked on the children, who now cuddled together in front of the hearth, sleeping soundly. Their cheeks had returned to a healthy shade of rose instead of the blustery cherry red caused by the horrific winds and cold.

Sarah walked into the kitchen just in time to see Rand

attempt to pick up a pot of boiling water with a tea towel. Surely a man who dealt with red-hot coals all day long would make sure he had plenty of padding before grabbing a hot piece of metal . . . wouldn't he?

"Sonofabitch!" Rand dropped the teakettle on top of the stove with a heavy clang and jerked away the rag. Even from a distance, Sarah saw an enormous area of reddened flesh on his right hand.

"Damn it—" Rand glanced up, and seeing her, he cut his words short. He looked a little like he'd gotten caught with his hand in the cookie jar, and before she could respond, he simply said, "Sorry, ma'am. I'm not accustomed to anybody being within earshot."

"They certainly aren't words I'm unfamiliar with, but—"

"But not around the children, right?"

Since he obviously saw the error in his ways, she just nodded gingerly. "Let me help you. Addie Claire and Damon are asleep, so no need for the milk, but I'd still enjoy some tea, if you don't mind. May I fix some for you, too?"

Rand raised his brows as if she'd asked him if he wanted a cup of arsenic, then said, "I drink coffee."

"You need that burn tended to." Boldly she stepped his way and seized his hand, and to her surprise he didn't jerk it away. "Do you have some salve?" She hesitated a second, then added, "Of course you do, you deal with fire all day long."

"And rarely get distracted enough to burn myself." He pulled his hand away and doused cold water over it. "I've had worse sunburns. I'll doctor it later."

"I see you've already put out cups and the tea, so while you go tend to that burn, I'll finish the tea and coffee."

A frown crossed his face. Although she'd just met him, she had little doubt this was a show of his displeasure with being bossed around in his own home. She had little doubt he wasn't a man who easily took instructions from anyone, man or woman.

Rand opened his mouth, but before he could say anything, rapid-fire knocking came from the door to the blacksmith's shop. Whoever was there wanted to make sure they were heard, and Sarah could bet the ranch, if she had one, that it wasn't a traveler needing the services of a blacksmith.

From the obvious frustration on Rand's face, he wasn't all that happy about another intrusion in his life.

Before Sarah could fill the china teapot that Rand had put out for water, she heard a piercing female voice snarl, "I guess you forgot that you were to let me know the *moment* my niece and the twins arrived, Mr. Humphrey."

Stepping out of the kitchen, Sarah walked into the shop and stopped in her tracks. The person covered in snow who pushed her way through the doorway of the shop reminded Sarah of a snowman who had escaped a snowdrift and come lookin' for trouble.

Sarah glanced from the woman to Rand and back.

Without acknowledging Sarah's presence, Edwinna Dewey wheeled her umbrella in Rand Humphrey's direction and said, "You did, didn't you."

"No, ma'am, I didn't forget anything." He looked squarely in her face, and his eyes narrowed suspiciously. "And I suspect this is a night I'm apt not to forget for a long time."

Chapter 4

Rand clenched his jaw and glanced in the direction of Sarah. He wasn't sure what she was thinkin', but from the pained looked on her face, it was anything but pleasant.

Maybe he'd be better off backing down from Edwinna, but he wasn't known for walking away from anything, and this wild woman, full of accusations, had just about used up all of the patience Rand allocated for any given person.

"No ma'am, I didn't forget. They've been here only a few minutes. Whether you are in a mind to believe me or not, I was on my way to tell you." He wasn't sure the woman even deserved that much of an explanation. He reckoned he was in a more charitable mood than he realized.

She didn't bother to answer, but turned in Sarah's direction. "I'm glad you are here." Glancing around the room, she continued, "Where are your bags, dear? I'm ready to leave."

"Nice to see you too, Aunt Edwinna." The hurt in Sarah's voice could be heard above the roaring fire. "Our bags are—"

Edwinna cut her off and whirled back at Rand. "I have a room at the hotel, and I'll send my driver to pick up her carriage and a fresh team first thing in the morning, so make sure it's ready."

Casting his gaze over to Sarah, Rand saw tears well in her eyes. She took a deep breath and looked away, emphasizing her hurt. He suspected that she bore rejection somewhat like a war hero might wear a badge of courage.

He'd walked slap-dab into a sticky situation. As much as he hated to admit it, he was a lot of things, but allowing a woman to be mistreated, if only with words, was something he would not tolerate. He'd seen too much of it in his life.

Rand had been raised to respect women, but Edwinna Dewey needed a serious dressing down, and it didn't matter whether she ever spoke to him again or not. As a matter of fact, if she'd ignore him for being a gentleman and sticking up for her niece, he'd ignore her being a total battle-ax . . . the rest of his born days wouldn't be too long.

"Edwinna." It felt good to go one-on-one with the ol' hag on a first-name basis. "You can either stew in the pot of your own making or join Sarah for tea. It makes no never mind to me, but the kids are asleep and Sarah is extremely weary and doesn't need any of your malarkey." He remembered his manners before Sarah had to remind him, and continued. "Sarah's been from hell to Georgia and back just to come see you, so I'm thinkin' you could make her visit pleasant. The choice is yours." He took a deep breath. "While you two talk, I'm gonna see what is taking Jim so long getting the team settled in."

Rand might as well have tossed kindling and a match on Edwinna's outlook on life. The older woman took two steps backward, and if a look could kill, he'd rightfully be laid out at the undertaker's by the time the snow was over. She whirled toward her niece.

"Well, are you going to let him talk to me like that?" Edwinna closed the umbrella and crossed her arms over her ample chest.

By the look on Sarah's face, Rand suspected it took every bit of courage for her to face her aunt and try to avoid a nasty confrontation. "Rand, we need to talk about your brother—"

"Half brother," Edwinna interrupted, and patted her foot impatiently.

Sarah looked at Rand for confirmation. He nodded.

"I apologize. I should have realized your and Mr. Crockett's kinship, since you don't share the same last name."

"Different mothers," Rand interjected. The why and what for of his older, wayward sibling's existence wasn't something Rand relished talking about to anyone. The fact that Jim was conceived in a night of heavy gambling, free-flowing liquor, and loose women many years before their father married Rand's mother was nobody's concern. Big Jim Crockett was a grown man long before Rand was ever a gleam in his father's eyes.

Checking on the horses could wait. He needed to find out what Sarah wanted to discuss concerning his half brother. Jim Crockett did a lot of things Rand didn't approve of, particularly his carelessness with money and his reckless behavior, but he'd never known him to be anything but a gentleman when it came to women and children, or to be derelict in his duties handling animals. Unfortunately, those were about the only good qualities Rand could think of at the moment. Surely he had more.

"Let's go to the kitchen and get some coffee. We can talk there," said Rand.

Before Sarah could answer, Edwinna piped up. "My dear Sarah, your dilly-dallying has made it abundantly clear that you have no plans on returning to the hotel with me at the moment, but since they will stop serving supper shortly, I'm going back, and I expect you to join me the moment the children are awake." With her fingertips, she pushed a tad of melting snow off her hat and let it slip onto the floor. "Although you could wake them up and come along now, saving yourself a lot of embarrassment. Just so my position is clear, I do not approve of you spending any more time than is absolutely necessary with Mr. Humphrey, and certainly not another second with Mr. Crockett, either."

"Aunt Edwinna, I'm painfully aware of your feelings toward Mr. Humphrey, but I am a grown woman who knows how to handle myself. I can assure you there will be no improprieties, but we have important business that must be discussed."

Huffing like the wild, west Texas wind in a foul mood, the old maid grabbed for her umbrella and in doing so knocked it to the floor. "I expect you at the Springs Hotel within the hour."

"Miz Dewey, I'll walk you back to the hotel." Rand grabbed his hat. "I sure as hell don't want to be blamed should something happen to you along the way."

"No need." Edwinna snatched up the umbrella from where it had landed and popped the dern thing open. "I'm a grown woman." She mocked Sarah as she stomped out the door into a wall of stark white snow.

A gust of strong north wind stampeded across the room.

"I wonder if your aunt knows that if you open a black umbrella inside it'll rain bad luck on you." Rand walked to the door and slammed it shut before returning his Stetson to the hat rack.

"Or if a woman drops one she must ask someone else to pick it up, because if she is single and picks up an umbrella herself, she'll never marry," Sarah added.

"It's gotta be black. And it's sure good to know there's a bunch of single men out there who can breathe a big sigh of relief right about now." Rand chuckled.

They locked gazes and both burst into laughter.

Rand enjoyed the way Sarah laughed. As much as he

desperately wanted to resist her captivating smile, her warm and enchanting humor drew him to her like a hummingbird to sugar water.

As much as Rand hated to find out what Sarah had to tell him about his half brother, he couldn't delay it much longer. They walked to the kitchen.

"Okay, tell me what Jim did this time." Rand placed two cups on the table.

"It's easy to see you're nothing like Mr. Crockett, so that makes it harder for me to say what I have to say." Sarah wrapped her hands around the hot cup of tea.

The more Sarah talked, telling Rand about how Jim Crockett had brought her and the children to the edge of town and literally dropped them off, explaining that he had business to take care of, and that his agreement with her aunt Edwinna only called for getting them to Kasota Springs safely, the madder Rand got.

Furor rose from the depths of his stomach, and he clenched his jaw. "So he just dumped you off to walk from the edge of town to my place?"

She nodded. "But it wasn't all that far, and he gave me good directions."

Rand corralled the anger milling around inside him. With a town consisting of a square with buildings surrounding it and a railhead at one end, even an infrequent visitor wouldn't need directions . . . except for tonight with the snow. About the time she arrived, unless one was very versed with the location of the various stores in town, the lack of visibility would make it easy to go off in the wrong direction and end up lost in open range. Lucky, the blacksmith shop was a straight shot into town.

"Regardless, he should have made sure you were safe and sound before he went off to do God only knows what." He wanted to add, *probably to drink whiskey and take up with some loose woman . . . just like his father—our father.*

"Rand, he was really a gentleman, kind to the twins, and I honestly think the trip took longer than he'd anticipated because of the weather." She looked up into Rand's eyes. "So please, don't be angry at him."

Anger continued to rise within Rand. "Did he say what was so important?"

She shook her head. "Just that he'd make sure our luggage and the carriage were returned the first opportunity he got."

"And that was about an hour ago." Rand tried to put things in chronological order. Although the walk from the edge of town to the blacksmith's shop didn't take all that long, with the deplorable weather conditions, not to mention two children to contend with, Jim would have had time to steal the money from the bazaar and disappear. The carriage would be too burdensome, and certainly noticeable, so he probably dumped it near the hotel and walked the rest of the way into town. The only thing Rand could do now was go find Jim Crockett and see that the money raised for the orphanage was returned.

"I'll be right back." He pulled his big frame to his feet and shot her an almost smile. "I've got to go check on the horses. Make yourself at home. If you're hungry there's chicken and dumplin's that my helper's mother sent over for dinner. After I get back, I'll take you and the children to the hotel." He stopped, then topped it off with, "If you want."

She returned a smile that set his heart racing. Unlike the storm brewing outside, her eyes were as radiant as summer lightning, but it was her words that caught him off guard. "Hopefully, it won't take you long. It's been a while since I've had such enjoyable company."

On his way out, Rand stoked the fire to make certain it

would keep the great room warm while he was gone. He wasn't sure how to respond to Sarah's comment, since he wasn't accustomed to receiving compliments, so he had only nodded. Sarah Callahan must be *loco* or lived a very boring existence if he was the best company she'd enjoyed in a while.

Sarah followed him to the door, and he felt her eyes on him as he pulled on his heavy sheepskin coat and Stetson and headed into a flurry of white, wet snow. He pulled the door closed, separating him from the most pleasant woman he believed he'd been around for a long time.

At least not since . . .

He took a deep breath, closed his eyes, and forced himself to remember his pledge. He'd never be guilty of comparing one woman with another.

Circling the building, even through the heavy snow he spied the carriage that Jim had driven to Carroll Creek to fetch Sarah and the children. Rand got busy checking it out, making sure the buggy was protected from the elements and that the horses were properly cared for.

But everywhere the blacksmith turned, flashes of Sarah got in his way. Visions of her slender, willowy body with a strength that didn't overshadow her femininity danced in his head. From the second he saw her, even with a big coat on and a hat covered with snow, he knew she was somebody he wouldn't mind riding the river with.

He couldn't keep his mind off the way she looked when she knelt down to put the socks on the children. Wisps of hair the color of a wheat field framed her face. And when the lace at her throat had parted, he hadn't been able to keep his gaze away from the hollow of the neck filled with soft shadows. Then she looked up at him with fiery blue eyes the color of the Texas sky on a clear day. Eyes that glowed with a challenge.

Dang it, and the only thing he was able to come up with

was some cockamamie question about fixin' some milk for the children.

What a way of making sure old feelings didn't have a chance to surface.

Frustration reared its ugly head. Rand found her nearness disturbing. Yet, in only a matter of minutes, she'd managed to open wounds that he thought were well on their way to healing. The sickening, familiar swell of pain ripped through him. Sarah had penetrated his being and touched his soft core in record time. Generally, he would never enter into another's family business, but he recognized the hurt in Sarah's eyes and felt the need to protect her from her own aunt.

A flash of unadulterated guilt ripped through him. Damn it, he'd thought he'd managed to steer clear of the wrenching pain and shame for the loss of his wife, especially since the anniversary of her tragic death was on the horizon—Christmas Eve. Three days short of three years. Maybe holding on to blame was his way of keeping the hurt at bay or covering it up or ignoring it . . . or at least a way to make sure he never got hurt again.

Walking into the stables he saw Big Tex and Bushwhacker, the horses who had brought Sarah and the children to Kasota Springs, in their stalls. Apparently happy to be out of the snow, they kept their heads in the feed sacks, more interested in the oats than Rand.

Near the door sat a relatively big trunk, not nearly as large as Rand's mother's Saratoga, along with two smaller traveling bags. So far, Jim had kept his word.

Rand took another gander around. Everything seemingly was in place, yet something was missing.

Rand almost ran back into the corral near the wagon yard. Jughead, the most temperamental mule between the Canadian River and the Rio Grande, was nowhere to be found. With plenty of able-bodied horses around, why in the hell had his brother—correction, half brother—stolen a dumb-as-a-stump mule?

Rand sat down on a bale of hay just inside the lean-to and stared out into the night, watching the howling north wind whip the snow around. He dusted snow off his beard. He'd been too busy to take good stock of the deteriorating weather conditions. Flakes no longer fell straight to the ground but blew horizontally, hurling into huge banks. He almost couldn't make out his hand in front of his face.

Jim Crockett couldn't have made it far without losing his way in the snow. Rand had seen it before. Soon the town would be isolated and paralyzed. Only a fool would try to go anywhere . . . not tonight, not tomorrow, and most likely not the day afterward.

Chapter 5

Sarah tried not to think about her confrontation with Aunt Edwinna. She hadn't been around her for a while, and as far as she was concerned, another three or four decades wouldn't matter in the least. She was the most condescending woman Sarah believed she'd ever met; and since the birth of the twins, things had gotten more stressful between them. The worst part was, they were family and there wasn't anything either of them could do about it.

Shuddering, Sarah chastised herself for allowing her aunt to even talk her into coming to Kasota Springs in the first place. She would have been better off to have kept the twins in Carroll Creek and forgone the holiday festivities. A nice quiet, uneventful celebration of Christmas was more to her liking, but the twins needed to know their family . . . what was left of it.

On the other hand, if Sarah had not come she'd not have met Randall Humphrey, probably the most intriguing man she'd ever come across. On the surface he was as pleasant as a rattler with a tummyache and the mind-set of a hungry coyote. Yet inside, he had to be a warm, caring man. For whatever reasons known only to him, he apparently didn't want anyone to see that side of him. She found his displeasure with about everything around him amusing. Yep, she suspected the man had to work hard to uphold his beastly persona.

The children were again asleep in front of the crackling fire. Sarah had taken Rand at his word and put the chicken and dumplin's on to warm. She had located a chamber pot and had seen that the twins' needs were taken care of. After washing their hands, they eagerly gobbled down the best dumplin's Sarah believed she'd ever eaten. Quickly, the twins had settled back on their pallet and gone back to sleep while she cleaned up the kitchen area.

Sarah found herself nodding off as she sat in the chair made for a big man, someone like Randall Humphrey. She didn't want him to find her asleep for fear he'd think she wasn't watching the children like she should. She picked up the book on the candle table. *A Tale of Two Cities*, and it'd been years since she'd read it. Once she opened the leatherbound volume, she found herself enthralled with the prose all over again.

Minutes turned into an hour or more as she read, enjoying the opportunity to be drawn away from reality into a world of make-believe, something she had been doing quite religiously of late.

She batted her eyes, but when they got too blurry to continue reading, she closed the book and returned it to where she found it.

The weather worried her, and she paced the floor. Finding herself at the window that looked out across the town, she wiped a circle of moisture off the glass but saw nothing but white. Raging winds battered the panels of glass.

Not having seen Rand for a while, Sarah prayed he was safe. The snow-laden winds could easily knock down the strongest of men. And no doubt Randall Humphrey was one strong man.

After making sure the twins' blankets were tucked warmly around them, she slipped back into the comfortable chair. Sarah snuggled deep inside the rough blanket, and in minutes she drifted off to sleep.

Sometime later, after depositing Sarah's trunk and two small bags just inside the door, Rand walked through the work area, removed his wet coat, gloves, and Stetson before warming up at the low-burning forge.

He was as ready as he'd ever be to face his visitors.

Although thoughts of Sarah hadn't left him for long, he now dwelled on what he'd do with the little ones, who he figured to be about three or four years of age. He had little experience in that part of being around kids. Hell, he'd been stripped of that possibility three years ago. Even the town's kids seemed to hide behind their mothers' skirts when they saw him comin' their way.

After warming up both his body and his courage, Rand walked back through the blacksmith's shop and pulled the heavy wooden doors shut behind him. Separating the work area from the living quarters would keep the great room warmer.

He wasn't sure what he expected to find inside, but a feeling of coming home certainly wasn't it. The smell of coffee and tea hovered in the air, and for the first time he could remember, he actually smelled the wood burning in the hearth. What was wrong with him? Had his brain frozen just from being out in the freezing weather?

For the life of him, he couldn't bring himself to wake the angel sleeping in his chair. He looked down at the children. He couldn't take the chance of having the fire go out during the night, because sleeping on the floor would be much like sleeping in a frozen creek bed. Besides, he needed to get them from underfoot as soon as possible. He didn't want a couple of fussy honyocks around come morning.

After all, Rand had work to get done, and if luck was with him, he could spend a quiet Christmas all by himself.

He scooped up a child in each arm and climbed the stairs two at a time. When he reached his mother's bedroom, he kicked the door open. His biggest concern, that the children would wake up and be frightened, didn't materialize. Both nestled their faces close to his neck. He settled them in the bed before he located two quilts and carried the covers downstairs.

Now he needed to do something with Sarah. She could sleep in the chair or he could take her to his bedroom upstairs. He kneeled down beside her, but for some reason he couldn't bring himself to wake her up. She looked so peaceful, and no doubt she had had an exhausting day just traveling, without adding having to traipse through the snow to get to his place. The run-in with her aunt would have caused anxiety to even a rested person.

Rand touched her arm with his finger kinda like he used to see his mama poke a loaf of bread dough when it was rising. He jerked his finger back, as though he thought she might snarl at him. He wasn't sure he could handle a screaming, terrified woman waking up the whole town.

He stepped back and stared down at Sarah. She didn't move an iota. Hmm, what should he do now? He could swoop her up and carry her to his bed, but if she woke up she'd probably clobber him and might never speak to him again, so what to do?

"Sarah." He again squatted down and spoke softly. "Wake up." He poked her again, then gently grasped her arm and shook her gingerly.

She opened her eyes for only a second and drifted back to sleep, leaving him with two choices—let her sleep in the chair and possibly get a crick in her neck, or he could whisk her off to bed . . . his bed.

He really didn't have a choice. He wouldn't be responsible for anything happening to her that would make it impossible for her to leave come morning.

Rand didn't have to sleep in his own room. Right now a hot cup of coffee, or some warm milkth, as Addie Claire called it, and a bed off the kitchen was good enough for him.

Besides, he'd always liked the tiny cubbyhole to the more spacious room upstairs because he could hear any disturbances from the livery. It had an ol' bed taken from a bunkhouse that was solid as a rock and somewhat comfortable.

Tonight it'd be best anyway, because that way he'd know if anyone got up in the middle of the night. It'd also be quicker to get up at daybreak, so he could get everyone out of bed and, hopefully, dig out enough to get them to the Springs Hotel and to their aunt Edwinna.

But first things first, moving Sarah without scaring the wits out of her.

Not even becoming winded, Rand lifted Sarah into his arms and carried her to his bedroom.

Weighing little more than a young fawn, Sarah folded into him and slipped her arms around his neck. "Thank you," she whispered. She smelled sweet and innocent and oh so welcome in his arms. The warmth of her words and the feel of her body against his caused unexpected sensations to rush through him, settling somewhere just as unexpected.

Getting her settled in, he covered her with one of his mother's quilts. Oh, how he was tempted to take advantage of her and see if her skin was as soft as he imagined and her lips as yielding as he figured they'd be, but he chastised himself for even the bastardly thoughts.

The way he was feeling right now, one touch could stir up emotions he was determined to never feel again—not with a woman that wasn't his wife. Maybe he needed a long walk in the snow to put out the fire raging in him.

Reality set in. For all Rand knew, Sarah could be a married woman. Edwinna had only referred to her as her niece and the children as the twins. There was nothing in her appearance that screamed married—no wedding ring, but she wasn't wearing widow's weeds either. Sarah seemed much too proper to have children and not be wed.

Rightfully, the whole issue should have been moot to him.

By morning, if the weather cooperated and he could dig out, Sarah Callahan and the twins would be safely out of his life . . . and out of his bed.

Chapter 6

Somewhere between midnight and sunrise, Rand rolled over on his side and looked out the open door into the kitchen. Light flooded the room. It was early, very early. Long before sunrise. It'd been a while, but he recognized the weather phenomenon he knew as whiteout, where heavy snow turned night into day.

Be it a one-inch or one-foot snowfall, nobody with any smarts about them would venture out, because they could get turned around in a heartbeat and never find their way to safety.

There was no urgency to begin his day in this weather. Although there was a chill in the air, it wasn't as cold as he thought it might be. The fire needed to be tended to, but since the room was still fairly comfortable, he'd stay put and enjoy the warmth of his bed. He rolled to his back and pulled the covers over his chest.

Sleep had evaded Rand.

First, he worried that the children weren't warm enough, so he'd ventured upstairs to make certain they hadn't thrown their covers off. Then, of course, he'd stopped on his way back to check on Sarah, who was snuggled deep beneath the quilts. He'd added logs to the fire twice. Once back in bed, he tried unsuccessfully to get some sleep.

After what seemed like hours passed, Rand had pulled on his boots and a jacket to check on sounds coming from the livery. Finding nothing out of order, he returned to his bed figurin' that the dang mama cat that had a litter up in the hayloft was probably playing around upsetting the horses. He supposed her kittens were big enough to wean, although he hadn't seen hide nor hair of them. A family of felines was another thing he wasn't too keen on inheriting.

Rand couldn't remember the last time he had slept late. Typically, by the time the rest of the businesses opened their doors, Rand had already put in several hours of work. As far back as he could remember, a hard day's work never scared him. Even when he worked on the Waco suspension bridge and came home exhausted, with little rest, he was up and raring to go long before sunrise.

Taking a deep breath, he exhaled, relishing his memories.

That's when he sensed someone beside his bed. Generally, that would put him on full alert, even make him reach for his Colt, but this smelled of peppermint, probably coming from the supply of peppermint sticks he'd been saving for a while from bags of Arbuckle coffee.

He kept his eyes shut and tried not to move, although he could make out the twins between his thick eyelashes. Lying flat on his back, most likely all they saw was his beard, sideburns, and mustache, so what were the little tarts up to?

"Is he dead?" the tiny girl's voice said.

"Naw, he ain't dead," Damon said, barely above a whisper.

Rand felt pressure on the side of the bed as they leaned down on their elbows and used the mattress to support their chins. He could feel their minty breath against his cheeks.

"Bet he is, and now I won't get any warm milkth," Addie Claire said with tears in her voice.

"Don't begin that cryin'. He ain't dead."

"How do you know?"

"'Cause the hair in his nose is still movin'." They both leaned closer. "See, it's twitchin' around, so he ain't dead."

"How'd you know that?" Addie Claire asked.

"Saw a bear asleep one night, and he looked jest like that." Damon had obviously fabricated an explanation.

"But Mr. Frumpy isn't a bear."

"Nope, but there could be a bear under all his hair."

A bear! Heaven to Betsy!

Rand couldn't contain temptation. He let out a hearty "grrr," and sat straight up in bed, stretching his hands out in front of him.

The twins returned bloodcurdling screams, louder than anything Rand believed he'd ever heard out of such small mouths. He was pretty sure they stirred up dust when they leaped up and ran for the door.

Rand doubled up with laughter that echoed off the closed-in walls of the tiny room. He couldn't recall the last time he laughed so hard.

From the smell of coffee brewing, the day had begun, and it wasn't even sun-up yet.

"What in the Hades is going on?" Sarah appeared in the doorway with her hands on her hips. Addie Claire peeped from behind Sarah's calico skirt and Rand spied Damon's boots on the other side. Sarah protected her chicks like a mother hen.

Well, true to form, he'd sent more kids hidin' behind their mama's skirt tails, but this time they had a reason to be scared of him. Not on purpose, mind you, just something he couldn't resist doing.

From her red cheeks and her blond hair perfectly in place, he'd say Sarah had been awake for a while, so the screaming hadn't sent her scurrying down the stairs to see what was wrong with the children.

Sarah looked him up and down. When she realized he was in his drawer tail, she directed her attention away from him and onto the children, instructing them to go back into the kitchen.

"I'll be there in a minute," she said.

Once they were gone, Rand tossed the quilt back and stood up.

She ducked her head, as though she'd never seen a man in his union suit before; but then he'd imagine she'd probably never seen a man in first-thing-in-the-morning condition before either.

Rand grabbed for his pants and stepped into them. "Sorry if I upset the little ones. I was just funnin' with them."

"They aren't upset as much as scared." She looked down at him, now that he was sitting on the side of the bed putting on his boots. "Children scream at anything that surprises them, but you shouldn't have deliberately scared them."

"Well, they shouldn't have been lookin' at the hair in my nose." He ran his left palm over his thick beard. "All men have hair in their nose." He quickly changed the subject. It certainly wasn't appropriate for discussion between a man and a woman.

"I've got to go feed the animals." Rand snorted, a tad upset that she didn't see the humor in what he'd done. It'd been on a whim and out of character for him. He'd never been spontaneous, and now he knew why.

One thing was certain, the priorities of his day had just changed. A haircut and shave jumped to the top of his list. Unless a miracle happened, from the amount of light streaming in the window, they wouldn't be going to Sarah's aunt's hotel anytime soon, so he might as well not tempt the children to further investigate his facial hair.

"I'll make sure the twins play quietly and not bother you again." She pushed back a tendril of blond hair and tucked it back behind her ear. "I have coffee made."

"I can smell it," he replied in the only way he knew how: with a minimum of words.

She took a deep breath and shot him a polite, yet brittle smile. "The children's clothes are dry, so as soon as I can get our things together, we'll be ready to go to the hotel." She stiffened her back and squared her shoulders, obviously trying to show him there was no compromising. "I appreciate your hospitality and letting us barge in here, but I'll not bother you for breakfast. We can eat with—"

"The children need breakfast," he interrupted.

"I know how to take care of the children, and I think it's best we get out of your way as soon as possible. I didn't mean to be a burden on you." She swallowed hard. "The weather is something I had no control over."

He read in her voice . . . "And neither do you!"

"You're not going anywhere," he snapped much too quickly.

Sarah set her chin in a stubborn line and raised her eyebrow in surprise. He'd been too sharp, and he realized it.

Rand tried to soften his tone, which was somewhat like toning down the sound of an approaching steam engine. "If you've looked outside, you'd know we're smack-dab in the middle of a blizzard and nobody is going anywhere for a while."

"I should have realized that. I hope the train gets here with the Christmas bell," she said in a much friendlier voice. "The children were looking forward to hearing it ring on Christmas."

"Not likely. If it's as bad outside as I think it will be, it might be days before we can dig out."

To his surprise, he didn't see any disappointment in her eyes, rather a glimmer that he took as relief.

"I need to tend to the horses," he again said.

Rand swore she smelled of sugar and spice as he passed her, or was it the biscuits in the pan on the sideboard?

"Coffee sure will go good with those biscuits. There's a jar of jam in the cupboard." Stopping, he turned to her. "I don't know what kind of jam. Might be plum or chokeberry. And I meant what I said about making yourself at home. We're stuck together for a bit now, so as long as you and the kids are here, my home is yours." He stopped, and after giving his next statement a little thought, added, "Up in the bedroom where the twins slept, you'll find a trunk that belonged to my mama. There's knittin' needles and yarn, also some hand towels to stitch on, if you get bored."

"Thanks. Please don't let us be a bother, we'll be fine."

"You're no bother." Without looking back at her, he walked through the great room directly to the forge and added wood. He used the bellows to fuel the fire.

Flames leaped higher and higher.

Fuller and fuller.

Hotter and hotter.

He pumped the bellows as though they would relieve some of his frustration, but for once, it couldn't lay the blame on others. He'd now have to wallow in a mess of his own making.

The words of his father came to mind. "Doesn't matter how high the manure is, it's how even it's spread out in the end that counts." At the moment, Rand sure as hell had created a lot of manure for one man to handle.

For just a flash, Rand considered jumping into the roaring fire to see if he was as tough as he thought he was. He'd never been soft and cuddly, probably not as a baby, not as a companion, and certainly not as a husband.

He'd managed to handle the whole morning pretty dern lousy, but he'd reacted the only way he knew how—bossy and unyielding.

Fighting heat, smoke, flames, and noise for so many years contributed to his roughness, but nothing had prepared him to be snowed in with two kids and a gorgeous, strong-minded woman.

After he finished his chores, he'd go back in and drink coffee with Sarah and try to mend things with her, make her understand that what she saw was what she got with him. That is, if she hadn't already bundled up the children and sloshed their way to the hotel.

Rand reached for his apron, but an envelope caught his eye. It was weighted down by a pothook he'd made a few days before. He picked it up and read "Mr. Humphrey. Personal," written in what Rand could only describe as hen scratching.

Who would have left him a letter?

Just as he was about to open the envelope, a terrifying scream, as shrill as Rand had ever heard in his born days, echoed through the air.

Rand dropped the envelope and rushed to the great room where the commotion was coming from.

One word followed another scream . . . *FIRE!*

Chapter 7

Addie Clare's scream seemed to go on forever. Sarah's heart nearly jumped out of her chest and fright washed over her, yet she knew she wasn't nearly as frightened as the little girl.

"Fire!" Addie Claire stood in the doorway separating the great room from the blacksmith's shop staring at the ferocious fire in the forge. She covered her eyes with her arms. Trembling, she screamed, "Don't touch. Don't touch or you'll burn up, too."

Damon appeared out of nowhere. "A bear cain't be burned up."

Addie Claire pounded her brother on the chest. "He can, too." Tears rolled down her cheeks, landing on her blouse, while her little fists continued to hit at her brother.

Sarah took Damon by the shoulders and squatted down to be on his level. "Leave your sister be." She swatted him on the backside and he scurried off.

She quickly turned to the little girl and took her into her arms. "It'll be all right, Addie Claire. I promise."

Addie Claire sank into Sarah's arms and rested her head on her shoulder. Tears soaked through Sarah's blouse. "Mr. Frumpy might get burned to death," she cried.

Sarah pulled the little girl to her and rocked the child until she settled down a bit.

Things happened so quickly that Sarah didn't even notice Rand had left his post at the forge and rushed to their side. He now squatted down beside Sarah.

"Hey, little lady," he addressed the child. "The fire won't hurt anybody, as long as you are careful and know how to handle it. It can be your best friend or your worst enemy."

"It hurts you to death." She looked up for only a second before burying her face again in Sarah's arms.

While she respected the fact that Rand was experienced and comfortable around fire, he wouldn't understand why Addie Claire was so terrified unless he knew what she had gone through.

Since Sarah and the children would be leaving Kasota Springs as soon as the snow subsided and would probably never see Rand again, there was no need to explain anything to him.

The little girl stopped shaking and dried her eyes on Sarah's sleeve before she looked up at Rand.

Sarah followed her gaze up to the giant of a man, and by the expression on his face she considered that he just might have a heart as big as his frame and understand much more than she first thought.

"Little lady, how about coming with me and I'll show you and your brother what a blacksmith does?"

She looked over at Sarah. "Can I, Mummy?"

Sarah nodded approval. The child didn't need to go through life being scared of fire, be it a candle or a blaze in a forge. Rand seemed genuinely concerned.

"Go get your brother and meet me in the shop, and I'll let you touch some of a blacksmith's tools."

Addie Claire looked at him in a leery way before she scampered off yelling, "Bubba, Bubba."

Rand pulled to his feet. "While she gets him, I'll bring in your bags. They are in the shop."

Sarah exchanged a smile with Rand. "Thank you. You haven't eaten breakfast."

"I'll eat extra dinner, then." Beneath his scraggly beard and mustache, a boldly handsome face smiled warmly down at her. "I'm sorry she got scared."

"It's not your fault." She tugged at the threadbare apron around her waist. "Are you sure you have time to mess with the children?"

"From the looks of the weather, all we have is time." As though he suddenly realized he was exposing his venerable side, he set his jaw and let a half frown form on his face.

Turning from her, he walked away.

In short order, Rand returned with her bags and took them upstairs.

The twins met Rand at the foot of the stairs and followed him into his shop.

Sarah smiled to herself. No doubt the children were in good hands, and she'd better get busy fixing some dinner. The chicken and dumplings were nearly gone, but there was enough for a noonday meal. She'd nosed around earlier and found plenty of supplies to prepare supper.

Before she did anything, she had to change out of her day-old traveling suit into something more suitable. She went upstairs and, after locating her trunk Rand had left, dressed in a brown calico day dress accented with red and trimmed in ivory lace. She touched a sprig of mistletoe Addie Claire had pinned on the lapel before leaving Carroll Springs, then tied on a red apron she had sewn especially for the holidays. That made her feel more festive, but what she saw next ruined the moment.

The small bag carrying the children's Christmas presents

was nowhere in sight. She knew for certain she'd left Carroll Creek with it, but apparently somewhere along the way, it'd been misplaced or lost.

How was she going to explain to the children that there would be no Santa that year?

With disappointment weighing heavy on her heart, she went back to the kitchen. It would work out somehow, she just knew it. There would be Santa, but how? Maybe the weather would break and she could buy some things from the local mercantile. After all, it was two days before Christmas. Surely Mother Nature would cooperate. Surely.

Sarah pulled a bowl from the cupboard and sifted flour in it. She deliberately switched her thoughts to Rand. She'd never been so smitten by a man in her life. She shuddered. Of all the complications she didn't need right now, a man's attention topped the list. She'd come twenty-five years without one, and now wasn't the time to fix what wasn't broken. She'd been caring for the children just fine without anyone else's help.

Her thoughts wandered from one thing to another for a while before settling on just how secure she'd felt the night before when Rand had taken her upstairs and put her to bed. Although she had been so exhausted that she'd barely responded, she recalled enjoying being in his arms and wished it had been longer.

In a state between sleep and being awake, she had snuggled deep against his hardened chest, and her head fit perfectly in the hollow between his shoulders and neck where she could feel the beating of his heart. Rand had smelled of leather and outdoors in a manly way.

Just remembering last night set her heart to racing.

Enthralled in her thoughts about Rand, she forced herself to focus on the task of making bread for supper.

Remember, Sarah, you do not need or want a man in your life!

Rand wasn't exactly sure he could convince the little girl that fire was something to respect but not be scared of, but he'd do the best he could. No doubt something had happened in her life to make her so terrified of the flames.

Damon rushed over to a sledgehammer leaning against the wall. Although he could pick it up, he couldn't lift it high enough to do any damage. He grunted and tried to lift it up again, but failed.

"That hammer weighs somewhere around thirteen pounds, so you'll have to grow up a bit, tadpole, before you can sling one over your shoulder," Rand said.

"I'm big enough." Damon grunted and tried it a third time before allowing Rand to pick up the hammer and return it to where it belonged.

Rand stepped over to the worktable and put a file and ball-peen hammer in their proper places.

Addie Claire's gaze never left the fire, but after a while she turned her attention to what Rand was doing, then said, "Mr. Frumpy, I can't see."

"Mr. Humphrey," Damon corrected her.

"That's what I said . . . Mr. Frumpy." She stomped her feet in a show of frustration with her twin brother.

"Just a minute and I'll see what I can do," Rand said.

He considered letting the children stand on a crate, but they might fall and get hurt. He couldn't take the chance on that happening, so he cleaned away some of the soot from the table.

Picking them up one by one, he set them on the bench, letting their legs hang off the side.

For only a second a thought flashed across his mind. He should be lifting his own child up onto the table and teaching him the craft of blacksmithery.

He sloughed off the thought.

A child of his own wasn't meant to be.

"It's sorta dark in here," Damon complained. "I cain't see good."

"It's necessary, so I can cipher the temperature of the iron by its color."

"You cain't make much more than horseshoes," the little boy remarked.

"I make a lot of things people need besides horseshoes. Pots, kettles, and ladles to cook with. Farming equipment, latches, nails, and hinges." Rand put away the remainder of the hand tools. "All sorts of things."

"Betcha cain't make a big ax, big enough to kill a bear," Damon continued to rattle on.

"Don't know that I'd want to go after a bear with an ax, but I can make about anything," Rand responded.

"Betcha cain't," the little boy challenged.

"Bet I can," Rand replied.

The test was on, with Damon rapid-firing items he was determined a blacksmith could not make.

Rand countered on every thing . . . so far.

"Christmas tree?" Addie Claire said.

That stumped Rand, but only for a second. "I'm not sure that I can, but—"

"You told us you could make anything," Damon interrupted.

"And decorations, please." Addie Claire piped up.

Pish-posh! Rand had told the children he could make anything, but anything didn't include a Christmas tree and ornaments.

Now what in the heck was he to do?

Rand was a man of his word, so in order to stay that way there was only one solution—he had to come up with a Christmas tree for the children. A task that wasn't as simple as it seemed.

Chapter 8

Sarah finished kneading the bread and placed the dough in a crockery bowl to rise, covering it with a tea towel.

She felt odd having nothing to do, something that rarely happened to her, but with the snowstorm raging and Rand to ramrod the children, she had a little bit of time before she needed to heat the leftover chicken and dumplin's for their noon meal.

The idea of sitting quietly and reading *A Tale of Two Cities* to pass the time away was appealing, but doing some handiwork actually sounded like fun. She could use the distraction; and hopefully, the busywork would ease the nervousness that crept over her for allowing the children out of her sight for so long and not being there to protect them. No telling what might be lying in wait for them in the shop and livery. An animal could step on them or they could fall. The mother cat could bite them, and God only knew what types of varmints lived out there.

It didn't take her long to locate the trunk and discover what she presumed to be Rand's mother's hidden treasures, especially an exquisitely pieced quilt top she recognized as

Grandmother's Flower Garden. A needle was threaded in the last square that had been stitched; or at least Sarah presumed that she'd done the sewing, since Rand said the trunk held some of his mother's handiwork.

Finding a thimble and a spool of thread, Sarah lit the kerosene lamp beside the bed and moved to the rocking chair. Time passed quickly as she worked away on the project. Since it had already been partially stitched, if Sarah focused, she possibly could have the quilt finished before Christmas Day. What a perfect thank-you gift to Rand for his hospitality during the blizzard.

Unaware of how long she'd worked, Sarah stopped to check the time. Two hours had flown by, and not only did she need to prepare a noon meal, but she was certain the children's presence had worn thin on Rand.

She hurried down the stairs into the kitchen. After pouring two cups of coffee, she crossed the great room to the blacksmith's shop and came to a sudden halt.

Where were the children? Searching the room with her eyes, she was unable to see or hear them. They must be missing! Her heart skipped a beat.

"Where's Addie Claire and Damon?" Sarah almost demanded.

Rand lifted an item out of the fire and walked to the anvil. "Up in the loft playing. I had to do some work in order to make a frame for a Christmas tree," he said, as though it was part of his regular duties to cast such an item.

She took a deep breath, but that still didn't relieve the uneasiness she felt with the children being unsupervised. "A metal Christmas tree?"

"Yep. The kids wanted one and challenged me, so I have

to live up to my word. Don't worry, there's nothing up in the loft except hay and a stray mama cat and her kittens. They can't get hurt up there."

"I'm, um, not so sure." She hesitated, feeling her ever-present need to protect the children slack up a tad. "Thanks for letting them help you, but I'm uncomfortable with them up in the loft alone."

"Sarah, they're fine. Just doing what kids do. You needed some rest, and they got bored a little faster than I thought they would." He bent the iron into a dome shape before stepping toward the forge and setting it in the slack bucket. "Are you a double-fisted drinker today or is one of those for me?"

"Coffee's for you." She sat a cup on the worktable. "I'm sure you're famished, so I'll go pull together a noon meal." She took two steps toward the great room before turning back to Rand. "Are you certain the children are safe?"

"Don't be so protective of them, Sarah. You'll smother the kids. They need to be free to explore and learn things on their own. Getting banged up is part of growing up. I can hear everything from down here."

"You know nothing about what my children need."

A muscle flicked angrily at his jaw. His expressive face changed and became almost somber. Removing the piece he was working on, he said, "I hear them coming now."

Damon appeared first, pulling a length of barbed wire formed into a ball. Hot on his heels, Addie Claire let out one wail after another.

Sarah rushed to her. "What are you doing with that wire? It'll cut your hands to shreds if you're not careful. Put it down right now!" She almost yelled at the little boy while squatting down to Addie Claire's level to comfort her and soothe away the tears.

Addie Claire shook her shoulders, as though shaking off her pain. Her tears dried up as quickly as a creek in a drought. She lifted her hands palm up for Sarah to show off the blood prickling up from several scratches. "See," she said, as though they were warrior injuries.

"Got the wire off a sleepin' bear," said Damon proudly. "And the bear almost bit off Sissy's hand. Cain't you see the claw marks?"

"Well, I suspect you didn't get the barbed wire off any bear—sleepin' or not. Figure you found it up in the loft where my helper Timmy stored it thinkin' it might be useful someday." Rand folded his thick arms across his chest and frowned down at the children. "But it gives me an idea on how I can use it to make a Christmas tree."

In unison they chanted, "We're gonna have a Christmas tree. Gonna have a Christmas tree." Addie Claire jumped to her feet, and the twins grabbed one another and danced a circle around their mother.

Suddenly, Addie Claire pulled away and shook her hands, "Hurts, Bubba." Peering up at Sarah, she said, "Kiss my ouchy away, Mummy."

Sarah pulled the child into her arms and kissed her little hands. Seeming happy her scratches were healed, the child scampered away, saying, "I wanna see what Mr. Frumpy is doing."

"Mr. Humphrey," Sarah corrected the child, who only shot a withering look back to her before joining Rand at the slack bucket.

"That's my girl. You're tough, little lady," Rand said.

"Addie Claire, come with me so I can tend to those scratches," Sarah ordered before adding, "I'm going to fix you all something to eat. Damon, go clean up any mess you made and don't dally. You both need to wash up and get ready to eat and take a nap. You're both dirty as little pigs."

"And as happy as ones playing in slop," Rand added, a tad too condescending for Sarah's liking.

Damon aggressively tackled his cleanup project, picking up pieces of paper they had played with. Before she knew what was happening, he ran toward the forge and tripped, but not before he managed to toss the scraps into the flames . . . along with an envelope.

Rand caught the little boy by the seat of his pants and pulled him to his feet.

She gasped at the thought of what might have happened if he'd fallen into the hearth.

Turning to Sarah, the big man said, "Take a deep breath. He's fine, although I wish he hadn't tossed in that envelope since I hadn't read whatever was in it."

"Damon, apologize to Mr. Humphrey," Sarah ordered.

"No need. It shouldn't have been on the floor. If it was anything important, they'll send another one," Rand said.

She knew she was frowning at Rand for making light of something that could have been a serious injury, not to mention Damon needed to apologize. However, since Rand had reasoned things away, she could hardly require Damon to say sorry for something Rand didn't seem all that concerned over.

"I've got some lanolin right here that'll work." Rand directed his comments to Addie Claire, then picked up a tin can and opened it. "To make your mommy happy, let's put on some of this."

The child followed Rand's instructions, and in no time wore the gooey, smelly stuff like a big girl.

Taking in a deep breath, Sarah studied Rand before she shot him a look of disapproval just in case he'd missed the first one. She returned to the kitchen still concerned the children could have been seriously harmed, yet finding it strange that she knew Rand wouldn't allow that to happen.

Why couldn't it stay like last night forever?

For whatever reason, he was so grumpy and unyielding to her, while almost acting fatherly to the children. Her heart skipped a beat at her thoughts.

Fatherly! Jumpin' Jehoshaphat!

On second thought. . . . How dare Rand tell Addie Claire to come to him when Sarah had made it clear she wanted the little girl to go with her to treat her scratches?

Rand had just taken over, ignoring her wishes.

Howling wind and snow assaulted the windowpane, causing it to rebel with a concerto of rattles and bangs, somewhat like the storm brewing inside Sarah.

She inhaled and exhaled twice, trying to corral her thoughts. Nobody had been there for the children but her since they were born, and they didn't need a hero now. She hated to admit it, but she probably felt a bit threatened. Was it that obvious that the need to protect the children shrouded her like widow webs masked pain?

Sarah couldn't recall ever being as frustrated with a man in her whole life. Not even her father. Rand agitated her in ways that he must deliberately set out to do. Why in heaven's sake hadn't she gone on to the hotel with her aunt when she had the opportunity? If she'd had any inkling what an unpredictable man Randall Humphrey was, she might have put up with her aunt Edwinna's antics in lieu of imposing on him.

Why question her decision now? But then she'd been questioning every decision she'd made for a while; however, the one thing she had never questioned was her decision involving the twins. No matter how hard her parents and others around her pleaded, she'd stuck to her guns. She knew she'd done the right thing in keeping the babies, regardless of how

hard it had been on her or what persecution she had to face
from some of the Bible-thumping citizens of Carroll Creek
for being an unmarried woman raising two children alone.

"That was yesterday and this is today," she whispered.

Once the weather lifted, Rand would be out of their lives,
and she couldn't allow them to become attached to him . . .
nor should she.

About an hour later, after having eaten and Sarah having
put the children down for their afternoon nap, Rand sat at the
kitchen table and watched as she poured him a second cup
of coffee. He mustered up a thank-you, which seemed to fall
on deaf ears.

Although he had tried to make conversation during the
meal, Sarah suddenly seemed cold and aloof to him, exchanging only necessary pleasantries while hovering over
the children like a mama jaybird protecting her nest. She
made sure their every need was met before they even recognized they had one.

Of course, he'd seized the opportunity to mull over what
had happened to his half brother and why he'd taken Jughead when there were a dozen healthy horses there to steal.

Rand would never admit it, but he had finally concluded
there had to be a reason, and Jim Crockett was not involved
in the theft of the money for the children's home.

An idea struck Rand. Once the weather improved, he'd replace the missing money, but nobody—absolutely nobody—
would know. He could clear Jim's name while helping the
children.

Humbug, hellfire and brimstone, surely Sarah's children
hadn't succeeded in weakening his resolution to keep his
heart closed to anything or anybody who could hurt him again.

One thing was certain, he'd be glad when Sarah was out of his hair; but when she left, so would the children. He didn't relish the idea, and definitely wouldn't own up to it if he got between a rock and a hard place.

Sarah returned the pot to the stove with a thud, drawing his attention back to the moment. After placing the plates in the sink, she picked up the dishcloth and began washing glasses and silverware.

Rand drank his coffee but couldn't keep his gaze off her. He ran through the events of earlier in the day and couldn't figure out what she was so put out at him about, except that he'd allowed the children to go up to the loft unsupervised.

That was it . . . she was angry because she didn't think he'd taken good enough care of the little ones.

He needed to clear the air with the stubborn and very beautiful woman washing dishes in his house.

Drawing to his feet, impulsively, he jerked up the tea towel and picked up a spoon. He wiped it dry.

"Sarah, I don't know what in the blue blazes I did to get you so out of humor with me, but it wasn't intentional, and if you're waiting on an apology for something I don't even know what I did, it'll be a cold day in hell before it'll happen." He set the spoon down on the counter with a clang.

"Sorry you feel that way, but I don't owe you or anyone else an explanation for how or why I feel the way I do." With a quivering lip, she turned to face him.

"I can see you're more like your aunt Edwinna than I first thought." He immediately hated himself for lashing out at her.

"I'm nothing like my aunt!"

Now, that was certainly the pot preaching to the kettle, since I've been compared all of my life to my rascal of a father!

"I'm sorry. I shouldn't have said that." He threw the towel down. Never turning his gaze away from Sarah, he continued, "I'm going back to work, so if you want to talk about what's eatin' on you, you know where to find me. Got a Christmas tree to make for the children."

"You mean *my* children," she corrected.

Fury flashed through him. She'd confirmed his fear. She really didn't trust him to be left alone with the children. It wounded him deep down inside. If only she knew how he hurt every day because he had so much love in his heart for the child he was never able to lay eyes on, much less hold in his arms.

Maybe he'd lost focus of the fact that Sarah's children weren't his, only the same age as his own, if the child had lived.

Rand stormed out and spent the next few hours working in his shop, drawing, shrinking, bending, and upsetting iron over the bright cherry heat until he'd formed a star, several round ornaments he figured represented balls, and two small bells that would eventually hang from his makeshift Christmas tree.

Deep inside he wanted to shed the whole charade of trying to celebrate the holiday. He could always 'fess up to the children that he didn't know how to make a Christmas tree, but something inside wouldn't allow him to seriously consider that as an option, since it wasn't true.

It wasn't his pride at having already told them he could make anything that halted him.

It wasn't their challenge.

It was simply his heartfelt desire to show the children that he wasn't a big, bad bear, plus a need to please Sarah, which was a fairly foreign feeling to him.

All he wanted was to make the best of a bad situation and provide Christmas for the little tykes.

Yet way down in his soul, he recognized it wasn't just the twins and Sarah he wanted to make happy—but Rand, a man who had a heart overflowing with unleashed love.

Changes had to take place, and he'd be the first to make them.

Chapter 9

Tears welled up in Sarah's eyes, and she leaned against the counter to support her shaky legs.

What had she done? From the look on Rand's face when he stormed out, there was no doubt that she'd alienated him because of her own insecurities. Why couldn't she let anyone in? Was she that scared of getting hurt? Or was she that scared of hurting someone else?

Moving to the table, she covered her face with her hands, determined not to cry. His comments hit hard. She'd been morally judged about her decision to not put the children up for adoption and to keep them for so long that she'd become obsessed with any possibility of losing them. But why should a well-intentioned man like Rand have to pay the price for what others had done?

After composing herself, she went upstairs to check on the children. Finding them fast asleep, she sat in the rocking chair and began working on the quilt. Absorbed in her own thoughts and stitching away, time passed quickly.

"Mummy," Addie Claire mumbled. "Gotta go find Mr. Frumpy." She yawned.

Sarah didn't bother to correct the pronunciation of Rand's last name. "I think it's best that you and your brother play upstairs for the rest of the afternoon. Mr. Humphrey has a lot of work to do."

"But Mummy . . ." The child trailed off, likely realizing she shouldn't argue with an adult.

Sarah kept them entertained making some ornaments for the tree out of yarn. They were rather primitive, but kept their little fingers busy and corralled where Sarah could supervise them like she thought they needed.

Maybe she was overly protective?

Rand might well be right; children needed room to investigate and explore, and she was smothering them.

Had she always viewed the kids as being her possession, instead of a gift loaned to her by the Good Lord?

A new perspective flooded over Sarah. She had taken on not only the responsibility of raising the children, but of sharing them. Whether Rand was in their life on a temporary basis or not, she should not withhold the opportunity for them to get to know the blacksmith and let them learn a little about his trade, while celebrating the joy of Christmas.

Sarah set the quilt aside. "Children, let's go downstairs. How about making some cookies and maybe even gingerbread men to hang on the tree?"

Addie Claire and Damon jumped to their feet and shrieked of happiness so loud that Sarah was afraid Rand would come running to see what was wrong.

"Let's go wash your hands and I'll gather up things to bake with." Sarah scurried to the kitchen with the children close behind.

In short order, she had the bread for dinner ready to bake, then mixed cookie dough. Using a glass for a cutter, she formed several cookies, added extra sugar, and tried to talk the kids into believing they were balls for the tree.

"I'm tired of makin' plain ol' cookies," Damon whined. "Cain't you make an angel or something else?"

After several attempts to cut freehand angels, Sarah sighed in defeat.

"Those cain't be angels," Damon spouted. "Can you make a bear instead?"

"I'm sorry. I'm not very good at making angels out of dough, but I tried," Sarah said, then added, "So a bear is out of the question."

"Betcha you could if you had a cutter that looked like one," Damon said. "One shaped like a bear."

"I know. I know." Addie Claire jumped off the chair she was standing on and headed toward the shop. "Mr. Frumpy can do it. He can make anything."

Damon joined his sister before Sarah could wipe the flour off her hands. Rand was much too busy to deal with their request for a cookie cutter.

Hopefully Rand had gotten over his annoyance with her, but he still didn't need the children to be underfoot when he had work to be done.

She caught up with them about the time they got to the shop, but came to a sudden stop. The sight before her took her breath away.

The metal tree frame she had seen Rand working on earlier had come to life at his hands. Strands of barbed wire created a beautiful and impressive Christmas tree that stood about the same height as the twins. The blacksmith had worked small pieces of metal into the shapes of balls and bells, then had added accents of a silvery metal, making them look festive and decorated.

"Rand, that's beautiful," she said.

He rubbed his hands on his heavy black apron and studied the tree. The warmth in his smile echoed in his voice. "Thanks. It turned out better than I imagined it would."

Both children ran to the tree and began examining it.

"But there's no angels," Addie Claire proclaimed, while touching every ornament one at a time.

Before Rand could explain why there were no angels, Damon pulled a work stool close to Sarah and climbed up on it, then piped up and said, "And bears. Cain't have angels without bears. Big ones, too."

Rand stepped over to where Sarah stood and under his breath said, "Are you sure they are twins?" Before she could answer, he continued, "There's no way Addie Claire survived nine months in the same womb with her brother. He would have driven her to an early birthing to escape him, I suspect."

Sarah peered up at him and saw a softening to his face, yet an unspoken pain was alive and glowing in his eyes. His smile weakened a little when he noticed her watching him.

"Memories?" Sarah wanted to put her hand on his arm but refrained, not wanting to pry, plus she had her own memories she wasn't ready to share with anyone . . . especially Rand.

"We all have 'um." Rand seemed to shake off whatever thoughts were going through his head, and changed the subject. "Something smells really good."

"Cookies," she said.

"Bears!" Damon cried, jumped from the stool and headed for the loft with his tagalong sister. "I see the bears."

Sarah opened her mouth, then clamped it shut, remembering Rand's warning about stifling the children, but it didn't help relieve the fact that her heart was in her throat seeing them climb the ladder to the loft.

"Kittens," Rand said in a matter-of-fact way. "Think he's found the kittens and calls them bears," he said with a trace of amusement in his voice. "Might be 'cause I taught them the nursery rhyme Fuzzy Wuzzy the bear."

"I see." She tried not to stare at him, but failed miserably. "Don't worry about making any cutters, I can manage."

"It's a challenge, and I told them—"

She finished his sentence, "That you can make anything!"

He nodded.

"Gotta keep a promise. I've got an idea. It'll take me a little bit, but I think I can do it."

"Make an angel?" Sarah asked.

"No, a bear," he said. "Remember, Fuzzy Wuzzy was a bear?"

"Fuzzy Wuzzy had no hair," she said. Then he added, "Fuzzy Wuzzy wasn't fuzzy," before she finished with, "Was he?"

They shared a good hearty laugh.

She stole another glance at his profile and stayed focused just a little too long on the seductive looks buried behind all of his facial hair, thinking he might favor a big, lovable bear on the outside, and decided he must have a heart as big as his physique.

"I, uh . . ." Sarah hesitated, confused with the thoughts that stampeded through her mind. "I need to check on the bread."

Hastily, Sarah turned around to leave and caught her foot on the stool Damon had moved next to her.

Rand grabbed her from behind, his arms locking around her waist to keep her from falling. He was so close she could feel the heat and strength from his body. His breath hot against her ear, he whispered, "I've got you. I'm not going to let you fall."

Turning her around, he gathered her into his arms and held her snugly. Surprised at her own eager response to his body against hers, she relaxed, sinking into his cushioning embrace, and had no desire to have him release her.

His lips brushed against hers as though by accident, but suddenly he gently covered her mouth, pressing his lips hard against hers. A delightful shiver of wanting ran through her as she responded, enjoying his kiss much more than she should. Wrapped in invisible warmth, she seemed to be drifting along on a cloud while her heartbeat throbbed in her ear.

Suddenly, Rand pulled back and tucked a couple of wayward curls behind one ear, then placed a light kiss on her forehead. "I'm not sure this is a good idea."

Her heart screamed that she wanted another kiss, while her mind reminded her it wasn't the right thing to do. With confused thoughts, she could only whisper, "Very bad idea."

Rand released her, setting her on her feet, but looked down at her with a smoldering flame in his eyes. "But if you ever—"

"I won't." She rushed out of the room.

Once out of sight, Sarah leaned against the wall, perplexed at the burning, aching need running through her body. She wanted, desired another kiss and longed for the protectiveness of his arms.

She crossed her arms and pressed her palms against her chest. Closing her eyes, she rested her head against the wall and whispered, "He wouldn't understand that I've never been with a man."

Chapter 10

Rand returned to his project with a new lease on life. He was still trying to figure out why he suddenly had a new-found way of thinking about a woman—not any woman, but Sarah Callahan. He took a deep breath. His promise to never have feelings for another woman surfaced again; but when he had least expected it, Sarah came into his life.

Came into his life! Had he gone soft in the noggin? She was only temporarily in his life because of circumstances. In a few days she'd go back to Carroll Creek and he'd never see her again.

The thought knotted his gut. Did he really want her to leave? In only a matter of days, she and the children had made a huge difference in lifting the darkness that he'd grown accustomed to. They gave him a renewed purpose and joy. So what would the future be like when they were gone? He wasn't sure he wanted to find out.

He thought back on the kiss, which was totally out of character for him. Oh, he'd kissed women before, hell, lots of 'um, but there was something innocent and special in the way Sarah responded. Almost as if it was a new experience for her, which of course was ludicrous, since she had born two children.

Picking up a piece of cooling metal from the slack bucket, he began bending and shaping it with pliers.

I'd sure like to kiss her again to see if my notions are way out in left pasture or not!

The pliers slipped and he slashed himself on the sharp metal. Not a big cut, just enough to bring blood. He wiped it off with his handkerchief.

How in the blue blazes had he worked all these years as a steel worker and blacksmith and never gotten seriously hurt, yet since Sarah had walked into his life, he'd managed to bang himself up twice? All because of having the sensual, tempting lady on his mind. If he wasn't more careful, he might end up chopping his nose off to spite his face, and that'd put him in one mell of a hess.

As he worked, the aroma of supper wafted through the air and the sounds of children's play filtered down from the loft. A concerto of giggles, whispers, and cries of happiness melded together, adding to the blacksmith's contentment.

How could two children and a lady like Sarah change his mood from one of loneliness to being high-spirited in such a short time? He knew he hadn't been happy for a while, but never thought when it returned it'd come from such an unlikely source.

He was filing off the jagged edges of a cookie cutter that somewhat favored an angel, when he heard footsteps descending the ladder to the loft.

"Mr. Frumpy, we need some warm milkth, please." Addie Claire held a young, fuzzy kitten wrapped up in a threadbare printed flour sack. The animal rested on its back in the crook of her arm, purring like a newborn baby.

"I'll go get some milk—"

"Warm milkth, please," the little girl corrected him.

"Warm for sure, but guys, don't take the kitten out to the stables, because he's really little, and the horses might step on him accidentally," Rand warned. "He'll come out and pester them when he's big enough."

"What's their names?" Addie Claire asked.

"Ain't got no names," Damon responded. "They're horses."

Rand spoke up. "That big chestnut roan is called Bushwacker and the dapple gray gelding is Big Tex, and—"

"Them are all boy names," Damon spouted.

"You don't have any girls." Addie Claire looked up at him with sad eyes.

"Remember that pretty little bay with the black mane and tail? That's Spit Fire, and yep, she's a girl." He wanted so badly to add, "A pretty little gal, just like your mama," but resisted. Instead he said, "See, they all have names."

Spying a small woven basket, he walked over and picked it up. "Looks about right for a bed for him."

Addie Claire squealed with glee and placed her little charge inside and covered him up.

To Rand's surprise, the calico nestled deep into the fabric. He was certainly more tamed than his mama, although he imagined the poor critter was exhausted at being played with by the children.

Holding the basket close to her, Addie Claire leaned against the workbench and eyed the angel Rand had made.

Damon stepped to her side and looked over the angel cookie cutter that Rand had just finished. "That cain't be no angel. Don't look like one. Need a bear anyhow."

"Mr. Frumpy, we gotta have an angel for the top, please."

Rand studied what could be an angel, but possibly was a bear. It gave him a notion on what he could do. "You guys don't touch anything, and I'll be back in a minute with some milk for," he looked at the brown, black and orange splotched kitten, then added, "for Bear."

A plan continued to form. He could use his failed attempts at making a cookie cutter to create a large cone shape where he could add wings, creating an angel for the top of the tree. He wasn't sure whether he was more eager to make the ornament or eat dinner, but both promised to be worth the wait.

Rand grabbed the cookie cutter and headed to the kitchen, where he found Sarah elbow-deep in dough. Her cheeks were rosy from the kitchen heat. Oh, how he wanted to take her into his arms and kiss her, but on second thought, he probably had scared her silly when he did that earlier. Rubbing his beard, it occurred to him that she might not like the feel of all the hair on his face, which gave him a justifiable reason to refrain from making a fool out of himself—again!

"Try this." He handed the metal cutter to her. "I've got to get warm milk."

She looked up with strikingly beautiful blue eyes as bright as twinkling stars on a clear night. He couldn't resist temptation, and reached over and dabbed away a splotch of flour from her cute little chin.

"Thanks." An easy smile radiated across her face, and she raised a questioning eyebrow. "Milk with your cookies?"

"It's for Bear." He located a shallow dish from the cupboard and poured a tad of milk out of a small crockery pitcher Sarah was using to cook with. Then he added more, thinking maybe mama cat and the siblings might enjoy a little. "Sure glad Timmy managed to get some milk over here before the blizzard hit."

"So, you're now hand-feeding a kitten?"

"No, a bear." He shrugged in mock resignation.

Rand returned to the shop and gave the milk to the children, who immediately rushed up to the loft, dribbling liquid all the way.

It was time for him to check on the animals and break up any ice that had formed in the water trough.

Grabbing his sheepskin coat, he walked out into the open. The wind let out a mournful howl. Snow continued to fall, but there might possibly be more snow and less wind, so the worst could be waning.

With a little luck and a bunch of prayers, the train bringing the church bell from Boston could arrive in time for Rand to get it installed at the church. He mentally crossed his fingers because he really wanted to see the faces of the children when the bells rang on Christmas Eve.

Dang, what was wrong with him? He'd gone from praying for snow, so he could be left alone with his memories, to wanting to make them with someone, and it all seemed to be tied to the pretty lady in his kitchen baking cookies and making bread.

For the first time in a lot of months, he had a reason to shave. He grabbed a clean pan near the watering trough and dipped fresh snow out of a drift near the door to the livery. He took it to the forge and set it on the hearth. Once it melted, he'd use the water to shave. Or at least that was his plan.

Just as he neared the ladder to the loft, both children jumped down, and in no time they were beside him. "Whatcha got there, Mr. Humphrey?" Damon stood on tiptoes to see inside the pan he was holding. Rand had little doubt that the child knew exactly what he had.

Rand lowered it for them to see inside, and answered, "Snow."

"Can we eat some, Mr. Frumpy?" Addie Claire asked. Standing on tiptoes like her brother, she had to clutch a handful of the blacksmith's pants leg to keep from falling over.

"Sure can." Rand smiled to himself, recalling his mama making something she called iced cream out of fresh snow and milk. She probably added some flavoring, but that he wasn't sure of. Maybe Sarah would know.

"Gotta wear something warm to go outside or you'll freeze." Rand pointed to the coats hanging near the door.

With the help of the twins, he gathered a pail of snow. After returning their jackets to their proper place, they headed for the kitchen.

Sarah had finished baking the cookies and had cleaned up the mess, which he suspected was mostly made by the twins.

The savory aroma of stew and hot bread welcomed them, and the table was set for supper. In the middle sat a Mason jar filled with what he first thought was holly berries, but after a closer look he recognized it as the mistletoe Sarah had been wearing on her blouse earlier in the day. She'd added some greenery and a red bow tied around the neck of the jar.

"Mummy, Mr. Frumpy is makin' us some iced cream from snow." Addie Claire grabbed a chair and pulled it up next to Sarah at the table.

Sarah looked at Rand with amusement in her eyes, although a perplexed look crept across her face. "Iced cream?"

"It's something Mama used to make. Snow, milk, and some type of flavoring."

"Vanilla," she said in a nonchalant way and turned to the twins. "Tell you what. Supper is almost ready, so if you eat all of your meal and don't bother Mr. Humphrey, you can make some right after we've finished eating."

Although their supper was a meager pot of stew, consisting mainly of canned vegetables, and hot bread, Sarah felt as though she'd eaten from a banquet table fit for a king.

The children bantered with one another, and even Rand

joined in wiping broth from Damon's face. The big man told the kids that if a bear smelled food, he'll try to eat them. He turned to Damon and warned, "But a tadpole like you would only be a snack to a big bear."

As much as Sarah wanted to fuss at him about scaring Damon, she refrained.

After the table was cleared and the dishes were in the sink, she spooned off cream that had risen to the top of the milk and placed it in a bowl. She stirred in sugar and a tad of vanilla, then drizzled the mixture over bowls of fresh snow.

"Hey, tadpole and little lady, tonight is the day-day before Christmas, so let's have an iced cream picnic." Rand placed a spoon in each dish and handed them to the children before he grabbed up a handful of cookies and walked to the hearth.

"Wait just a minute. I need to go get something." Rand headed for the little room off the kitchen. Returning, he placed divinity that he'd purchased from the bazaar on top of the plate of cookies.

"Candy!" the twins yelled and snatched pieces of the sweet stuff before Rand even knew what had happened.

"I guess I had a premonition when I got some of Aunt Dixie's divinity from the bazaar yesterday."

Rand found a comfy spot on the rug and sat cross-legged close to the fire. Damon was quick to join him, while Addie Claire lagged, staying close to Sarah's side, alternating eating the sugary treat with iced cream.

The blacksmith elbowed Damon and kidded him about how much iced cream he was eating on top of candy. In turn the little boy tried to elbow Rand, but only managed to smack the bowl, causing it to tip. As quick as if he was handling red-hot coals with his bare hands, Rand caught the dish and licked the splashes of syrupy snow from his hands.

* * *

Sarah tried not to laugh out loud but failed miserably. Biting her lip, she studied Rand.

Rand threw back his head and smiled warmly at her before he let out a hearty laugh.

Addie Claire joined her brother and they rolled on the floor in hilarity, no doubt to impress their new buddy, who elbowed Damon again.

Peering back at Sarah, Rand shot her a mischievous smile, stoking a gently growing fire within her. A slender, delicate thread of understanding began to form between them.

He turned back and gathered the twins and tucked them, one at a time, under his arm and tickled them until they could no longer squeal.

As much as Sarah hated to separate the children from their newfound friend, she had little choice but to begin getting them ready for bed. It was later than they usually went down for the night, but as Rand said, it was the day-day before Christmas.

"Go put your bowls on the table. It's time for bed," she forced herself to say.

"Do I have to go, too?" Rand good-naturedly asked.

"You're a big man, and I think you're old enough to make a decision when you want to go to bed without my help." Sarah stopped before she added, *Indeed, a very big, forceful man, who sets my heart to racing just thinking about going to bed!* She drew in air, held it a second or two, then exhaled, praying her wayward thoughts had returned to their hiding place within her heart.

"Skedaddle, tadpole, and take little lady with you," Rand said as he drew to his feet.

The twins were halfway to the stairs when they whirled

around and ran back to him. Catching him by his pants legs, they both gave him a hug and in chorus, said, "Thank you for the snow."

He patted them on the head like little puppies. "You're welcome. Sleep tight." He limped back to the stairs dragging a kid on each leg. "Don't let a bear get you."

Sarah almost ran into them, but with a little nudging they released their hold on Rand and scurried upstairs.

"Thank you." She pulled up her skirt a tad to take the first step, then turned back to him. "I think I'll sit with them and tell them a story. Sleep tight, yourself."

She thought for a flash he just might kiss her, but he suddenly stepped back without taking his eyes off her. He seemed to be appraising her like she was a prize mare he was considering adding to his stables. He finally said, "I have some things to tend to before bedtime."

After dressing the twins in their nightclothes and brushing their teeth, Sarah let them help her thread yarn through the holes she'd put in the top of a few gingerbread men cookies that she'd brought upstairs earlier in the day.

Sarah tucked the children into bed, told them a story, and within minutes they were fast asleep. She put the cookies back in the box and set them aside. They were ready to put on the tree Rand was making.

Picking up the quilt to begin work, Sarah thought back on the last two days.

The children had enjoyed themselves and had experienced some of the best times they had ever had in their three years of life, and she'd felt relaxed and happy for the first time in a while. There had been no good-meaning citizen, with an overly active imagination and a burning need to protect the children, around. Nobody to question her decision to keep the twins. And certainly, no one to judge her.

The howling wind drew her attention to the small window. Outside, the snow danced around and seemed to have lightened up as the day had worn on. A sure sign that their time in Kasota Springs would come to an end before long, and she'd return to the nothingness of her life in Carroll Springs.

Sarah prayed for more snow.

Chapter 11

Reenergized and with some ideas on how to make a merry Christmas for Sarah and the children, Rand worked in the shop until way late into the night.

He stepped back and studied his creations. Pleased with himself, he could only visualize how the tree would look once it was decorated with the ornaments Sarah had told him about over supper. Rand could hardly wait to see the children's faces.

For the first time in a long time, he had a reason for being. And it was to make sure the children and Sarah had a Christmas.

Ambling into the great room, he immediately noticed light coming from underneath the door to the children's room. He presumed that Sarah had fallen asleep in the rocker and he relished the idea of picking her up like last night and taking her to his bed. Perhaps she was already in bed, and if so, he needed to turn down the lantern and check on the twins.

He climbed the stairs and, as he neared his mother's room, heard soft humming. Gingerly he knocked so as not to wake the children.

No answer. He eased the door open and halted in midstep

shocked to find Sarah sitting in the rocker with a quilt lying across her lap, humming softly.

Rand took a step backward and tried to control the rampart hammering of his heart. Inhaling deeply, he stared more at the quilt than Sarah.

The quilt in her lap! Not any ol' quilt, but the one that he kept stored in his mother's trunk . . . the cherished coverlet that he didn't plan on another woman touching.

Sarah peered up at him.

Setting his jaw, Rand clenched his fist, then took a deep breath before he was able to corral his thoughts enough to say, "Sorry, I didn't mean to disturb you."

His first inclination had been to rip the quilt out of her hands and light into her about touching something that wasn't hers. But his earlier words rushed in and tapped into his brain. He distinctly remembered telling her about some of his mother's handiwork stored in the trunk. And he hadn't lost sight of the fact that he had made it plain that as long as she was staying with him, his home was hers.

Sarah continued to stare at him. "That's okay." Before she could say anything further, Rand closed the door and headed for the stairs.

In a flash Sarah was by his side. When she touched him on his arm, he stopped in his tracks. "What's the matter, Rand?" Not giving him a chance to answer, she continued, "Did I forget to do something before I retired?"

He turned his head slightly. The fringe of her lashes cast shadows on her cheeks, and unwelcome tension loomed between them like the heavy drifts of snow outside the window.

In a broken voice, she said, "You're angry with me."

A lump came to his throat. There was actually a woman holding on to his arm who had done everything possible to please him since she came into his life, yet he was angry at her for something she didn't even know she had done.

"Just surprised that you were still up," he lied. "I was checking on the children."

Sarah grabbed the neck of her dressing gown in her fist, apparently feeling uncomfortable that he was staring at her in her bedclothes.

"I'm going back to work." He wasn't sure if his frustration was because she found the quilt or because he had a burning need to take her in his arms and apologize in a very physical way.

She frowned as if dealing with a temperamental child and placed her hands on her hips.

"Randall Humphrey! You're acting like a jackaninny! And you're *not* going to go hide from me every time a subject comes up that makes you feel uncomfortable." She took one step toward him, and with defiance etched on her face and a challenge in her voice, she said, "Not this time you won't."

Rand smiled inwardly at her outburst. She might well be right about him not wanting to discuss certain matters in his life, but he'd never run away and hide from it. Or had he?

Managing a meager smile, he hoped to ease the tension between them, but from the look in her eyes he'd failed miserably, so he turned and walked down the stairs.

After stoking the fire, Rand located a bottle of whiskey in the back of the pie safe. He grabbed a glass, then on impulse picked up another one. Intuition told him that Sarah wasn't finished with him.

No doubt she was not only as stubborn as a mule, but wouldn't be happy unless she had the final word. He could bet money that he wouldn't be drinking alone tonight.

Rand barely finished pouring two shots of Tennessee's finest when he heard Sarah's footsteps descending the stairs.

Looking up as she entered the kitchen, he noticed she had put on a light blue robe over her gown, which only emphasized the sparkle in her sapphire eyes.

"Aren't you going to pour a drink for me?" She eased in the chair opposite him.

He slid his glass to her, then commenced pouring three fingers in the other one for himself. "I didn't figure you for a two-fisted drinker, but more of a mint julep sipper." He kept his gaze on her as he belted back a pretty hefty slug, praying it would wash away the unadulterated desire for Sarah that burned below his belt. For some reason neither his heart, nor anything else in his body, was listening to the warning his brain gave.

To his surprise she took a healthy swig. Although he expected her to make a funny face, shiver, and upchuck, she didn't. She took a second swallow. "I haven't had any Black Jack in so long I'd almost forgotten how smooth it is."

"Now that we have the formalities out of the way, Sarah, I'm really sorry for making you think I was mad at you."

"Don't take me for a fool, Randall. I could see it on your face and in your eyes." Sarah finished off her drink and slid her glass to him for a refill. "It was the quilt, wasn't it?"

"No—not really." Rand dilly-dallied a little before he poured her no more than half an inch of whiskey.

Rand didn't offer her further explanation and changed the subject. "I looked everywhere I could think of for your missing bag and couldn't find it."

"It's okay. At first I was a little upset because it has Christmas gifts for the children in it. But we'll manage. They're young enough that they'd toss aside the toys to play with the wrapping paper and bows." Sarah pulled her robe closed and crossed her arms across her chest. "Addie Claire and Damon have never had much of a Christmas, so just being here will make it special."

Rand ached because of the sadness that seeped into her voice, making him more determined than ever that the twins would have a Christmas to remember.

As if frozen in time, not knowing what to say, they stared at one another. Sarah broke the silence. "It's time you tell me the truth, Rand. You were angry about the quilt, but why? I just thought it was so close to being finished that I could have it done and it'd be a nice surprise for you. I wanted to thank you for taking us in and being so patient with the children, and thought that'd be a way to do it. I'm sorry. I had no right to lay a hand on your mother's quilt without asking first."

"If you'll stop talking and take a breath, I'll answer some of your questions." He picked up the Jack Daniel's cap. "The quilt didn't belong to my mother."

Baffled, she blinked. "Not your mother's?"

Taking a deep breath helped him organize his thoughts. He considered whether there was a need for him to explain further, because it'd open up a hole in his heart and let out the pain and memories hidden so deep for so long. But if he didn't explain, Sarah would likely pry until he came clean.

"This will take a while, so I might as well fix us another drink before I begin. I have questions for you, too."

And he began . . .

"It's my wife's."

"You're married?" She barely spoke above a whisper.

"No. Not anymore. Dad, Mother, and I came down to Waco to work on the Waco suspension bridge project. Shortly after, my half brother, James Crockett who you know joined us. It wasn't long before I began courting Jenny. We married and I got her in the family way. I was pretty happy about becoming a father." His memories made him stop for a second or two. "My father got his leg mangled on the job, and it changed him. Jenny and the baby she carried died three years ago tomorrow—"

"Christmas Eve?"

He nodded. "Yes. She was going over to her mother's for dinner just a few miles out of town and I didn't want to go. Thought I was too busy, something I've regretted ever since. Dad was supposed to make sure her rig was in good shape and drive her over. I knew the axle needed repairing and took him at his word that he'd make sure it was done before they left.

"Later I found out that something came up and my father didn't take her, nor did he fix the carriage. Might've been a need for some pain relief, which seemed to always come with a woman attached to a whiskey bottle, but I don't know. Jenny was pretty stubborn and ended up driving herself without any of us knowing. Something must've spooked the horses, because they bolted. Her rig went off the road and she was thrown out." He inhaled deeply, and tried to stay strong enough to confront his memories out loud. "When she didn't return, I set out to her parents' place and found her. She was lying in a ravine, and there was nothing the doctor could do to save her or our baby." As much as he wanted to fall into Sarah's arms and cry until he had no more tears, he couldn't do that to her. "I never knew if the child was a boy or a girl."

"I'm so sorry, Rand. I had no idea." Tears welled in her eyes. "Then what did you do?"

"I quit my job and wandered until I thought the break in my heart had somewhat healed. But it hadn't. Since Dad wasn't fit to work anyways, we picked up stakes, and much to Mother's encouragement we came to Kasota Springs and set up shop."

"Did you build this building?"

"Sure did. Board by board. Stone by stone. And before you ask, I pretty much considered my life over with and had no desire to make friends. Mama made a lot of 'em, but she died a few months back. My father moved on to greener pastures, and I've tried to take care of Jim the best I know how."

"He was very nice and considerate of us."

"Considerate enough that he left you and the babies to walk to my place in the snow."

"I'm not sure what was going on, but right before we got in town a big cowboy met us on the road. I couldn't hear everything, but I did catch a few words. Jacks Bluff for one, and I think James called him Tegeler. They talked briefly about the storm coming and something about a bazaar in town, which I found odd. That was all I could hear with all the wind before the cowboy rode off."

"Then what happened?"

"He got us to the edge of town, gave me directions to your shop, and said he had something he had to do and drove off. I never saw him after that."

"He was here some time or another because he exchanged the horses and the rig for my mule, Jughead. Guess that answers one question."

So far, Rand had mixed feelings. He'd talked about something very personal that gave him a sense of relief, but at the same time he felt wounded by the account of James on the road. He would have had enough time to get to town and steal the money for the orphanage. That's the only reason he and Teg Tegeler would have discussed the bazaar. The foreman of the Jacks Bluff outfit had a reputation as a stand-up cowboy, so Rand figured he had nothing to do with what James was involved in.

Sarah ran her index finger around the lip of her glass. "Rand, I'm sorry that I forced you to talk about something so private. I'm truly sorry."

To Sarah's surprise, Rand looked up and she could almost see relief on his face. He smiled at her in a different way than he'd done before, so enduring and understanding.

"It helped to talk. That's probably what I needed long before now, but just couldn't bring myself to show the world anything but a headstrong, tough guy who didn't give a damn whether he was liked or not. It shielded me from having to care again; but Sarah, I have a notion you might well know how it feels. Are you married?" He stared straight in her eyes.

Tightness came to her chest. "No." That was all she could manage to say.

"No, not right now or no, never?"

"No, never." She felt tears choking her. "And please don't judge me before you hear all of the story." She hesitated, then said, "I'm not the twins' birth mother."

"You . . . how? You didn't kidnap them or anything like that?" He raised an eyebrow.

"No, of course not. The woman who gave birth to them was my cousin, niece to Aunt Edwinna. She worked as a saloon girl in Carroll Creek, and I think she delivered a little more to the customers than their drinks. She found herself expecting and couldn't care for the babies, so she gave them to me to care for. The next thing I knew Viola rode out of town with the first railroad crew headed west."

"So that's why you're so protective of them. You're afraid she'll come back and take them away from you."

"Something like that, but I didn't realize it until I met you. The kids never had a man around them, so I guess I was a little jealous seeing them drawn to you so quickly. I don't want them to get hurt when we have to go back and they won't see you again."

"Does Edwinna know any of this?"

"Some. I think she won't allow herself to believe that

Viola would ever have had a baby without being married and certainly couldn't even think about her walking away from them. I'm afraid my aunt may have talked me into coming here hoping to force me into putting the children in the orphanage and walk away, too. Or worse yet, she wants to take them away from me to raise herself. She thinks she's a more fitting mother."

Rand took a drink and leaned back in his chair. "That would explain a lot. The folks in Carroll Creek probably didn't think much of the situation, I suspect."

"You could say that. I certainly didn't receive any invitations for Christmas dinner. I couldn't have been ignored any more if I were a pot of rotten garbage."

"Temperance society, I've heard."

"Bible-thumpers, I call them. But I can handle their disapproval most of the time."

"What do you do for money to provide for the kids?" Rand didn't mince any words asking.

"I had a little saved up, and my parents left some in the bank when they had all they could stomach and packed up and left town. Then they withdrew the money and had it sent to them, but nobody at the bank will give me their address. So when I get back, I'll find a job. But don't judge Viola too harshly. At first I received a little money from her every now and again, but that eventually stopped. She must've forgotten where she left the children."

"So, everyone went on with their merry lives, leaving you and the babies behind." Setting his jaw, Rand seemed to make a statement rather than asking.

"I don't want to lose the children, Rand. That's one reason I was almost happy for the blizzard once I seriously considered the possibility that Edwinna might have a plan to take the children from me. I thought I could get back to Carroll Creek without seeing her again. That way she can't take them away from me. Even the folks back home aren't a overbearing and critical of me as she is."

"And why is Addie Claire so afraid of fire?"

Sarah really didn't want to answer, but she'd come thi far, so there was no reason to withhold anything from him She took a sip of her drink praying for courage. "A grou of mean-spirited folks set a prairie dog on fire in my yard But before I could shield the twins from what was happen ing, Addie Claire realized it was an animal. Although it wa just a big rodent, it was still a living creature. She's bee scared of fire ever since."

Rand stood and put his hands flat on the table. Leaning forward, he looked her square in the eye. "You're not goin back to Carroll Creek with limited funds and nobody t watch after you and the kids." A comfortable smile came t his lips as he said, "And nobody is going to take your kid from you. My home is yours. Sarah, you need me and I cer tainly need you and the children, so I don't want any back talk. You'll stay with me."

Sarah felt exhilarated, yet apprehensive, as she jumpe up to give him a hug of thanks.

Suddenly feeling light-headed, she rubbed her forehea and before she knew what was happening, her knees buck led and she fell into Rand's arm, mumbling, "Take care o the babies."

Chapter 12

Enjoying the early-morning hours of Christmas Eve, Rand sat at the kitchen table, drinking coffee. Amused, he smiled, thinking back over having to tuck Sarah in his bed two nights in a row. It could become a habit, one he didn't mind going on for a long time.

Daybreak peeked over the horizon, as if skeptical of showing its face after so many days blinded by snow. Today might well prove to be the first day of the rest of Randall's life—if he had his way.

Although Sarah hadn't accepted his offer to stay with him. He could be just as stubborn as the pretty lady, and he wasn't about to let her go home without a plan for survival. Finding a job, since undoubtedly nobody in town would be amenable in hiring her, was probably not going to happen. But even in the best scenario, who would care for the children during the day? Not many bosses would want two little ones hanging on to their mother's coattails on the job, and certainly no one would want to care for the children during the workday.

To him the issue was settled—she would stay in Kasota Springs, and not with her aunt either. However, he had an inkling Sarah's feelings weren't as etched in stone as his.

Before she and the children rose for the day, he had shaved and prepared some of the things he thought he needed to create a special Christmas they would all remember.

Rand began breakfast. While the bacon was cooking, he went to the great room and moved the table next to his chair over by the fireplace, then brought in the tree he'd made out of metal and barbed wire. He set the angel on top and took a moment to admire his creation. Not bad for an ol' grouch of a blacksmith.

Now, as soon as everyone was up, he'd go upstairs and locate two toys he had stored. Ones he'd gotten for his own child, be it a girl or a boy. One for each.

When he returned to the kitchen, Sarah stood in front of the stove, tending the meat and buttering bread. "Good morning." She looked up at him with eyes as clear as the Texas sky on a summer day. Sarah wore a red and green plaid dress trimmed in lace, making her look fit to be Santa's helper.

"Good morning. Sleep well?" Rand squatted down to fetch something unrecognizable under the table. "Hmm," he said, after examining the sprig, "Mistletoe—and where did that come from?"

It was as if Sarah hadn't heard him, but he wasn't about to let a great opportunity like this go to waste. "My dad taught me if you find a pretty lady under mistletoe, then it's your responsibility to see that she's kissed."

Sarah laid her knife aside and peered back up at him. The glow of her smile radiated across the room as she looked up to the ceiling over her head. "I don't see any mistletoe."

Rand stepped in front of her and held the mistletoe high over her head. "Oh, but I do." He dropped the sprig of greenery with red berries and pulled Sarah into his arms. Crushing her to him, he kissed her with all of his heart. Her lips were warm and sweet on his. As he roused her passion, his own grew stronger.

Youthful giggles floated through the air.

Startled, Sarah and Rand quickly parted to see the twins standing by the door with their hands over their mouths, snickering to high heaven.

Rand saved the day. "Come on, guys, there's nothin' to giggle about. I was gettin' the speck of bread crumb out of your mama's eye. She's fine. So let's go upstairs, get dressed, and when we get back, breakfast will be ready." He gave Sarah a wink.

"Hey, Rand, I see you shaved. It felt—looks much better." Then she added, "Thanks for the help with the kids. Breakfast will be ready shortly." Red-faced, Sarah returned to her chore.

Once alone, she buried her face in her hands, feeling the flush on her face. What did the children think? Had they bought Rand's explanation? She was totally mortified, yet thrilled with his attention.

And what daring good looks he had that morning. Since she first laid eyes on him, she could only visualize what she thought he looked like behind his heavy beard and mustache, but nothing prepared her for what truly existed underneath all the facial hair. She remained engulfed in his chocolate eyes—warm enough to melt her heart, which still beat out of control at the thought of how handsome he was, standing before her with mistletoe in his hand. The big, rugged man reeked of strength, tall and straight like a towering cottonwood.

Rand had put on a fresh white store-bought shirt that clung to rippled muscles, making her want to touch every inch of his powerful body. Passion set her body on fire at the image she planned to keep in her mind for a long time—maybe forever.

The sweetly intoxicating musk of his body wafting through the air didn't help her pounding heart to settle down an iota.

A few minutes later, Addie Claire appeared holding her clothes and said, "Dress me, Mommy."

Sarah's heart sang with delight at her little girl's words. "Did you say Mommy and not Mummy?"

"Mr. Frumpy taught me to say it right." She gave her mama a big hug.

Rand walked in about that time. "I helped her pick out clothes, washed her teeth, and sorta fixed her hair, but think it's best you dress her. I don't have much experience in that area." He took over scrambling the eggs.

Sarah felt a zing in her heart, and escorted her daughter into the little room off the kitchen and dressed her. She adjusted the crooked bow in her hair. At least Rand had tried.

It wasn't long until everyone sat at the kitchen table enjoying breakfast as they chatted about Christmas Eve. The kids squealed with excitement about their wait for Santa Claus. Trying to stay on a level they could comprehend, Sarah delicately explained that Santa couldn't go everywhere on Christmas Eve, but he'd get there as soon as he could. Her explanation didn't seem to deter their excitement in the least. That would give her some time to get some store-bought gifts for the kids from Santa.

A jar of chokeberry jam seemed more important to them. Rand put an extra spoonful on Addie Claire's toast, and within seconds she was a drippy mess of sugar and spice like any three-year-old child.

"Here, let me clean off your face," Rand said, picking up a wet cloth Sarah handed to him.

A few scrubs later Rand laid down the washrag. "Little lady, you look much better."

"Thank you, Mr. Daddy."

Rand and Sarah locked gazes.

Cocking an eyebrow, his mouth twitched in amusement. "I didn't tell her to say that."

A warm glow flowed through Sarah as she took stock of how much she loved his gentle camaraderie, his subtle wit.

They shared a deep, jovial laugh that set the children into silly hoots mimicking the adults.

"Okay, kids." Rand shot them a purposeful frown that only made Damon sit up in his chair military style, then gave him a salute. Addie Claire followed suit.

Once they settled down and began eating again, Rand told Sarah that when he went out to check on the horses, the weather had improved, and as they could see from the kitchen window, the sun now was shining. He had shoveled a lot of the drifts away from the front door and planned to traipse through the snow toward the mercantile and see if it was opened.

"Do you want to go with me and see if Miss Allison has the mercantile open today, or can I pick up something for you?" Rand addressed Sarah.

Before she could answer, the children piped up insisting they tag along. "So, what do you think?" Rand asked Sarah.

"I need to stay here and do a few things."

But before she finished, Rand ruffed up Damon's hair and said, "If it's okay with your mommy, you can tag along with me."

Sarah gave her permission.

"You guys get in your coats and boots. I've got something to do first." Rand headed up the stairs and entered his mother's bedroom, where the children slept.

* * *

With no wind and no snow to hamper Rand and the children, the walk to the middle of town was pleasant. They stopped along the way to share in a goodhearted snowball fight, then made angels in the snow, which he was pretty certain Sarah wouldn't disapprove of. They were dressed warmly, and he had never known of anybody getting sick from being a snow angel.

Finding the mercantile closed, they began their trek back to the livery, but first he wanted to go by the church to see if anyone had heard whether the train carrying the bell was expected in.

To his delight, Reverend Johnson told him that the search party had sent word that the train was just a few miles outside of town up by the Sullivan ranch. A passel of men were diggin' it out and the train was expected to arrive in time for Rand to get the bell installed.

Christmas Eve candlelight services would be held as planned.

"I've got a couple of things to take care of in preparation for the candlelight services, but if I hear anything further, I'll send word to you," Reverend Johnson said, then turned back to Rand. "Thank you for all the work you did." He offered his hand in friendship.

Once the minister was out of sight, Rand took the kids up to the manger scene near the pulpit and let them look it over. That gave him time to take the deerskin pouch he'd retrieved from his mother's trunk and place it behind the exhibit.

Rand jerked upward as if shot out of a cannon when he heard footsteps coming into the church.

"I thought I might catch you here," Sarah called from the door. "I just heard that the train is due in shortly."

"Yep, but when it arrives I'll be busy setting the bell in the tower."

"Since we might not see you for a while, let's take a minute while we have the time and tell each other what we're thankful for this Christmas." Sarah gathered the children on the front pew and leaned down in front of them.

Rand joined her.

"Damon, go first," Rand prompted.

"You're not really a bear."

Rand wanted to laugh out loud but since he needed to show by example proper decorum in the church house, he went on to Addie Claire.

"That I have a daddy."

A knot formed in Rand's throat. He had resigned himself to the fact that he'd most likely never be called Daddy.

"Thanks, angel. Damon, how about a Christmas wish? Maybe something you want really badly for Christmas."

The child's answer was simple. "Cain't think of nothin' except to stay here with you forever."

Addie Claire was more realistic for a three-year-old. "To have more little bears."

Rand wasn't all that sure he wanted more bears in the loft, but if he had his way there would be two little kids to care for them.

Light flooded the church as both doors were flung open. With the sunlight blinding Sarah and Rand, they could barely make out who marched their way. The whiny, nagging voice gave away the identity of the intruder.

Without a hello, kiss my foot, or go to blue blazes, Edwinna Dewey headed down the aisle, having a conniption fit along the way.

Before she could say anything, Rand asked the little ones to go up to the front of the church and make sure everything was in place in the manger for the candlelight services.

In a matter of seconds, Edwinna Dewey turned into a full-fledged ring-tailed tooter, having a hissy of her own. "Get your things together, Sarah. I'll have my driver get you and the babies in an hour. I'm takin' the children where they can be cared for properly." As an afterthought, she said, "I just knew something like this would happen."

Fury rushed through every inch of Rand's body. "What has happened? We're in the church house, for heaven's sake. Why don't you just go to . . . ?" He still had some choice words on the tip of his tongue that were anything but appropriate to say in front of ladies, not to mention children.

"You know what happened." Edwinna raised her umbrella and pointed it at Rand to make her point. "I don't need any sass out of you, Randall Humphrey. This is between me and Sarah."

Sarah took Rand's arm, and with a steely glare she said, "I'm sorry, Aunt Edwinna, but Rand is as much a part of this as I am—and I am not going with you. I've decided to stay in Kasota Springs."

Edwinna puffed up like a horned toad with a tummyache. "He's taken advantage of you. I just know it. It's despicable putting your children in harm's way because of your own selfish needs. Exposing the little darlings to this . . . man!"

"Mr. Humphrey has been nothing but a gentleman." Sarah stiffened her back and placed her hands on her hips. "What would you have suggested I do? Sleep in a snowdrift?"

"You should have come to the hotel where you would have been safe with me."

"In a blizzard where I couldn't see my hand in front of my face? No, thank you!" Sarah spat out.

"It's just not right. He's made a tainted woman of you." Aunt Edwinna stepped up her voice level two notches.

Rand butted in and asked in a rather calm voice for him, "What would make it right in your mind?"

"The only way to make an honest woman out of her would be to marry her," Edwinna frowned. "But that's out of the question, I am certain."

Rand and Sarah looked at one another and a consensus formed between them. He raised a questioning eyebrow and she nodded slightly.

Reverend Johnson opened the door, then began backing out, but Rand asked him to come in.

Almost before the minister reached the gathering, Rand asked, "Are you available after the candlelight service to marry us?"

"I have some things to take care of to prepare for this evening's services, but if you'd like, I could do it in an hour or so," the minister said.

Sarah and Rand gathered the children. After thanking Reverend Johnson and assuring him that they would sign the county clerk's book of marriages as soon as it thawed out, they stepped outside, leaving Edwinna in a flit.

While Sarah put the children down for a nap, Rand finished the Christmas tree and decorated it, putting the angel he'd made on top. Out of a sack, he pulled out a string toy and a doll he'd bought three years ago. He put them under the tree.

Rand checked his pocket to make sure that his mother's wedding band was there, along with a bracelet he'd made for Sarah.

A knock on the door startled him a bit. When he opened it, he saw James Crockett, a head taller, pounds heavier, and years older than Rand. Wearing a heavy coat with moisture dripping from his shaggy eyebrows, he looked like a buffalo that had just come through a snowstorm.

Without any familiarities, Rand said, "I hope you brought Jughead back."

"Sorry I had to borrow him, but I had something I needed to take care of."

"Not a very good excuse."

James handed him Sarah's lost bag. "I found this when I backtracked from the train to town. I guess she didn't see it."

"What was so important that you had to leave them on the side of the road to get to my place in a snowstorm?"

"I left you a note, didn't you read it?"

A lump came to Rand's throat, thinking that he probably should explain that it'd been accidentally tossed in the forge, but he wasn't the one needing to explain anything to his half brother. Finally, he said, "Didn't read it." Just the fact that he didn't bother to open the envelope should make his position clear on how he felt at the moment about his half brother.

"Hmm." Jim shot him a questioning look, and ran his hand along his jawline. "I saw Teg Tegeler on the trail and he told me about the Christmas money for the orphanage comin' up missing. He heard they thought it was me. I didn't want to cause you any more trouble, so I thought it was about time I moved on out and went back East. That's why I took Jughead. I didn't want to take any of your good horses."

Rand wasn't any more sure of Jim's story than as he was of his own excuse for not reading the letter.

Sarah appeared at the door.

Raising an eyebrow, Jim said, "I see Miss Callahan got here safely."

"Without any help from you," Rand said in a harsh tone.

Before Jim could say anything else, Sarah began, "Rand, the most important thing is that we are safe. Mr. Crockett had business to take care of, so it's fine." She smiled up at Rand. "I think I'll go fix something warm to drink."

"Sarah, please stay just a minute." Rand put his arm around her waist and tucked her to his side. "She knows everything. No secrets between us. James, I want to know the truth, and now!"

"If that's the way you want it," James countered.

"You gentlemen need some time to think things through. I'll be back in no time." She scurried off and in only a matter of minutes returned with mugs of coffee.

James seemed to have gathered his thoughts during the silence that hovered between the two brothers before Sarah returned. Then he took a deep breath and began, "I just left, not wanting to bring any more shame than I already have on the only family I've ever known. I should've been a big brother to you, but I wasn't. Seems more like you looked out for me than me taking care of you. You always blamed our father for Jenny's death, but it wasn't him." He hesitated, taking a long time before he could continue. "It was me. Pa asked me to fix the carriage and take Jenny out to her parents' house. I didn't repair the axle like I was told to do. Once Pa found out about her death, he just took the blame so nobody would ever know the truth. After your mama died and his health got worse, he decided it'd be better if he didn't stick around, so he ventured off. Don't know where he is."

Rand swallowed hard, trying not to reveal his anger in front of Sarah. "So I should have blamed you instead of our father all of these years?"

James nodded. "I spent too many years at the Andersonville prison during the war to face living the rest of my life confined. Couldn't stand the idea, so being a coward, I ran."

"You should have kept running." Fury mixed with relief hobbled the rest of the things Rand wanted to say.

For some reason, knowing the truth seemed to have suddenly set Rand free. He no longer had questions. They were all answered, so with Sarah's help, he could heal—forever this time.

"That was my plan, but when I ran across the train snowed in up by the Sullivan ranch and met those fine folks who invited me in to share their grub and heat, I knew that if they could do such an unselfish deed without even knowing me, I had to come back to Kasota Springs and make things right with you.

"And I didn't steal the money from Doc Mitchell's wife. I suspect it might've been Sheriff Raines, but I don't know for sure. Boss Adler and his drunken low-life hooligans were hanging around, but I heard Louis and Barney were in the hoosegow and Adler was on the run." He stopped and for a minute Rand thought James might have tears in his eyes. "Can you forgive me, Randall?"

Rand took Sarah's arm and pulled her closer to him, then looked down at her, as if she'd provide the answer. The glow in her eyes told him all he needed to know.

"Seems to be the season for new beginnings. I think we're both in need of a brother, and since you're ready and able I'd just as soon have you as my big brother than anyone around." They hugged in a very manly sort of way. "Think there's some breakfast left over, so if you're a mind, would you stick around to be our witness? Because I'm gettin' hitched in about an hour."

"Gotta clean up first." James didn't seem surprised at their unexpected announcement. He just reached down and lifted the lost bag to Sarah. "This yours?"

Sarah could hardly contain her excitement and rushed to James and gave him a big hug. "Thank you. This has the presents for the children from Santa Claus." She turned toward the tree. "But I see he came early."

Spying the quilt wrapped in a red bow, Rand smiled. "And I see Mrs. Claus plans on taking good care of Santa."

From out of nowhere, Addie Claire and Damon appeared and rushed to the tree, ignoring everyone else in the room.

"We have a Christmas tree," Addie Claire said. "Even an angel on top." She turned, took a hold of Rand's leg, and hugged him. "Thank you, Mr. Daddy."

"Cain't be no real tree without bears." Damon stared up at his mama and Rand.

"Go look in the box on the table," Rand said. "There's ribbon bows, cookies, and bears that your mama made to decorate the tree, and a bell or two."

After finding Rand's crudely made bear ornaments, the little boy shouted with glee, "You didn't forget them bears."

Rand picked up a twin in each of his arms. With Sarah by his side, as if on cue, the new family began to sing,

> *"Away in a manger,*
> *No crib for His bed,*
> *The Little Lord Jesus*
> *Laid down His sweet head. . . ."*

Without warning, Rand's helper Timmy appeared at the doorway leading to the shop and joined them in song. When they were finished, he announced that the search party had just sent word that ol' No. 208 of the Fort Worth and Denver City Railroad carrying the Christmas bell was on its way to Kasota Springs.

"How's your mama?" Rand asked.

"She's doing lots better. Doc Mitchell thinks that a miracle happened 'cause her color is better and most of her hacking has stopped." Timmy smiled. "Saw you got back, Mr. Crockett, and I'm sure happy to see ol' Jughead. I saw they were fed, so I gotta amble on over to the church to be ready to unload the bell when it gets here." He tipped his hat and hurried toward the door, then stopped. "Merry Christmas, you all." Timmy dashed out, headed toward the train depot.

Rand turned to his almost wife and said, "I gotta go help unload the bell, but I'll be back in time to get hitched."

Putting the little ones down, he kissed Sarah on the forehead.

James grabbed his coat and joined Rand. "Not without me, little brother."

Damon jumped up and headed their way. "Not without me, too . . . Daddy."

Rand looked at Addie Claire, who had followed in her brother's footsteps. "Nope, little lady, you and Mommy need to stay here to do some of the girlie things a mother and a daughter do together."

Addie Claire grabbed Sarah's hand and said, "Let's go get hitched, Mommy."

An outburst of joy decked the hall of the Kasota Springs Livery and Blacksmith's shop.

Two hours later, accompanied by their witness, Jim Crockett; the bridesmaid, Addie Claire; and groomsman, Damon, Sarah Callahan and Randall Humphrey were pronounced man and wife.

Bundling up immediately after the vows, the new family hurried to the little white church with a steeple reaching up to the heavens, and squeezed into seats next to Tess Whitgrove and Sloan Sullivan. The townfolks filled every pew to celebrate the miracles of Christmas with a candle-light service.

After Reverend Victor Johnson concluded the service, he turned the pulpit over to Emma Mitchell, who reported that the money stolen from the bazaar had been returned tenfold.

The doc's wife ended with, "Kasota Springs is blessed

to be filled with angels." She held up a shiny double eagle to the congregation, but kept her gaze on Rand. "Particularly the one who put a pouch of double eagles near Baby Jesus in the manger."

Suddenly, the toll of the new Christmas bell sounded from the bell tower.

Shivers ran up Rand's spine. He moved his arm from the back of the pew and touched Sarah on the shoulder. Looking down, he smiled at his two little angels, who were tucked safely between him and his new wife.

Damon rested his hand on Rand's thigh, while Addie Claire held tightly to her mother.

His attention was drawn back to Emma Mitchell when her whiny voice joined the toll of the new Christmas bell. . . .

"I heard the bells on Christmas Day
Their old familiar carols play.
And wild and sweet the words repeat
Of peace on earth, goodwill to men."

And Rand whispered to Sarah, "My home will always be your home. Merry Christmas, wife."

Epilogue

Two years later
Christmas Eve 1889

Rand wasn't sure how many times he'd climbed the stairs and sat in the rocker he'd toted out of Sarah's and his bedroom, but it had to be a zillion.

The twins, now five, played quietly in the great room with the toys they had opened earlier in the day. Their uncle Jim looked like a big bear sitting cross-legged on the floor playing with what appeared to be a doll. Surely not!

Rand knew his wife's time was nearing, but had no idea Sarah was this close to having their baby. She'd been healthy, but as her time neared, ol' Doc Mitchell worried that she'd put on a lot more weight than he thought was good for her. But then Rand came from a family of big men, and if it was a boy, he might well just be a big baby.

Cry after cry, moan after moan came from inside the room. In between labor pains, he could hear Sarah's heavy breathing through the door. Then the pain would return and her cries were more screams of agony instead of a labor of love.

He knew the logistics of labor—after all, he'd delivered

his share of foals—but he had no experience with a woman's birthing process.

As time went on without any word coming from inside the bedroom, Rand became increasingly worried. He was about to wear the area between the bedroom and the stairs thin by walking the floor waiting on news about Sarah and their baby.

A shrill wail, more painful than Rand had ever heard in his life, echoed off the walls, followed by the sweetest sound he knew he'd never forget—his baby's cry.

Suddenly a second cry joined with the other one to create a concerto of bawling. Perplexed as to how one baby could make so much noise, Rand jumped to his feet and cupped his ear against the door. All he could hear were instructions from Doc Mitchell to his wife, Emma, who was helping him. Directions more perplexing than the baby's cry. Relief settled all around Rand. The new baby had to have healthy lungs to let out so many bellowing wails so close together.

Suddenly the door opened, almost making Rand fall inside, and Doc Mitchell stood in the threshold.

"Randall Humphrey, congratulations on being the proud father of a healthy baby . . ."

He stepped aside to allow Rand to enter the room. Coming to an abrupt halt as though he'd suddenly got bogged down in knee-deep mud, Rand stared at Sarah—and not one but two babies!

"I, uh." He had no words for how he felt. "Two babies."

"Come meet your daughter and her brother," Doc Mitchell said.

"Brother!" Rand almost shouted. "Twins!" He rushed to Sarah's side as the doc and his wife exited the room.

He gripped Sarah's hand and took a wet cloth from the bowl beside the bed and dabbed at her forehead. "You're exhausted." He couldn't keep his eyes off the little ones.

"But it was worth it." Tired but radiant, she looked up at him. "Oh so worth it. I love you, Rand Humphrey."

"And I love you, Sarah Humphrey, more than you can imagine."

"You know I always get the last word. I love you more, but we need to give them names before Addie Claire and Damon come in."

"We only talked about names for a boy." Rand finally scrounged up the courage to touch the forehead of one of the babies lying in the crook of Sarah's arms. "But with two—"

"What do you think we should call her?" Sarah smiled up at him. "Edwinna is out of the running."

"Well, if I can't use your aunt's name, then I'll have to think about it a minute." Rand pulled the quilt Sarah had made for him two Christmases ago from the quilt stand, and spread it over his precious wife. "How about the little tadpole there being Christian Alexander and our little lady Abigail Rebecca?"

"Exactly what I was thinking." Sarah pulled both babies tight to her and whispered, "Your mother's name. I like that."

"What could be more perfect than celebrating our second wedding anniversary with the addition of two little ones?" Rand said.

The Humphrey family was complete with a total of six. And they had received the perfect Christmas present: two bundles of joy to add to their inquisitive and rambunctious siblings.

In the distance, the toll of Christmas bells sounded through the falling snow.

Romantic Suspense from
Lisa Jackson

See How She Dies	0-8217-7605-3	$6.99US/$9.99CAN
Final Scream	0-8217-7712-2	$7.99US/$10.99CAN
Wishes	0-8217-6309-1	$5.99US/$7.99CAN
Whispers	0-8217-7603-7	$6.99US/$9.99CAN
Twice Kissed	0-8217-6038-6	$5.99US/$7.99CAN
Unspoken	0-8217-6402-0	$6.50US/$8.50CAN
If She Only Knew	0-8217-6708-9	$6.50US/$8.50CAN
Hot Blooded	0-8217-6841-7	$6.99US/$9.99CAN
Cold Blooded	0-8217-6934-0	$6.99US/$9.99CAN
The Night Before	0-8217-6936-7	$6.99US/$9.99CAN
The Morning After	0-8217-7295-3	$6.99US/$9.99CAN
Deep Freeze	0-8217-7296-1	$7.99US/$10.99CAN
Fatal Burn	0-8217-7577-4	$7.99US/$10.99CAN
Shiver	0-8217-7578-2	$7.99US/$10.99CAN
Most Likely to Die	0-8217-7576-6	$7.99US/$10.99CAN
Absolute Fear	0-8217-7936-2	$7.99US/$9.49CAN
Almost Dead	0-8217-7579-0	$7.99US/$10.99CAN
Lost Souls	0-8217-7938-9	$7.99US/$10.99CAN
Left to Die	1-4201-0276-1	$7.99US/$10.99CAN
Wicked Game	1-4201-0338-5	$7.99US/$9.99CAN
Malice	0-8217-7940-0	$7.99US/$9.49CAN

Books by Bestselling Author
Fern Michaels

___The Jury	0-8217-7878-1	$6.99US/$9.99CAN
___Sweet Revenge	0-8217-7879-X	$6.99US/$9.99CAN
___Lethal Justice	0-8217-7880-3	$6.99US/$9.99CAN
___Free Fall	0-8217-7881-1	$6.99US/$9.99CAN
___Fool Me Once	0-8217-8071-9	$7.99US/$10.99CAN
___Vegas Rich	0-8217-8112-X	$7.99US/$10.99CAN
___Hide and Seek	1-4201-0184-6	$6.99US/$9.99CAN
___Hokus Pokus	1-4201-0185-4	$6.99US/$9.99CAN
___Fast Track	1-4201-0186-2	$6.99US/$9.99CAN
___Collateral Damage	1-4201-0187-0	$6.99US/$9.99CAN
___Final Justice	1-4201-0188-9	$6.99US/$9.99CAN
___Up Close and Personal	0-8217-7956-7	$7.99US/$9.99CAN
___Under the Radar	1-4201-0683-X	$6.99US/$9.99CAN
___Razor Sharp	1-4201-0684-8	$7.99US/$10.99CAN
___Yesterday	1-4201-1494-8	$5.99US/$6.99CAN
___Vanishing Act	1-4201-0685-6	$7.99US/$10.99CAN
___Sara's Song	1-4201-1493-X	$5.99US/$6.99CAN
___Deadly Deals	1-4201-0686-4	$7.99US/$10.99CAN
___Game Over	1-4201-0687-2	$7.99US/$10.99CAN
___Sins of Omission	1-4201-1153-1	$7.99US/$10.99CAN
___Sins of the Flesh	1-4201-1154-X	$7.99US/$10.99CAN
___Cross Roads	1-4201-1192-2	$7.99US/$10.99CAN

Available Wherever Books Are Sold!
Check out our website at www.kensingtonbooks.com

Thrilling Fiction from

GEORGINA GENTRY